ISBN 978-1-84728-865-3
First Edition, First Printing

Copyright ©2006 Jesse Hajicek

Cover illustration copyright ©2006 Sarah Cloutier

Through all its incarnations, this book has always been dedicated to Spider, who will be my Grand Vizier when I rule the world.

The God Eaters

Prologue

In the middle of Hasher Street, just past noon, four large boys were beating a small one. The good citizens of the town of Burn River walked by on either side; this was no more remarkable than a cat worrying a bird's corpse. It was the nature of boys; it was the nature of the world.

The leader of the four was big for his twelve years, blond, red-faced with the heat of the Iavaian sun. He huffed and sweated as he kicked.

"You think you're better than us? Do you?"

The boy on the ground made a small sound. He was thin and brown, dressed only in a pair of ragged trousers. His black hair was matted. He curled protectively around his fingers and face, waiting for it to be over.

"Do you?" the leader demanded, and put the boot in again.

"*Inai...*"

A harder kick. "Speak Eskaran, damn you! You're in the Commonwealth now. This is *our* country. It's our job to civilize you filthy people. You oughtta be grateful. Are you grateful? Are you?"

"*Inai... aman ka'ashai...*"

"Shit," said another of the boys. "He don't even know what we're saying."

"Then I'll teach 'im." The leader applied the boot with great fury several times. When his cronies failed to join in, however, he grew embarrassed and stopped. He spit on the native boy's bruised and dirty back. "Stupid cow. It's our country now. You better learn that." He scuffed some dirt at his victim. Then he shoved his hands in his pockets and whirled away. "I'm bored. Let's go back of Maley's and see if we can kype some oranges."

His cronies concurred with varying levels of relief. They were new to the South, not yet accustomed to casual cruelty. They would learn soon enough, though. You couldn't be too easy on these natives. Had to pound 'em down when they got too proud. Even the Church said so. They were devil-worshipers and savages, and it was a righteous man's duty to civilize them. He'd been doing that boy a favor, really. His friends would understand that before too long.

Meanwhile, the blond boy showed them that there was plenty of fun to be had here if you were Eskaran. He showed them that you could do just about anything you wanted. Flip up darkie girls' skirts, and their mothers would just catch up the girls and look around with wide eyes, they wouldn't even yell. Steal from farmers' stalls right in front of them -- what were they going to do? The whole province was a free lunch for a white boy with some time to kill. They strutted and crowed, and the day passed in a fevered spin of power.

The new boys had to go home at supper time. Their folks were still trying to keep to Northern customs. The blond boy sneered at them for obeying these rules, then wandered on alone.

He had no fixed idea of what to do -- there was no need. He'd find something. Maybe one of those native girls, those brown girls in white dresses whose mothers had learned better than to object to what a white man wanted from them. Lately he'd been having new ideas about what he could do to those girls to make their eyes go big, make them whimper like puppies. He strolled through the emptying streets, meandering toward the native quarter. What if he went in one of their houses? What could they do to him? He could take anything, or smash everything. He wandered along the river front, roads pounded stone-hard by ore wagons, thick with the smell of the smelteries, empty now after the end of the work day.

Not quite empty. A small, dark form darted into the road in front of him, appearing from a loading alley: the boy he'd beaten before.

He chuckled. He'd wanted to scare a girl, but this would work too.

"Hey! You! You looking for another beating?"

He expected the kid to jump and run like he had earlier that day. But the kid didn't run. He grinned. He shifted from one foot to the other as if excited.

"Yes, please," the kid said. Perfectly clearly.

"You slimy little -- you speak Eskaran?" The blond boy lengthened his steps, still thinking the native would break and flee. Any second. But he didn't, and the northerner stopped when he loomed over the smaller child. The native was still grinning. His thin, sharp-chinned face was decorated with old bruises, bruises far deeper than any he'd gotten today. His eyes were huge and mad, and *green;* though all natives had black eyes this boy's were green like river mud. There was no fear in them. Apparently more threats were needed. "You uppity little shit. Didn't your mama teach you not to sass your betters?"

"My mama's dead. You got any money?"

"Bet she was a hoor."

"Yes," said the native boy, and his grin widened. "I'm a whore now too. You got any money?"

With an exclamation of disgust, the blond boy stepped back. "You filthy --"

The native's grin, impossibly, widened even further. He was showing every one of his sharp, crooked teeth, all the way to the gums.

"I asked you," he ground through those teeth, "do you *have any god damn money!*"

With the last word he lashed out his small fist, and where he struck, a pain blossomed that was enough to freeze the blond boy in panicked stillness with half a breath in his lungs, afraid even to scream lest it make the pain worse. He looked down in dawning horror to see blood running off the native boy's knuckles in a thin stream. He whimpered.

"No," he whispered as the knife pulled out -- and out -- had all of that been inside him? "You can't. You can't."

"I did," said the native. His fist flashed again, and everything stopped.

༄ ❀ ༄

Kieran Trevarde looked down at the body in the road and felt nothing. Not even satisfaction. Not even relief. He hadn't planned anything like this. He hadn't planned anything else either. He knew he ought to be sorry, but couldn't remember what it felt like. It would be only fair to cry for the dead boy, but he couldn't.

Used to be, he cried over stupid things, like a stomachache, or a toy his mama wouldn't buy him. Then his mama's pimp Barton had said Kieran had to earn his keep, and Kieran had cried at the look on Mama's face, and again for fear and pain during the rape, and with shame after, as he'd given Mama the money. He'd been crying the whole time Mama and Barton fought; and after Barton kicked her, while her stomach swelled up and turned shiny and bruised, they'd wept together until she fell into silence, away from him, alone. After Mama had stopped crying, he'd stopped being able to.

He threw his head back, swallowed a breath, choking back a swell of nausea.

Then he bent to empty his victim's pockets.

He had just turned nine years old.

"Relax, son," Kinter chuckled. "I think you and I could help each other. I hear you've done a fair bit of the permanent, considering your age. That true?"

Nearly sixteen now, tall for his age but twig-thin, Kieran Trevarde didn't relax. He didn't know how. He stood straight with his hands at his sides and looked at the leader of the White Rose gang with eyes like a coyote's. "Yeah," he said.

"So how come you're selling ass, boy? Don't you know you can make better money with me?"

Kieran shrugged. "Here I am."

The gang leader, Kinter, laughed at him. It was a pleased laugh. "Shrike tells me you have some kinda magic."

"He thinks so." Another shrug.

"How'd you get it past Survey?"

"Late bloomer, I guess."

"How 'bout you show me this magic."

"Don't know how."

The pleased look went from Kinter's face.

"Not sure it's not just luck," Kieran clarified. "I wish for someone to die, and he does. Takes a while, sometimes."

"How long?"

"Six months, once. Another time it was the next day. I can use a knife, though."

Kinter frowned, then waved a hand dismissively. "We'll see, I guess. You're hired. I'll pay you twenty a week, and you can stay at the Tall House. Don't bother the girls."

The boy stared for a moment more, then gave a curt nod. His leaving was an insectile sort of operation, maneuvering arms and legs too long and thin for grace in a strangely graceful manner. Shrike had told Kinter that the boy had grown at least six inches during his year in Tiyamo despite scanty prison food and constant abuse; durable. And he was pretty, would be gorgeous if given a chance to fill out.

Watching him go, Shrike echoed Kinter's thought loud enough for the boy to hear: "If I'm wrong about the magic -- I'd guess a face like that is worth at least ten-five a trick."

Early the next morning, Shrike died of a sudden apoplexy while in the bath. Kinter noticed the strange smile on the new hand's face and ordered the boy's pay raised. He sent old man Beatty to instruct the boy in various types of combat. He also let fall the word that he'd like the boy introduced to the pleasures of the poppy. It looked like the kid was a real thing. Kinter was the only opium bootlegger in history to have a ghoul-witch on the payroll. He wasn't about to let Kieran get away.

Just when it couldn't hurt any more, the pain got worse. It was amazing, really amazing, and funny in a stupid way. Black things crawled around the edges of the room, everything smelled of shit, the ceiling was getting lower, and still it kept hurting even more. Kieran could see his abdomen rippling with the cramps. *Just cramps*, he told himself, *I am not host to giant parasites...* But as soon as he'd thought it, he knew there really were worms in there. Great toothy worms eating his guts, and only one medicine would drive them out.

"Please! Just a little, just to tide me over, be logical -- God! Why are you doing this to me? Do you hate me so much?"

"I'm doing it 'cause I like you, actually," said a voice with a laugh in it, while a cool cloth stroked Kieran's cheeks. "And for the zillionth time, you told me you wanted to kick. You said not to give you any no matter what you said. I ain't got none, anyway." A face loomed, an ordinary face, tanned sand-colored, haloed by dirty blond curls, with blue eyes that seemed to dance and spin with the humming of Kieran's nerves. The blue-eyed boy gave him a smile full of sad humor, which transformed his ordinary face into something remarkable.

But Kieran was past taking comfort from that. "Why? It hurts --"

"You don't care why right now. Let's talk about sumpin else, okay?"

Kieran subsided, panting. Wondering if he'd chosen right, this first time in years he'd made a choice. He'd defied Kinter because of that smile. Kicking his tar habit was imperative because until he did he would be Kinter's slave, and if he remained Kinter's slave he would eventually do as Kinter ordered and kill this boy.

"It's for you," Kieran said hoarsely. "Shan, I'm doing this for you."

The cloth paused on his forehead. "No you ain't. You're doing it for you. But I'm glad if it'll keep you from drawing down on me again. For a minute there I thought it was all up."

"No. I'll never hurt you. I swear, Shan."

"I don't believe you," Shan said lightly, and dropped a kiss on Kieran's sweating forehead, and for a moment doubt vanished. Then the cramps started again.

"Whoo-ee! Will you lookit all that money!" Shan sat on the edge of their bed, chin in hand, staring at the pile of bank notes on the floor. They'd just knocked over the payroll shipment to the Dogtooth Mine. "Who'd a thought it? Did you? I sure didn't."

"You didn't?" Kieran, cross-legged beside the pile, looked up from cleaning his gun. "Forty workers times eight weeks times fifteen signets a man. Should be exactly four hundred eighty thrones there. Count it if you want, but the math's not hard."

"For you, maybe." Shan was sullen for a moment, but he never could stay mad. He grinned again the next moment. "I knew teaming up with you was a good idea. You're so damn smart, Kai. I done made more money with you --"

"That's not why you took me on, though," said Kieran wickedly. He tossed the revolver aside and seized Shan's wrist.

There was a brief tug-of-war to determine whether they'd end up on the bed or the floor. Grinning, Kieran gave in and let himself be pulled up. Smothered Shan's laughter with his mouth, surrendered to the defiant purity of plain desire. For someone who'd spent half his childhood as a whore, he'd been remarkably ignorant about sex when Shan had taken him in. He'd thought all he had to do was show up. He'd certainly never made love, never multiplied pleasure by trading it back and forth, until Shan had taught him. Even after months of Shan's tutelage, he was rarely the one to start anything. This time, he thought maybe he was finally starting to trust his lover. He hoped so; Shan deserved that.

Later, when they lay sweaty and content together, Shan asked, "What are you gonna do with your half?"

"Dunno. What're you?"

6

"Well, the shotgun rider kilt my horse. Gotta get another one. And then... Dunno. Maybe I'll buy you a diamond earring."

Kieran laughed. "Don't buy me presents. I've got my own cut."

"Well, what're *you* gonna do?"

"Waste it." Then an idea came to him. "I know. Remember how when we were at Dindy's that one time, he had this engraving behind the counter? That new gun, that you could order custom?"

"Yeah. You gonna get one of those?"

"It takes nine bullets, Shan. Ten if you carry one in the chamber. Self-cocking, and it has separate magazines like a Lockeart. I could do some real wrecking with that."

Shan raised himself on one elbow to look down into Kieran's face. "You like wrecking way too much. One of these days, babe, you're gonna wreck the world."

"Not the part you're standing on," Kieran said, but for once Shan didn't smile.

~ ❋ ~

The cops had stopped firing. Into the silence came the sound of wind and the small clicks of Shan reloading.

"I'm just about spent," Shan muttered. He snapped the cylinder into place and looked ruefully at the handful of bullets he had left. Then he raised his eyes to meet Kieran's. "How you doing for reloads?"

"Two. More than you. They gotta be running low too, though."

Shan risked a glance around the edge of the bit of broken wall they cowered behind. A bullet whined overhead as he pulled quickly back. His look was bleak. "Guess why they shut up."

"Aw, shit."

"Yep. Reinforcements. And... uh..." He lowered his eyes. "I saw a white coat."

"Shit," Kieran repeated, with more feeling. "It figures they'd call in the Watch. I'm a rogue Talent, after all."

"Think you can take him?"

"No."

They looked at each other for a time. Kieran saw his own understanding mirrored in the sky-blue of Shan's stare. This was it. Well, they were highway robbers; they'd never expected to live forever. If it wasn't the cops, it would've been Kinter's gang, out to prove that nobody was allowed to quit. So he'd die before he turned twenty; he'd never figured to live even this long. When Shan seized him by his shirt front and kissed him hard, he knew what it meant.

"I love you," he said, and realized it was a lie.

"Cover me," Shan replied, and shifted his weight.

It all seemed to have been planned in advance -- Kieran knew exactly what would happen in the fraction of a second before it did, and knew as well that his part in it was also ordained.

Shan sprang to his feet in a movement meant to propel him in a long, diving leap from their small bit of cover toward the right, where he might be able to see past the wagons that sheltered the police. Kieran jumped up too, reaching for a handful of Shan's jacket to pull him back into cover. And then came the wet smack of a bullet hitting flesh, and the side of Shan's head dissolved in brilliant scarlet.

For the rest of his life, Kieran would remember how the blood glittered in the sun. It hypnotized him as he shouted, as he curled around Shan's wretched empty house with its flopping limbs. Shan's blood coming down more slowly than his body, pebbling in the dust; blood and brains and bone. Running down the side of Kieran's face, mingling with his own blood where shards of shattered skull had laid open his brow and cheek.

It was intolerable. He'd thought that the world was harsh because it was indifferent, but in that moment he realized that the world was deliberately cruel. Let it win; let it have him. Kieran didn't care. He didn't want to play this stupid game anymore.

And then there came up inside him someone who did.

Kieran felt himself begin to stand; then he was pushed back from his senses so that everything went pale. Gratefully, he let go of himself as the bullets began to sing in earnest. He was going to die now.

When, some vague eternity later, the fog cleared and dropped him into a body bound with cold-iron chains and tortured by a Healer's efforts to keep it alive, his groan was one of despair. It was followed in the next bubbling breath by a screech of rage.

Someone said, "How 'bout you heal 'im up, and we'll

shoot 'im again."

Nearer: "You've done your job. Now it's out of your hands."

Outraged: "That fucking savage took out five of my men! He deserves --"

"We have a use for his kind. That's all you need to know."

Kieran willed them all to die, but his will was caught in some sticky nowhere and lost; his insults and threats were ignored. His screams of pain and outrage likewise. At last, when he'd stopped bleeding from the lungs and they'd loaded him on a wagon, he fell silent.

He began to smile. He knew his teeth were red.

Someone in a sand-colored police uniform clouted him on the ear. "What are you so happy about, you murdering freak?"

Kieran spit blood before answering. "Now that Shan's dead," he said, "I've got no reason to be nice anymore."

They hit him again, but he could see them trying to figure out how he could be any worse than he'd been before, and he went on smiling.

༄ ❈ ༅

In the bare desert a hundred miles northeast of Trestre rose an immense table mountain of banded golden stone. It stood more than twice as tall as any other land form in the area, nearly circular in shape, too steep to climb. Its distinctive form and size had earned it a place in the mythology of the natives. They believed it had once been the castle of a god. It was riddled with tunnels, but they claimed not to have done the digging, nor did they know who had. They called it Iaka'anta, and would not approach it.

The Eskarans called it Churchrock, and they had made it into a laboratory and a prison.

Staffed and maintained by the elite government mages of the White Watch, the Churchrock facility provided an excellent place to study magical Talents and the people who possessed them. Its natural properties made it easy to set up and maintain a ward to keep the prisoners from using their magic. Though far from water sources, it was situated on a flat plain not far from a major rail line; the ancient tunnels simplified building and provided some inherent shielding.

Most important -- at least to Watch Director Thelyan -- was the fact that it had once belonged to the devil-god Ka'an, and no longer did.

Thelyan did not, of course, inhabit it. He only rarely visited it; twice yearly for routine inspection, and occasionally to satisfy his curiosity about the progress of some experiment or to view an interesting subject. He had left standing orders that he was to be notified if the facility received a Threnodist, Stormcaller, or Oneiromancer who fit certain criteria, but as these were rare Talents and his criteria rather strict, such a case occurred only once in a long time. Even more rarely -- only once before in this incarnation -- he came to visit a subject who'd been held here far longer than any of the researchers knew. Iaka'anta's best qualification for being made into a prison, when he had ordered the Churchrock facility built, was that it had been one already for centuries.

In the bowels of the mountain was a door that looked as if it might lead to a storeroom, uninteresting, distinguishable from all the other doors in the place only by the fact that it could not be opened. Hardly anyone could even see it. Now Thelyan put his hand to the latch and watched with satisfaction as the shape of the locking spell rearranged itself to accommodate him. He opened it and slipped through, letting it lock itself behind him.

Beyond, a stair led up. He had carved this stair into the stone with his own magic, alone, long before his chosen people officially occupied this territory. There was no source of light. Thelyan didn't need one. He could see the stone around him with senses far finer than sight. The only other individual in the world who possessed these senses, at least to such a degree, awaited him at the top of the stair.

Climbing the long spiral high into the mountain, he reached another door, this one of thick copper. This one had greater protections on it. He could not simply slip through, but had to provide a key, an intricate idea-form that completed the waiting spell. Any magic directed against the door itself would simply ground in the copper. Only this particular password would trigger the lock, which was a masterpiece of spellcrafting. Thelyan believed that not even the one beyond the door could have set a spell in grounded metal. He built his structure of thought and fitted it into the pattern; the door swung open with a screech of metal.

He made a light, a tiny whorl of a sigil which lifted free of his fingers to float above him, hissing faintly and emitting a blue-white glow. This revealed an ovoid room, just large enough to contain the null sphere that held the prisoner while giving Thelyan room to stand and observe it.

The null sphere was an invention he hadn't shared with the world. It was the only structure strong enough to contain one of his own kind. A lacy cradle of brittle iron clasped what looked like a drop of mercury twelve feet in diameter. Seals were fixed at each intersection of the iron straps, each made of a different material: jade, wood, granite, ice. As he inspected it for signs of wear or damage, the mirrored sphere rippled from time to time. It was not mercury; it was a thought-thin but absolute divide between inside and outside, which not even light could cross. Once he'd satisfied himself that the device was in good working order, he touched two of the runes, releasing them, so that light and sound could pass through.

Now a shape was visible hanging motionless in the middle of the sphere. A naked human form, curled fetal and inert. In appearance, it was a boy of fifteen years, chalk-pale, shrouded and tangled in hair the color of cherry wood. The boy's fingernails were ten-inch corkscrews. Thelyan had stopped him from aging, but could not remove him completely from time. Even though he was never fed or given water, he somehow managed to obtain substance from somewhere. Thelyan had never been able to induce him to part with the secret of how it was done. It was in hope of obtaining such secrets that Thelyan kept him embodied and imprisoned rather than absorbing him. Sometimes, more often as he descended further into madness, the creature could be tricked or bullied into parting with useful information.

"Chaiel." Thelyan's voice disappeared into the tiny space, barely sounding in his own ears. "Chaiel. Wake. Chaiel. I wish to speak with you."

This went on for some time. After many more repetitions of his name, the boy in the sphere at last responded. Sluggishly, he opened his eyes and turned them on Thelyan, iron gray and perfectly insane, as round and unthinking as a lizard's.

"Chaiel. Speak, so I know you can hear me."

"Speak so I know you can hear me," the boy echoed. His voice was dull.

"Answer, so I know you understand me."

After staring at Thelyan for a minute or two, the boy

gave a flat imitation of a giggle without changing the blankness of his face. "No. I don't like you."

"Of course you don't. However, I suspect you're bored. I have a puzzle for you to play with."

That had the usual effect: the boy straightened with a sudden knifing motion, twisting in the air to face Thelyan, suddenly eager. "Give it!"

"My precognitors have recently begun to see a major change affecting me. The lesser Talents put faces on this change, telling me they foresee a war, or bad weather, or a rebellion. Those I rely on, though, tell me they can't understand what it is they're seeing. They say that changes emanate from a blank place, or from a thing so alien they can't describe it. Several have gone catatonic. You may not be able to see the future, Chaiel, but you know all the past. I wonder if you can figure out what they're seeing."

Chaiel began to laugh. Thelyan waited patiently for him to finish. Eventually, the boy said brightly, "That's easy. They see your death and they're afraid to tell you."

"Unlikely. There's no force on earth that could kill me."

"I could."

"Perhaps. If you weren't in the null sphere. But you *are* in the sphere, Chaiel, and you won't get out."

That might have been a mistake. It sent the boy into a convulsion of babbling and weeping that lasted nearly half an hour. Thrashing like an overturned insect, he strained to reach the sphere's surface. He knew he could not, but tried anyway. Clawing at his face with his helical fingernails, Chaiel drew bleeding scratches down his cheeks and brow as the nails broke off. Once they were no longer part of him, they fell clicking to the floor beneath the sphere to join a litter of similar scraps there. He watched their fall with an expression of anguished longing.

When Chaiel had calmed somewhat, Thelyan rephrased his question. "What sort of thing would appear to a Precognitor as a blank space radiating change, or as a thing too alien to describe?"

"One of us," Chaiel answered promptly.

"There are no more of us."

"You didn't eat us all. Some of us you lost."

"Who?" Thelyan knew the answer, but there was a chance of some new information.

"Medur."

"Incarnated. Powerless. She was never a threat."

"Ka'an."

"Also lost in incarnation."

"How can you be so sure? We all start incarnated. Maybe he's getting his power back, did you think of that? Maybe he fell into his Burn and sucked it up." Chaiel made a rude slurping noise. "Like a fly on an eyeball. And he's going to come for you and twist you around until you're inside out and you have to look at yourself and see that there's *nothing in there!*" This was followed by another spate of giggling.

"I would have sensed such an event. In any case, I doubt a personality as fractured as his has survived repeated incarnation."

"Because he's full of smaller gods?" More giggling. "That's unstable? *You're* a *menagerie*. You should be in here. You could keep yourself company. You'd never be lonely." An abrupt shift to anguish. "I wish I had another of me! Oh, Thelyan, let me out, I promise I'll be good!"

Thelyan ignored this. "What is it my Precognitors are sensing, Chaiel?"

"Lemon drops. Penwipers. Go to hell."

"If you don't tell me, I'll leave, and I won't talk to you anymore."

"Good." Sulking, Chaiel curled up again and put his arms over his head.

"As you wish." Thelyan reached for a seal.

"Wait! I can tell you something else important!"

"Yes?"

"Medur is male this time!"

Thelyan shook his head at this useless information. It wasn't important, and Chaiel knew it wasn't important. He was just wasting time. Thelyan touched the seal that controlled the passage of light; he heard the beginning of Chaiel's wail just before he stopped sound as well.

The weakest of his enemies, Medur was no threat to him, and he'd made no effort to seek her out. If she could have been controlled, her abilities in the realms of agriculture and the cementing of community ties might have been useful, but she was irrational. She would lack the strength of personality to emerge as herself; she'd remain encysted within the mortal body's mind, dormant. He'd had his chance to swallow her, centuries ago, but had chosen instead to scatter her power and kill her body rather than poison himself with her sentimental weakness. The only possible threat was Ka'an, and that devil-being could be dangerous only because his Burn had not dissipated as the others had. Even so, the evil one would have to emerge and subdue his mortal vessel's mind, a difficult enough task even for Thelyan, who retained all his power from life to life.

No, the source of change couldn't be another immortal. It must be something else, some complex system or train of events that a mere human mind couldn't grasp. Thelyan would meet the threat and deal with it when it occurred.

He locked the door behind him, thinking that it would probably be decades before he opened it again.

Chapter 1

The sound of the train was hypnotic. It dulled his mind and made his limbs feel heavy. It made it easier to pretend he wasn't here, and none of this was happening.

It was, after all, patently ridiculous that he, Ashleigh Trine, minor rebel and utter clueless nobody, could ever be treated like this. Like a dangerous criminal, a rogue Talent, too nasty to hang. It had to be some kind of stupid dream. A very *long* stupid dream, a prank that had gone about three months too far. Any minute now one of those Watchmen in the white coats would come in and announce that it had all been very funny and now he could go home, and they hoped he'd learned his lesson about gossiping behind the government's back. He was a good sport. He could take a joke.

They'd taken his chains off at a whistle stop somewhere in West Mauraine. He'd been allowed to use the station lavatory, but not to buy a candied apple from the vendor on the platform. Not that he had any money. Or bootlaces, pen, pocketknife, etcetera; he supposed they'd take his clothes when he got to prison. Thinking about this made him increasingly fond of the yellow shirt and brown corduroy bags he'd been arrested in. He'd been wearing them for months now while awaiting trial, and they'd been a bit ratty to begin with, so there wasn't much left of them. But now they were just about all that remained of the world he belonged in. His clothes and his glasses -- *If they were going take my glasses they would have done it already, wouldn't they?*

Ashleigh leaned against the swaying wall of the prison car, peering out the tiny slatted window, picking at the scabs the cold-iron manacles had left on his wrists. There was desert outside. It had been interesting to see how the slushy end-of-winter snow of Eskard had given up on the way west. Not gradually as he'd imagined, but all at once, so that he would have missed it if he'd had anything better to do. For instance, a bloody *crayon* to write with -- how could you kill yourself with a pen, and ought he to be worried that they'd thought he'd want to?

He was going to be eaten alive in prison. He'd realized

that shortly after the shock of not being executed had worn off. He was pale, skinny, freckled, redheaded, and myopic; he was certain to learn new definitions of pain, fear, and degradation. There was nothing he could do to stop it. He could only try to distract himself from worrying.

A sort of shack thing flashed by, and he saw a farmhouse farther off, skimming along between the stationary mountains and the speeding scrub. A plume of smoke rose from an intermediately distant valley beyond the farm, growing closer as acres of dry plow-furrows slipped by. Ashleigh could discern a sharp new smell under the reek of the engine and the desert's alien scent. Something chemical. A city; or at least a giant refinery. He'd heard that most of the iron and coal and so forth for the Commonwealth's military machine was produced out here. He scrubbed his glasses with an already filthy shirttail and peered hard at the plume of pollution as it grew closer. He sincerely hoped this wasn't his destination.

When the train stopped at a roofless platform surrounded by grayish adobe shacks, his heart sank. He told himself they were just taking on fuel and water, but it had only been four hours since the last stop. Then one of his white-uniformed guards came and banged on the compartment's iron door to get his attention, and he knew: he was being sent to wheeze out his last months in slavery at some asbestos mine or something. He wondered whether, if he made a break for it, they'd just shoot him.

"Back on the bench, Trine," the guard said. "Hands on your head."

Ashleigh did as he was told. The man came in with his gun trained, as if his slight, bespectacled prisoner might perform some amazing feat of derring-do and wrest the weapon from him. He was followed by another, who carried the hated manacles.

"Oh, no," Ashleigh groaned. "Do we have to?"

Ignoring him, the man fastened the chains on Ashleigh's wrists. As he stepped away, he said, "You better keep that big mouth of yours shut from now on. We're taking on a couple of real baddies. They won't be nice to you like we are."

"If I'm not a real baddie," Ashleigh muttered, "why am I here?" Naturally he got no reply. The Watchmen just slammed the door, leaving him to scratch his wrists and remind himself that none of this was actually happening.

The engine sat on the tracks, humming to itself, for a

long time. His watch was another of those things he didn't have, but it was long enough for the sun to get behind a ridge of furrowed hills a couple miles west of the train. The desert, which had been all rust and mustard before, went suddenly purple. The warmth of the day was instantly gone. Some kind of demented dog started howling somewhere nearby.

A clang of footsteps on the metal connector-thing outside his moveable cell made his heart jump with apprehension. The 'real baddies' coming aboard, no doubt. A Watchman stepped in first, establishing a field of fire throughout the tiny room. Then a big, saggy pig of a clearly nasty man, who glared at Ashleigh with a sort of hateful avarice, obviously hoping he'd get a chance to do some violence as soon as the guards were out of his hair. He had to be threatened before he'd take his seat against the opposite wall.

Ashleigh was watching pig-man as carefully as someone allergic to wasps watches a buzzing blot on the windowpane, so he was turned away from the door, but he heard a third set of footsteps enter. Then an amazing voice spoke -- a young baritone, sandy and smooth at once, with a strong Iavaian drawl, lazy as a wolf gnawing a bone.

"No, I wanna sit over *there*," the voice said. "I don't wanna sit by Burdock, I been sitting by him for fuckin' weeks, it's real stale."

There was a sound Ashleigh had learned to recognize: the thud of a rifle butt into someone's kidneys. The inevitable grunt followed, and then something that sounded suspiciously like a fragment of a laugh. Ashleigh ripped his gaze from the evil stare of the man across from him to watch as the possessor of this razor-blades-in-the-candy voice was shoved into the car.

This was the tallest human being Ashleigh had ever seen, and the most beautiful, and the most frightening. His hands were chained at his belt. As a sour-faced Watchman fastened the back of that belt to a ring behind the bench, the tall boy gave Ashleigh a cool half-smile and a small nod. Ashleigh tried to nod back like a normal person, while reaction ran through him from eyes to loins like boiling honey.

The Iavaian could not have been much older than Ashleigh's eighteen years, might even have been younger, but he looked as if he'd been through several wars and was eager for another one. He had the angular features typical of his race, the brown skin and black hair, but his eyes were a dusty, yellowed green, like the sky before a bad storm. Pale scars streaked his face: divided one of his sharply angled brows, nicked the bridge of his nose, drew dashes along one cheekbone. His hair was matted into waist-length ropes What shredded clothing was left on him was so caked with mud and dust and what looked like dried blood that it was impossible to tell what color it had been. Beneath the dirt, his arms were scrawled with more scars and spiky red-and-black tattoos. His long legs made the low bench awkward for him, and he had to sit sideways to keep his elbows out of pig-man's way. His skinned-knuckled hands were huge. He was lean and menacing as a wild dog, and no matter how he hunched on the bench his presence crowded the jail car until it was hard to breathe in there.

The car gave a lurch and the engine's vibration changed pitch. The guards had left long ago, but Ashleigh, busy staring, hadn't noticed. Even the movement of the train only registered peripherally. The Iavaian stared back patiently while Ashleigh gawked at his face, his corded forearms, his long throat, his many scars...

"You done yet?"

Ashleigh felt his face go hot. He jerked his gaze away. "Sorry," he muttered.

"Not much else to look at," the Iavaian said forgivingly. "I mean, there's the floor, and Burdock's ugly mug."

"Hey." Pig-man spoke for the first time, in a high, nasal voice that didn't fit his exterior and perhaps explained his attitude. "I about had it with you, boy."

The scarred boy grinned at pig-man, teeth crooked but perfectly white. "You think you're pretty?"

"Shut up. I don't gotta take shit from you no more." He turned his scowl on Ashleigh. "Quit staring, you pansy."

"I wasn't."

"You calling me a liar? You saying I lied?"

"No, of course --"

"Then quit fucking staring."

"I -- dear god, I'm back in grammar school."

"What's that supposed to mean?" Pig-man, Burdock, stood up. Ashleigh tried hard not to cringe back against the wall. He was wondering, despairingly, whether there was any incentive for a man already on his way to prison not to beat him to death right there in the jail car, when Burdock took one step and went sprawling on the floor.

The Iavaian reeled in a mile-long leg and smiled. "Means

grow up," he clarified.

Burdock began to get up, turning, clearly about to launch in the Iavaian's direction. He never made it past the first half-syllable of his retort. The Iavaian kicked him under the chin hard enough to snap his head back and send him over to smack the back of his skull against Ashleigh's bench with a sickening thump.

Ashleigh edged away from the man's still bulk, and back from the Iavaian who'd downed him while still chained to the far wall. A small bubble of blood appeared at the corner of Burdock's mouth and commenced growing and popping with every rattling breath.

"Quit cringing. I ain't gonna hurt you. Just saved your ass, didn't I?"

"Yes... thank you."

"You should probably kill him. I would, if I wasn't locked down." He sounded as if he meant it.

Ashleigh looked to him in horror. "Kill him?"

"If where they're taking us is anything like normal prison, he'll kill you later if you don't get rid of him now."

"I can't do that!"

"Sure you can. Step on his neck. Easy."

"That's not what I mean."

"Oh. Scruples." The Iavaian shrugged. "Probably want to get rid of those pretty quick here."

Ashleigh decided not to ask, after all, what the boy's name was, or why he was chained to the bench. Carefully training his eyes on the small square of window that glowed above the other's head, he made himself very still.

This isn't happening, he told himself. *It isn't real. I'm not here.*

"Trine. Wake up, boy. What the hell did you do?"

Ashleigh pried his eyes open, wincing in the glare of a Watchman's hissing gas lantern. Sleeping with his head against the compartment's vibrating wall had given him a headache. The wall wasn't vibrating now, though. They'd shut the engine off. They had arrived.

All at once, he came awake and sat up, half panicked and none too coherent.

"Whoa," said a guard in a different uniform, a tan one. "Easy, kid. Man asked you a question." With a jerk of his head he indicated the slumped form of Burdock, still blowing bubbles.

Across the car, the Iavaian chuckled. "That Trine, he's a madman. I'm scared."

"Shut it, freak," the Watchman spat.

Ashleigh opened his mouth to explain, but the Iavaian was looking at him expectantly, scar-bisected eyebrow slightly raised, and he changed his mind. "He had some kind of fit," he said instead. "He was banging around, and then he fell down."

"Huh." This news seemed to surprise no one. "All right. Come on out, kid. Watch the step there."

Feeling a thousand years old, Ashleigh climbed out into the desert night.

It felt like a dream because it was too real. He was raw, a bunch of naked nerves and infant emotion. The chill breeze with its freight of unfamiliar smells overwhelmed him. The sounds of strange insects hurt him.

They had stopped at a platform of bare concrete roofed with corrugated steel. It was lit with a painful profusion of lamps. Two white-uniformed sentries watched the distance, too disciplined even to move their eyes. Ashleigh was marched down a set of steps and onto a gravel road which led toward a small constellation of lamps. Overhead, the stars were huge. There were too many of them. He felt as if he might fall into them. Between the stars and the lamps there was a huge square blackness where something blotted out the sky.

At first he thought it was a building. A few steps later, he realized he'd misjudged the scale by several orders of magnitude. It was a mountain. A flat-topped mountain that could have swallowed his home town of Ladygate with room to spare for a couple of suburbs if you stacked them. Stopped at a gate in a wire fence, half-hearing his guards exchanging formalities with the heavily-armed men inside, he saw his new home and wanted to cry. It was built into the base of the mountain. It had no windows at all.

They were let through the gate. Ashleigh took a last look at the stars, said goodbye to fresh air, and walked into prison.

There was a series of checkpoints with metal gates, and then a bare white room where he was made to sit on a bench. There his escort left him.

"Bye," Ashleigh said forlornly.

One of them turned at the door. "Keep your head down and your mouth shut and you'll be all right," he advised. He didn't sound as if he believed it.

This room couldn't be his cell, because it had doors at either end. He wasn't waiting long before the second door opened, and a man in a tan uniform motioned for him to come through. In the room beyond was a man with a clipboard, and neither instruction man nor clipboard man were armed. There were, however, a couple of slots up near the ceiling. Maybe the guns were behind them. Besides the men, this room had another bench, a couple of big bins, an alcove with a drain in the floor, and a long row of shelves of folded blue-gray clothing.

"Hands," said the first guard. Ashleigh offered them, and his manacles were taken off and tossed in a bin. "Clothes." Shivering naked, he said farewell as his friendly clothes went into another bin. "Put your glasses on the bench. You can get them later. Step into the shower."

Squinting now as well as shivering, he went into the alcove, the floor of which was slimy with what he hoped was soap. Suddenly he was deluged with freezing water. His startled squawk made the guards laugh. *Probably the high point of their day*, he thought sourly, *dumping cold water on people*.

"There's a cake of soap behind you. Make sure you work it thoroughly into your scalp and all body hair."

The soap was a poisonous yellow and smelled like tar. He supposed it killed lice. He also guessed that there was no point explaining that he'd never had lice in his life, so he rubbed the nasty stuff into his scalp and armpits and groin, wincing as the skin began to itch.

"Good. Now make sure you rinse off all of it."

Another icy deluge was enough to rinse everything but his hair; the thick curls trapped the soap, and his scalp still itched. Was, in fact, beginning to sting. "May I have a little more water?" he begged. "Please?"

The guards looked at each other and shrugged. Clipboard man pulled a little handle and Ashleigh was allowed to finish rinsing his hair.

While Ashleigh dripped and shivered, instruction man produced a tape measure. "Stand there. Arms and legs apart."

Ashleigh tried a joke, to see what would happen. "A summer ensemble in fawn linen, if you please, and none of those garish brass buttons this time."

This got a wry quirk from clipboard man, who spoke for the first time: "Sure, we've never heard that one before." Then he commenced writing as instruction man called out Ashleigh's measurements. He was far more thorough than Ashleigh thought necessary, considering that the clothing he could see in the shelves was rather formless. It was as if he actually were being fitted for a suit. They even measured his neck and wrists, the length of his hands and the circumference of his head.

"Um. Excuse me," he said when they were finally done. "Why all the measuring?"

"This is a research facility," clipboard answered. "We study you fellows here."

"What, criminals?"

"Talents." Instruction man handed Ashleigh a stack of blue cotton cloth, with his glasses perched on top. "Through there." On cue, another door opened.

A long series of rooms ensued. Ashleigh was weighed, prodded, gagged with a stick, had his kidneys and throat and testicles kneaded, his eyes and ears peered into, was stared at through colored lenses and exposed to magnets. Bizarre though it all was, after a while he found himself losing interest. He was tired. He was hungry and cold. He wanted to put his ugly new clothes on and go to sleep in a nice, safe cell.

At last he got his wish. The series of humiliations came to an end and he was allowed to dress -- drawstring pants and a sort of peasant blouse which, despite the measuring, didn't fit at all well -- and to put his glasses on. He'd had them off so long that resuming them made his head hurt.

A final clipboard man checked the spelling of his name, then called some armed men to take him into a maze of stairs and tunnels carved out of honey-colored stone. At last, past yet another metal gate, they came out into a cavernous space that echoed with snoring and smelled like despair. Yellowish lamps provided just enough illumination for Ashleigh to see a broad central corridor lined with metal gates, and steps leading up to a second tier of gates set back from the first. Each gate on the ground floor revealed a cell with two sleeping occupants; the ones on the upper right level seemed mostly vacant.

"I'm going to hate it here," he mumbled.

"Trine. 2-E. Up the stairs, kid."

Dragging himself up the steps, he was let into a cell that was, blessedly, empty.

"Home sweet home," the guard told him, and the gate clanged shut.

Too tired to even pace out the size of his cell, Ashleigh picked the left-hand bunk, wrapped himself in its scratchy but mercifully clean blanket, and went to sleep.

A clang of metal woke him. He fumbled for his glasses, dizzy with fatigue. Morning already? It was still dark, but maybe it was always dark here.

No, the air was still full of snoring. The guard was talking to someone right outside Ashleigh's cell. "I heard about you, you son of a bitch. You just give me an excuse to shoot you."

The gravel-and-honey voice from the train replied. "Those that ask don't get. All right if I sleep now?"

The cell door opened; a dark form came in; the bars clanged shut. Ashleigh found his specs and rammed them onto his face, bringing the spidery shape of his cellmate into focus. The Iavaian bounced on the edge of his bunk a few times, making it creak, then sprawled out on it. His feet hung off the end. He rolled his head toward Ashleigh to show him a glint of teeth.

"Trine," he said. "How about that. We're alphabet buddies." He flopped out a long arm, and after an awkward hesitation Ashleigh understood and mirrored the gesture. The Iavaian's hand engulfed his. "Trevarde. Kieran Trevarde."

"Ashleigh Trine."

Trevarde continued to hold his hand. "You seem like a smart kid. You smart?"

"I guess so."

"So you recognize I could squash you like a bug, right?"

Ashleigh didn't like where this was going. "I can see that."

"All right. You don't give me any attitude, Ash, we'll get along just fine." Trevarde finally let go. He put his arms behind his head and closed his eyes, apparently at ease.

Burrowing back into his blanket, Ashleigh considered this new development. On the whole, he concluded, it was disastrous. Trevarde was apparently extremely dangerous, from the way the guards behaved. Ashleigh was inclined to agree with them. And Trevarde's undeniable charisma added an extra danger, for he was sure that if the tall Iavaian guessed that Ashleigh was attracted to him, an ass-kicking would be a best-case scenario.

The advice everyone kept giving him was right. Head down, mouth shut. Just keep repeating: *This isn't happening. This isn't happening.*

Chapter 2

The punishing noise of an automated bell woke him in a panic. Flailing free of his blanket, Ashleigh tumbled off his bunk, to the laughter of his cellmate.

"Not a morning person, Red?"

"Oh god," Ashleigh groaned. He climbed back onto the bunk, rubbed his eyes, fumbled for his glasses. The cell was so small that his nearsightedness had little effect. He could see Trevarde's face well enough. It was still nice to have a layer of glass between himself and the world. "No descriptive nicknames, please."

Trevarde gave a rolling shrug. He'd clearly been awake for some time already; his hair was no longer matted, and he was quite a bit cleaner. There were wet handprints on the front of his shirt. "Sure thing, Ash," he said easily. "But *they're* all going to call you Red. Or Specs. Or the catch of the day. What did a mouse like you do to get the Watch's attention? No, let me guess. You're a firestarter."

"No," Ashleigh said miserably. "Empath."

"Harsh. You're doomed." Trevarde stretched, yawned, scratched himself. "Concealing a Talent? That can't be all you did."

"Insurgent writings. Treason."

"For real?" This seemed to catch Trevarde's attention. "What kinda stuff did you say?"

"Oh, ah..." Ashleigh doubted Trevarde really wanted a political lecture. "I reported abuses of power by the Watch, things like that."

"You ever kill one?"

"Excuse me?"

"Watchman. Ever kill one?"

"Er. No. I've never killed anyone."

"Too bad," was Trevarde's reply.

Ashleigh nearly asked how many people Trevarde had killed, but bit his lip instead. Mouth shut, head down.

A massive clang echoed through the cavern. He went to the door and looked out through the bars. The huge room was illuminated by dirty skylights in its vaulted ceiling. By this gray glow he could see that the entire tier opposite and below had opened its doors by means of a mechanism that connected the row. Prisoners were filing out of their cells, lining up like soldiers.

"Breakfast," Trevarde guessed, right in his ear; then added, at Ashleigh's reaction, "Jumpy, aren't you?"

Ashleigh tried to be still. "Do you blame me?"

"Nah. Not surprised you're scared. But you know... tell you what. You stick with me, I'll take care of you."

He turned to find himself nose to chin with Trevarde, trapped by the taller boy's hands gripping the bars on either side of him. He swallowed hard, and managed to speak without a quaver. "What do *you* get out of that arrangement?"

"Excuse to beat on all the idiots that'll be lining up for a piece of your tender ass." At Ashleigh's skeptical expression, he let go of the bars and stepped back, smile fading. "No joke. I did a year in Tiyamo when I was a kid. I know how these places work. When you're the new boy, you have to be hard or they'll walk all over you. But you go around picking fights, they decide you're *kaiyo*, you're sick, they all gang up on you. So now you're my little pal and I'm going to protect you. Get me all the fights I need."

Unable to think of an objection that wasn't moral in nature and therefore probably incomprehensible to Trevarde, Ashleigh settled for grumbling, "I'm not little. I'm six foot one and three quarters; they measured me rather precisely last night."

"You're no bruiser, Trine." With an echoing crash, the doors on their tier opened, distracting Trevarde from the conversation. "Breakfast," he confirmed.

The line that formed on their tier was shorter than the others. Ashleigh also noticed that the men on this side were cleaner than the rest, fatter, their eyes more defiant and wary. New, like him. Opposite and on the ground floor, the prisoners were thin and worn, and when they moved they shuffled. This did not bode well for the future. A strutting man in a tan-colored uniform strode up and down the line, poking people into place with a wooden baton. As he did, he lectured them.

"Welcome to Churchrock, boys. Welcome to the beginning of the end of your lives. You will never leave here. You are here for good. The sooner you get that through your thick heads, the longer you'll survive.

"Each one of you has committed a hanging offense, and

for all anyone knows, we hanged you. You are dead to your families, your friends, and the world. You should be thankful you're still breathing. It ain't because you deserve it, though. You're alive because the White Watch needs test subjects, and that's all you're good for, because you are the scum of the world, a fact you'd better not ever forget.

"Every morning, you will wake when the bell rings. You'll be up and dressed and ready to get in line when the tier opens fifteen minutes later. If you make me come in and get you out of bed, you will wish to God you hadn't. There will be no talking in line. You will wait for permission to go, at which point you'll march in an orderly manner to the mess hall. There you'll be given your breakfast, which you will eat neatly and quietly. Don't bother asking for seconds, because you won't get any. You'll have half an hour to eat. After that, you'll line up again, and that's the high point of your day, because you get to go outside. Exercise period lasts one hour.

"After that it's back in the cells until five, when we do the whole thing again. That's the routine, boys, two meals and two hours outside, and the rest of the time is yours unless the Testing folks want you. We expect you to be grateful as hell. Now move it out."

Encouraged by prodding from the guard's baton, they were marched through a different tunnel and up a different set of stairs. A nauseating smell reached out to reel them into a communal dining hall, where inmates sat in rows eating ugly food from tin trays. Ashleigh lined up with the rest to receive a portion of grayish scrambled eggs, watery ham, and weak coffee, all of which he was apparently supposed to eat with a spoon, since that was the only utensil he was given.

"Over there," Trevarde suggested, indicating an empty table. "Let 'em get used to us before we get near 'em at meals. Like dogs."

"Good idea." Beginning to follow, Ashleigh felt something hit him behind the knees, and suddenly he was sprawling backwards, tray flying out of his hands. He hit the ground first, and then the food followed, a streak of hot coffee scalding his face. "Ow! Dammit!"

Laughter surrounded him. The men at the nearest table were laughing loudest. A moment later, as Ashleigh was picking himself up, the culprit identified himself by feigning anger: "Hey faggot, you got eggs on me! Ain't you gonna apologize?"

Ashleigh knew better than to point out the ruse. It was really just like grammar school all over again. But this was the sort of situation Trevarde was looking for, wasn't it? When the Iavaian reached to help him up, he knew it wasn't consideration for him so much as calculated rudeness to the others.

Eggs stood up. His cronies leaned forward in anticipation. "Well?"

Trevarde dusted Ashleigh off a little, then pushed him aside to give Eggs and company an odd half-smile. "I got a better idea. How about *you* apologize for tripping him."

This struck everyone as funny. "To him? Oh, that's a good one." Eggs chortled. "The hair farmer wants me to apologize to Carrots here. That's good."

"No, you apologize to *me*. The kid's under my protection and nobody touches him."

Ashleigh edged backwards, wondering whether Trevarde was actually as dangerous as he seemed, or whether he was about to have his bluff called. Meanwhile, the prankster and his pals were savoring this new humor. "Your protection, huh? Oh, I'm so scared. We supposed to be scared of you? You supposed to be somebody special?"

"Name's Kieran Trevarde." He spread one of his hands, displaying a row of dots tattooed around it. "Nice to meet you."

The laughter suddenly died. Prankster had a go at scoffing, but he moved back a step while he did it. "You're not him. He woulda died before he let 'em put him in a place like this."

Trevarde pulled down the neck of his shirt, to show a shiny, star-shaped scar on his chest. "They got Healers, fuckwit. My breakfast is getting cold."

Prankster looked from Trevarde to Ashleigh and back again. "Sorry," he grunted.

When they were seated at their lonely table, Ashleigh asked, "What was that? I don't understand."

"Boring. Guess he must be lower on the pecking order than he thinks he is. See, I wanted to give the main hardass an excuse to back down. But I blew the element of surprise on a wimp, and now the actual top dog is going to have time to talk himself up to facing me." He shoved his tray over. "You eat this. I lost my appetite."

"But -- uh, thanks. But I still don't get it. Are you famous or something?"

"Guess you could say that. Ever heard of the Dyer

Brothers gang?"

"No."

"How about the White Rose?"

"No. Sorry."

"It's okay. Don't figure folks up north hear that stuff anyway, not if they're not in the business. You're too clean for this place, you know that? I still don't get why you're here. Churchrock's where they send the worst of the worst. Folks who use their Talents to hurt people."

"You did that?"

Trevarde looked at his tattooed hand. "Yeah. I'm a jinx. You know, a ghoul witch."

"You're *what*?" Ashleigh edged away.

Trevarde looked annoyed. "Get back here. I won't hurt you. Can't use my Talent in here anyway. It's warded. Or haven't you noticed?"

Ashleigh shook his head. "I didn't even know I had magic until they tested me at my sentencing."

"Huh." Trevarde was rubbing his thumb across the dots on his palm. "You high up with the rebels, then?"

"Not really. Propaganda. I just had a handful of contacts." He winced at the memory. "The Watch sucked them right out of my head. I'm sure they were all arrested. I'm sure most of them are dead now."

"But you were good at it?"

"I guess."

"I was good at what I did too."

"And that's what you're famous for?"

"Every one of these dots is a dead man, Ash. You want to count 'em?"

"Uh. No."

"You're not eating," Trevarde pointed out, and laughed.

After breakfast, they were taken outdoors. Ashleigh was so glad to see the sky again that he didn't, at first, realize the potential for chaos. They were let out into a big fenced square of dirt, in the baking heat, with nothing to do, and no supervision except the distant guns on the watchtowers, but all he could think about was the gorgeous blue of the sky.

Trevarde was more alert. "This is where the fights happen," he observed. "Somebody gets in my face, you step back."

"Sure."

They walked around a bit, passing knots of two or three or five men standing together and the occasional pathetic creature huddled alone. A couple of those were talking to themselves. One was pressed to the bars of the fence as if trying to squeeze himself through. He looked almost emaciated enough to succeed. Ashleigh wondered how long it would be before he himself went mad and ended up like that.

Trevarde seemed to be appraising each of their fellow prisoners as a trader appraises another man's horses, with an educated but distant eye. To Ashleigh, they all looked equally terrifying.

He watched Trevarde instead; the way the sun gilded his skin and struck poison-green sparks from his eyes, the way a dusty breath of hot wind lifted strands of his hair and twined them into the glyphs of an alien language. In this bright light his scars were less apparent. While Ashleigh watched, Trevarde stretched, arms behind his head, arching his back. This caused a gap between his shirt and trousers, showing a smooth brown expanse of finely muscled stomach. Ashleigh looked away, wondering if Trevarde could possibly have done it on purpose to bother him -- dismissed that as wistful paranoia -- realized he had no clue whatsoever, and felt suddenly as if he'd been struck blind. He'd never noticed his Empathy, never intentionally used it, but now he felt its absence; anesthetized, colorblind. Everyone's motives were a mystery.

No wonder they were all so scary. When he couldn't sense the humanity of them, they all seemed like automatons. Greasy homunculi. The set of some sadistic play.

And you were wondering, he told himself wryly, *how long it would take you to go mad.*

A more purposeful kind of movement among the aimless wandering distracted him from his thoughts. It was with something like relief that he nudged his companion's ribs with his knuckles. "Here comes your fight, Trevarde."

"Call me Kieran." He spoke through a yawn, turning to see the approaching men with no sign of apprehension. "Nobody I like uses my last name."

"All right. Kieran." Ashleigh took a step back, out of the path between Trevarde -- Kieran -- and the three men who were stalking toward him. It didn't seem like a good idea to be within arm's reach of anyone right now.

The lead man was also a Iavaian, a bit lighter of skin than

Kieran was. He had a similar ranginess, though not nearly as tall, and wore his hair in two braids. He had a patchy mustache, and a cool arrogance in his eyes. His two followers were a red-faced blond of the dockhand variety and a bald, bearded fellow who had a vaguely demented air about him. When he got close, the leader put an extra bit of saunter in his step and raised his chin an extra notch. Ashleigh thought this might mean he was scared, but it was too hard to guess these things now.

"So," said braids, "You're Kieran Trevarde." He made it sound like a test.

All Kieran said was, "So?"

"I heard you killed Ama Sona."

"So?"

"He was good. Better than you. You're nothing without your magic."

"That's what you think, huh?"

"Yeah. It is."

Kieran shrugged. "All right."

Braids turned to Baldie with a grin. "You hear that? He admits it."

"Nah," said Kieran lightly, "I just said it's all right if you think that. I don't actually care what you think."

Braids stepped in closer. "You should care. I'm Duyam Sona. Ama was my brother."

"I know. You didn't like him much, either." This revelation was delivered with the same cool as anything else that came out of Kieran's mouth. "I had a contract on you too, but you got bagged before I got my advance."

Duyam Sona clenched a fist between them. "Is that all my brother's life meant to you? Money?"

"All it meant to him, too. You don't pony tar through Burn River for the retirement benefits."

"Fuck you, you son of a fucking --"

"Uh-huh. Are we going to fight, or what?"

Sona replied with a snarl and his fist. Kieran slid aside and hit back with the heel of his hand to the center of Sona's chest. As their leader flew back, knocked breathless, the other two charged.

Ashleigh, backing farther away, looked around to see if any intervention was forthcoming. Most of the inmates in the yard were watching the fight, but none seemed interested in being involved. That was good, right? But it seemed vaguely horrific, the impassive way they watched.

When he looked back, the fight was over.

Baldie, bleeding from the nose, was helping Sona to his feet. The blond backed away hugging his ribs, with the self-absorbed expression of a man in pain. Ashleigh found he was surprised that they were all still alive. Kieran was rubbing the point of his jaw.

"You clipped me. That's good. You might make a fighter someday." This was apparently directed at Baldie, because that one spat a gob of blood and a garbled obscenity.

Sona wasn't done. "I'll kill you, Trevarde. You better watch your back, because I'll kill you."

"All right." Kieran put his hands behind his head again and walked over to the fence. No one followed but Ashleigh.

Ashleigh said tentatively, "That looked easy."

"Yeah." Kieran sighed. "I was hoping for a good fight. Ama was pretty good."

"So you really did kill that man's brother."

"Yeah. Ama Sona worked for a gang out of Trestre, tried to expand into Burn River. Gang I worked for didn't like that."

"That's these Weavers you mentioned?"

"Dyers. But no, that came later. This was when I was, what, seventeen, I guess. When I was with the White Rose."

Ashleigh was starting to feel sick to his stomach. "So you were a drug runner? That's how you got this reputation?"

"Nah. I was a killer. I worked for the drug runners. Opium's big business down here. We slaughter each other so you white folks can have pretty dreams."

"Hey, it's not --"

"I know, up East you got people shooting each other over the paint thinner that leaks out the bottom of the corn crib. Down here we do it for tar. And you know, I think half these operations are backed by the government. You try to make some kind of moral sense out of it and you'll just tie your head in a knot."

Ashleigh struggled to contain his judgment, but one look at Kieran's bland expression and it jumped out of his throat: "Does that make it okay, in your opinion? That the world is corrupt and you murdered corrupt men, that makes murder all right?"

"I never said it was all right," Kieran said coldly. He stared until Ashleigh dropped his gaze, then turned his back.

After an exchange like that, Ashleigh would've liked to stalk off somewhere by himself for a while, but instead he was back in his cell with Kieran, trying not to make eye contact. Lacking privacy, his next choice would have been to hide in a book, but a brief conversation with a guard informed him that there was no reading material whatsoever to be had. Not even a newspaper.

He killed a few minutes exploring the cell. There was a tin pitcher half full of water and a washbasin still sludgy with the remains of Kieran's morning ablutions. A steel toilet of the sort found in outhouses -- he supposed a water closet would have been too much to ask for. A slab of polished steel intended to function as a mirror, but no razor. What on earth was the mirror for if it wasn't to shave by? In a tray attached to the bottom of the mirror was a tin cup and a damaged comb, just one of each, which they'd apparently have to share.

His bed was a narrow frame of steel tubing, bolted down, with a mattress that felt like it was stuffed with raw cotton. There were mysterious stains on its tan-striped fabric. There was a drain under the washstand and an air shaft above the mirror, both too small to admit his head and both covered with metal grills. And that was it. That was his entire world. The only interesting thing in the cell -- hell, the only object with moving parts -- was his cellmate.

It was time, he decided, to make peace.

"Look, Trevarde -- I mean, Kieran --"

"Forget about it."

Taken aback, Ashleigh only managed, "Um?"

Kieran gave him one of those false smiles. "Any sentence that comes out of nowhere and starts with 'Look --' is doomed to end with 'sorry'. I'm not mad. My past isn't a secret, I just get tired of talking about it."

"Oh." Ashleigh looked down at his hands, made them stop picking at the hem of his shirt. "Then -- if you don't mind -- just so I don't keep blundering into it -- could you tell me? Who you are. Why you're here." He waved a vague gesture. "What the world looks like from where you are."

"What, you don't want to drag out the mystery?" Kieran stretched out on his bunk, hands behind his head, showing the skin of his waist again, so that Ashleigh had to look away. "Nah, you're right, better to lay out all the cards. Puts us on more even terms. And I have a feeling you can help me as much as I can help you."

"How?"

"Dunno. Now shut up so I can tell the story."

"Sorry."

"So. Me. My mother was a prostitute. Then she died. So I was turning tricks for a while, actually quite a while, and that's why I was in lockup the first time. Prostitution. Would've been a fine and a work sentence if I was a girl, but you know, they tacked the extra sodomy charge on. Tiyamo was a giant dogfight, and that's all you need to know about it. That's where I found out about my Talent. Missed the normal fourteenth-birthday Survey on account of not officially existing."

"Didn't they do a Survey when you were arrested?"

"Yeah, but they didn't find anything. I don't know why. Either they fucked it up or mine grew late. I noticed it the end of my first year in Tiyamo. See, I was this scrawny little guy, and everybody knew why I was in there -- anyway, there were some folks I really wished would just curl up and die. And they did. One guy got bit by a snake in the yard. Another guy got sick, and a couple guys stabbed each other... I probably woulda killed off half the inmates and got caught, except this guy Shrike noticed what I was doing and clued me in. Got me a job when I got out. 'Course, I ended up killing Shrike pretty much right away. I didn't like his attitude.

"Kinter -- that's the boss -- he gave me whatever I wanted. Drowned me in girls and liquor and poppy. I don't like girls, and booze bores me, but the tar was all right." Kieran gave a snort of bitter laughter. "Mistake. Once he had me on the leash, well -- you get it."

What does he mean, doesn't like girls? He can't have meant it the way it sounded. Ashleigh must've made some sound, because Kieran turned to give him a disapproving stare. "Don't look so shocked, Ash. Most of the world lives like that, one way or another."

All Ashleigh could think was that he was starting to like being called Ash. He'd declined the nickname as a child because of the dumb jokes people made about it, but it was all right now.

"I'm sorry. I didn't mean to interrupt."

"Sure. Anyway, I had to learn to kill folks up close and personal, because Kinter didn't want to overuse the magic thing. Gets too obvious, certain people get too interested. I learned to shoot, use a knife -- use it right, I mean -- and they had this old guy who knew *kengdan* -- you heard of it?"

"Iavian boxing, right? It's illegal."

"It's dirty fighting. Stuff like you saw today. First thing Kinter had me do when he figured I knew enough was beat some guy to death over a bad deal that cost him about fifty signets. You believe that? Five thrones. My guess is he didn't care about the money, he was just trying out his new toy.

"So I hated him, of course. But he held the leash.

"That was how it was when he sent me after the Dyer brothers. White boys from Rainet. Cal, Mack, and Shanin. They weren't in the poppy game, they were just holdup men. You know, highway robbers. I was supposed to shoot two and disappear the third, make it look like they jacked each other. Maybe to distract the cops from something, I dunno. The point is, when I found them, watched them, listened to them, I couldn't do it."

He paused, looking Ashleigh over, as if deciding how much to tell. Then he looked away. "Actually, it was Shanin Dyer's face that stopped me. He had this way of smiling, like he knew what you were thinking but he liked you anyway...

"I told Kinter no go. He cut off my supply. Three days without it and I was begging to do the job. Went back to the Dyers' hangout and found I couldn't again, sat there debating with myself until they came out and caught me. That was such a damn relief -- I figured they'd just kill me -- but they didn't. Shan talked the others out of it. He helped me kick.

"Cal got killed a couple months later, Mack settled down with a native girl who'd already had a couple of his babies, but me and Shan kept going. Had some good times, made a lot of money. Got famous, too. I hear we made the papers all the way out to Helermont when we hit the Red River mail train. We didn't get hardly nothing out of that one, but I guess it looked flashy or something. Wish we'd kept our heads down more, 'cause after that the cops got serious about catching us. Probably the fuckers who killed Shan got a medal."

He sighed. Levered himself off the bed and went to the bars. He stood there for a while, looking up at the dirty skylights. Then he put his back to the cell door and stared at Ashleigh for a time. Suddenly he reached out and set his hand on Ashleigh's hair. Ashleigh flinched, and Kieran snatched his hand away. He went back to his side of the room as casually as if he'd done nothing strange.

"I'm tired of this story. Shan's dead, and I'm in here." Kieran threw himself on his bunk. "I'm taking a nap." He rolled over to face the wall.

Ashleigh stared disbelievingly at his back for a long while. He'd never encountered such confusing behavior before. One thing he was sure of: Kieran was nowhere near as in control as Ashleigh had at first assumed. His calm had been deceptive. Just because he'd kept a straight face while blurting out the story of his sordid life didn't make it any less blurt-like. And what was that thing with the hand?

Had Kieran meant what it sounded like he'd been implying? That the late Shan Dyer had been more than a partner in crime? Maybe more than a friend? Was he mourning a lover? He didn't act like it. Besides, no one would have admitted so lightly to being an invert; surely such proclivities were subject to floggings and cagings in the south just as they were in the rest of the Commonwealth. Probably Kieran had just wanted to make contact with someone, anyone -- but with his Empathy damped, Ashleigh knew he was just making blind guesses. It could have meant anything at all.

Ashleigh bitterly regretted flinching. Kieran was probably tired of people being afraid of him. But he *was* scary. And he clearly had a few gears loose, though after a life like that he was certainly entitled to be a bit batty.

Ashleigh tried, for a while, to imagine what it must have been like to live that life. He couldn't. He thought he'd probably gawped like a goldfish the whole time he was listening; which hadn't kept Kieran from telling him. Maybe it didn't matter who he'd been talking to, as long as he could spill his story and get rid of it. Maybe he'd even wanted to be stared at. To have someone care enough to be shocked. Or maybe the case was the opposite: that Kieran was so incapable of feeling as to part with the wretched garbage of his past as easily as anyone else might discuss the price of onions.

Ashleigh found he was chewing his nails, and made himself stop. *What does it matter?* he told himself. *It's not as if he cares what you think. Or what anyone thinks, or says about him.*

Nevertheless, Ashleigh had to wonder whether the reason Kieran had given for offering his protection, as an excuse to fight, had been a cover for something a little kinder... or for something more cruel.

Chapter 3

Kieran studied the texture of the wall, working on his calm. He'd cracked a little bit, there; explained too much. Given in to impulse. That had been a junkie thing to do. All day he'd wanted to know what those rusty curls would feel like to his hand, and so he'd just gone ahead and found out.

There was a chill feeling he could wrap himself in, if he could find it, that would make it too much trouble to talk like that again, not worth the effort to reach out to the poor, doomed, pale thing he shared his cell with. Once, he'd been good at it. After Shan, though -- having friends had been a mistake. He couldn't remember exactly what he'd done after watching a bullet take Shan's head apart, but when he'd come to his senses there'd been five cops and a Watchman dead and he himself had been discovering the joys of a sucking chest wound, which sort of indicated a loss of control.

Blaming himself wasn't going to help. The reasons never mattered. Excuses only made you look like an idiot. He had to close up the gaps.

Was Ash going to pry now? Kieran could feel him staring. Maybe telling him all that stuff had scared him; that would be good. He'd keep his distance. Having a clever little mouse on payroll was one thing; getting attached to him was another, and Kieran had no intention of doing that. Ash was going to be useful. The guards seemed to like him, he was intelligent, he was weak and needy, he was an excellent tool. But only if he stayed a tool. His ignorance of the true nastiness of life could be a liability, otherwise.

It was too bad, really. In other circumstances... No. That was a bad place to let his thoughts go. There were no other circumstances.

If wishes were horses, Kieran thought, *I'd be the only one walking*.

So he chose a spot on the wall in front of his nose, a vein of darker orange running through the yellow stone, and examined it with all his attention. It was a trick he'd invented as a child. He didn't move his eyes, refused his thoughts, concentrated on that one little orange swirl until all the useless anxiety and useless hope had faded. Until he could look at his cellmate's freckled, innocent, blue-eyed face and not want to smash it in or devour it.

When someone spoke his name at the door, he was almost ready to handle it. He almost didn't give a damn why, or what was about to happen. Almost was going to have to be good enough; they weren't going to give him time to finish collecting himself.

"Trevarde," the guard's voice repeated. "Get a move on, freak. Unless you want a taste of this." There was a slapping sound.

Something touched his shoulder. "Kieran?"

"Don't touch me," Kieran said. But he didn't jump. He didn't hit. That was going to have to do.

He got up, and discovered that 'this' was a baton the guard was smacking into his palm, making a show of impatience. Kieran could've easily taken it from him and made him eat it, but knew he would've been perforated by a dozen bullets the next moment. Since he supposed he didn't want that, he came along peacefully instead.

"Where are you taking him?" Ash asked.

"Testing," the guard replied. "You'll get your turn. Probably tomorrow." Ash must've looked fearful, because the man added, "He'll be back by supper, so don't rent out his room just yet." He made up for this non-regulation reassurance by prodding Kieran in the small of the back. Kieran responded with the obligatory cold glare, but inside he was smiling. *Good mouse*, he thought at Ash. *They like you. Make them tell you things. Use your innocence to help me, and I'll see you get to keep it as long as possible.*

An explanation was a very tiny victory, of course, but Kieran could never have gotten one, no matter how sweetly he asked.

Testing. That didn't sound like fun, but it was apparently nonfatal, and since he couldn't do a single thing about it he saw no reason to have an opinion. Another guard fell in behind him at the end of the tier, and they marched him down the stairs and through the gated door he'd been brought in by last night. It seemed like they might be taking him outside, to another building, but then they took a left turn and he gave up guessing.

It grew colder as he walked, and the light changed. There was a flight of stairs, the stone painted with glossy gray industrial paint. Up, but still in a tunnel carved out of solid rock. They were inside the mountain.

The walk ended at a metal door that felt cold to look at -- what a weird thought. There they waited for a time. "Now, you mind your manners when you meet the Colonel," the guard said, apparently just to fill the silence. "Or I'll take it out of your hide."

After a while, the door seemed a little friendlier, and then it was opened by a man in a White Watch uniform. Two pins on the collar and one loop of scarlet braid on the shoulder. Not a colonel. "This is Trevarde?" said the uniform. "Come in. Sit down."

As Kieran went in, his mind opened up like the view from a high hill. Like a fever ending. Like waking.

"God," he said.

"Sit down," said a man behind a metal desk. "Chaler, you can go."

"Sir," said the uniform, and went.

Kieran went to the empty chair that faced the desk and fell into it, a little stunned. The sensation of being imprisoned had gone entirely. He knew that he was farther from freedom than at any previous point, locked into a small white-painted hollow in the middle of a mountain with only one well-guarded exit, and yet some oppression had paradoxically lifted. It left him feeling light and strong and wide-awake.

This room was outside the wards that kept the inmates from using their Talents. He'd barely noticed them, coming in, but it seemed the pressure had built up, and letting his mind unfurl brought a sensation of pleasure that was slightly painful. It threatened his composure.

"Aren't you afraid I'll attack you?" he said.

The man who was undoubtedly the Colonel smiled at him pleasantly, as if they were just chatting in a bar somewhere. "I think you're smarter than that, Mr. Trevarde."

"Well, yeah. But people don't usually bet their lives on it."

"I'm also rather better shielded than those you've attacked in the past. Your Talent would have little effect on me." He waited for a response. When he didn't get one, he turned to taking things from the drawers of his desk.

He was a fleshy man, the Colonel, with gray hair in a tidy queue and half-round spectacles perched on his nose, a bit past middle age, not at all what Kieran expected from a high-level White Watch officer. The Watch mages who'd grabbed Kieran from the local police had been damn near faceless in their pseudo-military perfection. Maybe this was what they'd be when they grew up.

"I'm Colonel Warren. I'll be performing a series of tests with you, some of which may be unpleasant, but they'll be less unpleasant with your cooperation. I'm aware that being a prisoner tends to make one wish to rebel, to cause difficulty for one's captors, but I think you have a strong instinct for self-preservation, Mr. Trevarde. I think you'll find it in your best interest to follow my instructions and cause as little trouble as possible. Do you understand?"

"Sure. What's this for, anyway?"

"For the greater good, Mr. Trevarde. You should be thankful you have this chance to work off a little of your moral debt, though of course it can never be paid in full this side of the Final Judgment. Now, we'll begin with a simple Survey. You've been through this before, so I expect you to remain calm and facilitate my task by opening up as much as possible."

Oh shit, not one of these. Kieran closed his eyes as the Colonel came out from behind the desk. *Okay, you can handle this. It's just another trick, you remember how to do this, you just wait it out...*

The Colonel's chilly fingers touched his head, and suddenly Kieran knew he couldn't open up to this. Something in him that wasn't subject to will rebelled. And so the mental rape of the Survey was every bit as painful as it had been at his hurried excuse for a trial.

Icy, alien thoughts like blunt metal instruments battered at his defenses, tearing his thoughts apart. The agony was nothing physical, but something worse; a pain like grief, like shame. Then the probing penetrated below the level of thought to a place in the mind that Kieran knew was never meant to be groped like this. The cold manipulation of a stranger's thoughts dissected his selfhood; peeled apart layers, poked and squeezed, cut and bruised.

Fighting was impossible, but he fought anyway. Not consciously, because volition had been the first layer to be shoved aside, but with an automatic response, like vomiting when poisoned. When at last the alien thoughts stopped pushing, this reflex ejected them, doing as much damage on the way out as they had done coming in.

A scream choked off, and Kieran recognized that it had

been his own. He was sweating, shivering, hoarse. He tasted bile in the back of his throat, and bitter hatred, and his stomach hurt. He tried to speak, and only groaned.

The Colonel was back behind the desk. "I did warn you not to fight," he said, in the kind of smug pretense at apology that Kieran had used on men who'd tried to kill him.

"Ah, shit," was all Kieran could get out.

"We'll have to repeat the Survey from time to time, you see. I hope next time you'll make it easier on yourself."

Kieran tried to swallow, couldn't, spat instead. "Anyone who could keep from fighting that," he croaked, "is a sick, sick person."

"Well." The Colonel looked at some of the things on his desk; picked up a pen, moved a piece of paper. "I believe we're done for today."

As if he'd been eavesdropping, the lesser uniform who'd let him into the room a million aching years ago opened the door and said his name. It was an effort to get out of the chair, and when he walked he stumbled.

"Kieran! What did they do to you?" Ash caught his arm as the cell door slammed, to steer him to his bed.

"Quit touching me," Kieran grumbled, but didn't pull away.

"I'm sorry. Here --" The redhead rushed to take the blanket from his cot, and when Kieran lay down he spread it over him, looking even whiter than usual. "You're shaking. You look terrible. What did they do?"

"Survey." Kieran swallowed. "Just a Survey."

"Look how you're sweating. God. Do they do that to everyone?" Ash went away, came back a moment later with a tin cup. "Here. They brought more water while you were gone."

Kieran levered himself up on one elbow and drained the cup. He remembered to be polite, reward the favor: "Thanks. I'm all right now. Just let me sleep."

"Sure." Ash went away, but his voice came back after a moment's pause. "I hate that they call it that. It's a lie. As if they're just asking questions. As if it's your own fault that it hurts."

"Let me sleep," Kieran repeated, too scattered to put any force into it.

When he woke, it was dark, the darkness filled with snoring. He had turned over in his sleep; what he saw when his eyes opened was Ash, sitting on the edge of the cot opposite, chin in hands, watching him.

"What the hell are you looking at?" The words came out milder than he'd intended.

Ash sat up straighter. "Huh? Oh. Sorry. Thinking."

"How long have you been doing that?"

"All my life." Ash sounded embarrassed by his own weak joke.

"Well, stop it."

"Sorry."

"And stop apologizing."

The lost look that had been Ash's default expression since the first moment Kieran had seen him went away then, finally chased off by irritation. "Well, what do you *expect* people to say when you bark at them?"

Ash, Kieran realized with a sinking feeling, was damned good-looking when he wasn't doing his kicked puppy impression. Maybe it was just the dark. The freckles weren't so obvious, the haloing curls weren't as red, so it was easier to see the clean lines of his face.

No. I already decided no. Kieran sat up, then put his hands to his head. "Shit. I am so hung over. I hope the Colonel was just trying to scare me when he said they were going to Survey me again later."

"Is that who did it?"

"Yeah."

"Tell me about him."

"How does it matter? You'll find out soon enough."

"Maybe I can be a little more prepared."

Kieran's laughter brought a guard to tell them to shut up. When the guard's footsteps had gone far enough down the walkway, he made an effort to speak quietly. "What makes you think," he muttered, "that any damn thing you can do will prepare you in any way for the reaming you're about to get? What good would it do?"

"I'd be less scared," Ash whispered back. "If I knew what was coming. I don't know. I just don't feel like giving up yet."

Kieran thought about it, and at last agreed. "I guess making trouble staves off boredom."

"I was thinking more along the lines of analyzing them the way they're analyzing us. If we can figure out what they're looking for, maybe we can mess with them."

"Don't see how."

"Not yet."

Kieran sighed. "Fine. Something to do, anyway. Not much to tell, though. Bastard's name is Warren, and he's got a mind-probe like an ape with a sledgehammer."

"Clumsy, eh?"

"As bad as the jackass who did me at my trial. The last one, I mean. I think worse than the first time, but maybe because back then I didn't have a Talent yet."

"You think he found what he was looking for?"

"How the hell should I know?"

"Ssh! I don't know, but when I was Surveyed I could kind of tell. He was mucking around in there, and he hit something that kind of -- flashed -- and then he stopped."

"Huh. Nothing like that."

"I wonder what that means."

"You go ahead and wonder. I'm going back to sleep."

"All right, but Kieran?"

"What?"

A pause. "Never mind."

"No, what?"

Ash's eyes were hard to read in the dark. "I forgot what I was going to say."

Sure you did. You were going to cross a line, I'll bet. Say something personal. Smart mouse, figured out where to quit. Nevertheless, Kieran found some of his bitterness had faded. He was still angry, but he had it contained now. Futile as it was, Ash's idiotic hope had cooled some of the burn inside his head.

The next day, Ash outlined the first stage of his plan.

"We should find out what Talents these other guys have. They don't send everybody here, right? We can figure out what they're studying."

"Sounds about right." Kieran watched oatmeal drip off his spoon. "What's stage two?"

"Uh... I'll figure that out when we get the results from stage one."

Kieran chuckled. "Genius." He bent to gulping down his breakfast while considering who to approach first. Not that he was real excited about this scheme of Ash's, but it would be interesting to see how people reacted.

No one had bothered them so far today, but it was only breakfast. It would take people a while to work up their courage after he took down three big guys the day before without breaking a sweat. Maybe, just maybe, they'd all figured out he was tougher than the lot of them, and there'd be no more fights at all. But Kieran didn't believe in miracles. The structures of power would be more complex than that, and harder to shift. Very few of these men would be able to admit they were outclassed unless the lesson was spelled out in blood.

"That guy," he said at last, pointing with his spoon at one of the half-mad loners no one ever talked to.

"Him?" Ash looked skeptical. "What, are you collecting wimps?"

"Loser unity." Kieran grinned. "No, actually I just figure he won't waste our time with attitude."

"Loser unity. I like that."

"W-what do you w-want?" The man had cornered himself by the fence and was shaking like an angry kitten. "I d-din' do nothing."

"Must've done *something*," Kieran said. "You're here, right?"

"Din' hurt you none. Got no fight with you."

"Fine. I just want to know what your Talent is."

"Why? I never done nothing to you!" His voice climbed to a squeak. "I got no fight with you!"

Exasperated, Kieran leaned closer. "Look, just answer the damn --"

The man's eyes rolled up in his head, and he folded into a heap.

Ash cleared his throat nervously. "Um. Maybe you should let me talk to the little ones."

Behind them, a familiar voice said, "You won't be satisfied until you've killed us all, will you?"

Kieran turned with a sigh to confront Duyam Sona, this time with only his broken-nosed monkey to back him up. "What happened to that fat yellow-haired bastard you were dragging around yesterday?"

"*You* happened, you shit! He never came back from Testing yesterday. Guess they figured it was easier to get rid of him than stick a plaster on those ribs you broke. Now I see you're picking on the crazy ones."

"He's okay. I just spooked him." He looked to see if the fainter was up yet. He wasn't. "Ash, give him a hand, would you?" Then he made a startled noise as something hit him in the stomach hard enough to hurt.

His body reacted before his mind; the back of his fist sent Sona sprawling. He caught himself beginning the long stride that would lead into a kick to the jaw as Sona started to get up, and was able to turn it into an ordinary step. He planted his feet and waited for Sona to be vertical.

"I'm bored of fighting you. I gave you a free shot and you didn't even break anything."

Sona spat a string of pink saliva. "You killed my brother. You killed my friend. And I'm going to kill you."

"So *do* it, for fuck's sake. Don't make a speech first, just grind a spoon handle nice and sharp and stick it in my back. Explain why afterwards, if you have to talk about it. Though you oughtta recognize nobody gives a shit about your reasons. Nobody cares whether you kill me or I kill you."

"*Kaiyo*," Sona accused. "You don't care any more for your own life than for any of the poor bastards you murdered."

"Should I?"

Sona stared for a long moment. Then he gestured to his monkey and turned away; that stiff-shouldered walk that meant they were trying not run.

"Kieran, was that a good idea, telling him that?" Ash was doing his puppy face again. "He just might take your advice."

"So?"

"I see."

"You try and get some sense out of the fainting flower. I'll take my scary self somewhere else. If anyone fucks with you, scream like a girl."

"Oh, yes, very good," Ash said dryly.

No one started anything with Ash. Kieran pretended to bask by the wall, while with half-closed eyes he followed the coppery gleam of Ash's head around the yard. The white boy got barked at a few times, but no one got physical. When they were back in the cell, he reported his results.

"I talked to four Pyrokinetics and an Entropist. I mean, firestarters and a breaker. Also a bunch of guys who wouldn't tell me anything." A flush rose in his cheeks. "Anything useful," he amended.

"Did they talk shit to you?"

"Yeah. But that's not important."

"No, it is. You're under my protection, I can't let people trash you."

"Aren't we getting a little sidetracked here?"

"Yeah, just point 'em out tomorrow and I'll take care of it."

"I really wish you wouldn't."

"Don't you listen? That don't matter. Now, you were saying."

Ash thinned his lips, annoyed, then deliberately relaxed his face. When he spoke, his voice was emotionless. "I was saying. There were a hundred and four men in the yard. So it's possible the percentage of Pyros was about on the mark. Rebel intel said the Watch had six percent fire Talents, and I think we can expect the proportion to be roughly the same among men who evaded Survey. Which would be our friends here. With me so far?"

"Sure."

"But considering that *eighty* percent of the ones I *spoke* to were Pyros --"

"And the other one a breaker, which is also a destructive Talent. But you don't end up in Churchrock just for skipping a Survey. We all got grabbed off the gallows. So I'd say we learned jack shit today."

Ash looked a bit taken aback, as if he hadn't expected Kieran to actually grasp what he was talking about. He rallied, though, and went on, "What about Kinesis? It's the most common Talent. Maybe I just missed them all, I know the data pool is too small for any kind of conclusion, but Kinetics are very common and there were none. Kinetics do crimes too, right?"

"I wish we had something to write on. Or with." Kieran flopped down on his cot, pondering.

"I'll pester the guards."

Kieran raised an eyebrow. "Think that'll work?"

"No harm in trying."

"Not for you, I guess. Anyway, unless you can keep all this shit in your head, it's gone, because I have a brain like a sieve."

"I can remember what we have so far. If the sample reflects the general case at all, we know they've been studying fire Talents, and our inclusion indicates a new direction. I'd like to know what Talent that blond man had, the one who disappeared." After a while he added, "That Burdock fellow, the one from the train -- I haven't seen him."

"Maybe I killed him after all. I sure as hell concussed him."

Ash looked disturbed. "Why did you, anyway? You hadn't decided to make a pet of me yet. What did you care if he attacked me?"

Kieran opened his mouth to reply, but hesitated. Ash probably knew what reactions he inspired, how everyone who didn't want to abuse him needed to protect him, but Kieran didn't feel like admitting out loud how reflexive it had been. "I knew him in Burn River," he prevaricated. It was technically true. "The man was a stain."

"Old grudge?"

"Just never liked him. He was muscle for my old boss. Pyro. He was the favorite toy before I came along. Didn't see a lot of him, but when I did he always acted all yessir-nosir, 'cause he was scared of me, and then he'd talk shit behind my back. Guess when he called you a pansy it reminded me."

"Oh." Ash studied the floor, while his ears slowly turned pink. That was interesting. "So you don't think he really believed..."

"Nah. He would've called you a cocksucker, if he thought you really were. That's what he liked to say about me when he was sure I was out of earshot." Kieran chuckled. "Closet case if I ever saw one."

Blushing in earnest now, Ash said, "Is there any other kind? I mean, it's illegal."

"Well, there's me." Kieran shrugged, pretending not to watch Ash's reaction. "I'm a fucking murderer, what do I care if people know who I sleep with? You got a problem with it?"

Ash's eyes flashed panic, and he babbled. "No! Of course not. You are what you are, right? I mean, thank you for being honest. Not that you care what I think."

Kieran laughed. "Didn't mean to spook you."

"I'm not spooked. It's just you don't often hear someone just come out with it like that. Roughly never, in fact. I wouldn't presume to judge -- if I thought there was a judgment to be made, which of course -- what I mean is --"

"Okay."

"Quit laughing at me!"

"Can't. You're too fucking funny." But Kieran was laughing at himself as well, and at circumstance; after he'd decided not to develop an interest in Ash, it looked like Ash already had an interest in him. But the northerner didn't want to admit it, which was only reasonable, so he figured he could get away with ignoring it a while longer. Maybe it would go away.

Footsteps approached their cell. "Ashleigh Trine."

Ash sighed. "My turn."

"Good luck," Kieran said wryly. He knew that there was no such thing.

Roughly an hour later, he heard a sound like a child crying. As it came closer, he went to the bars; the bawling noise was Ash, walking ahead of the guard with a stiff-legged gait like a broken machine, arms dangling, mouth wide open and emitting periodic gasps and hiccups.

Ash looked like a congenital idiot. The guard looked ashamed.

"Step back from the door." The guard had to repeat himself before Kieran moved. Kieran backed away, staring horrified at the red-eyed, wet-faced *thing* in front of him.

Ash was let into the cell. He went to the back corner, where he put his face to the wall, hugging himself. After locking the door, the guard stayed for a moment before stomping away. Kieran hesitated quite a bit longer.

There was a dark streak of sweat down the back of Ash's shirt. His rust-colored hair was almost straight now, strands plastered to his thin white neck. His narrow shoulders were shaking irregularly, his fingernails white where he clutched his elbows. Spectacularly pathetic. Seeing Ash like this this made Kieran want to tear down the world and stomp on the wreckage.

The impulse rushed through him to rip the weeping boy apart, to make him *stop*, to make him cease to be as if he'd never been. He made himself take a deep breath, waited for the urge to pass. Then the second impulse came: to clutch this fragile creature tightly in his arms and never let anyone come near him again. He conquered that as well. Only when he'd let go of both rage and pity did he reason a course of action. He needed Ash to be sane, and to depend on him, to use his harmlessness on the guards and weaker inmates. He had to be helped. But Kieran must not betray the weakness in himself.

Taking the blanket from Ash's bed, he approached with the care one used on an unfamiliar dog. "Hey," he said softly.

Ash sniffed. "Don't look at me." His voice was small.

"Sure. Okay." Kieran draped the blanket around Ash's shoulders. "Come out of there. You should lie down."

"Don't want to." But he let himself be steered, clutching his blanket. On the bed, he curled up in a ball. There he continued to bawl intermittently.

Not enough. Kieran searched his memory for ways to calm a distraught person. There weren't many. It had been a long time since he'd cared whether anyone was upset, and longer since anyone had given him that consideration. After several minutes of watching Ash shudder with sobs, he remembered something -- far too intimate, it would be taken wrong, but he *had* to make the crying stop.

He went and got the gap-toothed wooden comb they had to share. He sat on the edge of Ash's cot. Steeling himself for the disturbing touch of another person's damp skin, he slid his hand under Ash's sweaty hair and began dragging the comb through it.

At first this just made Ash cry harder. Eventually, though, his sobs subsided to hiccups, then to even breathing. It took forever. By the time he finally cried himself to sleep, his hair was dry enough to curl again, and Kieran's hands were tired.

And Kieran had spent way too long looking down on planes and curves of milk-white skin spotted with tiny freckles, the infant delicacy of Ash's red-bitten mouth, the slender smoothness of his curled hand, and now had to fight with himself to put the comb away and go back to his own side of the cell.

No, he told himself. *No. Absolutely not. Never again. They will kill him sooner or later. You will not allow this to scratch you.*

Chapter 4

Ashleigh didn't trust himself to speak for a long time after that. Kieran made no attempt to break his silence, for which he was grateful. The tall Iavaian hovered protectively near him whenever they were taken out of the cell, a powerful shadow to shield him from the stares and laughter of those who'd seen him crying. Ashleigh thought that if he had that dark, quiet presence beside him all the time, he could bear these violations and not go mad, but it was a near thing. By lights-out on the third day, he was ready to talk.

"I want to thank you," he whispered. Curled on his side in the dark, he could still feel Kieran's protective presence. Strange, that he could sense it despite being without his Talent. It crossed his mind to wonder if he would find Kieran so comforting if he could feel the ghoul-witch's morbid power; he'd never been near one before. But then, he'd never been near a murderer before, and that didn't seem to matter either. "You've been very kind to me."

There was a rustle and a creak. The mattress shifted; warmth of Kieran's hip beside his thigh; hair draped over his hand, telling him the tall boy had bent his head nearer. "Feeling better now?"

"Yes." Without turning over his hand, he spread his fingers and felt strands of heavy black hair slide between them, fascinated by the tenuous sense of connection it brought. "I didn't... I didn't expect... I'm very grateful."

"You want to tell me what happened?"

"No. But I'm going to anyway. I think I have to."

"I'm listening."

"I learned why I'm here. Me personally, as opposed to all of us."

"Yeah?"

"I met that Warren person you mentioned. He wasn't alone. He had some students with him. Other Watchmen. Surveyors. Recent Collegium grads, I think, because you know they take the braid off when they wash their uniforms, and these guys had one loop brighter than the other."

"You don't miss much," Kieran praised him, and he felt

warmer for it.

"I want to figure these things out," he explained. "If I know more than they think I do... There were three of them. Warren probably did his explaining before I came in so I wouldn't hear it, but he had to instruct them a little bit. He told me not to fight, then went into my head. Which of course I didn't like. But he just went in and touched something and came out.

"Then he told one of the students to go in, 'Paying special attention to the inflamed state of the linkage.' And that one went in and blundered around a bit. When he came out he said he couldn't find any Talents."

"Wait. He said Talents, plural?"

"Right. I know, that's weird now that I think about it. I haven't heard of people having more than one."

"Me neither. But go on. Couldn't find it."

"Warren told him that 'a marginal Talent is sometimes eclipsed by flaring in a periodic stress environment,' whatever that means. And he should try again. Um. I kind of lost track after a while, but I think they each made two or three attempts. I don't remember exactly what I heard after that, but I gathered the impression that the reason I'm of interest is that my Talent is so small. Hard to detect. They were practicing." He hesitated, because if he went on and Kieran was indifferent... but he remembered the gentleness of Kieran's fingers, gathering up his hair, smoothing it back from his face. Caring wasn't guaranteed, but it was possible. He took a deep breath and continued. "One of them was enjoying how much it hurt me. That room's not warded. I had my Empathy -- more sensitive than before, sort of rubbed raw -- and one of the students, he really liked that the Surveys distressed me. The more upset I got, the more excited it made him. I mean... sexually. Excited. And. And he. He was being. Hurting me on purpose." Ashleigh held very still, waiting to learn whether his pain mattered to anyone but himself.

A large hand landed on his hair, the sympathy he'd hoped for but hadn't expected. Gratitude and relief made his heart clench, and suddenly he was fighting tears. Kieran's rich voice was soft and near: "You're okay now. It's over now."

"They'll do it again," Ashleigh choked out. "Again and again, until I crack. And then they'll kill me. Or, worse, they won't."

"No. We'll think of something, Ash. I --" The hand

tensed, there was a swallowing noise, then a long breath. "I'm angry too," Kieran murmured at last. Ashleigh got the impression he'd almost said something else. "Look, I know you're scared of me. But you have to trust me. That's *why* you have to trust me. Because I'm mean enough to take what these sadistic fucks deal out and keep going. So you have to lean on me, and learn from me, and you have to keep going too."

Ashleigh rolled his head to search for Kieran's eyes, but couldn't read what he found there. "What are you saying?"

"I'm saying I'm going to keep you sane. Don't be afraid of me anymore, I'm not going to beat you up if you step wrong or something. When trouble's flying from everywhere, I'll be the direction it's not coming from. I'm saying you do what I tell you, and maybe... maybe we can get out of here."

Though he knew it was a lie, it helped to hear it. "Thanks," he said. "For trying."

Kieran snorted. "At least try to take me seriously, okay? Sure, we have about a housefly's chance in a hurricane, but I for one am going to give it everything I've got. You should decide whether or not you're with me."

"Of course I'm with you," Ashleigh said instantly. "A fly's chance is still a chance, you're right. What do you need me to do?"

"Whatever it takes. For now, sleep. Get your head straight so you can function tomorrow. And no more crying. They pity you now, but do it too much and they'll peg you as a nutcase." His hand stroked Ashleigh's hair once more, and then his presence receded. A creak from across the room; a rustle of blankets. Eventually, his slow breathing: sleeping as if his conscience were clear.

Ashleigh lacked that ability. He lay awake, thinking so hard his head hurt.

Earlier, he'd tried to understand what made Kieran how he was. Now he thought he was beginning to see it. The first Survey he'd suffered had been painful and humiliating, but he'd been sure it would be the only one. When the rawness in his mind had faded, he'd just been glad it was behind him. This time, though, to have it done a dozen times in an hour, by amateurs, and to feel their emotions at the same time -- clinical indifference from three and perverted joy from one -- he'd been gang-raped, whatever they chose to call it. No wonder he was a mess.

He wondered if shame like this was something Kieran

had lived with all his life. Why hadn't it wrecked him? Ashleigh was afraid that one more white uniform would drive him screaming, head-banging, eye-clawing mad. Might have done this time, if not for Kieran's kindness. Whatever inspired that kindness, be it pity or calculation or -- he wasn't sure whether to hope for or fear this -- desire, it was the only thing in his world that didn't hurt.

So he would take Kieran's advice. Learn from him. Become someone who could do what was expected of him. The person Kieran wanted him to be. Someone who could swallow horror and keep walking. Who didn't care if people didn't like the truth. Who didn't need to be protected like a child.

"Ash," he whispered, trying it out. "Ash Trine. Good to meet you, I'm Ash Trine."

"What's that?" Kieran mumbled sleepily.

"Nothing. Just changing my name."

"Um, 'scuse me?"

The guard paused outside their cell, throwing a suspicious glance past him to Kieran -- who was, by agreement, nonthreateningly washing his face at their tin mirror. "Need more water?"

"No, thanks, we're fine for water. But I wanted to ask you if there's any way I could get some paper."

The guard gave him a wry half-smile. "Sure, but it won't do you any good without a pen, and I can't give you one of those."

"How about a pencil?"

"Nothing sharp. Sorry." He began to turn away.

"Um." Ashleigh would have given up, but he was being Ash now, and Ash didn't mind if the guard got annoyed. "A crayon? Stick of charcoal? Please? I'll owe you bigtime."

That made the guard get a funny look. "Owe me what, Trine?"

"Whatever. I'll shine your shoes. Come on, I'm going bugs in here with nothing to do."

"Look." The man was getting exasperated. "If I give you a pen, and they find out, I'll lose my job."

"They won't find out. I can hide it." He did his very best needy-kid look. Today, unlike previous instances, it was a mask. "Please?"

The guard's face closed up. "I'll see what I can do." He

went away.

"Worth a try," said Kieran when the guard was out of hearing.

"He'll get it. Tomorrow, probably."

"He didn't sound real cooperative."

"That's how I know. Did you hear how he called the prison authorities 'they'? And if he didn't think it was possible, he wouldn't have bothered arguing with me. When he got all stiff, when he left, he was feeling guilty. We can start our census tomorrow. Bet you anything."

Kieran looked impressed and skeptical at once. "You sound like you still got your Talent."

"I guess I learned how to read people, sensing what was behind their faces. I still feel blind, though."

They were confined to quarters today. There had been neither breakfast nor exercise. An earlier attempt at charm had determined that the guard didn't know why either. From time to time the sounds of conversation rose to shouting, always followed by the click of a guard's boots and a barked order to break it up. Everyone was restless.

"Hey," Ash began, not sure what he was about to say but knowing he wanted to talk.

Kieran was cleaning his fingernails with the handle of a mess hall spoon. He just grunted in reply.

"Can I mess with your hair?"

"Mess with it how?" Kieran examined the spoon.

"I don't know. Comb it or something."

"If you're returning the favor from the other day, save it for when I need calming down."

"What, like there's a limited quantity of hair-combing in the world? I'm just bored. My hands want to be doing something."

"Guess I don't care."

Ash fetched the comb. When he turned around, Kieran was taking his shirt off. Ash goggled. "Um."

"Just a second." Turning the shirt inside out, Kieran lifted one of the shoulder seams to his teeth and snapped a thread.

"What are you doing?"

"Alterations." He bit at the seam of the other shoulder. "What are you looking at? Never seen tattoos before?"

"Um. Not that kind. They're nice." *And so is the skin they're on*, he added in his mind. "What do they mean?"

Kieran looked surprised, as if no one had ever asked that

before. Ash couldn't imagine why; the tattoos were mystifying. There were bands of dots and slashes and symbols all over his arms, a sawtoothed spiral curling down his left forearm, and a large black glyph that covered the upper left part of his chest, as well as the band of dots around his hand that he'd explained before.

Kieran tapped his chest. "This is a wind knot. It's a really old symbol, you find it carved on ruins and painted in caves and stuff. It's kind of a clan thing. This," he indicated two bands of symbols around his right bicep, "is a poem. These here --" the dots and slashes -- "are memorials. And, um, this zigzaggy thing is just decoration, and I did it myself, so it's not deep enough and it's fading. Why, you want one?"

"No. Thanks."

"It would stand out nice on that white skin of yours."

"I'm sure it would, but --"

"I'm just playing with you. Here, do your fidgety hair thing." He turned sideways on the edge of the cot, making room for Ash to sit behind him.

Ash gathered up the thick, black length of Kieran's hair, preparatory to starting the comb through it. It was nothing like his own chaotic mop; it felt smooth and cool and heavy in his hands, and it was all he could do not to bury his face in it. He wished he could find out if tattooed skin felt any different. If it *tasted* any different. With what Kieran had said the other day, there was even a small chance that such a thing would be welcomed -- *Right, because a twiggy freckle-faced twit like you is just what he needs to take his mind off his dead outlaw boyfriend. Stick to combing.* But since Kieran's back was turned, he could gorge himself on the sight of it. He could imagine what it would feel like to run his fingers down the furrow where muscle met spine.

He could sit with his knees up and pull his shirt down in case Kieran turned around, or things might get embarrassing.

"When you're done playing," Kieran said, "Make two braids. You know how to braid, right?"

"I guess so."

"You guess? You never braided yours?"

"I mostly had it short. That's -- well, up north anyway, that's how everybody under thirty's wearing it. What you're seeing now is three months waiting for my trial and not being allowed scissors. I managed to talk someone into shaving me before I went on the dock, or else I'd have looked like a complete bum."

"Oh. Fashion." Kieran sounded disgusted. His shoulders tensed, and there was a ripping sound. "Speaking of which, think they'll shoot me for wrecking my regulation shirt?"

Still reeling from the sight of lithe muscles rolling under cinnamon skin, Ash made an incoherent noise.

"My bet is they'll just give me a new one. You going to make those braids any time soon?"

"Uh. Yeah. Sorry."

Bending to his task -- and to conceal his discomfort in case anyone looked at him -- he ran the comb through in long strokes. Gradually, he realized he was happy. How strange, that in the middle of one of the worst situations he could possibly have ended up in, he could be content. But he was. To hell with the Watch and their Surveys, to hell with the bored nastiness of the other prisoners, the bad accommodations and worse food, despair and doom, to hell with it all. He was glad just to be near Kieran, to be touching him even if only a little, to be trusted by him even if only marginally.

Kieran liked him. He'd said so. 'No one I like uses my last name.' And 'Lean on me, I'm going to keep you sane.' Kieran was his friend.

"Kieran?"

"Yeah?"

No, that would be ridiculous. Even if Kieran were desperate enough to go for someone as boring and funny-looking as Ashleigh, there was no privacy whatsoever. "Never mind."

"No, tell me."

"I forgot."

"You have to quit doing that."

"Sorry."

Kieran made another ripping sound, and then another.

"Kieran?"

"If you say never mind --"

"What the hell are you doing to your shirt?"

"Show you in a second. Make the braids here, behind my ears, but leave the back loose. They should be about this thick." He held up his thumb to illustrate.

It took some doing, but eventually Ash managed to make a braid of the correct size behind Kieran's right ear, and he discovered what all the shirt-ripping was about: Kieran had removed the sleeves and torn them into strips, which he began wrapping around the braid.

"Fashion?" Ash said wryly.

"Tradition," Kieran returned. "These should be red leather, but you make do."

"What is it, a tribal thing?"

Kieran turned to give him a poisonous green glare. "Yes."

Ash leaned back from that stare, realizing what his words had sounded like. "I'm sorry. That was a stupid thing to say, and after all the anti-assimilationist pamphlets I've written too. It's just, you seem so --"

"White?" Kieran's tone was venomous.

"Cosmopolitan, I was going to say. Come on, I'll swallow my foot plenty without you shoving it in for me."

After a moment, Kieran's shoulders relaxed, and he chuckled. "All right. Cosmopolitan."

"I mean, everything you've told me about yourself was a city thing. Burn River or Trestre; unless I'm wrong, the two biggest cities in the South. And the government claims it's abolished all tribal customs. I think that's morally reprehensible, but I also thought it had succeeded."

"Well, it hasn't. We remember. Not that it does anyone any good. Nobody can afford to care who you're related to. We're all too poor. Maybe if you try for a job and the line boss is the same clan as you, he can put in a good word, but the guy doing the hiring is going to be white, and he probably hates taking advice from natives. Only reason to give a damn what blood you're from is pride and stubbornness."

He finished wrapping the second braid and turned around, and suddenly he was a different person entirely. Still dangerous, but somehow nobler. Not a criminal but a warrior. "In Iavaiah, lineage passes through the mother. Mine may have been a whore, but she was born Tama'ankan. Green Sky. Sun-Eater. And she might have called me Kieran Trevarde, but it isn't my name."

Ash swallowed hard, not sure what any of this meant. "What is it? Your name?"

Kieran hesitated, shook his head. "Outside. I'll tell you outside. When we get out of this place. Not before."

"Oh."

Then Kieran put his newly sleeveless shirt back on, and grinned, and was just himself with a new hairstyle. "You look stupidly impressed. Like I'm about to paint my face yellow and slaughter all the guards."

"I'm wondering what you're up to. You don't do anything just for the hell of it."

"What you said about the tribes being abolished -- that means if I walked down Water Street with my hair like this, I'd be wearing five new stripes on my back by sunset. Ten for a repeat, and they shave your head. So it kind of strikes me funny that short hair is the fashion where you come from. Down south, it means you were a dumbass and got flogged twice."

"And you want to find out if they'll do that here."

"Yeah."

"And *you're* going to keep *me* sane?"

"Well, I kind of get the impression that the normal rules don't apply here. Could be useful to know just what kind of shit they let you get away with. See, I figure --" He paused. "Did you hear that?"

"Hear what?"

"Ssh." Kieran held his hand up for silence.

Ash listened, but heard only the same noises he'd been hearing before. People talking, coughing, moving around. The click of guards' footsteps and the creak of someone's bed.

Then, beneath that, gently at first but rising, there came a thin whistling from above, which was joined by a rattling sound.

"*Yeah*," said Kieran, quietly but with deep satisfaction.

"What is it?"

"The sound of spring, my friend."

"What is?"

"Thunderstorm."

Ash went to the bars and looked up. The light looked no different. The skylights were too far and filthy for him to tell whether rain was falling. But the thought of rain made him sad. "It isn't fair," he muttered.

"Damn straight," Kieran replied automatically. "What's not fair?"

"That's why we're confined to quarters today? A little rain?"

"Never seen a storm down here, have you? There's no such thing as a little rain. Not this time of year. It comes down in bathtubs. Wind takes the roof off your house, then hail beats the crap out of you, then a tornado rips your arms off. Oh, and then there's the flash floods."

"I see." Ash peered harder at the skylights. "Is that wind

I'm hearing? Hey, what if it takes the roof off *this* place?"

Kieran made a snorting noise, but came up behind him and examined the skylights. "Have to be some storm. We're underground. Only about the top yard of these walls is actually built, the rest looks dug out. And if we didn't get killed by falling glass and shit, we'd still be behind these bars with guards everywhere. See that slit window over there? That's a gun post." He paused. "But I bet I could climb that wall."

"That one? To the roof?"

"See that metal box on the end? I think that's the thingy that opens all the cells on the tier, in the morning."

"Hey, if we did that, then in the chaos --"

Kieran sighed, his breath stirring the hair on the back of Ash's neck, raising shivers. "I can think of worse ways to die."

All at once, the light went strange. Ash cleaned his glasses on his cuff and looked again. "That thing you said about a green sky..."

"Means hail. Tornadoes sometimes. A bad storm for sure."

"That's what color your eyes are. Storm green."

Kieran moved from behind him to beside him and stared down solemn-faced. Stared long enough that Ash began to feel a fizzing in his blood, paralyzed and wanting. He couldn't breathe. He was afraid even to blink, lest Kieran realize what this looked like and stop. If they hadn't been standing right at the front of the cell for everyone to see... Ashleigh twitched with surprise when his fingertips brushed the warmth of Kieran's arm, because he hadn't meant to move.

Kieran's lips thinned and he turned away. "Whatever. Wake me if the sky falls." He flung himself across his cot, face to the wall.

Shame rushed in where anticipation had been. *What the hell did I think I was going to do, just now? I gave myself away for nothing.* Ash leaned his forehead on the bars. Above, wind shook the skylights in their frames. It grew darker and darker. The rattling sound stopped and started again, grew loud, then faded to a steady clatter. Gradually the darkness abated. Some time later, sunlight came back in a rush, bright through the newly washed glass.

That was when Ash noticed that the gun post above the second tier opposite was deserted. There were two guards on the floor, as usual, but no one up above. Surely Kieran could take two guards, if they were close together and didn't get a

lucky shot.
	Then the two of them could climb the wall up to the barred skylights, and hang there looking like idiots.

Chapter 5

"What, are you supposed to be Tama now?"

Duyam Sona had blocked their path to their table, and was doing a fairly convincing disdainful sneer. Kieran handed off his tray to Ash, just in case, but didn't bother replying. He just cocked an eyebrow and waited.

"You're a disgrace to your tribe, if you even have one."

"Tama'ankan," Kieran clarified mildly. "Sure I'm a bastard, but I knew my mother well enough. How about you? Let me guess -- Chamka?"

"Tallgrass," said Sona haughtily.

"Figures. Think you're better than the rest of us 'cause you got to keep your ranges, then you come into town begging for handouts the first time the rains fail. Well, in your case, I guess you got a job -- will you fucking quit?" This last because he had to block a halfhearted punch. "*Kaiyo* bastard."

"You're the one who's crazy. Walking around looking like that. You know what happens when you cross the line around here?"

"Tell me."

"Vivisection."

"Fun."

"Yeah, laugh it off, crowbait. You'll be screaming soon enough. And then your bumboy's anybody's meat."

It actually required a bit of effort not to react to that. He turned to Ash. "Is that what people were saying when they were talking shit to you?"

"Um. Pretty much." Ash was blushing again. He'd have to learn to control that sometime soon.

"You care if they think it's true?"

"Not really."

"Hey, *Tama*, I'm talking to you!" Sona gave him a shove.

Kieran considered his options. It would be easy enough to wreck Sona's day, but the food was getting cold. "All right. You're talking to me. Why?"

"Because." That seemed to stump him a bit. "I'm just warning you."

"I appreciate it," said Kieran solemnly.

With a snarl, Sona turned on his heel and stalked back to his breakfast.

Ash made an exasperated noise as they sat down to their own ugly food. "What is *up* with that guy?"

"You're the Empath. You tell me."

"I can't. I mean, you did kill his brother, you admit it, so of course --"

"They didn't like each other. It's not like it hurt him personally."

"Yeah, but family is family, right?"

"I wouldn't know."

"Oh. Well, I don't have anybody but my aunt, but if someone murdered her and I let it slide, I'd hate myself forever."

"You like her?"

"Kieran, it doesn't *matter*. I mean, yes, I do, but even if I didn't -- this is a tangent. What I'm saying is, he should feel like it's his duty to take revenge on you. What I can't figure out is why he doesn't just *do* it, like you said the other day. The way he keeps baiting you, it's like he wants something else. I can't figure it out."

Kieran shrugged. "Me neither. Eat your slop."

Ash stirred his oatmeal, watched the congealing mess plop off his spoon a few times. "Maybe I should talk to him."

"*You?*" But after a moment's thought, Kieran realized it might not be such a bad idea. "Okay. Do it."

So when they were all turned out to pasture, Kieran stayed by the wall and Ash wandered over by Sona alone. Kieran was surprised to see that Ash was the taller of the two by two or three inches. The pale boy *acted* so small, Kieran had gotten into the habit of thinking of him as little. The truth was that he was taller than most of the others in the yard. Not the thinnest, either; Kieran himself probably looked about that skinny with his clothes on. It was Ash's whiteness that made him look so fragile, and the little-kid freckles, and the glasses. He was the epitome of the kid the whole neighborhood picked on. Kieran wondered if he'd keep that wimpy look all his life -- then reminded himself that neither of them were likely to live long enough for it to matter.

Ash didn't seem to be having any trouble handling Duyam Sona. They were just talking. Sona looked angry, but then he always did. He was making tight, sharp gestures with his hands. Ash had his head tilted like a kitten. *That's it, kid. Be cute and harmless, and no one will have the heart to --*

Wrong. Just as that thought went through Kieran's head, Sona snatched the spectacles off Ash's face, threw them down, and stepped on them.

Then he looked straight at Kieran.

"Fine." Kieran pushed himself away from the wall. "It's your funeral."

Sona gave a sickly smile, watching Kieran come at him. With a deliberate, contemptuous gesture, he lashed out and backhanded Ash across the face, knocking the white boy sprawling.

The world abruptly shook itself into a new focus; a cold, tense state where the colors were washed out and the air tasted of metal. Sona ceased to be a person, became an offending object which must be broken down until it vanished. Options for achieving this flashed through Kieran's head with tight clarity. All the mobile obstacles in the yard scattered out of his path.

All but one. One of them got in front of him, mouthing noises at him. He grabbed its head to throw it aside. But the skin of his palm remembered this texture, and it yanked perspective back into him with a painful shock. For the space of one breath he was holding himself together on the verge of going feral and shredding everyone within reach.

Then he smoothed down Ash's hair where he'd disarranged it, and Ash's words began to be a language he could understand.

"-- what he wants, you can see that, I know you can, just walk away Kieran please you don't have to prove anything --"

"Hush," Kieran said, and Ash did. The relief in the sagging of those narrow shoulders, in the dimming of those sky-colored eyes, made Kieran ashamed. He felt sick to his stomach. He wasn't shaking, but a vibration in his nerves told him he might begin any minute now. Sona, beyond Ash's blocking body, was visibly trembling; awkward, as if he'd forgotten his lines. All the faces on the periphery were round-eyed, skittish like horses. Only Ash wasn't afraid. Why wasn't he? Kieran almost hadn't recognized him -- and he shouldn't have assumed that he was immune, whether recognized or not.

"I figured it out," Ash said. "What he wants. He wants to die, Kieran."

Kieran tested his voice. It came out too deep, but smooth and calm. "I gathered that."

"No, I mean it's a plan. He wants you to kill him." His voice dropped to a whisper. "For which the guards will probably shoot you."

"Clever," Kieran said. He raised his voice so Sona could hear. "But you're going to have to wait until I'm suicidal too. Until then, every time you lay a finger on Ash, I will break that finger. My guess is the Watch don't mind what shape your hands are in."

Sona's face contorted. He gave an incoherent bellow and rushed at Kieran, swinging wild, all pretense at skill gone. Kieran stepped out of his path and tripped him.

"Give it up, Sona. You're making us all tired."

"Just wait." Sona got as far as his knees and stayed there, head hanging, fists clenched in his lap. "You wait. You may think you're used to shame, but you don't know anything yet."

"Coward." Kieran picked up the remains of Ash's glasses. They were ruined, both lenses smashed, wire frame twisted. He dropped the useless thing in front of Sona. "Maybe you can slit your wrists with the pieces. *Inayaju*. You make me sick. Remember to cut up, not across." Then he took Ash's arm and hauled him away.

"That was cruel," Ash said when they were out of earshot. "Kieran, that was outright cruel."

Kieran spat on the ground. "You don't understand. He's not just a coward, he's a blasphemer. A hypocrite. See, if all he wanted was to commit suicide, there are plenty of ways around here. Spoon knife. Pants noose. Hell, you can bang your head against the wall if you get really desperate. But that's not good enough for him. He thinks he's a *heriye*, a noble knight, he wants to go down in battle. 'Cause we Iavaians have more Hells than you folks do, and suicides go to the basement." He spat again. "*Inayaju kamon.*"

"What's that mean?"

"I don't know how to translate it. Crybaby, sniveler. Somebody who spends all his time bitching about his problems instead of solving them. What about you, aren't you pissed? He broke your glasses."

"I'm just a little nearsighted. It's not as if I'll need to read street signs or anything. I can see well enough not to run into walls."

Kieran noticed a smear of blood on Ash's lip. Without thinking, he reached out and wiped it away with his thumb. He immediately regretted the gesture -- because of how it had probably looked to everyone else, and because Ash's sharp inhalation and dilated eyes were going to stick in his mind and bother him when he was trying to sleep.

He glanced at Sona to remind himself he was angry. "He's not forgiven."

"I just think, if we let ourselves get worked up, we'll end up like that --" Ash aimed a thumb in Sona's direction -- "sooner than if we keep our heads."

"You might be right." Kieran turned abruptly away from Sona's kneeling form, suddenly worried that anguish might be contagious. "Well, that was embarrassing. Let's pretend it never happened."

"Let's pretend we're fishing in Helermont Bay, while we're at it." Ash returned with a lopsided grin.

"Kieran Trevarde." The cell unlocked with a clank. "Get your ass out here."

"I'm getting to really hate hearing my last name," Kieran grumbled as he obeyed. He glanced back to see Ash looking apprehensive, gnawing his lip. Kieran gave him a bitter smile on the way out.

This time, as he was marched to the tunnel, he examined the features of the place as he passed them. The walls were clad in glazed brick to about eight feet up, but above that was bare stone, rough enough to climb, at least if you were a halfway decent climber. If he could get on top of the door-opening mechanism... then he'd be shot, and if he found some way to avoid that, the skylights had bars on them.

Well, there were two ways to look at that thought. It might be better to consider it one out of three obstacles potentially defeated. Two out of four if he counted the fact that these two guards with their guns were standing way too close to him. He could deal with them any time he wanted.

It was the same tunnel they took him into, the same stairs up, so Kieran was disoriented when they came to a turning that hadn't been there before. The hall should've gone straight to the door of Warren's little white room. Instead, it curved right, bringing them to a short cross-passage with a door at one end.

Again Kieran was made to wait until the door opened. Again it was the same Watchman who let him in, and again Warren was waiting. But this was a different room, longer, with two metal chairs bolted to the floor facing each other. One chair was empty; the other was full of Sona's fat blond friend, bound to his seat with leather straps. He looked mostly out of it, not red-faced now but grayish. The empty chair had straps as well. He really didn't like the look of this.

"Sit," Warren ordered.

"Make me," said Kieran.

Warren glared at him, just long enough that he began to wonder whether the officer had any means to force him into that unpleasant-looking chair.

Then the pain came.

Formless, sourceless, engulfing, thought-killing, it came inside all his defenses and turned him in an instant from rational being to suffering animal. It could not be fought, ignored, or endured. When it ended, he was lying in a puddle of vomit, too weak to even wipe his face.

His escort lifted him into the chair and strapped him in.

"Now," Warren said in that hideously reasonable tone he used. "We wish to study your threnodic Talent. The man before you is weak, close to death. Kill him."

Kieran considered several replies, discarding the ones most likely to cause Warren to torture him again. What he eventually said -- mush-mouthed with the pain's aftereffects -- was, "It doesn't work like that."

"Don't presume to educate me, Mr. Trevarde. You will remain in this room until that man is dead. Should you choose to try to outwait us, you will become very thirsty." He gestured, presumably to his minion, and went out of Kieran's field of vision. A moment later, the door slammed.

Kieran spent some time taking leisurely stock of his situation. Testing his bonds. They were solid, of course. Then he tried talking to Blondie, but the man was out cold. For a while he debated with himself whether to try offing the guy. On the one hand, the man was doomed. If Kieran refused or failed, the Watch would find another use for him. Vivisection, for instance, unless that was a product of Sona's diseased imagination. So it wasn't like there was a moral issue. On the other hand, Kieran didn't feel particularly cooperative after the nasty zapping he'd gotten. And he resented having to make this decision at all. The whole thing was sordid and idiotic and got him nothing either way, except maybe a few minutes of semi-privacy, if he could ignore the fact that Warren was probably watching him by some magical means right now.

So Kieran settled down in the chair as far as the straps would allow, let his head roll back, and took a nap.

Quiet. So quiet up here, bright and warm, on the mesa's top. Small, harsh plants grew in cracks and hollows, and he was the first person ever to see them. The sky was pale, the sun white, the air still. He could see all the way to the mountains along the western horizon, a gray unevenness along the bottom of the sky, pretending to be a cloud bank. All around him the broken land of the desert unrolled.

Someone said his name. He turned around. At the mesa's center stood Ash Trine made perfect; he glowed copper and ivory, his eyes were gas flames, his smile of welcome was brighter than the sun. Kieran's heart constricted with a delicious pain of longing, a righteous fire of resentment at his blood's lusting boil, his teeth ground together. He raised his weapon and pulled the trigger -- the sound slowed and rolling like a distant machine growling -- and the arc of Ash's body flying backwards was beauty in the raw, better than sex.

Ash was trying to speak, blood bubbling from his lips in lieu of words. Kieran bent to kiss him, swallowing the blood from his mouth. In it he tasted the words Ash had been trying to say.

He woke suddenly and without transition. He could still taste the blood; for a moment, he was unsure which was the dream and which was real. Then reason started its destroying engine and began to chop his dream apart. *That was outright sick,* he told himself. *Also largely meaningless. And could you possibly have picked a weirder place to fall asleep?*

He still smelled of vomit. The man in the other chair was still out cold. He had no way to judge how long it had been. But he was very thirsty.

Enough, he decided. He'd asserted that he wouldn't obey out of simple fear. Now it was time to do what he had to. At least the poor son of a bitch didn't have to be awake to feel himself being tipped over the edge.

Using his Talent never felt like something he did with his mind. It seemed, instead, as if a new kind of hand grew out of him, pulling from his chest, and reached into the other man as into a pool of water. What this hand actually did was hard for him to explain, even to himself. Perhaps everyone carried with them the seed of their own death; perhaps what this hand touched was the death that was already there, merely bringing it to the surface. Or perhaps he found the shortest path of possibility and steered his victim's time onto it. In this case, the man was so close to dying, so riddled with infection and bloated with internal bleeding, that Kieran barely had to brush him with the invisible hand; the man gave a long sigh, as if relieved, and it was over.

Despite the humiliating circumstances, he felt a sense of satisfaction. A clean job, more a mercy killing than a murder, no pain, no complications. Hangman's pride.

"He's dead," said Kieran loudly. "Can I go now?"

After a short wait he heard the door open, heard two sets of footsteps. Smelled one man's sweat and another's dusty breath. Felt hands wrap around his head from behind, and had just time to think *oh shit* before they both came in at once.

He woke partway when he hit the floor; just enough to guess by smell and sound that it was the floor of his cell. Not enough to move, though he'd been thrown down in a sort of awkward position. The floor was wonderfully cool, but not very clean. He hoped to god they'd leave him alone until he felt better.

He heard a small gasp and a choking sound. Hands shoved at him, got under his shoulder and neck, lifting him onto someone's knees; arms around him, pressing his face into a bony chest that was shaking with hoarse, uneven breaths.

Kieran swallowed spit until he was no longer too dry to talk. Then he said, very carefully, "Who are you, and why are you hugging my head?"

The hands shifted, cradling the back of his skull so he could look up. The light was dim and yellow, but he could make out a diamond-pale eye, recurved lips, a pointed chin speckled with metallic stubble. Ash. Of course. He was a shade alarmed at the thickness of the fog in his head now that he'd realized it was there. He'd thought, for a moment, that he was back in Tiyamo.

"Oh," he croaked. "This is *that* prison."

"I thought they'd killed you," Ash whispered. "I thought you were never coming back."

"No such fucking luck."

Ash took in a long, shuddering breath, let it out smoothly; composing himself. He set Kieran's head gently on the floor. Some noises later, he returned with a dripping rag.

"What did they do to make you throw up? Poison you? Did they hit you in the stomach?"

"Nuh-uh. Kinda... pain zaps. Brain torture thing." Caught between wanting to be cleaned up and hating the cold and wet of the cloth, he endured it until he felt he was no longer outright filthy, then tried to turn his head away. "Wanna sleep now."

"I can't move you. You're too heavy. Can you help?"

"I'll stay here." Kieran let his eyes close.

He meant the floor. But when his head was lifted and then lowered to be pillowed on Ash's lap, he found he didn't mind it much. It was pretty comforting, actually. He felt as if he were made of soft lead, sagging to conform to the surface beneath. He was nearly asleep when his human pillow shifted slightly; shortly thereafter a blanket settled over him. He realized he'd been shivering only when the shivering stopped.

Noises came and went. Sometimes he was moved a bit, and this annoyed him, but on no account was he going to bother waking up. Sleep was too safe and precious; even the dry sleep of empty, looping dreams that was the only kind he could get inside the prison wards.

But there came a time when he could no longer cling to sleep. The world was clamoring for his attention. Aches everywhere: head, throat, joints, muscles, stomach. Coughing sometimes. Light. Opening his gummy eyes, he saw the underside of Ash's chin, and the grayness of daylight. It took some effort to make a noise. When he managed it, Ash looked down and smiled with such proprietary gentleness that Kieran was immediately embarrassed.

"Ag," said Kieran. He tried again. "Hat." He choked on dryness and was taken over by a long, painful coughing session. Ash's hands were on him the whole time, smoothing back his hair, steadying his shoulders until it was over.

"Can you move now?"

As an answer, Kieran sought for and found his limbs, dragged an aching arm across the floor.

"Good. I'm going to sit you up now. Let's try to get you onto your bed."

That didn't sound like fun, but neither did staying on the floor -- the gritty stone that had seemed so comfortable before was now a literal pain in the ass. Not sure if he was up to the effort, Kieran resolved to do his damnedest anyway, because he remembered that when he'd gone through that gauntlet of examinations -- what was it, not even a week ago? -- he'd weighed in at a hundred and ninety pounds, and he was pretty sure Ash had never lifted anything bigger than a dictionary in his life.

Ash surprised him, though. The kid might not have been strong, but he was methodical, and not afraid to use what little strength he had. When Kieran proved unable to do much more than tremble and wobble, Ash uncomplainingly did the whole job himself, though it was awkward. Kieran indicated gratitude by a flopping gesture of his hand that probably didn't convey anything.

Ash brought him a cup of water. Kieran had to concentrate his full attention on simply holding his head up, but it was worth it; though the cup knocked against his teeth with his trembling, it was as good as a clear stream after a week in the desert. Which implied that he was badly dehydrated.

"More," was his first coherent word of the day.

Ash poured water down Kieran's gullet until he sloshed, then made him eat two slices of cold toast, clammy with congealed raspberry jam. "The guard got it for me," Ash explained to Kieran's questioning look. "I think it was his own breakfast. I don't think they hate you as much as they pretend to."

Kieran rolled his head, as much of a gesture of negation as he could manage. He knew that if a guard had shared his breakfast, it wasn't for Kieran's sake, but for Ash's. There was just something about those round blue eyes that made authority figures go protective. His theatrical selflessness might have had something to do with it as well. "Did you sit there all night?"

"Um. Well. Yeah. Don't worry about it. It's not like sleep's in short supply around here."

"The floor would've been fine."

Ash said nothing.

"Well. Anyway. I guess... thank you."

"You should rest."

"I did. I will. You missed breakfast so you could keep being my pillow, huh?"

"Yeah."

"Did *you* get any food?"

"No."

"Martyr."

"Maybe I just didn't want to go out there alone."

Kieran made an attempt at a laugh. "Nah. I think I'm getting the hang of you. You're like the nice little boy in those improving books. The one who's so kind and good that nothing bad ever happens to him. Was life really like that for you before?"

"Maybe. I guess. God watches over fools and children, and like that."

"Bullshit. Fools and children get jacked all the time."

"Well, I'm not going to get into philosophy with someone who can't talk with his eyes open. You get some rest. I've got work to do."

This provided a reason for Kieran to unstick his eyelids. "Work?"

Ash displayed a thin book with blue card covers. "Our friendly guard came through yesterday while you were in Testing. A whole empty account book and a brand new pencil. But he still won't tell me his name." Ash flipped the book open and offered it. "I've already started. See?"

Kieran squinted at the gibberish on the page; his first reaction was that he was even sicker than he'd thought. A closer look confirmed that the first word was, indeed, 'QNMAUUP,' and it just got worse from there. "What the hell is that? Some kind of code?"

"Cypher. Not that there's anything in here they don't already know, but I like the idea of the headache they'll get trying to read it."

"They teach that at rebel school?"

"I guess you could say that."

"So how am I supposed to read it when you're not around to decode it for me?"

Ash turned pages, the motion of his hands crisp and businesslike. "Here, I wrote the square on the first page. You encrypt the first letter using the line beside the first letter of the key, then move to the line beside the second, and so forth. Just try to avoid touching the letters as you go through it, or the smudged places will give away the key."

"Which is?"

"Something you said, actually. Struck me as appropriate. Loser unity."

"Perfect." Kieran's laugh turned into coughing. "Okay, I feel like hell. Go do your code thing and let me sleep."

"Right. Say -- you didn't go to school, did you?"

"You're joking. I'm Iavaian. They don't let us into school. Why?"

"I was just wondering how you learned to read."

"Taught myself. Had plenty of free time. Assassin's not a full-time job, you know; wouldn't be much of anybody left if it was. Now for fuck's sake let me sleep."

"Sorry."

Kieran thought for a few moments that all this conversation had made him too alert to go back to sleep, despite how rotten he felt. Then his thoughts began to wander, and he emerged from one long, confusing concept to realize it had been a dream. He drifted easily under the surface of dozing, lulled by the scratching of his cellmate's pencil. It was an oddly pleasant sound.

Chapter 6

Ash spent the next several days bringing his encrypted record up to date. There was, after all, very little else to do. He was allowed to skip dinner and exercise the first day in order to take care of his cellmate, and though he got a little hungry he preferred hunger to braving the yard alone. Someone would be sure to get nasty if Kieran wasn't around. So his motives weren't as altruistic as Kieran seemed to believe. Not completely, anyway. It was sweet, in a sick way, to have the gorgeous Iavaian depending on him -- not that he deluded himself that Kieran was enjoying the attention.

Kieran recovered from his exhaustion with surprising speed. The next morning he was nearly himself again; a bit wobbly and drawn, but able to hold his head up and greet the world with his usual cynical half-smile. He was able to put on an appearance of strength during meals and yard times, but these efforts left him shaking, and for several more days he spent the rest of his time in bed. He made no reference to Ash's tearful state the night the guards had thrown his unconscious body on the floor, and Ash was thankful for that. However often Ash might daydream about the hypothetical rewards of his loyalty, he knew a daydream from reality, and in reality Kieran seemed to genuinely hate emotional displays of any kind.

When pressed, Kieran had given a dry account of his six-hour adventure in Testing. It conveyed no useable data, but apparently Kieran saw Ash's research as a fidget to pass the time. There was no sense in being offended at this; it was probably the truth.

Nevertheless, as a device against boredom it succeeded, so Ash gave it his whole attention during the week or so it took for Kieran to return to full health. Every day he talked to a few people, and added a few lines to his account. He quizzed inmates and chatted with guards. When they were taken in small batches to bathe and be shaved, the prison barber turned out to be a font of useful knowledge, and once Ash got him talking the man went on endlessly about Talents he'd seen over the years. Ash had divided the book, front and back; recorded numerical data in the front, flipped it over and wrote his own observations in the back -- along with the things he had to get out of his head by dumping them onto paper, encrypted with a different key. He had not quite reached the point where he could encrypt his words without the square of letters on the front page, but he was close, sometimes going several words at once without having to look.

Sometimes he read his results to Kieran, and speculated about what they meant. There were a lot of Pyros who'd been there six months or more, but their numbers were slowly decreasing. The new arrivals were largely marginal Talents like Ash's own, the kind that could be missed completely if they manifested after the state-mandated Survey at the age of fourteen. What this implied was, on one level, obvious -- that the Watch had finished looking at fire talents and switched focus -- and on another opaque. Why had they felt the need to build this place at all? What was it they had failed to understand without it?

Kieran was the only ghoul-witch they had. Possibly the only one alive. Apocryphal accounts told that possessors of this Talent rarely survived its first manifestation.

That, according to Kieran, was because the Watch killed them. Apparently his tribe, the Tama, had produced several ghoul-witches and a great number of storm-callers, and that was one reason the tribe was nearly extinct now. In the first years of the Annexation, the Commonwealth had slaughtered Tama on sight, lest their dangerous Talents prove a military problem later. This was just hearsay, though; no records remained of that time except the heavily edited versions the government allowed.

Ash doubted that Kieran's rarity was relevant to the purpose of Churchrock, though, because the other Talents were mostly common ones. That irritating Duyam Sona, for instance, was a Kinetic. The only serious clue Ash was able to gather was that more than one inmate had been probed for Talents in the plural, or overheard reference to that concept, though none actually possessed more than one. That was interesting, but didn't seem to justify this elaborate facility.

Nor did it inspire any escape plans. But Ash thought it was sweet of Kieran to pretend that escape was possible.

Which is what he was doing the day after their baths, clinging to the bars like a monkey in a zoo, rattling every moving part he could find. "It's a simple lever thing. Really basic. They push that handle down and this bar up here slides. If

I jammed a rock or something in there just before they closed it, I bet this strut here would pop right off."

"Leaving us locked in for perpetuity." Ash sighed. "Kieran, *please* get down. How am I supposed to soft-soap the guards if you keep making them mad?"

"They don't care. I see people climbing on the bars all the time." Nevertheless he hopped down, bending to peer at the lock mechanism. "If I had anything heavier to pick it with -- maybe a spoon handle? No, too fat. The problem is the weight of the bolt."

"The problem is that they're not idiots. We're not going to be able to get out any way anyone's thought of before, because the designers of this place will have thought of it too."

"So we'll get creative. Chin up, kid. We're not like the rest of these poor fuckwits."

"Sure. We're smarter than the average prisoner, right?"

"Right. Hey, you got room in your book for the guard schedules? I notice there's one guy who goes to sleep on the gun post. He was napping yesterday when we went for out baths."

Ash made a sour face, fingers feeling for the scab on his jaw where the prison barber had cut him. "That lummox of a barber is full of fun facts, but he cut hell out of my face. You don't know how lucky you are that you don't have to shave. Maybe I should grow a beard. I'm going to end up looking like a taxidermy experiment otherwise."

"What's wrong with a few scars? You have a problem with looking like me?" Kieran scratched the white slash that divided one of his eyebrows, then smiled to show it was a joke. "At least we get baths. I was afraid we wouldn't."

Ash remembered yesterday's effort to remain calm despite the sight of Kieran naked, and the thought threw him off his stride, but he tried to keep up the bantering tone. "You think if I change my last name they'll let me in the bath *before* the water's brown?"

"If that worked, we'd all be named 'Aaaaaa.' I'm surprised we get to bathe at all. Water's expensive around here."

"I guess. Anyway, you were saying. The gun post. Was that Sunday?"

"Yeah. Huh. It just occurred to me it's kind of weird that there's no temple service."

Ash gave him a wry look. "Don't tell me you're religious,

Kieran."

"That would be funny. But no, it's just that at Tiyamo we had to sit through a sermon every morning, and three hours of it on Sundays. Like they thought it was going to reform us, hearing about all the bloody destruction Dalan visited on the Herenites or whatever. I just think it's weird that there's nothing like that here."

"I didn't really notice. I haven't been to temple since grammar school, myself."

"They let you get away with that up north?"

"Who? The Watch? Not much they can do about it."

"Really? 'Cause in Burn River, if the cops catch you on the street during worship time, they'll for sure make you go to the temple, and probably beat you up a bit first. They see you skipping temple a bunch of times, you're likely to get arrested for moral degeneracy. Or if you're a native they might charge you with demon worship. Which of course there's no way to disprove, so --" He sliced a finger across his neck. "What did you do, stay in all day with the curtains pulled?"

"Kieran, there's three and a half million people in Ladygate, if you count the suburbs. There aren't enough police or Watchmen in the whole Commonwealth to arrest them all. I don't think there are temples enough to hold everyone, if they all decided to go, so it wouldn't make much sense to try to force them. Of course, businesses have to be closed during worship time, you can really catch hell for being open on Sunday morning. At least, if you're too obvious about it. But a lot of places have the door unlocked and the curtains closed and serve people anyway, kind of unofficially, and the cops mostly let them get away with that." Ash paused, floored by a wave of homesickness. "I wish I'd taken a better look at the city when I got arrested. So I could remember it more clearly. But I couldn't bring myself to believe I wouldn't be coming back."

"When we get out of here you can go anywhere you want. And quit making that face. Every time I try to work on our escape plan, you get this look like you're telling a terminal case he's going to be fine. It doesn't help."

"Sorry." Ash wasted a moment trying to figure out what his face looked like when he did the expression Kieran was complaining about, but gave up. "What do you want me to do?"

"I already said. Take notes on the guard schedules. I'll be lookout."

Ash got out his book and opened it to a blank page. After a few minutes of careful printing, he looked up. "We have to make up names for the guards. They won't tell their real ones. Some kind of regulation. I think it's meant to keep them from getting friendly with us."

"So make up some descriptive nicknames."

He did that for a while. Some time later, another thought occurred to him. "Kieran? What day was it that we had that storm?"

"Huh. I lost track. About a week and a half ago? Day before Sona broke your glasses, I think. You're putting the weather in your book too?"

"I noticed that the gun post opposite was deserted. I need to figure out whether that was the day or the storm."

"Why didn't you tell me then?"

"You were being grouchy."

"Well, next time don't be such a baby. We should talk to someone from the opposite side and see if the post above us was vacant too."

Ash hadn't quite finished writing when the bell rang for dinner. At the sound, his stomach growled. They only got two meals a day, and that just wasn't enough. He thought he might be still growing. Not just taller, but bulking out a bit too. "Hey Kieran," he said as they waited for their tier to be opened. "Do I look any less skinny than I did when I first got here?"

"Probably," Kieran said without looking. "Starchy food. Starchy and greasy. Potatoes and pork. Eugh."

They had to be quiet while being lined up and counted, but Ash picked up the thread when they reached the mess hall. "What's your favorite food?"

"Aw, kid, don't do that to me."

"Come on."

"Rice balls. This lady I used to know, Shou-Shou, she made these rice balls that were so spicy they'd make your eyes melt right out of your head. You take the rice, see, and some peppers and onions and stuff, and whatever meat you've got, and moosh it all together like that, and you fry it --"

"That's not greasy?"

"Not if the oil's hot enough. You use oil, not lard."

"I miss cooking."

"Cooking? You?"

"Well, it's not like I had people to do it for me. Aunt Isobel and I split the chores between us, and cooking was one of my jobs. But I like it. When we're rich and famous I'll make you some of my Yelorrean beef stew. I'm Yelorrean really, you know."

Kieran snagged a lock of Ash's hair. "Naaah."

"Hey, not every redhead is. But my family's from there. They say real Yelorrean beef stew you should be able to stand the spoon in it. Mine, you can plant a flag and lean on it."

"This is a selling point?"

"It's good. It contains no grease. And plenty of pepper. You'd like it. How do you get rice in the desert? Isn't that expensive?"

"They grow it in the highlands, I guess. I don't know. As far as I'm concerned, food comes from the grocer's. Unless you shoot it yourself. Anyway, quit torturing me. You do realize that even if we talk ourselves delusional about good food, what we're really eating is -- what is this, anyway?"

"Casserole, I think. I'm fairly sure this rubbery white business is some kind of noodle. Unless it's tripes."

"Shit. Thanks *so* much."

"I don't care. I'm starving." Ash shoveled up a mouthful and chewed consideringly. "It's edible. Marginally. You know, for a hard case, you sure are picky about food."

Kieran shrugged. "Never gave a damn about gambling, girls, or liquor, so what else was I going to spend my blood money on? Well, clothes and weapons mostly, but I could afford to eat right. Not a lot of expenses when you're piling up a debt to society the size of mine." Kieran grinned, as if he found the mention of his crimes amusing.

"Oh." A bit embarrassed to have gotten them onto that subject, Ash gave his tray of -- whatever -- his full attention. But even with the sense of having tread on the edge of shaky ground, he felt as calm and happy as when Kieran had let him braid his hair. This was really pleasant, talking for no reason except to make conversation. Not to make plans or test each other's strength, just chatting. Because they were friends, or getting to be.

This, Ash thought, *is a little excessive. I'm in the Heaven of Serenity just because he's acting normal around me? A little amiable small talk doesn't make this a best-buddies-forever kind of situation. And it certainly doesn't mean he has the slightest romantic interest in me. Not that I'm sure I'd want him to under these circumstances, that could be really dodgy. Even an obvious friendship could be dangerous. I really shouldn't be smiling like this.*

Despite this reasoning, the feeling persisted, and Ash couldn't bring himself to fight it. It made the food taste better, anyway.

"Hey, Ash." Kieran sounded a bit hesitant, which made Ash's heart beat faster -- until the rest of the sentence turned out to be: "Watch past me and tell me when nobody's looking over here."

"Why?"

"Testing a theory. Here, stack my tray under yours."

"What are you going to do?"

"Probably something idiotic. Is anybody --?"

"Yeah, wait. Okay. Now."

Kieran vanished under the table. After ascertaining that no one seemed to have noticed, Ash bent over his supper to hide the fact that he was talking. "Kieran, what in the world --?"

"Ignore me," was the reply from the floor.

Ash borrowed one of Kieran's expressions: "Huh."

When the inmates were lined up for yard time, no one pointed out that they were one person short. Ash had thought Kieran's absence would be obvious; he was, after all, possibly the tallest human being Ash had ever seen. Surely someone would notice that there was no big grinning Iavaian sticking up over everybody's heads. But no one commented. The count after the exercise period would show Kieran missing, but for now the line shuffled out as usual.

They're not even paying attention, Ash thought. *Is that what he was testing?*

And now he was, for the first time, in the yard without Kieran. Without that tall shadow beside him, he felt terribly exposed. He sincerely hoped people had the foresight to realize that this didn't make him fair game. Maybe he shouldn't have declined to identify those who'd said nasty things to him out of Kieran's earshot. A little calculated retribution might have been a good idea after all. Although no one had been really obnoxious since Duyam Sona had broken down. Maybe it had sobered everyone.

Anyway, he had work to do. One of the men who'd been least hostile to Ash's previous questions was enough earlier in the alphabet that Ash thought he might have noticed about the gun post the day of the storm. It took a while to find the fellow; he was sitting down, over in a corner of the fence, obscured behind people's legs. He looked like he was trying to fall asleep and half succeeding. Or maybe, Ash amended when he got closer, the man was trying to wake up and mostly failing.

"Hartnell." Ash squatted next to him. "Hey. Hartnell."

"Um?" Hartnell's eyes opened a slit, then closed again.

"What's the matter with you? Bad morning in Testing?"

"Uh. Yeah."

"Sorry to bug you, then. But I just have a little question."

"S'okay."

"You remember when there was that thunderstorm last week?"

"Uh-huh."

"Did you notice whether there was anyone in the gun post above my tier? Because the one above yours was deserted."

"Oh."

"So did you notice?"

"What?"

"Come on, Hartnell. You're making me nervous. Pay attention."

"Go 'way. I'm fine."

"You don't sound fine. Maybe you should move over into the shade." He tugged Hartnell's arm, but couldn't get him to move.

"Nah. M'okay."

What was wrong with the man? Heatstroke? Food poisoning? Or was this what repeated Surveys would eventually do to everyone? This vague, sleepy stupidity reminded Ash of a girl he'd seen once who'd suffered a botched version of the Excision all female Talents had to undergo. But Ash couldn't think of any reason the Watch would want to Excise a prisoner's Talent; if they were done with him they'd just kill him. The situation was creepy, frankly.

A shadow fell over him. "What're you doing to that poor bastard?"

Ash squinted upward, shading his eyes with his hand, and recognized Sona's bald, bearded friend, Gibner. *Oh, this just gets better and better.* He aborted a motion to stand, thinking he had a better chance of avoiding a fight if he stayed down here, being harmless. "There's something wrong with him. I think he's sick."

"No shit. They have him out two, three times a week. Must have a real interesting Talent."

"But he's just a Pyro, like half the guys in here. And he was fine yesterday."

Gibner took half a step back. "If he's really sick, you better say goodbye. They don't waste medicine on the likes of us. Where's your sugar daddy?"

"He's not, not that you care. He'll be along shortly. He's not out of the picture, if that's what you're asking, so don't bother picking on me."

The bald man snorted. "He doesn't understand anything, and neither do you. Fighting's just about the only fun we can have around here. But Trevarde's so tough, he throws the whole thing out of balance, the way he knocks people back without even looking. I figure half the guys in this yard would love to stick a knife in him just so things can get back to normal. You can tell him I said that, too."

Ash shook his head. "I know what he'd say." Ash put on a blandly sardonic Kieran-face. "So fight each other. Long as you leave me out of it, I don't give a fuck what you do with your time."

Gibner chuckled in grudging appreciation. "Yeah, that's what he'd say, I bet. But who wants to spit teeth for second place?" The yard noise changed suddenly, and the man pointed at the door with his beard. "Speaking of spitting teeth..."

Ash followed his gaze, and what he saw made him leap to his feet, heart jammed like a rusty machine. Two tan-uniformed prison guards and one white-coated Watchman were hauling Kieran into the yard, half carrying and half dragging him. His face was slicked with blood. They threw him at the ground, and one delivered a parting kick that aborted his first effort to stand.

Not even conscious of who he was shoving, Ash elbowed and thrashed his way through the clustering prisoners. He reached Kieran as the tall Iavaian finally managed to get his feet under him. Trying to be helpful, he grabbed Kieran's arm.

The next thing he knew, he was sprawled on his back, tasting blood where his teeth had cut the inside of his cheek.

"Ow," he said mildly.

Kieran swayed over him, unapologetically offering the blood-smeared hand that had bruised Ash's face a moment earlier. "Shit, don't jump me like that. I coulda killed you." He hauled Ash upright, then did a strange little shimmy, as if shaking his bones back into place; rolling his neck and arms, making faces. One of his eyes was in the process of swelling shut, and the lower part of his face was so bloody that it was hard to tell exactly where he was hurt. The hand he hadn't offered looked puffy and awkward. He stood with a slight stoop, listing like a sinking ship.

"My God, Kieran. What did they do to you?"

"They tried to sell me opera tickets. What do you *think* they did? They beat the living shit out of me. What are you assholes staring at? Do you need your asses kicked too? Because I can provide that."

Ash put a tentative hand to Kieran's shoulder. "Let me help you over to the shady side. You should sit down."

"Quit hovering." Kieran shook him off. "You're making me seasick. Go play somewhere else."

"But -- Kieran, you --"

"Fuck off! Anybody gets within ten feet of me, I'll eat his fucking eyes!" With a vaguely threatening gesture and a vicious scowl, Kieran limped off toward the wall.

"Fine," Ash said to no one. He went to the opposite side of the yard and stood there with his arms crossed, doing his best not to look. Trying especially not to think of how attentive and sympathetic he'd be if Kieran weren't being a macho jerk about it. He understood that it would be foolish of Kieran to show weakness in public, but couldn't he have taken a friendly hand? Or at least not bit Ash's head off for offering?

Gibner made a deliberate detour around the yard just to pass by Ash and say, "Trouble in paradise?"

"I dare you to go make friends with him," Ash returned, and that ended the conversation.

When they were rounded up at the end of yard time, Ash didn't even stand near Kieran, let alone help him walk. Back in the cell, he busied himself with his book. The first couple of times Kieran said his name, he pretended not to hear.

Kieran gave up for a while, washed his face and hands, combed dried blood out of his hair. Then he tried Ash's name again. Getting no response, he threw the comb, bouncing it off Ash's forehead.

"Don't," Ash snapped, sweeping the comb onto the floor.

"Well, quit sulking."

"I'm not sulking. I'm just leaving you alone, like you wanted. So I don't make you *sick* anymore."

An exasperated sigh. "That's not what I meant, and you know it."

"Oh, I know. You can't let anybody help you, or somebody might challenge you for the King Shit of the Barnyard title. And then you might have to *hit* somebody again, which of course you *hate* to do."

"Oh for -- all right, I'm sorry, already."

"Well, *that* sounded sincere."

"Don't you want to know what I found out?"

"What, that if you stay behind the guards beat you up? I gathered that from visual evidence."

"No, dumbass, that the guards eat right after we do, and they get their coffee out of the same kettle. If I could get hold of something nasty and drop it in the coffee urn, I could poison them all."

"Too bad your personality's not water-soluble."

"Now look, you --" Kieran paused, then snorted. "Okay, that was funny. But you can stop now. I mean, would *you* be all sweetness and light after -- no, I bet you would. 'Oh, I might be bleeding internally, but that's not *your* fault.' Why am I apologizing to you? Do you know how hard it was to just lie there and let them kick me? But I guess that wouldn't be hard for you."

"No," Ash said sourly, "getting picked on kind of comes naturally for me." Then the rest of Kieran's speech penetrated, and he finally looked Kieran in the face. "You think you have internal bleeding?"

"Nah." He pulled up his shirt to examine a series of ovoid bruises on his torso, each the size of the toe of a guard's boot. "I was worried about it for a few minutes there, but it's not swelling." He tried to grin, but it turned into a wince when his split lip began to ooze. "The look on your face is priceless. You can't decide if you want to go 'oh poor baby' or spit on my shadow."

"Sounds about right," Ash admitted.

"You care too much. That's going to wear you out if you keep doing it. So, did you find out about the gun post being empty?"

"I tried to ask Hartnell, but he was sick or something."

"Yeah?"

"Kind of vague and sleepy. He talked, sort of, but it wasn't really what you could call a conversation. Gibner said the Testing people have had Hartnell out two or three times a week. Which struck me kind of odd, because he's been here longer than we have, and he has a really common Talent, so why do they want to examine him more often than they do us?"

"That *is* weird." Kieran got thoughtful. "Any other symptoms?"

"Not that I noticed."

"Did he seem upset? Scared?"

"No, that was another strange thing. He wasn't at all alarmed by his illness. He seemed pretty happy, actually. Made me wonder if he managed to get hold of some liquor, but he didn't smell of alcohol."

Kieran frowned at the dried blood under his fingernails. "No. He wouldn't."

"What do you mean?"

"Tell you later."

"No, I want to know."

"I won't tell you until I'm sure."

"But --"

"You think you can change my mind?" Kieran looked Ash straight in the eyes, and for just that moment his face was naked of masks; no wry superiority, no intimidation, not even the half-irritable patience with which he endured injuries. He looked like a boy cornered by a man's world, in that instant. Whatever he was refusing to tell Ash, he was scared to death of it. His voice was mild as he went on, "It might not be something I want to get you into. Leave it alone."

Ash didn't answer, because he couldn't breathe. Only when Kieran looked away was he able to draw breath. He let it out wordlessly. Not a single one of the things he wanted to say would have been welcome.

The next day, guards and inmates alike seemed to watch Kieran especially closely. Not surprising, Ash thought, after the stunt he pulled. A few more like that and the best escape plan in the world would fail because everyone would be watching for him to try it. Kieran didn't seem bothered by it, though. It was, Ash was beginning to understand, just the way Kieran operated, shutting out everything he didn't perceive as relevant. He moved through his constricted world like a forgetful man in the middle of a complex task, ignoring anything that might obscure his mental list.

Ash was glad, at this moment, to be excluded. He had some thinking of his own to do, and being ignored was the closest he was going to get to privacy. Time had given him a little perspective on yesterday's events, and now he wanted to know why he was riding an adolescent pendulum between elation and despair where Kieran was concerned. Was it just boredom and confinement exaggerating his feelings? *An attraction and a friendship do not necessarily add up to True Love. I had better stop thinking like a moonstruck schoolgirl, or I might begin to act like one, which would get me killed in short order. But how, when every time I look at him I lose the rest of the world?*

To say Kieran had a forceful personality was understatement. Not a pleasant personality, but powerful. He had such strength, but it seemed brittle somehow. More flint than steel. Maybe it was the fragility Ash sensed beneath the armor of Kieran's cold confidence that made him so compelling. To be trusted with even the slightest glimpse of that breakable self was the highest honor. To be sent out of that trust was a slap in the face. Kieran was more real than anyone Ash had ever known.

He watched with careful eyes the way Kieran moved, slow and smooth and deliberate. The way he talked, soft and low in his amused drawl, but with a chill in his eyes that warned against taking that quiet for granted. The way he ignored his hurts, never probing his bruises or tonguing his split lip, favoring a pair of sprained fingers automatically but without tenderness.

No wonder he'd been famous as an assassin and highwayman. It had nothing to do with his Talent. He simply had no opinion about pain. Not only did he not pity the suffering of others, he was not interested in his own.

Sick, Ash thought. *Very sick, and beautiful, and horribly strong. I hate the people who made the world in which he had to become this thing.*

During their exercise periods, Kieran spoke to several people. Ash, told to stay by the wall, heard none of these conversations. He could only watch expressions pass over everyone's faces but Kieran's. The others were variously belligerent, frightened, suspicious, obsequious. Kieran smiled sometimes, or raised one peaked brow to indicate some skepticism or irony, but these couldn't really be called expressions. They were as constructed as his long, slow stride and casual speech. Ash wondered, in retrospect, whether even the cornered look of yesterday had been calculated.

When, in the evening, Kieran would not tell Ash what

he'd been talking to people about, Ash wasn't surprised. Hurt and worried, but not surprised at all.

Chapter 7

*B*lue; *infinite floating blue. Soaring, wingless, effortless, white-hot, straight up. A feeling of being known, of being crucial to the world, a piece of landscape or type of sky or subtle color without which nothing functioned. Coming home.*

Then there was Ash, far below, stuck on the ground and searching for his anger. "I know where it is," Kieran told him, "but I'm not telling." As Ash studied how to change his mind, the first sweet breath of approaching rain took Kieran by the back of the neck and folded him inside out...

Back to the smell of sick-sweat and the taste of bile. Distant, a door noise, a quiet voice: "Sir, he's regained consciousness."

Testing. He was in Testing. He'd refused some order. The pain had given him such visions... what was it they wanted him to do?

He was strapped into that chair again. In the other chair, the one that faced him, that poor bastard Hartnell hunched with bloodshot eyes. There was a smell of vomit and feces around the man, and he was shaking. Shaking and sick as Kieran himself had once been, which was why, Kieran now remembered, the order to kill Hartnell had caused him to demand payment. A useless smartass remark. But he remembered too well what it felt like in there. Hartnell was in opium withdrawal.

"Are you ready to cooperate?" The Colonel's tone hinted that more torture would not be difficult to arrange.

Kieran caught Hartnell's eyes and held them. Hartnell shook his head convulsively, muscles in his jaw writhing. He wanted to live, despite his discomfort, even if only a few minutes more. Kieran could respect that. To Warren, he said, "Hit me."

Maybe he'd hoped that giving the order would cause the Watchman to withhold his power; people didn't like to do as they were told, especially when they thought they were in charge. Warren, however, had his method.

The pain clawed through Kieran's guts, into his eyes and the roots of his teeth, every nerve in his body sending up distress flares at once. He felt his whole flesh go into instant rebellion, and an instant later he was nowhere to be found; absent and flying.

He'd never told anyone about this, about how he sometimes left his body to its fate and went somewhere else. Even Shan hadn't known, though Kieran had done it several times while kicking his tar habit. It was a sort of cowardice, he supposed, but what purpose did it serve to stay and endure? It had happened off and on since he was small, since he spent fourteen hours watching his mother die. He couldn't do it on purpose, but when things got bad enough it just occurred. There were places in his life that were blank, such as the missing time between Shan's death and his own capture. In those times, he was someone else, and had nothing to do with Kieran Trevarde's squalid scrabbling for survival.

High above the mesa, so high it was just one more blotch in a scrawled carpet of reds and yellows and green-grays. Moth-eaten lace of stone and sand. Brighter green in streaks where water ran. All of it belonged to him. His house, where he had always lived, his true body, his source. Due west, his heart beat, smoldering in slow rage like a coal-mine fire. Farther, over the mountains, clouds came skimming. Rain coming. A small, hard rain. Tonight, or early tomorrow morning. He longed for it to wash the dust from his soul.

He didn't have to wait. He could go there, ride it down the mountain and across the world. He could go anywhere -- but the vision was breaking up, and he woke to the ache and stink of his mortal flesh.

He supposed he must look like Hartnell now; twins in sweat and shakes and twisted muscles. Warren was no longer in the room. He must have gotten involved in something else, which meant Kieran must have been out for a while. Hartnell was still conscious, though not so wide awake as before. Kieran took the chance to talk to him.

"Another one of those," he said, "and they'll have to give up on me for today. What are they going to do with you?"

"Dunno." Hartnell swallowed and blinked, too dehydrated now for it to do any good. His voice was a sticky rasp. "How come you're... why?"

"Why not?"

Hartnell managed the ghost of a laugh. It was obvious why not. "You'll have to. Sooner or later."

"Yeah."

"It'll hurt."

"Probably."

"More than this?"

"No."

Hartnell let his head hang. Kieran found himself hoping the poor doomed bastard would give up, because another shot of that pain might cause some kind of permanent damage. But he'd already made the decision to let Hartnell decide, to cut Warren and his minions out of the loop, to prove a point. He wasn't going to go back on that. So there was no point anticipating.

Door sound. Footsteps. Hartnell brought his head up, glaring hatred past Kieran at someone behind him. Then his eyes flicked to Kieran's face. He bared his teeth. "Do it. Do it quick."

Kieran was ready. He slammed into Hartnell's chest like a shotgun blast, found the edge and shoved hard. The snap as life's thread broke recoiled back into Kieran with nearly as much force as he'd put out, like bouncing a ball against a wall, and he swallowed it down. That quickly, Hartnell was gone.

"Did you see that?" The assistant sounded excited. "Did you see him catch that recoil?"

"I did indeed." Warren came around to take Kieran's pulse and peer into his eyes. "When the Director arrives, we shall have to see if Mr. Trevarde can reproduce the result. Preferably, next time, without a tedious show of childish defiance."

"Fuck you," said Kieran generally. When Warren and his assistant began the inevitable Survey, Kieran held in mind until the last moment his awareness of Warren's bad breath and the bags under his eyes. It was a tiny revenge, but it made him feel a little better.

They had to carry him back to his cell again, but at least he was awake for it this time, and knew where he was. When they dumped him on the floor, he was coherent enough to catch himself on his hands and knees rather than sprawling on his face. He grasped at Ash's offered hands, climbed up the white boy's clothing, and launched a headlong stumble from there to his cot.

Ash knelt beside him, hand on his arm. "Do you want to talk about it?"

The warm hand on the spasming muscles of Kieran's

forearm felt far better than it should have. Knots all over him started relaxing. He watched Ash's face as he told the truth, curious to see the exact moment of rejection: "They had me kill Hartnell. He was just about all in, but he didn't want to go. They zapped me a couple times. Then Hartnell said do it, so I did. Poor stupid son of a bitch."

Ash went still, eyes blank as blue sky, and stayed like that for most of a minute. He didn't look away, though. When he came to life again, it was to say carefully, "I'm surprised that a mercy killing would seem worse to you than this kind of torture."

It was his stubbornness Ash objected to? Not the fact that he'd killed Hartnell in the end? "I don't want to give in too easy. Gets to be a habit."

"What were you going to do, die in his place? Would it have saved him? Spare yourself the pain. It doesn't do any good."

"Sure it does. Warren got so pissed off, he used adjectives."

Ash set his teeth in his lip, pleading wordlessly. Kieran instantly felt like a complete asshole. *Master manipulator, this kid, and I don't think he even knows he's doing it.*

"It really bugs you, huh?"

Ash nodded.

"Guess if I go down, you're screwed. Pretty much literally."

"That's not it! I just don't like to see you like this. No one likes to see a friend get hurt. We *are* friends, right?"

Kieran felt a dose of treacherous warmth run through his exhausted body, and knew he had to squash this line of questioning before it went any further. He forced casual heartiness, knowing what a slap in the face it would be. "Sure, we're friends. I got your back. Now get off my blanket." But he couldn't meet Ash's eyes as he said it, and he was too aware of where in the room his cellmate went when he retreated. He could feel Ash's wounded silence; leaning on the bars, not looking.

He reminded himself that he had more important things to think about. He now had the final confirmation of what had been wrong with Hartnell, and incidentally several other inmates, all of them young, thinnish, beardless -- their physical similarity was a clue to how they got the stuff. Kieran was not surprised to find that business going on here, just as it had in

Tiyamo.

Kieran knew that he could insert himself into that group easily enough. Though his height and reputation made him less attractive to the type of guard who liked to relieve his boredom that way, he could use his pretty face   and a few other tricks he knew -- to entice the suppliers to add him to their string of slaves. But it had been a long time. He'd believed he was done selling ass forever, and it wasn't fun to contemplate doing it again. And then there was the question of the tar itself. Could he touch it, possess it, and not use it? He would have to build up an enormous stash if it was going to do him any good as a poison. Just thinking about it made his stomach clench with desire. It would make this place bearable, being opiated, it would make it *easy*, he wouldn't have a worry in his head until his day came to die -- which was, of course, the problem. Was he strong enough not to become what he would pretend to be?

He didn't know. He wasn't sure.

Well, there was time to think it through. A stash of poison was not an escape plan. There was work yet to do. That was comforting -- to line up his puzzles and chew through them like a sawmill through a tree. Made him feel like he was doing something more productive than lying in bed listening to his eyelids twitch.

Warren had said 'When the Director arrives.' Someone important was coming here. Security would no doubt be tighter during the visit. Would it be more relaxed afterwards?

Another thought: though he was exhausted, he was less drained than the first time he'd been tortured, almost as if he were building up a tolerance. Was that possible? Or was this a fluke, would he end up weak from it, get sick -- what if he had to rely on Ash for their escape? In fact, even if he himself were in prime condition, Ash would still surely have to do some climbing or running.

"Hey Ash." His voice was thin and dry, but his cellmate rushed to him as if he'd shouted.

"What do you need?"

"You're not going to like it."

"So? Just say it."

Poor idiot. Ash sounded ready to jump off a cliff for him. And after getting barked at and dismissed, too. Kieran wondered if he was one of those pathetic people who just got more loyal the more they were abused, and felt guilty. But it was still amusing to see Ash's bewilderment when Kieran said,

"I need you to find out how many push-ups you can do."

Ash blinked at him a few times. Obviously not what he'd expected to hear. "What? You mean --" He pantomimed.

"Yeah."

"Now?"

"Yeah, now."

"Why?"

Kieran grinned. "'Cause you can't dance, it's too wet to plow, and it's a little windy to be stacking chickens."

After a moment's shocked silence, Ash gave a startled laugh. "You what?"

"'Cause I said so."

"Oh, hell, fine," Ash said. He got down on the floor and did a few push-ups. "Sixteen," he grunted when his arms wouldn't lift him.

"Could be worse, I guess. Rest for a minute, then do five more."

"I'm never going to be as strong as you."

"And you'll never be as weak as you were before you met me. Bitching won't change my mind. You know how stubborn I am."

"I know," Ash sighed, "but I also know I'm going to disappoint you."

"What's that got to do with anything?" Kieran was scornful. "You care way too much about stuff that doesn't matter."

"So you said before." Ash shook his arms out and got back down for another five.

When the bell rang for dinner, Kieran made himself stand, though his thigh muscles were twitching in the most irritating way. Ash told him he looked bad, gray, and his own smell nauseated him -- acrid fear-sweat dried and itching -- but he'd be damned if he was going to live like a victim. Anyway, he was starving. He ate everything on his tray, even the canned vegetables in a sauce that tasted like snot.

Outside, the sun's warmth revived him further. He was no longer shaking, just tired. The still, hot air tempted him to sprawl in the shade, as so many others were doing, but he had something yet to do, and he'd decided he wanted this part to be public.

"Hey Ash," he said. "Hit me."

"Sorry?"

"I want you to hit me."

"Hit you? You mean -- pow? Are we faking a fight?"

"Like that would be real convincing. No, I just want to see how you hit."

"Er. Where?"

"Stomach. Won't hurt me. Go ahead."

Ash hesitated; opened his mouth and shut it; shrugged. He fixed his eye on Kieran's midsection. Winding up, he thumped his fist into Kieran's ribs. His knuckles stung a bit, bony as they were, but Kieran doubted it would even bruise. Ash shrugged again. "Bad, I know."

"Wrong in many ways," Kieran agreed. He saw out of the corner of his eye that people were looking at them. Good. "For one thing, you looked too hard at where you were going to hit. But it takes a while to get over that, so in a real fight aim for the face, since you're going to be looking there anyway. For now, let's deal with the fact that you hit like a kid."

"Of course I do," Ash said defensively. "I haven't been in a fight since I was about ten years old. And I lost that one."

"Well, you're not a kid now. Put up your hand. Like this."

Ash did. Kieran gave it a little tap, just enough to set Ash shaking his wrist and wincing.

"Did you see that coming?"

"No. You're a lot faster than I'll ever be."

"Well, you could be faster than *this* at least." Kieran mimicked the wind-up and swing that Ash had performed. "You waste energy swinging around like that. Not to mention you tell everyone what you're up to. Just throw it straight out. Get your shoulder behind it. Straight out." Kieran demonstrated more slowly.

"Wait. Do it again." Ash's eyes traveled back and forth along Kieran's body as Kieran smacked his hand a couple more times. "Okay. Let me try."

Kieran spread his arms, leaving his torso wide open. Ash looked a bit worried, but shrugged and raised his fists, stepping forward. Then Kieran was knocked back a long step, grunting as the breath was knocked out of him. "God *damn*, boy," he huffed.

"Good?"

"Shoulda had you hit my hand. Yeah, good. You're a fast learner."

"Thanks." Ash glowed.

"Shove up your sleeve. Let me see your arm."

Ash flushed as Kieran probed his way from wrist to shoulder. Kieran was glad he himself was not prone to blushing; the skin of Ash's arm was too smooth, too soft, starred with tiny freckles and downed with fine coppery hairs, the muscles rounded and not large but definitely present. He let go quickly when he was done.

All he said was, "You're not as skinny as I thought. You're never going to be a bruiser, but it won't be hard to put some more muscle on you."

"That means more push-ups, I suppose."

"All sorts of shit like that. For now let's work on your form." He held up a hand -- then, realizing it was the one with the sprained fingers, hastily switched it for the other one. "Don't worry about hitting hard this time. Just make sure you hit where you're aiming, and concentrate on speed."

"Hey kid," a spectator called out. "What do I gotta do to get lessons too?"

"Fly up and get me a chunk of the moon," Kieran told him shortly.

"Now, that ain't fair," someone else said. "If you're gonna start a little school, oughtta be open for everybody."

Kieran speared the speaker with a narrowed glare. "Ash Trine stood by me every second since I got here. Who the fuck are *you*?"

That engendered some muttering, but no more actual protest. Later in the yard hour, he heard someone sneer the words 'true love' in a mocking tone, but didn't feel like interrupting the lesson just to beat respect into some random asshole. Let them think Ash bit pillow for Kieran's protection. It'd make others less likely to try climbing into his shadow.

When they were returned to their cells, Ash was full of questions. Kieran, too tired to stand anymore, flopped down on his cot and answered, "You need to be stronger. That's all. The way things are going, it's possible I'll be weak like this when we get our chance. I might need your help."

"Oh." Ash raked his sweaty hair from his forehead, then flexed his fingers, frowning. "Aren't we pushing it a little hard? My hands hurt."

"If you can still move 'em, you're fine. We can't be sure how much time there is. There's going to be climbing at least, and maybe fighting."

"All right." Ash smiled that sickly smile that said he didn't believe in any escape plan, was only doing this to be agreeable.

That was fine. Kieran didn't need him to believe as long as he did the work. But he'd probably try harder if he had a reason he could understand. "Work yourself sick, Ash. I don't know how much longer I can protect you."

"You're not giving up, are you? I'm sorry, that sounds like I'm just using you to hide behind -- I'll do what you want, I'll learn to fight and everything. Just... Kieran, tell me you're not going to quit trying. Without you, even if I were as strong as you are, I'd still be in trouble."

"Course I'm not fucking quitting," Kieran snapped. "Can the damn melodrama and grab some floor, stringbean."

Ash flashed a relieved grin before getting down and forcing a few more push-ups.

Lights-out came too early, as always. Kieran had been dozing; the creak of Ash's cot springs woke him. He yawned, twisting his back, hearing his spine pop, then looked to find Ash staring at him again. He considered snapping at the kid for gawking, but figured he'd used up his bossy license for the day. He made idle conversation instead. "How's the book coming? Got the guard schedules down yet?"

"Pretty much. Tomorrow, when we can see, I'll show you what I've called them, so you can understand the lists."

"What I really want to know is which of them get their supper after us. I think it's going to have to be supper."

Ash's expression was hard to see, but his tone was skeptical. "You're still thinking about dosing their coffee."

"Like to know if it would be useful, at least."

"With what, Kieran? What are you going to do, pee in it? Get sick and spit in it? If we had access to anything poisonous..." There was a pause. "You've thought of something."

"Don't worry about it."

"Something dangerous."

"I said leave it alone." The conversation had stopped being idle, and he didn't want it anymore.

"Kieran --"

"You just get me that information, and leave the ugly shit to me, okay? You can't handle it." He rolled to face the wall.

"Kieran," Ash said softly.

Kieran ignored him.

"Kieran, please don't. I don't know what you're

planning, but I can tell it scares you. I don't want to think about how bad something would have to be before it could scare you."

Exasperated, Kieran threw his blanket off and glared at his cellmate. "Exactly how the fuck does that matter? I'm not staying here. You help or you don't help, but don't you try to tell me what's too hard for me. If I'm still breathing when it's over --"

He was interrupted by a sharp crash that rattled the panes of the skylights, a flash that printed Ash's crumpled face on his retinas. His first thought was: *Dammit, crying again, you big baby*. Then he remembered something that seemed to fling the prison doors wide open.

"I dreamed this."

Ash was illuminated by another lightning flicker, dragging his hand across his face. "What?" His voice was muffled. "Storms?"

"This one. When Warren zapped me -- it'd take too long to explain. The point is I knew it would hit about now, about this hard, and last about a quarter hour."

"Fascinating," Ash said in a dull tone.

"Damn straight it is. This puts a whole new spin on everything."

"Then you don't have to do the thing that scares you?"

Kieran didn't answer. He watched the lightning through the bars. He pretended he couldn't hear Ash sniffling.

The storm was short and sharp, just as he'd predicted. He didn't think it was a coincidence. Somehow, by dreaming in an unwarded room, he'd actually seen the weather rolling across the world.

There had to be a way to use that.

When the bell woke them, he was sore and stiff, but nowhere near as wrung out as he'd been after his last trip to Testing. That was interesting; he'd only been zapped once that time, whereas he'd got three jolts yesterday and here he was perfectly functional. *Maybe you build up a tolerance*, he thought. *The way you do to poppy.*

Which he had to think about. One thing he'd learned, living the life he'd lived: you have to know your limits. Determination by itself was useless. If you didn't have the abilities to back it up you were just going to get yourself in trouble. So he had to be dead certain he had the strength to possess a great fat wad of tar and not taste it. Not even handle it with his fingers, let it seep into his skin. Not argue himself into using just a little to ease the ache of abused muscles, settle a rebellious stomach, calm the dry sting of his dreams. He wasn't sure yet.

He would be sure soon. He had already decided that he could handle what he'd have to do to get it; soon he'd know he could handle having it. When he was sure it was necessary, when it fit together with his other plans.

"Show me the guard schedules," he ordered when they were locked in for the day. "Show me who's who."

Ash, drooping a bit from the morning's *kengdan* lesson, dragged out his book and opened it to a page of the usual gibberish. "If you want, I can write it plain for you. We'd have to rip out the page after --"

"Just tell me. I'll remember."

"All right. Here's what I have so far..."

But he had only gotten through naming the guards, and hadn't yet begun translating the schedule, when they were interrupted by purposeful footsteps on their tier. This happened every day but Sunday, and sometimes more than once, and usually the guards stopped before reaching them or passed them by. Nevertheless, Kieran's stomach tightened, and he saw that Ash's hands shook a little as he hid the book.

Two tan uniforms appeared. And stopped.

"Ashleigh Trine."

Ash froze like a rabbit. Kieran stood aside to let him get up, but he didn't move.

"Ashleigh Trine. Come on, kid."

In a whisper that cracked to a squeak, Ash said, "I can't."

One of the guards gave a long-suffering sigh and jangled his keys. "Trine, don't make me come in there."

Ash stood, but it was to back up, not to obey. He shook his head slowly, big-eyed. "I can't. I can't. Kieran!"

"Trevarde, why don't you come over here and put your hands through the bars." The guard beckoned his partner forward. "You cuff him. I'll get the kid."

Kieran knew he'd save himself trouble by complying, and he really wasn't in the mood for trouble this morning. But Ash had backed himself to the far wall and was shivering like he'd shake himself to pieces. Kieran just knew Ash would scream when the guard touched him.

He didn't want to hear that sound.

"Be right there," he told the guard. Then he went to where Ash cowered. The redhead let Kieran take his wrists, even stilled his shaking some, but shrank back when Kieran leaned to speak into his ear. "Hold your head up. Sooner you go, sooner you come back."

"I can't." Ash was breathing in little gasps. Kieran was ashamed for him. "I can't. I can't. I --"

Kieran slapped him across the face.

"Hey!" a guard shouted, and keys clanked. "Dammit!"

The slap had driven a look of shock and hurt into Ash's eyes, but at least they were focusing. Kieran wrapped a hand around the back of his thin white neck, feeling cold sweat beading there. Lips to Ash's ear, he whispered, "You're not here. You're not here. You're somewhere else. Don't come back until you can come back to *me*. Understand?"

He drew back to see Ash nod in numb bewilderment. Then Kieran's arm was twisted up behind his back and he was clouted across the side of the head; he had to use all his attention to keep from fighting. He could get out of this grip so easily, could take both these guards like a dog killing chickens, but it wasn't time yet.

"What were you whispering about?" demanded the one who had Kieran's arm. "Planning something?"

"Just --" Kieran grunted as his arm was twisted so the bones creaked. "Just doing your job for you."

"Yeah, well, next time you do as you're told. Stupid fucking natives." His legs were kicked out from under him.

Kieran heard the swish as the guard raised his baton, and had a moment to wonder whether Ash was feeling guilty for causing trouble, or too scared to care. Then came the sickeningly familiar sensation of a blow to the head, knocking his vision skewed and making his ears ring. When he felt steady enough to get off the floor, he was alone in the cell.

He wasted half an hour or so being angry. At the guard who'd hit him, naturally. At the institution of Churchrock for creating the situation, and at the whole Theocratic Commonwealth for allowing it. But mostly at Ash for turning chicken like that. It reminded Kieran of situations he preferred not to think about.

Eventually, as it always did, the anger faded. Anger was a waste of energy. It never changed anything.

Making sure there were no guards in the area, he got out

Ash's book. Ash had showed him how the code worked, sort of. He'd only half listened, so figuring out how to turn gibberish into words ate up a fair chunk of time. Kieran supposed he wouldn't bother with something this tedious if he'd had anything better to do. He translated the guard schedule into his head, trying to memorize it. Digesting the knowledge that a certain guard who'd been seen with Hartnell was on their tier tomorrow morning.

When he was confident he could remember the schedule, he started flipping pages at random, translating a word here and there to guess the subject of the page. 'Talents.' 'Arrivals.' 'Speculations.' 'Syyakwt.'

Kieran retried that last one several times, thinking he'd messed up, but he kept getting the same garbage. The page was densely packed with prose; not a list or a series of notes. It was encrypted with a different key.

Anger resurged in Kieran's gut, hotter than before. Ash was keeping secrets from him. How dare he? That sneaky little fuck! After everything Kieran had done for him! Well, it wouldn't stay secret long. Kieran would shake it out of him --

He flashed on a picture of himself grabbing, looming, threatening, and Ash cringing, that fear in his eyes not for guards or tests but for Kieran alone. Kieran's stomach instantly knotted. Slapping Ash's face to snap him out of a panic was one thing. Venting anger on him, though, raising a fist to him, leaving bruises on that pale soft skin -- *Never. Never.*

So he'd figure the code out himself. Ash would use some word as a key, some word that meant something to him personally. Maybe something Kieran would never guess, the name of his childhood dog or something, but he'd used 'loser unity' for the rest of it, so maybe it would be something equally topical. Something... he frowned as he groped after the concept... something that *felt* secret. He wouldn't use something that would enforce the feeling of being imprisoned, so it wouldn't be a simple I-spy clue like 'bars' or 'guards'. Something that reminded him of freedom.

Going faster and faster as he got used to using the letter square, Kieran tried the words that came to his mind when he thought of freedom, reasoning that the same thoughts would occur to Ash. 'Sky' and 'home' didn't work. 'Freedom' and 'out' and 'death' and 'life' didn't work.

'Storm' worked. Then stopped working. Kieran chewed his lip for a moment, thinking back along the days and nights to where 'storm' came to mind, then bent to the page again.

The key was 'storm green'.

I'm going crazy, the text read. *I have to write this down to get it out of my head. Or try at least. He's driving me insane. Sometimes I think I'll scream if he comes near me; sometimes I think I'll explode if I don't touch him. He scares me senseless, and I want him more than I want to keep breathing. He doesn't like me at all, though. I think he hates me for being weak. He could never respect me, let alone love me. I never imagined anyone could be so beautiful or so broken. Last night I sat up watching him sleep until dawn...*

...How could hands that have killed be so gentle? Maybe I was wrong about his opinion of me. Could he be so kind to someone he holds in contempt?...

...It's ridiculous of me to develop a crush and nurse it in my little diary, it's absolutely ridiculous. This is a prison, for god's sake. I'm absurdly lucky that I'm still alive, and the fact that I haven't been beaten or raped is beyond belief. I have no right to borrow pain...

...Those eyes. Those incredible eyes. I fall into them, they tear me apart. And oh his razor smile, his earthquake voice, his starless night, his terrible strength of soul, perfect proof against the arrogance of my pity...

...How does anyone survive this? I would walk a hundred miles to make him look at me, I'd bleed out for a smile, every time he touches me I have to think of snow. If the Watch take the time to decrypt this, they'll all die of disgust I'm sure. Yes, you bastards, I'm a disgusting deviant, get your hands out of your pants. Let me describe, imaginary reader, what I would do if he'd let me...

Footsteps in the hall. Kieran snapped the book shut and jammed it into its hiding place behind the mattress.

The guards let Ash into the cell and left. Ash stood where they'd put him, staring at nothing. He wasn't crying this time. His eyes were circles of blue paper, pasted on slightly wrong.

Kieran just sat there on the edge of the bed for a while, looking at him. Thinking: *You rat. You rat bastard. How dare you fall in lust with my face when you don't have clue one what's going on behind it!* But as Ash kept staring, unmoving, Kieran's anger slipped away. It was spooky, the way he looked. Shut off, like an engine in the repair yard. The way he breathed long, shallow breaths, as if sleeping, gaze fixed on something past the back wall, deep inside the mountain.

Standing, Kieran walked into Ash's line of sight. Ash's eyes tracked him, but blankly. Had Warren and his students broken something in the boy's head? Turned him into a permanent idiot?

"Ash. Hey." His voice was unacceptably hoarse. He swallowed and tried again. "Ashleigh. You in there? Come on, kid, you're scaring me."

Ash blinked several times, slowly. Slowly, awareness came into his stare. Slowly, by stages, the porcelain mask of his face crumpled, melting to helpless anguish.

He let out a choking gasp, grabbed two handfuls of Kieran's shirt and buried his face in it, bruising Kieran's collarbone with his forehead. Then he just clung there. Not crying. Just hiding.

"Hey." Kieran took Ash's shoulders and pushed gently, but without effect. It would apparently take some force to pry Ash off his shirt, and applying it didn't seem like a real good idea at the moment. "You're fucking scaring me, Ash. Say something."

Ash's voice was a dry whisper. "You said you'd keep me sane. Now would be a good time."

"Okay. Okay." Kieran wrapped his arms around Ash's tense shoulders; awkward at first as if reading instructions from a book, until fury at helplessness -- Ash's and his own -- made his grip tighten convulsively. He was thinking it might be a little late for the sanity thing. He bent his face to Ash's neck, getting a mouthful of hair when he spoke. "I've got you. I have you now."

"Tighter," Ash gasped. "Squeeze me so small I disappear."

Kieran obediently crushed Ash even more closely. Ash's clutching hands pulled his shirt all askew. It was hard to breathe. Ash was strung so tight he was vibrating, drenched with cold sweat. It wasn't right that he should feel so very good in Kieran's arms. It was sick to enjoy this. It was wrong to let Ash's frantic heartbeat shake him this way.

It was also impossible to change. This pale, needing creature huddled against his chest was a thing like a new addiction, the first dose that awakened a craving, and Kieran had always been weak on that front.

They leaned into each other for what felt like hours, long enough for Kieran's back to cramp and his legs to start trembling. He had to swallow several times before he could speak. "Let's sit down," he offered.

Ash didn't let go or raise his head, even though it made moving less than graceful. On the bunk, he curled against

Kieran's side, fists still knotted in Kieran's shirt. Kieran wrapped the blanket around his shoulders, smoothed his dirty hair. He couldn't forget what Ash had written about the gentleness of his hands, and it made him self-conscious, far more careful than he might otherwise have been about enfolding Ash's shivering body in his arms. He rested his cheek against the top of Ash's head; caught himself about to plant a kiss on Ash's brow, which would have been a bad idea even if Ash weren't playing at being in love with him. He whispered soothing nothings -- whispered nursery rhymes in Iavaian, since he couldn't think of anything coherent to say. Gradually, the tension in Ash's body began to abate, until all at once he slid down to rest his head on Kieran's thigh, and Kieran wondered if he'd fainted.

He hadn't. "I didn't cry," he said dully.

"I noticed."

"I'm not okay, though."

"Well, no. We're not going to be, while we're here."

This made Ash open his eyes, but he didn't look up. Kieran watched him frown and chew his lip in profile.

"The trick to staying sane," Kieran went on, "is to accept the pain. Not the thing that caused it, but the pain itself. You just say, fine, this fucked me up. What do I have left to work with? Don't run from it, Ashes. That never helps."

After a long time thinking, during which expressions flickered across his face like shadows, Ash rolled his head to look up at Kieran. "Ashes?"

"Oh. Sorry."

"No. I like it." He went back to staring across the cell. "It's descriptive."

"Thought you didn't like descriptive nicknames."

"I like this one. That's what I have left, you see. I'm a burned-out house."

"What did they do to you?"

"I don't know. I wasn't there." Ash lifted his hand and flexed it before his eyes. "Even when they were in my head I wasn't paying attention. I was spread out all over. More in their heads than mine. And when I came back home, I found my house burned to the ground. And all my stuff is gone."

"I know the feeling. But you've got the things you need. You know who you are, and who I am, and what we have to do."

"What we have to do..."

"We have to leave. And I know how."

This made Ash sit up and fix his faded blue stare on Kieran's eyes. What he was looking for, Kieran didn't know, but not finding it seemed to make him tired. He put his forehead down on Kieran's shoulder. "You won't tell me what you're going to do."

"No."

"Why?"

Kieran smiled bitterly. "You might talk me out of it."

"Then maybe I should."

"No. Trust me, I can handle it. I'm good at getting over things. I haven't thought about Shan for weeks..." He sucked in a breath, horrified at himself. At the things that rolled steaming and shrieking through his head at the sound of that name, at his own ability to have set them aside.

He'd forgotten the scar that cut his eyebrow. The sound and smell and hot wet slap and sting of a large-caliber bullet demolishing his lover's head not twenty inches from his face. He had a scar from a piece of his lover's skull, and here he was cuddling with *another* blue-eyed white boy as if Shan could be replaced --

But the shudder that went through him was a solitary twitch, not the beginning of a shaking fit. *That's not how it is,* he said to himself. *Shan was my friend, and I miss him, but he never needed me like this. I offered Ash my help, and now I have to follow through.*

"Let it slide," he said at last. "All you have to do for the next couple hours is breathe. I'll stay here if you want, but, uh, your head's kind of on a bony place."

Ash hauled himself away. He lay down, pillowing his head on his arms. "I'll be okay. It's enough to know you're near."

"Guaranteed," Kieran said with a nod to the bars, getting the ghost of a smile for it. Released from the role of comforter -- and its attendant sneaking temptations -- he got up and started stretching out. "I'll try not to make too much noise."

"I don't care. Make noise. So if I fall asleep I'll still dream you're here."

So Kieran made a point of slapping his feet against the floor as he did some forms, feeling a bit of an idiot, but at the same time oddly glad. That puzzled him. It wasn't a good time to be glad. But there was an unfamiliar joy in being trusted so much, untrustworthy as he was. Either Ash was a singularly trusting soul, or his crush was based on something real. Kieran chose to believe the former. The latter would mean it was already too late to keep from wrecking what was left of Ash's life.

Chapter 8

I don't like the way my head feels.
I don't like it.

Ash was peripherally aware that his thoughts were simple as a child's; a vague nauseous ache of the mind. He didn't have the strength for it to matter.

I don't like what happened to my head, to me, going outside myself. In other people's heads. It was all so loud. Some of me is missing.

His own panic had embarrassed and unnerved him when the guards had come for him. He'd been well aware that it was pointless, that he'd save himself humiliation by going willingly, even as he'd been utterly unable to do so. Then Kieran had saved and damned him with one breath.

'You are not here.' The same mantra he'd repeated through his first few days. Coming from Kieran's lips it had become the truth. He'd felt Kieran's breath on the skin of his ear and been drawn into that sensation, even while it lost its meaning. Sounds echoed and distorted, the act of walking had absorbed him, and when he'd passed through the intangible membrane of the ward he'd flown apart.

If Kieran's voice had not recalled him, he didn't think he would ever have come back. He would have become one of those peripheral prisoners who were moved around like stiff-jointed dolls, waiting to die. But... he *had* come back, gathered into himself by Kieran's enfolding arms and sawtoothed voice. He knew that memory would make his heart ache later, but the feeling was lost in the general soreness now. Sensation was muffled. Where he lay with his head on his arms, blanket tucked around him, he wasn't sure if he was cold or warm, bleeding or whole. He looked past the small mountain of his knuckles to where Kieran flowed through a series of mock-fights, underwater-slow.

That grace soothed his eyes. Kieran's heartbeat still echoed in his head. Just yesterday he'd been pleasantly miserable debating with himself whether he was in love or merely infatuated. Now it was obvious that none of those words had any real meaning. He knew one simple thing, and of that he was certain beyond the need to think about it: *I'll die without him.*

He meant it without metaphor; literal death waited beyond Kieran's protective shadow. Whether his mind or his body broke first, it was clear he lacked the strength to survive the damage without Kieran's help. It should have frightened him, but instead it seemed to help a little, knowing what it was he needed.

I know how things are for you, Kieran. I know how you can swallow emptiness and hold it inside. What I still don't understand is how you draw strength from that void. Are you unhappy like I am? Or are joy and sorrow two more of the things you don't perceive?

The dinner bell filtered through many layers of detachment and reached him after it had stopped ringing. It took a moment to remember that he had to do something in response to the noise.

Leaving the cell made his skin crawl. The sight of tan uniforms worried him. He dealt with it by copying Kieran, doing what Kieran did, and by this means managed to line up with the others and march to the mess hall, and did not panic and bolt. He got his tray, allowed food to be put on it, went to a table and sat down where he could see Kieran's face. Nothing else was quite real. Kieran scooped up a chunk of overcooked potato on his spoon, so Ash did too. But when he considered putting food inside himself, in his mouth, chewing, feeling it slide down, he thought he might vomit.

"Eat," Kieran ordered.

He almost said 'I can't' again. But the sound of those words in his head was more disgusting than the thought of food in his mouth. He ate. It tasted like wet paper.

Outside, it seemed offensive that the sun was shining. *I'm in the desert,* he reminded himself. *That's what the sun does here. It shines with a hard high-pitched whine and burns away everything soft on the ground. I am a soft thing being burned. Kieran is not.*

"Square stance," Kieran said.

Ash frowned, trying to make these words make sense.

"First one I showed you. Feet apart and parallel."

They were going to practice fighting? Ash didn't think there was much point. "The thing I need to fight is in my head," he murmured.

"So show it you're a badass. Square stance." Kieran waited a moment, then barked, "*Today,* Trine."

Because it was easier to obey Kieran than argue with

him, Ash did as he was told.

Kieran put up his hands, palms out. "Start where we left off yesterday. Right straight, right cross, left straight, left cross. We're working on accuracy again."

Weakly, he knuckled Kieran's left palm, then missed the right one entirely. Took a moment to remember how to use his own left hand. *Pathetic. I'm pathetic.* He kept missing the straights with his left, missing the crosses with both hands, until a short segment of a small-child whine escaped him and he broke stance. "I can't do it today. I'm so *stupid* today."

Kieran's hand darted out and smacked Ash's forehead. He put his hands up again. "Start over."

Ash made one weak swing, forgetting his form entirely, then turned away. "It's useless."

A hand on his shoulder spun him around, a slap stung his face. "That's useless," Kieran growled. Another slap; Ash reeled back, tears threatening. "*That's* useless." Showing teeth, Kieran darted slaps at Ash's cheeks and forehead, shoves at his chest and arms. "You going to let me win? You going to let me do this to you?"

"Ow! Kieran!" Ash flailed instinctively at the next hand that came near him. The blows were coming too fast, he couldn't block them all, Kieran had turned against him, his shelter had become his enemy and it was all over -- fear sparked in his chest and everything went bright. He slapped away what seemed like a hundred hands at once, and in his panic followed this flurry with a blow of his own.

Everything went still. His fist was wrapped in Kieran's, and the tall Iavaian was smiling.

"Feel better now?" Kieran asked gently, and Ash realized that despite the alarming speed of the blows, Kieran hadn't hurt him. He couldn't even feel where Kieran's hands had landed.

"Define better." But in his own grumbling, Ash heard that his hopelessness was gone, at least for now. "You're a mean bastard, Kieran. You didn't have to hit me."

"Okay." Kieran released his fist. "Square stance."

Gritting his teeth, Ash lined up his feet, bent his knees, and smacked a fist into Kieran's palm. Right, right, left, left. His form was sloppy, but he didn't care. He was supposed to be working on accuracy, not force, but he was throwing his shoulder behind each punch, and it felt good.

Kieran's palms were reddened by the time they were

done, and Ash's knuckles swollen, and his despair had vanished. And, somehow, he hadn't missed once.

"What are you doing?"

Kieran turned from the washbasin, water running off his elbows, the muscles of his back shifting deliciously. "Conducting the Gevarne Philharmonic. What's it look like? I'm washing my shirt."

"Why?"

"It smells. How many sit-ups was that?"

"Thirty."

"You did thirty-five yesterday."

"I'm just resting." Ash settled his chin on his knuckles and watched the movement of Kieran's shoulders. It came to him that he was more resilient than he'd thought. Just yesterday he'd been half mad with fear and hopelessness, but already his libido was back. He wasn't yet sure he forgave Kieran for hitting him, however little physical damage he'd done, but if the point had been to awaken Ash's urge to survive the ploy had succeeded. His mind still felt bruised, though. He hadn't slept particularly well, had woken before the bell today; it still hadn't rung. The sky was just starting to go gray. He'd been a little surprised to find Kieran up before him, but no explanation had been offered and he didn't feel like asking for one. He waited until the ache in his gut subsided and did ten more sit-ups before looking at his cellmate again.

"You going to wear it wet? Or go to breakfast without?"

"Without." Kieran wrung out the wad of blue cotton, then turned with a grin to snap it at Ash, spattering him. "You look better today. How're you feeling?"

"Peaceful."

"Peaceful! And you think *I'm* a nut job." He made a shrug into shaking out his shirt. "Whatever works for you, I guess."

"And you? How are you?"

"Same old. Bored. Whiffy. Wish they'd let us in the bath more than once a week. Clean water would be nice, while I'm wishing."

"When we get out, let's go somewhere there's a lake, and swim until we get all pruney. And burn our clothes."

"I thought you didn't believe I can get us out of here."

"I trust you."

That put something into Kieran's eyes that was halfway between anger and worry, and only lasted half a second. "Good," was all he said.

The bell rang. Kieran spread his wet shirt over the rim of the washbasin, then tugged at the string of his trousers, with a jerk of his chin toward the door. Ash obediently looked away. Having to share a toilet was no longer embarrassing; there was a certain etiquette to it, that was all. When Kieran muttered something in Iavaian, Ash pretended not to hear. That was how you made your own privacy, in a place like this. Still, he wondered what it had been -- Kieran had never talked to himself before.

All the doors opened. Ash stood, yawning. He was too sleep-deprived to be hungry, but it wasn't as if there was a choice. "It better not be sausage today," he began to say, but lost his train of thought as Kieran walked out past him.

The difference was subtle, but shockingly effective. Pants hanging an inch too low, stride fractionally shorter, leading with the hips just a little, tilt of the chin somehow saucy instead of arrogant today -- *What the hell is he up to? He looks like a slut.*

Ash wasn't the only one staring. Several inmates, more likely woman-starved than fey, were gawking at the spice-colored spans of Kieran's skin. And one of the guards had his eyes fastened on the jut of Kieran's hipbones with an anticipatory, gloating look Ash didn't like at all. Ash tried desperately to marshall his thoughts, to understand this change, but he'd been walloped by the same hormonal sledgehammer. It made him feel simpleminded -- as well as too hot all over, so he was undoubtedly turning bright red.

As they took their places in line, someone snickered. "Looks like *somebody* got some last night."

"Shut it." The guard who'd been staring sauntered down the line until he reached Kieran. He raked his gaze up and down Kieran's body. "Where's your shirt, Trevarde?"

"Washed it, sir." Kieran's voice was different too. The razor blades buried just a little deeper in the candy. It had a purr in it. Ash was beginning to be frightened.

"Getting domestic, are we? Thinking of starting a business? Taking in these lads' washing?"

"They don't have anything to pay me with." Kieran's smile was a challenge; the guard's was a threat.

"Back in your cell, boy. No breakfast for you today."

Kieran gave a liquid shrug. Though Ash tried desperately

to catch his eyes, he only stared at the guard. The line moved out without him.

Sick to his stomach, Ash picked at his breakfast. Halfway through the period, someone sidled up to his table as if to drop some smartass remark, but when Ash looked at him he went away without saying anything.

In the yard, he punched the air three hundred and thirty-two times, and didn't think about anything but counting. He didn't dare. He didn't even try to tell himself that Kieran would explain, that it would be all right, because he knew it wasn't all right and there was nothing he could do about it.

On the way back to the cell, he kept counting; steps, prisoners, skylights, anything. He felt light with fear, unreal and floating, moving by habit. He half expected the cell to be empty, but Kieran was there. Ash walked into the cell like a clockwork toy and sat down on the edge of his bunk, opposite where Kieran sprawled, and didn't let himself feel relieved that the tall boy was at least still alive. There were worse things than dead, in this place, and Kieran looked like he might have discovered one of them.

Kieran was lying on his back with his eyes open. His color was bad, and he blinked too often, but there was no mark on him. Except for the blinking, he looked like a corpse. One arm trailed over the edge of the cot, the hand dangling limply. After a long time, Ash leaned out to touch that hand, to find out if it was clammy or fevered; it must be one of the two, the way Kieran looked.

"No touching," Kieran murmured. His lips barely moved.

"What happened?"

"Ask me later."

Moving carefully, so as not to startle, Ash knelt on the floor beside Kieran's bed. As he did, he noticed something under it: the tin cup they had to share, with a pellet of something brown and wet stuck to the bottom.

"Put that back," Kieran said sharply, though he didn't move. "Don't touch it. Don't move it, don't look at it, don't talk about it. They find out I have that, we're fucked."

"What is it?"

"Poison."

Ash slid the cup as far back under as he could reach. He stood, and looked down at Kieran for a long time before Kieran looked back. "What did you do, Kieran?" He was proud that his voice came out quiet and even.

Kieran sighed, his eyes wandering away again. "Remember how I said I used to have a habit? It never really goes away, you know."

"That's *opium*?"

"Quiet! He wanted me to eat it while he watched. I had to put it under my tongue. I'm going to have to put it under my tongue every time."

"Every time what? Kieran --"

"It's costing me to let it sit under the bed. You understand? Don't make it harder."

"I see." Ash backed up until the edge of his bunk hit him behind the knees, and folded. "How many more times is this going to happen, Kieran? How much do you have to hoard before you can use it in your plan? How can you stand --"

"Not that." Kieran blinked at the ceiling. "That one you don't get to ask. Your other question -- at least three more like that. More would be better. He gave me a fat dose. Guess he figured if I was lying about how big a tar habit I had, lying so I could share it or something, a big wad like that would kill me."

Ash hadn't thought his heart could shrink any further, but at this it squeezed down to pebble-size. "How much did you swallow?"

"Don't panic. I didn't even fall asleep. Used to eat suicide doses like candy. That's not the problem. The problem is I can't think about anything but the cup under the bed."

"Oh." Ash swallowed. "I could, I could --"

"No you couldn't. There's no place to hide it and I could take it away from you any time I wanted. Leave it."

"I could... distract you, I was going to say."

"What?" Kieran gaped at him, with a rasp of incredulous laughter. "You have the worst timing I have ever fucking witnessed. I just sucked cock at gunpoint, you dumbass. I'm not exactly in a cuddly mood."

"You --? But. That's not -- I didn't -- oh, god." Mortified, Ash buried his face in his hands. "I'm sorry. I'm so sorry."

"I told you you didn't want to know."

"Oh god, Kieran, isn't there any other --"

"Fucking drop it, Ash. I used to do it for a living, it's no big deal."

He sounded calm, even jocular. But when Ash dared to look up, Kieran was staring at the ceiling again, blinking slowly and too often.

Chapter 9

He'd been ready for two weeks.

The cup beneath the bed was half full now. He had a full-fledged low-grade habit again from holding doses under his tongue, but so far he hadn't given in to the urge to swallow. Poor Ash was a wreck; the kid had been to Testing twice more, and on top of that he didn't seem to be able to handle what Kieran was doing. But he hadn't lost it again -- yet. He didn't talk much these days, but he still wrote in his book, which Kieran guessed was a sign of life. Kieran didn't bother reading it. The white boy's poetic agonies would seem like a sick joke, compared to reality; unless he'd given up feeling things that strongly, which was sensible, but sad; Kieran really didn't want to know.

Every day that passed now, readiness deteriorated. Any minute, something could happen that would wreck their chances. Ash might crack. Kieran might talk himself into dipping into the tar stash. Either of them could get sick, or go to Testing and not come back. Or the little cabal of guards who supplied the opium could get tired of Kieran as they'd tired of Hartnell; there was no way he could fake withdrawal well enough to fool someone who'd seen it firsthand. However much he groaned and griped, he couldn't pantomime vomiting and loose bowels and sweats. They'd know he'd been hoarding, and then the game would be up.

The main consideration, though, was simply that he was tired of this place. Tired to death of it. The food and company, of course, the smells and grit and ill-fitting clothes, the physical confinement. More than that, the humiliations, threats and whoring. More even than that, the Colonel and his insectile persistence, his torturings and pryings, the constant fear that one of those Surveys would uncover the escape plan. But most of all, Kieran was tired of the wards that squashed his Talent. It was like never quite being able to stand up straight. He sometimes even looked forward to Testing, just so he could uncurl his cramped mind for a few hours. The Colonel's tedious tortures were almost worth the visions they brought.

It was on those visions that his plan depended.

The visions, the drug, and Ash's cooperation. The kid had put on muscle as spring wore toward summer, while the smoothness of youth melted out from under his skin. He was worn down fine, and the change was startling; though the sun had bleached orange and gold into his rusty hair, making it redder, and doubled his freckle density, he'd started to look dangerous. An odd beauty had emerged as well. More than the sharper lines of his face, the difference was due to the confidence that fighting lessons had put into his movements, and the haunted heat of his blue eyes, which seemed to see nothing but pain. The other inmates got out of Ash's way whether Kieran was near him or not.

As his body strengthened, though, it seemed his mind eroded. If the opportunity to use the plan took too long to arrive, Kieran feared that Ash would be useless. Would just sit and stare, the way he was doing now.

"Hey Ashes," Kieran tried, to see if this was one of the days when Ash was responding to stimuli. It wasn't. The redhead didn't even look up; he just kept picking at his cuticles. The beds of his nails were flayed to bleeding.

Across the tier, someone's name was called in an official tone. Time for Testing. Ash didn't tense or flinch the way he used to, didn't react even when the guards stopped outside their cell.

"Kieran Trevarde."

They'd stopped bothering to say goodbye or good luck when one of them was taken out. It was pointless. Kieran thought he detected some relief in Ash's expression. He couldn't spare the energy to be annoyed; after all, Ash was more damaged by these sessions than Kieran was. He was right to be glad it wasn't his turn. Anyway, it took all Kieran's attention simply to go quietly and not wear himself out with useless worry about what might be waiting for him. The last few times, he'd been in the room with two chairs, doing the Watch's housecleaning for them. Each time, he'd refused to use his killing Talent until Warren had dragged his every nerve through the fire enough times to make his joints ache and his head throb for hours afterward. Warren seemed to think it was plain stubbornness, but the truth was that Kieran needed the dreams he had when he was knocked out of himself by agony.

That being the case, he was both relieved and displeased when he wasn't taken to the usual room this time. Instead, the guards brought him to the first white room, the one with the desk.

This time, the desk was clear of papers, and Warren was not the one behind it. The Colonel stood to one side as Kieran was brought in and made to sit. In the place of power behind the desk sat the most creepily perfect man Kieran had ever seen, looking at him with a clinical interest that somehow turned his guts to water as nothing and no one had done since he was a small child. Kieran had the impression that it had been a mistake to meet the man's eyes, because now he was caught. There was something eerily familiar about those eyes, paler than Ash's, something that reminded him of past defeats and errors, humiliations, made him feel acutely how dirty and bedraggled he was.

The man behind the desk could have been anywhere between twenty and thirty-five. He was pale, everything about him pale as mist; his hair was blond as cream, his eyes so light a gray they seemed made of silver foil. Those eyes speared Kieran like a pin through a specimen insect, and Kieran could not look away.

Colonel Warren spoke to this man in a reverent tone. "Shall I put him through his paces, sir?"

"That won't be necessary, Colonel." The man's voice was as cool as his eyes, without accent or emotion. "You may go."

This seemed to startle Warren just a bit, but he collected himself with a sharp salute and a crisp "Yes, sir."

After Warren had gone, the stranger simply sat and looked at Kieran for a time. Kieran had no choice but to stare back. Belatedly, he realized that this was probably the Director that Warren had mentioned. Though his uniform was the same cut as other Watchmen's, the braid at his shoulders was white instead of red. Where others' collars sported small squares of red enamel to show their seniority, this man had a series of what looked like diamonds. Other than the insignia of his rank, he had not a single ornament, no indication of anything personal around him.

Kieran was scared of him.

It didn't make much sense. The guy was a little weird-looking, and obviously pretty high in the Watch, but he hadn't done anything yet but stare. Still, Kieran was irrationally certain that this man, out of all the Watch, was the one who knew how to really hurt him.

"Do you dream?"

The sudden question startled Kieran into a confused

113

reply. "What? Dream? I guess so. Sometimes."

"True dreams."

Visions. The man was talking about his visions. The game was up. "I don't think so," Kieran lied.

"Do you have any special connection to the weather?"

"Connection?" Kieran frowned puzzlement, avoided thinking of how his visions took him into the clouds to see whether any rain was coming. "Sorry, but what are you getting at?"

"Do you have any memories of past lives?"

"No -- I mean, that's heresy, right? Not that I guess that would matter here --" He caught himself and shut his mouth firmly. *You're losing it. He's just another Watchman, you big baby.* But he was sure that his answers had been wrong.

The Director rose. "Come with me."

The command was delivered in an ordinary tone, but it lashed puppet strings to Kieran's limbs and hauled him helplessly along. A passenger in his own body, Kieran fought a swell of panic.

Outside the room, Warren saluted some more. "Sir. Do you want a subject brought to the Testing room?"

"Yes." The Director glanced at Kieran. "Someone he cares about, if that's possible. A personal acquaintance."

The impending panic burst wide open in Kieran's chest; part of him watched while the rest shook to his pounding heart, sweated, made clumsy steps in the wake of the Director's will. The part that watched was able to remark that he'd known Ash would not last long in this place, that he should not have grown as attached as he had, that it was his own stupid fault if this broke him. The rest was an injured animal on a leash, thrashing in helplessness.

I won't do it. But he couldn't say it out loud. The compulsion to obedience was too strong. *I won't.*

He was taken to the room. Put in the chair. Strapped down. Hunched there shuddering and rageful, twisting at the bonds of the Director's command. There he waited for what felt like days while the man in the white-on-white uniform flipped idly through a stack of papers he'd brought with him. His vision blurred, his nose ran, his throat closed, but he couldn't even weep, the leash on his mind held him so tightly.

The door opened; footsteps entered. Kieran strained to see, escape, attack, anything, while the prisoner he was to kill was brought into his field of vision.

Duyam Sona.

It was all he could do not to laugh out loud, not betray his relief. Not Ash. It wasn't Ash. Ash was safe from his murderous power. Nothing else mattered.

The Director looked between the two Iavaians with mild interest. "Did you select this one for his resemblance to the subject? I require an emotional bond, Colonel."

"I'm afraid Trevarde doesn't seem to bond much with anyone, sir. But he won't wish to kill another native."

"You misunderstand me, Colonel. This is not intended as a form of psychological torture. But if this is the best you can provide, then I suppose the distant blood tie will have to suffice. Ready him."

Kieran couldn't believe what he was hearing. The Colonel must have known that he and Ash were inseparable. Anyone with eyes knew that. Warren had lied to the Director. Why? Not just so he could continue to train students on Ash's faint Talent. Could it be that he actually felt some pity for his charges? It didn't matter right now. All Kieran needed to know was that the man before him could die without breaking anything Kieran needed to keep, and that was enough.

The Director came over to Kieran's chair and wrapped a long, cool hand around the back of his neck, a strangely gentle gesture. "Kieran Trevarde, kill this man."

Compulsion was like cold water running down his throat; his intention could do nothing to halt it, and it slithered inside him unchecked by his resistance. He jammed his eyes shut and clenched his teeth, but already the hand of his heart was uncoiling. He had to fight, had to refuse, because he needed the visions, needed the pain to send him out, but it was all happening too fast.

Then it came to him. 'Kieran Trevarde, kill this man.' *Kieran's not my real name -- and by the way, which man did you mean?*

By his mind's sight, he found bright knots of life inside the room, felt them like breath on his skin. Sona's aching flame of fear, the glassed-in shape of Warren, and the icy serpent of the Director's will coiled around all their throats, familiar as his own nightmares. He would not touch that last, was afraid to touch it. But Warren -- he'd never realized how fragile those shields were all this time. A sharp shock easily shattered them. He heard a gasp as he dug his thoughts' fingers into the tough join between soul and flesh and pried with all his strength. Pain came, but it wasn't enough. Kieran dug deeper.

"Colonel, control your subject. Colonel!" A sharp sigh of exasperation; then a pain that made Warren's psychic tortures look like a head cold came pouring along Kieran's nerves.

Kieran lost his grip, his focus, his breakfast, and the contents of his bladder. The intensity of it, the shock, kept him present and aware long enough to hear his own scream fail into a rack of sobbing whimpers, heart straining, diaphragm convulsing, shredded thoughts crying *I don't want it after all, why did I want this?* Then the window deep inside opened and let him out.

Wind cleansed him, sweetly cold at this altitude. The desert was lush under him, blooming with pale flame colors, wallowing in the season of storms. Those storms' trails were apparent in scars cut into the earth, the red ropes and fans of erosion. The air tasted fresh, wet, full of ozone.

Where was that smell coming from? The sky was blue and empty.

He rose higher, until Churchrock was lost among the shadows of the ground. For the first time in one of these visions he was aware of his body, saw his own brown legs curled beneath him. Held out his arms before him and saw the skin blank of tattoos, scarless, and wound with a weight of gold that could buy the world, but which was not heavy. His strength was enormous. He inhaled and rose into the wind, laughing as his hair beat his back with a thousand gold-weighted braids. A king, an emperor of the air, all below belonged to him. He rose until the earth's curvature was visible, until the sky's blue darkened around him.

Now the only features he could make out were swaths of color, wrinkles and smooth places. To the west, the mountains blended into one snow-riddled scar that curled around the world out of sight, and beyond them there was only cloud.

It streamed through the passes and built high enough to smear against the sky, white above, purple inside, and roiling like a boiling kettle. Its shadow was solid black. It was the mother of all storms, coming to show the desert that spring was not a gentle season. This was it; this was what he needed.

Come! he commanded it. Come here to Iaka'anta with your hailstones, your sweet winds, your tornado claws to dig this abomination out of the ground and fling its dust into the sky. Come free me. Free me so well that I can never be locked in again.

And he felt the storm answer.

He came back to a body as weak as water, riddled with a thousand aches, reeking, and he didn't care. A voice was blabbering at him, but that was somehow soothing; after a moment he realized that this was because it was speaking Iavaian.

"All crazy," it was saying. "All of you. Why didn't you just do it? No wonder you're going extinct. I would have done it. But no, you have to do your Tama thing and spit in their eyes and make them kill you. Dumb bastard."

"I'm not dead," Kieran muttered. He pried his eyes open to meet Sona's bewildered glare. Was it his imagination, or did the man look grudgingly relieved at that?

"You will be soon enough, you keep pushing them like that. Why didn't you just do it?"

Kieran managed a wan smile. "I like to make them mad. It's a Tama thing."

"Well, they're mad. Now do the thing. Let me out."

Before Kieran could reply, the door opened and Warren and the Director came into his line of sight. Warren said, "Are you ready to cooperate now?"

"Wait," said the Director. He peered into Kieran's eyes, touched his throat and forehead. "I want him at full strength. It isn't often that I have leisure to observe one of these under controlled circumstances. We'll attempt this again tomorrow." He turned to Warren. "That will give you time to improve your personal wards."

The Colonel flushed from pink to purple. "Yes, sir." He gestured a brace of tan-uniformed guards into sight. "Put them back. Clean that one up first."

As Kieran was jelly-legging out the door between his guards, a white uniform jogged past and into the chair room. Kieran heard the rustle of paper, and: "Director Thelyan, sir, urgent message for you from the Central Office."

Thelyan? Thelyan... The name snagged in Kieran's mind, like a foreign word he'd once known the meaning of. He stumbled deliberately, lurching hard against one of the guards and letting his legs splay out from under him.

"How inconvenient. Why can't these rebels ever cause trouble on a weekend, eh, Colonel? I must leave immediately; we'll have to continue this another time. I won't be in Rainet more than a week, I expect -- I assume you can keep my subject alive for a week?"

The guards got Kieran upright again at that point, and Warren's reply to the Director's dry tone was lost in the clatter of their boots. But he'd heard enough. Director Thelyan was leaving, the storm was coming, and the only way it could be better would be if his muscles didn't feel so much like they were made of damp string.

Ash was sitting just as Kieran had left him, staring at the floor. Kieran laughed; relief, anticipation maybe. Ash looked up, dull-eyed, as Kieran stumbled to his bunk. The guards had thrown him in the bath with his clothes on, and he was still dripping. Wobbly, but not nearly as weak as he should have been.

"What's funny?" Ash demanded. He didn't seem much interested in the answer.

"Come over here."

A pause. Then Ash pried himself upright, dropped himself at Kieran's side. When Kieran's arm went around his shoulders, he twitched, then froze. Kieran put his mouth to Ash's ear and whispered.

"We're leaving tonight."

He drew back to watch expressions blossom across Ash's features. Surprise, then hope, then suspicion. Kieran remembered how it had been to think Ash would be the one he'd be made to kill, and tightened his hand on the pale boy's shoulder.

"You're playing with me," Ash accused.

"Get your book."

Ash blinked. His eyes began to regain their light. "My god. You're serious. You're actually going to stake our lives on this rickety plan you've been hinting at."

"Yes, I told you. And it's going to work. Get out your book, I need to see the guard schedules."

Ash obeyed, but his nostrils flared as he turned the pages. The smolder of dull pain in his eyes was waking to rebel fire, and it was beautiful to see. "You're going to get us killed. You're going to get me killed, and I'm going to die not even knowing how it was supposed to work, if it worked, which it won't, because you didn't tell me."

"I thought you said you trusted me."

"I did say that." Looking up into Kieran's face, Ash visibly snapped awake, finished the process of leaving his private fear. His pupils dilated, blood rushed to his sunburned cheeks and chapped lips, and he sat up fractionally straighter. "Yes, all right; of all the things I could do today, trusting you is one of my better options. I'm with you."

"Besides," Kieran went on, "so what if we die? It's not like we're going to lead long, productive lives in here. What have you got to lose?"

At this, a ghost of humor crept into Ash's expression. "Well, I'd rather not die a virgin."

Kieran snorted. "Figures. You act like one. Now quit sidetracking me and tell me who's overnight on our tier tonight."

"Uh... Blondie and Squarehead."

"Where are they for afternoon? Are they on at all?"

"I've never seen Squarehead pull an afternoon shift. I think he's strictly nights. Blondie could be anywhere."

"Shit. All right, if Blondie's out, who subs for him?"

Ash hesitated. "Look, you're not going to try that old dodge, are you?"

"Which?"

"Eek, eek, I'm sick, come in my cell so I can whack you on the head."

"No. Just find the sub."

After some study and mumbling, Ash gave a humorless laugh. "That would be either Fidget or Shithead."

"What? Who's Shithead?"

"Your *supplier*." Ash spat the word.

"Damn, kid. What a name. Jealous?"

"Angry. Look, let's just --" His hand flung air away.

"Okay, okay. Fidget would be the one who's always got his fingers in his eyes, right? That's fine. That's perfect." Kieran motioned Ash close again. He couldn't afford for anyone to overhear even the fact that someone was whispering, so he put his lips close enough to brush the skin and barely breathed the words. "It goes like this. Memorize it and don't ask questions."

"That's ridiculous," Ash said when Kieran had finished. He was bright pink and sitting sort of hunched over; Kieran had given him a thrill with the ear thing. "You're hanging it all on a hallucination? You can't possibly be that sure --"

"Shut up, for fuck's sake! Shit, blab it to everyone, why don't you?"

"Sorry. Okay. But the question stands."

"It's a risk. Yeah. But if I'm right, we'll never get a better chance. We won't live to see a better chance. I'd ask if you're in, but I'm not giving you a choice."

"Of course I'm in." Ash hugged his book to his chest. "And I do trust you. It's everything else I don't trust." His voice dropped to a whisper. "My god. Tonight. By this time tomorrow..."

"Don't think about it. Hope will just distract you."

Chapter 10

"Trying to start a fashion, boys? You won't get new shirts when winter comes, you know. You'll freeze your stupid asses off."

"Yes, sir." Kieran let the struggle to keep a straight face show; he'd look like that no matter what his reason for having torn the sleeves off Ash's shirt. He wasn't nervous yet; there was no way for his face to betray the fact that a scrap from one of Ash's sleeves was holding a flap of hammered-flat spoon over the lock mechanism of their door, poised to pivot when the tier was opened, and that Kieran had just heard it clink perfectly into place. The guard glanced between them, alike in sleevelessness, and at the rag of blue-gray cloth Ash was wearing as a bandanna, and let it go.

"Go on, get in line."

Ash muttered, "You mean it gets cold here ever?"

"Sure it does. Freeze the tits off a statue," Kieran replied.

"No talking! Straighten it out, there."

As the line moved out, Kieran darted a glance back, but couldn't see the rag or the spoon. That was good. No one else would see it either.

Padding barefoot along the stone, Kieran picked a particularly gritty bit of corridor and did a startled shuffle-step, went the rest of the way at a half-limp. Once inside the mess hall, he dropped out of line to lean against a table. As he pretended to pry a splinter out of his foot, he watched Ash go through the supper line in his usual place. He kept up the splinter act just long enough to be last in line.

Out of the corner of his eye, he saw Ash leave his tray and walk straight to Sona's table. *Not so obvious, idiot! It looks planned!* But neither of the two guards near the door reacted. Come to think of it, people really did plan that kind of thing, brooded for days before calling someone out, so Ash's awkwardness was right in character. The white boy bent over Sona, talking in a low voice, and Sona jerked upright with a look of angry suspicion.

Come on, come on, take the bait. It didn't look like Sona was going for it. Kieran was at the end of the line, the last lump of boiled vegetables was being dumped on his tray. If the distraction didn't happen, today was a no-go. If it happened late, this whole part of the plan would have to be reworked before they could try again. The cook shoved the ladle back in the pot of vegetables and turned away. *Now, damn it! Say anything, just get him mad already! It's not like the man is a fucking saint --*

Ash stepped back and threw his hands up, giving in -- then suddenly flicked Sona's tray into his lap with a nasty smirk. In an instant, the Iavaian was off the bench and swinging.

Perfect. Kieran didn't watch the rest. In that first moment of noise and sudden movement, when all eyes automatically jerked to the disturbance, Kieran's hands went to work. One to the coffee urn, one into the back of his collar where the opium was hidden in a ball of rag. Open the urn, shake out the rag; close the urn, hide the rag. The whole operation took two seconds, tops.

He drew off a tiny splash of coffee into his cup to keep anyone from remembering a suspiciously clean cup after the fact. He turned around just in time to see a bloody-nosed Ash floor Sona with a beautiful right backfist to the jaw.

The guards hadn't moved; a glance showed one slapping the other on the arm, waggling fingers in the universal sign for 'pay up.' Kieran grinned, lengthening his stride to cut off a handful of inmates who looked as if they'd decided to play too.

"That's enough, Ashes," he said.

Ash turned to him, wiping blood from his face, eyes shining. "How was that, Teach?"

"You won. That's all that ever counts. Now go eat your damn supper." He shoved his tray at Ash. To Sona, he held out a hand. "Not dead yet, I hope?"

"Unfortunately." Sona ignored the offered hand. He used the edge of the table to haul himself upright, rubbing his jaw. "You put him up to that?"

"Wasn't me who stepped on his glasses. Give people something to prove, they prove it." With that, Kieran went to join Ash.

"Did you see that?" Ash greeted him with a huge smile. A smile on Ash's face after the past few morose weeks seemed like a lucky omen. "I kicked his ass!"

"Good work. Keep your head, now. This is where it might get sticky."

Ash leaned in close. "You think they saw you?"

"No. But watch my back anyway."

"I see them. They're just standing there."

"One of them bet on you, you know."

"I wonder how much he won? Not that it'll do him any…" The redhead's joy at winning the fight crashed into the fact that people were going to die because of it. Kieran felt sorry for the softhearted little twit. If there'd been a way they could do this without killing, Kieran would have done it that way, for Ash's sake.

"Yeah, okay. Let's just hope they're all in a coffee mood tonight." *And that the coffee's bitterness hides the taste. And that I put in enough, and it dissolves fast enough, and they don't start dropping until they're at their posts, because if they get replaced right away this was all for nothing.*

He had to wrestle with himself not to stare at the coffee urn. Out of the corner of his eye, he watched it the whole period. No inmates went back for a second cup -- they seldom did, the stuff tasted like turpentine and they had no reason to stay awake. Halfway through supper, a cook opened the urn and poured in a fresh pot, and didn't seem to see anything amiss. Kieran imagined the swirl of boiling coffee stirring the dissolving drug, melting it into a potent soup of sleeping death.

"God," Ash said, "I'm so nervous."

"You're doing fine. Just remember to be a sulky bitch like you've been the past few weeks."

"Asshole." Ash made the insult sound affectionate.

"Eat. You don't want to do this on an empty stomach."

"I'm too nervous. I'll puke."

"No you won't, because I'll kick your ass if you do."

They both managed to force their food down. The bell rang, and they were let into the yard. Kieran imagined he could taste the heaviness of the impending storm, but that was wishful thinking. Through the side of the fence that faced west, he could barely make out that the mountains looked a shade smoother, a hair closer than usual.

"Are you sure --" Ash began.

"Yes. Quit talking about it."

"Sorry."

"Now we're going to practice like we always do."

"I'll screw up."

"So?" But he didn't need Ash acting weird, missing moves he'd had by heart yesterday. "We'll do kicks. Yours suck, so nobody'll be surprised if you do it wrong."

"Oh, thanks."

"Don't mention it. Floating stance. Bend your knees more, weight over your back leg. Good. Snap kicks, right here. And try not to break my hand, I'm going to need it."

He'd been right: Ash's kicks were awful, and no one noticed that it was because he was nervous.

"You kick like a constipated priest," Kieran said after a while.

"Well," Ash huffed between awkward efforts to reach Kieran's head-high hand, "you smell like one and the southeast tower's empty have a look."

Mentally congratulating Ash's even tone, which no one would hear even if they heard it, he circled under the guise of making Ash pivot. The kid was right; there was no one up there. The swivel gun was unattended, pointing at the sky. The other tower was still manned, and the guard there didn't seem alarmed. Those guards shouldn't have eaten yet -- could they be already shortstaffed? Better than he could possibly have hoped. He just knew something was going to go wrong to compensate.

Time passed. Kieran got tired, didn't have much strength to spare after getting zapped by the Director, so he stopped the lesson. There was nothing to do then but wait.

"Is it just me," he heard someone nearby comment, "or is it starting to get dark?"

"We shoulda been inside by now," was the puzzled answer.

There were no clocks, but the sun had fallen behind the cloud bank over the mountains, which at best guess made it nearly an hour later than they usually went in. Kieran imagined the confusion that must be occurring inside, as the prison administrators tried to compensate for the droves of guards that must be falling ill right about now. It rankled that this part of his plan's success or failure was invisible to him.

A careful study of the guard schedules had led him to decide that those who ate their supper after the inmates were a combination of two shifts. Both the afternoon people going off duty and the night people coming on would have a chance to sample his special recipe. Depending on how many came down sick, there might be almost no one in the towers or on the gates outside, because when missing half their staff their best option would be to put what guards they had as close to the prisoners as possible. Where Kieran could get at them. He hoped.

When the prisoners were finally let back inside, their escort wore white uniforms instead of tan. Kieran silently rejoiced. His brew must have been both potent and popular; they were so understaffed they'd had to pull people out of Testing just to get the inmates out of the yard.

They filed back into their cells. The White Watch men stood warily to their unaccustomed duty while a lone, nervous, tan-shirted guard went about hauling the levers that closed the cells. Kieran smirked at the Watchmen as he passed them. They couldn't use their magic inside the wards any more than he could. They were just men, in here, and they could smell a predator. One shifted his rifle to cover Kieran; the other stupidly stared at the business with the levers. Kieran hoped no one took advantage of this slackness to start a riot, because killing these idiots now wouldn't get anyone out of the cell block. But the only advantage the prisoners took was to talk and laugh while they were locked up, though they were supposed to be silent until the doors were closed. Only Kieran and Ash didn't have anything to say. They avoided each other's faces until, with a familiar clank and grind, the bars closed them in once more.

It was torture to wait until all the guards had gone down to the end of the tier, out of earshot. When he was sure it was safe, Kieran wedged his foot in the bars and hopped up to see how his clever little mechanism had worked.

It hadn't.

"What's wrong?" Ash backed away from the look on Kieran's face. "What is it? Oh, hell. I told you the lock bar was too heavy. It bent, didn't it?"

"Shut up." Kieran sat heavily on his bunk and put his head in his hands. "Shit. Shit. Well, there goes everything."

With his face in his palms, he couldn't see Ash's expression, and he didn't want to. He didn't want to see his misery mirrored there. He didn't look up even when the bed sagged under Ash's weight and a hand landed on his shoulder.

"Look, Kieran..." Ash's voice was careful. Humoring him, or afraid of him. Like everyone else. How could he have ever mistaken that for respect? "We'll think of something. Maybe the sickness dodge will work after all, what with everyone going down --"

"They'll know what it is by then. We have to wait for the storm, remember? If they can see us they'll gun us down, you know that." Kieran jerked his shoulder, trying to dislodge Ash's hand, but failed. "We're fucked. I fucked us. Quit trying to be nice about it."

"I'm not. Okay? Kieran, look at me. At least we're taking a bunch of them down with us, right?"

"Now you sound like me. Stop it."

"Kieran."

"I said stop!" Kieran forgot about not looking, but the expression he found on Ash's face was not the one he'd feared. Far from being miserable, Ash was burning bright again. The pale blue eyes were all the way alive, at this worst of times to lose detachment Ash was completely present. "Don't you care?" Kieran snapped.

"I don't believe it's over. Something will come up. We'll think of something. We're smart, we're smarter than they are."

With a shaky breath he regretted letting Ash hear, Kieran reached down behind the bed. He pulled a sliver of sharpened spoon metal from its hiding place inside the mattress and showed it briefly before palming it. "I'll send you off whenever you're ready, then do myself. I can do it so it won't hurt. I just want to hear that storm first."

Ash looked startled. He shook his head.

"Think about it, Ashes. When my 'supplier' talks, when it all comes out... they don't waste pain, around here. They'll probably make me kill you, then keep me alive to study how I did it. If I'm going to kill you, I don't want to have to live with it more than thirty seconds." He stopped, shocked at himself. Ash didn't speak for a long moment, biting his lip and searching Kieran's eyes. Then he nodded.

"Not until I tell you," Ash said. "I want to know for sure there's no hope first. Promise."

"I promise. Not until you tell me to."

There was nothing to say after that. They watched each other's faces. Kieran found himself oddly detached, caught by the complexities of iridescence in Ash's eyes, lulled into a kind of peace.

The lights went off. They sat together in the dark, not speaking or moving. Kieran heard the guards on the stairs, meaning they were walking both sides, just three guards for the whole place, but it didn't matter anymore. He thought of how they'd been planning to do it; sliding open their door under cover of the storm's noise, slipping out to catch the guards unawares, opening the cells and in the safety of a mob swarming through the mess hall into the yard, over the fence, capturing the towers, opening the gate, escaping into the wild dark while the rain erased their tracks...

It wasn't going to happen.

I'm going to die in this place, he thought. *But I gave myself up for dead months ago. All this has been borrowed time. Is there anything I regret?*

"Ashes," he whispered.

Ash's hand tightened on his shoulder briefly.

"Ashes, I read your diary. The other part of the book -- I guessed the key weeks ago."

There was no reaction. Ash continued to watch him without expression.

"So I know how you think you feel about me. And, um, I think I want to apologize or something. For not being who you think I am. I know I have a pretty face, it confuses people into thinking I'm pretty inside. I'm not. I'm all rotten in there. And I'm sorry for that."

Slowly, Ash's hand slid from his shoulder. "What is this, a deathbed confession? I'm not giving up yet."

"Don't tell me you're not mad."

"Livid. Mortified." He just sounded tired. "Kieran, I think I get why you can't believe I might be right about you. But I'm right. You're not nice, I know, you're a killer. But your mind, your soul, is beautiful. Like a storm is beautiful, like the desert is."

Kieran gave a short sigh. "I can't believe we're having this conversation. I know, I started it," he added to forestall protest. After all, it *was* something like a deathbed confession, even if Ash chose to believe they might still somehow escape. "I'm grateful, I guess. That you see something in me. But you don't understand, Ashes, I'm dead inside. Cold. Cold like a dead thing."

"I could warm you."

Anger sparked. "You think it's always cheap for me? You think I'm cheap? Say something nice and get it for free?" He had to take a calming breath to keep his voice to a whisper. "We're going to die tonight, I'm trying to be honest. Not that it'll keep me out of Hell. I just want to be honest right now, okay?"

"Okay. I'm sorry. You know I didn't mean it like that." Though the light was dim, he could see the shine in Ash's eyes, the tremble of his lower lip as words were discarded before they formed. Eventually Ash went on, "I wish I had my Talent right now. Then I'd know if you wanted me to believe you or not." He breathed a faint laugh. "It's a relief to have it out in the open. But it seems so much smaller, when it's not a secret. Hello, yes, I'm an invert too, and I want you desperately, I might be in love with you, is that all right? It seems... stupid."

"It's not stupid. I'm just sorry I can't deserve it more, is all."

"I won't waste time arguing whether you deserve it. I just want to see you smile and mean it, once. What do *you* want right now?"

"I want to leave," Kieran said. He heard sullenness in the words, the useless petulance, and perspective opened for him. He'd known it forever: nothing matters when you're going to die anyway. Why were they bothering to talk at all?

He reached, despite everything surprised that Ash didn't flinch, and brushed a tendril of dirty hair away from Ash's lips, which moved under his fingertips as Ash turned to chase the touch, eyes flicking closed. A hitch in Ash's breath caught Kieran in the chest like a bullet. He swallowed hard, heart suddenly hammering. He bent and covered Ash's mouth with his own.

Something strange ran between them in that kiss, some current of new energy. Contact shocked him; with its immediacy, with how incredibly good it felt to be touched, close, wanted. It hurt, it was delicious, it made him weak, he needed it more than breath.

He pushed Ash down on the bunk, one hand knotted in the soft curls at the back of Ash's neck and the other sliding down his hip. Ash's arms were around his waist, clinging desperately. As his weight bore down, pinning Ash to the mattress, Ash groaned into his mouth and shuddered all over, squirming, aroused beyond bearing and ignorant of what to do about it. Kieran released Ash from the kiss and moved to graze teeth along his jaw and neck, making him gasp.

At first, the thunder was buried under the pounding of his heart; the taste of the skin of Ash's throat interested him more. When he noticed the hiss of rain, it seemed only fitting, a background for the storm in his blood. His fingers were trying the drawstring of Ash's trousers, making the muscles of Ash's stomach jump in interesting ways. Nothing else seemed remotely interesting, compared to that. It was the hail that got his attention. It sounded like gunshots.

Half reluctant, half irrationally relieved, he pulled away

by stages until he could look at Ash's face. He wasn't sure what he was going to say, if he even meant to talk at all, but the option of speech was lost in a shock of breaking glass.

There were shouts, reminding him that they were not alone, that he had been about to undress Ash in full view of anyone who happened to walk past; more crashes sounded, and time returned in the clatter of debris striking the cell block floor. Lightning showed faces pressed against bars, eyes turned up, mouths round and black, rain and bigger things frozen in midair. The next flash was longer; he saw a jagged clump of ice the size of his fist hit the floor and blow like a grenade.

And behind all that noise, he sensed a different kind of sound. It reached him through the soles of his feet. The whole mountain hummed with it.

He took Ash by the arms and pulled him off the bed. Ash came trustingly, though he kept looking back at the spectacle of breakage in the middle of the cell block. They crouched in the back corner, against the wall. Kieran was grinning so hard it made his face hurt. "Come on," he growled through his teeth. "Come on, rip it down."

"What is it?" Ash shouted over the rising wind. Deep inside though they were, it was blowing into their cell and it was hot -- night in the desert and the wind was *hot*, and smelled burnt and wet at once. Rather than try to answer over its howling, Kieran wrapped Ash in his arms and pulled him down. Ash seemed to get the idea, tried to make himself small.

The wind's noise took on rhythm. It was a harmonic throb now, thrumming in his bones. It sounded like a race between the nine fastest trains in Hell, as heard from inside an oil drum the size of a cathedral. It reached inside Kieran, that sound, and shook him, more alien than the stars and at the same time just like coming home. *Tornado. A big one, a huge one. What a wonderful way to die!* Things were flying around -- paper, clothing, broken glass -- the air was cloudy with dust and mist, mud pounded to a vapor. Kieran bent over Ash's head, not trusting the northerner to protect his own eyes and lungs. He squeezed his own eyes shut against the abrasive air, snatched a handful of his hair over his mouth, wishing he'd thought to grab a blanket to cover them. It was too late now. Even in the back of the cell, the wind was buffeting them painfully.

The floor and wall gave a series of shudders, more tangible than audible. Kieran's ears popped. There was a dull, crunching thud, and everything got louder.

Time lost meaning. Everything was happening at once. A fine crack ran across the floor right between his knees, and he knew the storm would go on until everything was ground to dust. It felt right. He was aroused by the way Ash shivered against him, and that was not out of place either. The noise was infinite. There was no end to wind. His mind shuddered, and he knew that the wards were about to go, but they didn't.

And then the wind was not so loud, and nothing else was falling. The air went cold, and then there was only sighing rain, and distant rolling thunder. Darker than usual, because most of the lamps had smashed, the cell block looked strange.

He realized, abstractedly, that he was sorry it was over. Uncurling himself carefully, he checked Ash for damage. A few scratches, nothing even really bleeding. Ash was watching him expectantly, caught between fear and excitement. In the weird light, he saw with dismay that the cell was intact. They were still locked in. Voices were beginning to murmur, rising in astonishment; from the piles of debris on the floor, from the rain pouring in, he understood that the roof of the central area had been torn completely off.

"Holy shit," he said. His voice sounded strange in his aching ears.

Ash's mouth moved, and the words reached him from a long way off: "I thought it was going to kill us."

A flash of thought, his brain restarting -- hope bubbled up, unfamiliar and urgent. He launched himself at the front of the cell, scrabbling among the debris, and came up with a daggerlike shard of glass ten inches long. It was scary-looking, but not very sharp. He handed it to Ash. "Hold this."

Taking it, Ash was all eagerness. "You have an idea?"

Kieran couldn't find his makeshift knife. There was no time. He selected the thinnest sliver of skylight he could find and sawed it across the skin of his ankle, high up where his pants would cover it.

"What are you --" Ash stopped when he saw what Kieran was doing, ripping the cheap cotton of his shirt, smearing the blood on his hands and chest. Ash pressed the sharp tip of the shard against the floor until it broke off flat, held the larger piece out for Kieran to spatter. "You want me to yell for help."

"You're quick." Kieran placed the flattened end of the shard against his ribs, making sure it looked right. He dropped to his knees, curling over it as if in pain, and nodded. "Be realistic."

Ash took a deep breath, and for a moment Kieran thought he'd screech like a harpy and be totally unconvincing. But he started out only a bit louder than usual. "Kieran? Oh shit. Oh shit, okay, hold still." His voice began to climb and crack. "Help? We need help down here! Don't, don't, don't try to move it you'll make it worse -- we need some *help* here!"

The occupants of nearby cells took up the cry, moved by the usual human urge to be busy when things are weird. Kieran wanted to applaud. Instead he dabbed blood on his chin, set his teeth in his lip, and gave a hideous drawn-out groan for the pair of grubby, wild-eyed Watchmen who came to fumble at the lock of the cell.

"Hurry," Ash urged, hovering at Kieran's side.

To their credit, they were wary of Kieran. One covered him with a rifle while the other knelt to examine his wound. Their mistake was discounting his frantic, knuckle-biting cellmate. One moment, Ash was whimpering and fussing; the next, he shoved the rifle upwards and head-butted the guard in the nose, transformed in an instant from a comic-opera nancy-boy to a snarling fury.

Kieran made the nearer man swallow his exclamation of startlement, along with a few teeth. The angle was bad, so the beginning of the fight was awkward, and he took a solid punch to the ear that set his head ringing, but once he got his feet under him he dispatched the man in short order and turned to rescue Ash.

Ash didn't need rescuing. He was choking his man with the rifle. Seeing that Kieran was done, Ash flung his victim free and clubbed the man upside the head with the stock. He offered the gun over the Watchman's twitching body. "Got you a present," he grinned.

When they ran out of their cell, someone cheered. Another voice joined it, and another. Then demands and instructions swelled over the cheers and overwhelmed them. Kieran saw the one remaining guard running toward him and worked the rifle's bolt, but the man skidded and changed direction. He went for the exit on the far end. He'd be through it and raising the alarm before anything could be done about it, unless Kieran made a lucky shot; in the dark, with a pounding heart, using an unfamiliar weapon, he doubted he could drop the man in time. He chose not to bother shooting. They weren't going out that way.

Climbing over rain-slick piles of broken stone, he felt his ankle begin to twinge where he'd cut it. He shut the pain away. Reached the lock lever and hauled it down. With a clang, the tier unlocked, the doors swung open in unison. Ragged, dirty men swarmed out, cheering.

He wasn't going to waste time on the other three tiers. "Let everyone out!" he shouted over the general hollering. "The more get out, the less get caught!" A glance at the rifle showed him it lacked a strap, so he tossed it aside. He made a stirrup of his hands, nodding to Ash. "Go."

Boosted onto the lock box, Ash hesitated a moment, trying to fit his fingers and toes into the cracks in the wall. There had been no way to practice for this.

"Go!" Kieran bellowed, and somehow Ash found footholds. Kieran was right behind him.

It seemed to take hours to climb the wall. Below, faces swarmed and shouted. There was one gunshot, but it wasn't followed by any change in the general commotion. Kieran could see that Ash's limbs were shaking; his own were beginning to tremble as well, reminding him that he'd been through Testing that same morning. A moment's dismay broke in his mind. *We're not going to make it.* But right on its heels came the realization that half an hour ago he'd been making final confessions, and now he was halfway up the cell block wall heading for open sky. More than halfway. Almost there. And they were pulling themselves over a lip of broken wall, between twisted slats of metal that had once barred the skylights, into the full blast of the downpour.

Lightning flashed, showing him the wreckage all around. The tornado had broken down walls and snarled fences like yarn. He spotted a relatively clear hole and pointed it out to Ash, getting a nod in answer. Beside his feet, a knotted strip of torn blanket thumped across the top of the wall; the less limber prisoners had made a rope and thrown it up to him. He didn't have time to help them, but he did it anyway, tying the blanket rope to a solid-looking bit of skylight frame before he took off running.

A shout, several shouts from different directions, muffled and meaningless. Then a shot. He ignored it. The rain was bucketing down. No one could shoot straight in this; he could hardly see ten feet in front of him. They were running downhill, he could tell because rivulets of runoff were forming and flowing the same direction. Ash was pulling ahead despite his shorter stride, not bothering to pick his footing but trusting to pure luck. There were more shots, more shouting, falling behind. A heap of fence loomed on their right, eerily tall the way the winds had twisted it, and then they were through.

Suddenly he was no longer blind. Ahead of him, Ash stumbled and slowed, then settled into a smoother gait, subject to the same sensation: seeing with something other than eyes, *knowing* in a way he had never even noticed before it had been taken away from him. They had passed the ward's edge, they were finally really out.

And we're going right back in if we don't put some serious miles behind us, he reminded himself.

It was easier to run outside the ward. He had a general sense of the terrain around him, allowing him to pick smoother ground. He'd never thought about that ability before, but now he realized most people must not have it. He could sense that the ground here was flat and sandy, that the puddles and rivulets forming on it were shallow and solid-bottomed. Fluttering blue from the clouds showed him that it looked the same for a ways ahead; hard to judge distance in this light and veiling rain, maybe half a mile. Beyond that was just a dark jumble, which he could only guess must be a bit of hilly terrain.

Ash was faltering now. That first burst of speed had worn him out. Kieran took his arm, made him stop, and they took ten seconds to catch their breath. Put their heads back and gulped rain. Then Kieran clapped Ash's shoulder to get his attention and led him out in a brisk walk. He hoped Ash was a good walker. He himself could keep up this pace all night, even tired as he was, but Ash was looking worn. The climb had been hard for him.

"You're fine," Kieran said. "You'll make it."

In reply he got a wild-eyed look he couldn't interpret. It could have been fear or elation or anything. He darted a look back at the compound, but aside from a general impression of untidiness he couldn't see anything that was going on back there.

Downhill, the slope becoming more gradual as they left the vicinity of the immense mesa, they began to encounter knots of scrub, lumps of rock. His feet were starting to hurt; though he'd grown used to going barefoot, no amount of callus could save him from all this gravel. He hoped they didn't step on anything poisonous. In a rain like this, critters could get flooded out of their holes, and in their panic they'd sting or bite anything that got near them.

The rain seemed to be letting up, so what was that roaring? Water was doing something large up ahead. Kieran wanted to uncurl his senses and reach out to it, but he wasn't sure how. His mind was too sore, this particular skill too unpracticed. He slowed his pace, mindful of the dangers of a desert rainstorm.

It was fortunate that he did, because there was no lightning to show him the sudden river that cut their path. Only the sense of surroundings that came with Talent kept them from falling in. Not, he realized, that he could sense the river itself. In fact, it was blank, a wall of emptiness, snatching away any senses that were extended toward it.

"Now what?" Ash's voice was a shade too high. Starting to panic. "Can we go across?"

The experience of his whole life told him that you never, never cross unknown water in the desert, never go down in a wash in a rainstorm, never linger in a slot canyon at any time, because the water might not follow the regular water rules. It might suddenly swell, might drop on you a wall of water ten feet high, or it might do the opposite and be suddenly sucked away, leaving you buried in cemented mud. It might carry you off, slam you against rocks, wedge you in holes, and of course it would always do its best to drown you. In this darkness he couldn't tell how wide this flood was, but from the sound and the way it blocked his mind it had to be big. So the idea that came to mind was probably suicidal.

"It'll cover our trail. We go in."

"What? No, no we don't."

"Grab onto me. Here, not just my hand, that won't work. We'll lean on each other and try to stay upright, but if we fall -- can you swim?"

"Not in this!"

"Sure you can." Arms locked around Ash's waist, Kieran stepped into the water. Ash had no choice but to do the same.

The current snatched at their ankles, rose around their knees. Debris knocked and scratched, snarled weeds wrapped and tangled. Step by laborious step, they made their way downstream. The rain was beginning to let up. A glance back made his stomach clench -- there were lights at the prison again. The search was beginning. With luck, they'd round up the weaker ones first, the ones who hadn't made it this far, but he couldn't leave it to luck. He and Ash were still close enough that a searcher with a lantern might locate them by sight alone.

"We have to go faster."

"We can't," Ash protested. "We'll drown."

"You can swim, right? We'll ride."

"No. No. Kieran --" Ash's objection ended in a splutter as Kieran pulled him deeper into the rush of water. It snatched them both instantly, knocked their feet out from under them and whirled them away.

Aware only of his struggle to breathe and to keep hold of Ash's shirt, Kieran didn't know how long the flood carried them. Longer than minutes, less than hours. His strength was ebbing fast, the chill of the water stiffening his muscles. More than once, he took on a lungful of water and thought he had drowned himself. He threw a mental apology to Ash for his stupid idea, which had surely killed them both. But at last sandy ground scraped under him and rolled him over, and he was beached, panting in the icy night.

The darkness was total. The water had shelved, spread out maybe, and he lay on his back in inch-deep mud. He still had a handful of Ash's shirt; Ash was attached to it, and alive, wheezing and coughing. Relief turned his guts to warm jelly, making him feel even weaker than he already was.

"It's cold," Ash said shakily, when the coughing was over. "Where are we?"

"How should I know? It's as dark as the inside of a dog. We should get up. We should walk, to keep warm."

"I can't."

"Me neither." Kieran rolled over, spit out a mouthful of grit. He tugged at Ash's shirt, tried to get closer. By shuddering stages, Ash climbed into his arms and huddled there. It seemed forever before the space between them grew warm. Kieran would not have been surprised if his wet shirt froze to his back.

"This would b-be a s-s-stupid way to die," Ash chattered.

"We'll get up and walk in just a second. As soon as the moon comes out."

"Okay."

"Won't be long now."

"Okay."

Gradually, their shivering subsided. In the storm's wake, the damp air was not so cold, and clinging together like this was warmer than Kieran had thought it would be. With warmth, though, came exhaustion. He heard it in his own voice when he spoke.

"They won't find us. We must've rode that river for miles. We got out, Ashes."

"*You* got us out." A ghost of a laugh. "Kieran Trevarde, you are significantly larger than life."

Chapter 11

Discomfort woke Ash; a long list of discomforts. Heat; itching; buzzing; things were walking on him. One of his hands had gone numb. He kept his eyes closed for a long time, nonetheless, sleepily convinced that he was hiding.

Last night surfaced in little bubbles of memory; they were running away, were they still escaping? Or had they escaped? Was it safe to move? That was Kieran's bony shoulder under his head, Kieran's chest under his arm, which would have been lovely except that there were flies walking on his face. He snorted them away from his nostrils, rubbed at his eyes; mud flaked under his hand. It felt hot to the touch. When he opened his eyes, brightness gave him an instant headache.

Inches away, Kieran's face was dusty and gilded. This was, Ash realized, the first time he'd seen Kieran sleeping in a good light; that might account for the way Kieran's beauty shocked him. His eyelashes were astonishing. His lips, slack and soft in unconsciousness, were pure drunkenness, and Ash remembered with a surge of gladness that he had tasted them the night before. Kieran's long, callused hands were draped loosely around Ash's waist. His pulse beat in his throat. He looked about fourteen years old. He looked innocent. He was real, all this was real, they were really free.

Ash closed his eyes again, pressing his cheek a little closer against Kieran's shoulder, everything else flying away for one moment. It wasn't possible that it had all turned out so well. Things this good simply didn't happen.

He couldn't avoid the world forever, though. It was getting really, really hot out here.

Where was 'out here'? Ash moved to sit up, and discovered aches in muscles he didn't even know he had. The groan he let out woke Kieran, who immediately answered with a groan of his own.

"Ow. Shit. Ow. What died in my mouth?"

So much for innocence. Ash couldn't help smiling. "Good morning."

"Yeah." Kieran stretched, wincing. He scratched a shower of dirt out of his scalp. He looked at Ash and burst out laughing.

"What?"

"You should see yourself."

"What? I'm dirty, I know."

"You're the mud man."

"I can see *you*."

"Yeah, but your hair is doing this." Kieran grabbed a hank of his own matted hair and splayed it atop his head, making a face and a rude noise.

Laughing, Ash got himself vertical and dusted himself off. There was an Ash-shaped outline on the ground where he'd been lying, an imprint still damp in a field of mud cracked into irregular polygons. The sun was over some hills in one direction, there was nothing but cracked mud in all the other directions, and though he was fairly sure direction one was therefore east, that didn't help a whole hell of a lot. "Where are we? Are we lost?"

"For now. We'll get unlost later."

"I'm thirsty."

Kieran feigned surprise. "Don't shock me like that."

"And I want a bath."

"You should stay dirty, actually. Not that you have a choice. It'll keep you from burning. In fact --" Kieran grabbed a handful of mud and smeared it around on the back of Ash's neck. He conducted a thorough inspection of the public parts of Ash, anointing him with gritty slime. Ash squirmed when the process tickled, laughed, enjoying it, until he noticed that Kieran had suddenly gone serious.

"Something wrong?" Ash ventured.

Kieran stepped back, dusting his hands. "There. If it gets wiped off, or if you sweat it off, rub more dirt on. Otherwise you'll fry, you're so white."

"I didn't burn much when we were out in the yard."

"You're going to be in the sun for the next ten hours. Not the same."

"Oh. I guess so." That idea took a moment to sink in. "Ten hours?"

Kieran squinted at the sky. "Well, it's late spring, looks like the sun's been up for an hour or so. And we'll have to do it again tomorrow, maybe the next day, depending on where we are. I never saw Churchrock on a map. All I know is we're somewhere northeast of Burn River, maybe closer to Trestre. We're north of the main rail line -- that's what we have to find."

"Okay. And then where do we go?"

Kieran took a long breath and blew it out in a sigh. "*We* don't go anywhere. I go west. You go east. We hop freights in opposite directions."

Something unpleasant happened in Ash's stomach. He couldn't answer. Couldn't even breathe, for a long moment.

"Don't look at me like that," Kieran said. "You knew it'd end this way."

"No. I didn't."

"What did you think was going to happen? You were going to follow me around forever?"

"Yes. I guess I did think that."

"You want to be a killer too? You want to be a real criminal now? Should I teach you how to murder strangers for money?" Kieran sounded terribly tired.

"Kieran, if -- okay, I hear you, but I can't -- what *was* that then, last night? You kissed me, we almost --"

"I thought I was going to die. It doesn't count."

"It doesn't count." Ash gave a breathless, brittle laugh. He turned away, looking at the cracked dirt in the palms of his hands. "I see."

After a pause, Kieran said, "Maybe you believe me now."

Ash didn't have to ask about what. "So it meant nothing to you."

"Not nothing. It was a comfort. It wasn't a beginning. We don't have time for this."

Ash surprised them both by rounding on Kieran in a bellowing rage. "*Make* time! This is important! Explain it to me! Make up your mind! Waking up in your arms made me so -- *happy* -- how can you think I want to go back north? Do you care about me? Because I thought you did!"

For a long moment Kieran stared, and though he was stone-faced and cold-eyed, Ashleigh thought he might be about to weep. Then his lips thinned and his chin lifted. "Just 'cause *you're* wet don't mean it's raining." Kieran turned on his heel and strode off across the cracked mud toward the blank horizon, leaving splintered footprints in his wake.

Ash watched him go, momentarily overwhelmed by an urge to just sit down and let the desert have him. *So that's how it's going to be*. Wild, melodramatic thoughts coursed through him, the need to beg and plead warring with the resolution to go far away from Kieran as fast as possible. Underlining all of it was a shame so strong he wished he could murder himself with a shotgun, because thirst and hunger were too gentle a death.

These blind emotions faded as Kieran grew smaller in the distance. Others welled up gently beneath them: *He's got other things on his mind, like surviving, and maybe drug withdrawal. I expected something he doesn't have the strength to do. It was unkind of me. And he was right that there isn't time for this kind of thing; he knows how to find water and I don't.*

Wincing at the soreness in his abused muscles, Ash set off after him at the best pace he could manage.

They didn't speak until what was probably something like noon, when Kieran found a puddle shaded under a snarl of broken brush. Even then, he didn't say much.

"Don't stir up the bottom. I don't want to drink mud."

"Okay." Ash made a careful scoop of his hands and drank. The water tasted delicious as candy at first, but as his thirst was slaked he noticed a swampy flavor in it. When he was done, he looked into what was left and saw little squirmy motes wriggling in the puddle. "Ew. There are buggy things in this."

"Won't hurt you." Kieran bent to the little pool and slurped it right down to the mud layer; he must have finished off half a gallon of the filthy stuff. "Wish we had something to carry this in. Just going to piss it right out, drinking it all at once like this." He stretched, making his spine crack, then looked around. He pointed out a low violet irregularity between them and the far-distant line of the mountains. "We should make those hills in four or five more hours. Should be more water there."

"Without bugs in?"

"Probably not." Kieran started walking again, and that was the last thing he said for almost three days.

Time blurred into a nightmare spin of speed, with unkind slow intervals of clarity. Despite his coating of itchy mud, renewed periodically with dust, Ash's skin burned in streaks where his sweat revealed it. His scalp was especially vulnerable; the dirt in his matted hair made it itch furiously, and when he forgot himself and scratched, it hurt like fire. Sometimes he thought he must look like a sick monkey, what with the scratching and wincing and the gingerly way he walked on his flayed, blistered bare feet. All day he sweated and longed for night, and at night he cursed that wish while he shivered, as if night wouldn't have come if he hadn't wanted it.

When there was shade, they rested for long stretches during the day, which allowed them to use more of the night for walking. Exhaustion always claimed them in the end, though, and they had to find some hollow or corner, chase out the poisonous wildlife, and curl up as small as they could make themselves. They slept wrapped around each other like cats, but there was no affection in it.

The first time Kieran had embraced him against the night's cold, Ash had allowed himself some hope -- had snuggled close and whispered Kieran's name, begging -- but had been given only silence in return. Kieran was as empty of comfort and caring as the desert sky. He was only trying to keep warm.

Hunger was a constant sickness. Ash discovered that it didn't confine itself to his gut after a day or so, but spread through his body, so that he could amuse himself by listing all the parts of him that were hungry. His ankles were hungry. The backs of his ears were hungry. Sometimes Kieran killed something, barehanded or with a rock, and they ate raw meat that tasted of salt and metal, which only served to make him queasy for a few hours before the hunger returned. Ash thought snake meat tasted worse than bugs or mice, but it was fun to watch Kieran catch snakes in his hands. Sometimes they ate plants, usually dry chewy ones that did nothing against the hunger at all. Some flooded his throat with bitterness; others were simply something to have in his mouth for a while so it wouldn't be so dry. The best was a sort of cactus leaf that had to be carefully denuded of thorns and then broken open -- the pulp tasted horrible, but it was wet.

All this time, they didn't speak. There wasn't anything to talk about. There wasn't even anything to think about. The desert was beautiful and boring. Long flat bits of plain, covered with prickly weeds and scrub, divided strips of rocky hills paved with sharp gravel. Ash became certain that Kieran had no idea where they were going, and they'd just keep walking until their feet fell off and they died. Sometimes he looked forward to that, because it would be nice to be done.

At first he thought he was hearing the cry of some

strange desert animal. It sounded familiar, and a little frightening, and in his half-asleep state he pondered it until it faded into the distance.

Only then did he realize that animal noises didn't fade off like that. He sat up and shook Kieran's shoulder.

"Hey," he rasped.

Kieran sat up, squinting. They were hiding from the midday sun under an overhanging bit of stone; while they'd slept, the stone's shadow had shrunk, and sitting up put Kieran's head in the glare. Knuckling dust from his eyes, he gave Ash a questioning look.

"I heard a train."

Kieran thought a moment, nodded, and lay back down.

Frustrated, Ash considered shaking him again, but he doubted it would change anything. Hearing the train's whistle meant the end of the nightmare to Ash, but maybe to Kieran it meant something else. The end of quiet, maybe.

I'm an Empath, shouldn't I be able to tell? But in all this time, he'd sensed nothing from Kieran. His Talent was too weak to be any use. For a moment, he was bitterly jealous of Kieran's powerful ability, even if it was only good for killing. To have that kind of strength would make a person different inside, might make a person confident and cold like Kieran was. *Might make a person afraid to feel anything, lest he understand what he is.* Maybe Ash's weak Talent wasn't to blame. Maybe there was just nothing there to sense.

Weary with despair, Ash lay down to wait until Kieran was ready to leave.

The tracks had a smell. Ash was surprised by that. Growing up in Ladygate, the second largest city in the world, he'd seen thousands of trains and all their steely habitat, and never noticed the particular reek of tar and metal that rails had. He smelled it before he saw them. Now he copied Kieran, kneeling to put a hand on one rail's polished surface. It was hot; he snatched his fingers away. Kieran held the pose a moment longer. Then, with no word or look to explain himself, he turned and walked off down the embankment, toward the distant cut the train would eventually come from to take him away.

Exasperated, Ash began to trot after, until he saw what Kieran was doing -- gathering up fallen chunks of coal and pitching them idly into the undergrowth. He wasn't going anywhere, just waiting. Ash sat down where he was. He heaved an enormous sigh, the kind that ought to produce a feeling of relaxation. It only served to make him more tense. This was it, this was where he let Kieran Trevarde remove himself the way he'd come in. On a train. The irony of that kind of closure wasn't quite enough to make him smile. Not even a bitter smile. A grayish grasshopper landed on his knee, big enough that he felt the weight through his prison pants, but he was too tired to flinch. Dozens of the creatures fled before Kieran's footsteps, red underwings flashing. The whirring of their panic told him where Kieran was. He didn't have to look. Didn't want to. But he did anyway.

Weary as they both were, dizzy with starvation, Kieran still projected a large predator's grace. Nothing feline, he was too angular for that, but some kind of canine, something that was to a coyote what a tiger was to an alley cat. He had that loping stride, that swing-limbed inevitability. Some kind of skinny, hot-climate dire wolf. Ash shook his head at his thoughts. They were silly, not poetic -- what Kieran most resembled was himself, an overgrown child who had never once been safe. No wonder he wanted to part ways. Ash was just a liability to him. How could he protect someone when he couldn't quite protect himself?

"Damn it," Ash muttered. That wasn't strong enough. "Shit. Fuck." He snorted. He'd never been much good at cursing. "*Gwnorregh!*"

Kieran's laugh sounded loud over the hissing of his feet in the weeds. "What did you call me?"

"Nothing."

"No, seriously." He began wandering back, still flinging coal chunks across the tracks.

Scowling, Ash repeated the curse. "I don't know what it means, so don't ask. I just know my aunt says it when she hits her thumb with the hammer. And I thought you weren't speaking to me."

"News to me. I was thinking."

"For three *days*?"

Kieran looked surprised, as if everyone could keep their mouths shut for seventy-odd hours at a time. "What was that word again? Canorra?"

"Close enough."

"Yelorrean?"

"Yes."

"Know any other good swear words?"

"Yes."

He thumped down next to Ash and threw the last black rock of his handful. "Well?"

"Why should I bother teaching you? You're leaving me any minute."

"Leaving you." Kieran raised an eyebrow. "Okay, think of it like that if you want."

Ash felt his face burning, his eyes stinging; he knew his face was red, and childish tears were starting to run; he was too exhausted to care. "You know what? You want to know something?" He didn't wait for Kieran's indifferent shrug. "Not everyone is you, all right? Not everyone is numb and powerful and big and scary and hollow. And you can go around knocking people over all your life, and then you'll get old and sick and you'll know *exactly* why you're dying alone, because you're the kind of cold bastard who sees those things. And maybe you'll think of me and you'll wonder what my life was like. And you know what? I can tell you right now. For your future self. You tell yourself this: Ash Trine's life was *good*, it had *colors* in it and people *smiled* and there were dogs and flowers. And then you remember to tell yourself you could've been in it but you were too much of a stiff-necked paranoid prick to try."

Kieran was unimpressed. "Been saving that up, huh? You're such a kid. But I do love to hear you talk."

Ash put his hands over his face and gave up to crying. His heart was breaking; he understood that phrase now, because he felt the crack run through, ripping him apart.

"Oh for -- stop it, you baby!" Fingers closed on his wrists, jerked his hands down. Kieran was scowling at him, but beneath that there was...

Gasping, Ash reeled under a rush of understanding. "My god."

"What?"

"You -- you unbelievable asshole."

"What, already?"

"Half this pain is yours! You're all ripped up inside, you want me to come with you, you want it so bad -- god *damn* it, Kieran!"

"I want you to go home." Kieran's voice was flat and tight.

"My Empathy's back. It's been back all this time. I

thought it wasn't working, because all the feelings felt like mine, but that was only because yours are the same. You don't want to leave me behind."

"Bullshit."

"No, I know now because, because just now I was so hot and salty inside that finally it was different from you and there you were, right in front of me."

Kieran made a dismissive noise. "Think whatever you want, it doesn't --"

"But it hurts you so much, and all you have to do to make it stop is admit it! God, it makes me so mad! Do you *like* festering away like that?"

As an answer, Kieran went to touch the rails again. His voice was dry and hard when he said, "Here we go. Should be the 4:20 out of Salt Rock, so I'll be going first."

Ash scrambled to his feet. "You're such an idiot!"

"I could kill you right there, boy, and you are *baiting* me. Who's stupid here?"

"And don't call me boy! You're no older than I am!"

"Nineteen." Kieran looked bitterly amused.

"One year."

"Decades." The Iavaian threw his head up like a horse scenting the wind. "If you're done having histrionics, you better listen up 'less you wanna walk home. You let the engine get past, don't let 'em see you. Then you get up a good run. Pick a car where the door's all the way open or it'll slide and knock you on your ass. Grab the side and swing in. You watch how I do it. Your train oughtta be 'long in a couple hours."

Now that his Talent had returned, Ash understood that tone as he never had in Churchrock. When Kieran's drawl thickened like that, it was time to shut up, or someone was going to taste blood. The unfairness of it made him sick to his stomach. "I hate you," he said tightly.

"Good. Makes it easier for you. Now get back under that brush 'fore someone sees you." Kieran took another look up and down the track, then backed beneath a twisted miniature tree that was as hard and thorny as he was. A distant engine noise began to make itself heard over the other sounds.

Ash obeyed, shaking, still crying. How could someone be so stupid, so blindly wrong, so -- scared, so lonely, so certain that anything bright dangled before him was bait for a rust-toothed trap -- *and he's just as hungry and exhausted as I am, and look how that's making me act.* He took a shuddering breath.

"Kieran, I'm sorry."

"Okay. Now shut up."

"I don't hate you."

"Don't matter."

"Can we please say goodbye like civilized people? Please."

In his nest of thorny weeds, Kieran grimaced and stuck out a hand. Ash offered his own, let it be swallowed up, seeing its red-knuckled paleness folded in that big brown hand for the last time. That touch held a moment too long, and in it he felt Kieran digging down into his pain like a toad in mud, hiding in it, believing stubbornly that it sheltered him. He was ditching Ash *because* it hurt, because nothing that didn't could be trusted. There was no way to change his mind. Up until now, that assumption had always been true. Ash blinked his eyes clear and let his hand fall.

Kieran gave an explosive sigh. "Look --" he began.

"I forgive you."

"What?" A startled laugh.

"Any sentence that comes out of nowhere and starts with 'Look' --"

Kieran's laugh came again, a shade more genuine. "Yeah. Okay. I forgive you too. Just remember the good stuff, okay?"

"Okay."

"We *were* friends."

"If you ever run into me again, as far as I'm concerned we still will be."

At this, Kieran's face, for just half a second, showed something fragile before the bitter husk snapped closed again. And the sharp pain under Ash's ribs rang with harmonics, like a bell when its neighbor is struck.

The train came upon them suddenly. One moment a distant grinding, the next a swell of noise that rumbled the ground, it came burning out of the distance at a hellish speed. Ash swallowed hard. There was no way to touch something like that. The task was impossible. The noise was immense. As it drew near, he counted four engines pulling in tandem, and the back end was still not out of the cut. The first few dozen cars were coal hoppers, piled high and shedding dust and little coal lumps at every jerk of the chuffing engines. Behind those, there were boxcars, dull green and rust-red and gray.

Kieran burst out of his hiding place and worked himself up from a jog to a sprint. Ash staggered out of his own bit of cover, watching Kieran run away from him. Long legs flashing, Kieran matched speed with the train. He pulled even with a red-slatted wooden box like the side of a barn. Grabbed with both hands and hauled himself up and vanished.

Didn't even look back or wave or -- or anything --

Ash didn't mean to run after. Never actually decided. It was as if a hook was set in his ribcage and the line just fished him in. He was running as soon as Kieran's dust-bleached feet disappeared inside the car; maybe before. His lungs burned, he could hardly see, he stepped on sharp things and knew he'd lame himself, but that only made him tuck his head down and sprint harder. He'd never run so hard in his life. But he was doing it, was actually beating the train, if he could only keep it up long enough to reach that red car with the open door --

And he was there, and knowing it was going to get him killed he grabbed the door's edge and pulled as hard as he could. Rolled across filthy, humming boards. Raised his head to see Kieran slumped in a corner with his arms wrapped around his knees, misery still etched into the shape of his face.

"I'm coming with you," Ash gasped.

Kieran's eyes were enormous, and in the dusty shade looked more yellow than green. His voice was wondering, joyful, and a little frightened. "I guess you are," he said.

Chapter 12

The men guarding the platform snapped to attention and saluted as their visitor stepped from the train. Those engaged in the work of rebuilding the prison's defenses knew better than to stop work, but were still tempted into risking a few glances. The Director was a figure almost of myth, the ideal of all the Watch stood for. A young man, some said only thirty, he was wiser than the eldest of his advisors. He was said to have been selected by his predecessor from a group of children brought in for Survey and raised specifically for the office. He was said to be incorruptible, without weakness or mercy, more powerful in magic than any lesser officer could ever hope to become. It was said he could not be surprised, that he was bulletproof, and that he never slept.

All this was true.

Thelyan chose to allow these rumors because they were useful to him. He was aware that their whispered transmission prevented them from being taken seriously. Their truth could not hurt him. What he truly was, no one had the frame of reference to guess. This body was even younger than the thirty years ascribed to it. He'd accelerated the useless years of childhood; when he'd met the previous Director, he'd been an adolescent of six.

When he'd created the Watch, centuries past, he'd implanted in the arcana of the Director's secret knowledge a pass-phrase by which he could be recognized. Should a Talented child utter this phrase, he was to be trained to the directorship as quickly as possible. By this means, he'd assured he could take the reins of power personally whenever he chose to incarnate. There was a similar system in place in the Church proper, should he ever wish to be Heirophant. So far he'd never found that position useful; too much public scrutiny, not enough real power. If he needed the Heirophant to announce a new scriptural interpretation, he was perfectly capable of sending inspirations.

He waited on the platform until the head of the Research Division arrived with a four-man escort for him. Colonel Warren was bright red, huffing as he hurried in the desert heat.

His salute was adequate.

"Welcome back, sir. We -- er, as you can see, the --"

"Yes." Thelyan lifted his chin to indicate that he saw the wrecked fences, the shattered hole that was the cell block. "I'm not here to direct repairs. Is there anywhere sufficiently intact for us to speak privately?"

"There is, but I must warn you, there is a possibility of cave-ins --" He broke off at Thelyan's look, realizing that the Director could probably outright remove the mountain if he so wished.

"Are the wards intact?"

"Yes, sir. They held."

Thelyan nodded. He had set those wards himself. They were burned into bedrock. He had not expected a simple phenomenon of weather to break them, but it had crossed his mind that this particular storm might not have been natural. Later, he would examine the traces it had left, just to be sure. "And my particular test subject? I expect you've recaptured him by now."

Warren was too red to blanch, but his cheeks went blotchy. "I'm sorry to report that we have not, sir."

After two seconds' thought, Thelyan chose not to respond to this. Neither encouragement nor chastisement would affect the outcome in any way. The Colonel, like most others of his rank and many lesser members of the Watch, knew of the Director's particular scientific interest in Threnodic Talents. Trevarde was already their highest priority, Thelyan was certain. After all, no one was ever dismissed from the Watch. Those who failed in their duty were removed from the chain of command in other ways. Thelyan had learned, through long study, that the human animal was perfectly capable of threatening itself; duplicated threats merely made it surly and prone to rebellion. He gestured for the Colonel to lead him, and the man sprang to obey with the alacrity guilt provided.

The office to which he took Thelyan was not his usual one. On the way, Thelyan cast an interested eye over the damage the storm had wrought. It had been an exceptional bit of weather, apparently. In his long existence, he had encountered a storm of such destructive power only twice before, and thus it was tempting to ascribe this one to the same source. A clear mind could not succumb to such thinking, however; Thelyan had not, after all, made a study of severe weather. So he observed the cracks in the stone, the collapsed buildings and half-fallen tunnels, and remembered them, and made no judgment. Deeper within Churchrock's stone, the hollowed rooms and passages were intact.

It was a shame that some of it had been wrecked. He did not enjoy destruction, or indeed unnecessary change of any kind.

He took the offered chair in a room that had previously been a storage area. It was still lined with file cabinets. Thelyan made a mental note, if the various rebels and criminals ever left him some free time, to familiarize himself with the contents of these files. He let Warren sit, waved the escort away, and closed the door from a distance with a gesture and a word. Another gesture, a few more words, drew a veil of silence around the room that only he could penetrate. Warren looked impressed, as he should; magic outside one's Talent, pattern-magic, was nearly effortless for Thelyan. The same effect would have required a five- or ten-minute ritual for Warren. Thelyan didn't even have to stand up. But then, he was the one who had invented the method.

"I have your report," he said, "but of course it's out of date. Have you recovered all the subjects of special interest?"

"All but Trevarde, sir. And one Ashleigh Trine, who was classified special interest because we were using him as training material, but he's only an Empath."

Thelyan raised an eyebrow. "And a rebel propagandist, as I recall. He yielded us a large group in Ladygate this past winter. How do you suppose he managed to evade you?"

"My guess is that he's with Trevarde. The two were confederates in the escape. See, Trevarde used --"

"In a moment, Colonel. In your report you mention that the northern section was damaged and a number of subjects lost. The wording is vague. Do you now have a better understanding of the situation?"

Warren shuddered at the mention of the northern section. It wasn't his responsibility, and Thelyan got the impression he avoided it as much as possible. "The, um, the Section Head hasn't reported yet, sir."

"Very well, I'll speak with him later. Who's in charge of rebuilding? You? You've made the perimeter fence a priority, I assume."

"Yes, sir. I've made it clear that the placement must be exact."

"Good. Now. I believe you were about to tell me how

the most secure detainment facility in the world suffered an escape of such excessive scope."

Warren's jowls quivered, and his chin bobbed. "Your Mr. Trevarde was the instigator, sir. He somehow got hold of a quantity of prepared opium and introduced it into the coffee urn at the end of the inmates' dinner period. He was able to do this unobserved because he'd engineered a fight between two of his confederates, which distracted the guards."

"The confederates' names?"

"Trine and Sona. Sona's the one we brought in as a --"

"Yes, I remember. Has Sona been recaptured?"

"No, sir, but he isn't with Trevarde. We had his trail following the south road, but he lost us in a wash."

"Very well. Advance his capture to a priority just below Trevarde's. Were there other confederates?"

"No, sir."

"I presume the guards who allowed themselves to be distracted were reprimanded. The policy of nonintervention in prisoner conflicts exists to prevent just such an eventuality."

"They're dead, sir." Warren shrugged. "They drank the coffee."

Thelyan nodded. "Continue."

"The men went to their supper while the prisoners were in the yard. Nearly all of them drank the coffee and were poisoned. However, because the cooks refill the coffee urn several times during the course of the meal, the poison was diluted by stages, so that not all the men showed the same symptoms. Our initial diagnosis was food poisoning from the corned beef, which was the only item the guards ate that the prisoners didn't. The symptoms were consistent: dizziness, vomiting, sudden fatigue.

"This was in the report, but I'll recap: we had four fatalities, nine men unconscious, and three more conscious but too ill to perform their duties. I pulled everyone from Research to hustle these fellows out-Ward for Healing. I distributed our remaining personnel with an emphasis on the outer barriers, as per policy, and had the prisoners locked down for the night.

"We'd been aware for some time that a large thunderstorm was approaching. By ten-thirty, when it struck, the medical section had revised their diagnosis to opium poisoning, though they hadn't yet discovered which of the dishes had been poisoned. My judgment was that it was most likely introduced into the food stores during transport, as part of a rebel plot to attack the compound from outside." Warren's face was drawn with guilt. "I was disastrously wrong, as it turned out. Thinking that the attack might take place under cover of the storm, I pulled men from barracks to fully man the perimeter.

"The hail was between four and six inches in diameter. There were at least two tornadoes in the area, as well as straight-line winds and subsequent heavy rains. We lost eight men to the storm, sir. Another five were injured.

"The prisoners' escape through the broken roof of the cell block was detected immediately by a Watchman named Sarsen Cowder, who fired several shots and attempted to raise an alarm. Unfortunately, Cowder was immobile with a broken leg, having been thrown from a tower post by the wind. He was unable to give chase or shoot accurately. By the time others came to his assistance, forty-six of one hundred two prisoners had vacated the premises.

"I was out there myself, sir. We needed every gun we had, by then. This decimated us."

Thelyan nodded to indicate that he'd absorbed all this; he'd found that if he didn't give some kind of acknowledgment, people repeated themselves. "Have you discovered yet how they escaped their cells? Your report claimed the doors were opened from outside, with the tier mechanism."

"Yes, sir. It was difficult to ascertain when I wrote the report, because the three guards who were on duty in the cells are all dead. One apparently ran from the cell block and was killed in a tunnel collapse. The other two were beaten to death by escaping prisoners. They were found in 2-E, though. Trevarde and Trine's cell. I've since interviewed many of the prisoners who failed to escape or were recaptured. Apparently Trevarde feigned an injury and Trine yelled for help. I know, sir," Warren held up a hand to forestall criticism. "That kind of ruse shouldn't have worked on them. All I can say is that their knowledge of your particular interest in this prisoner might have been a factor."

"I see." He considered this. Knowing of Thelyan's intention to further study the subject Trevarde, the guards had most likely weighed the possibility of duplicity against the possible death of the Director's special project, and chosen to risk the former. A not illogical decision, if an unfortunate one. "Very well. How many prisoners were killed by fire from the gun posts?"

"Well, none, sir." Warren looked puzzled. "We couldn't man the posts during the storm."

"I would have thought those would be more essential than men on the tiers, Colonel."

"I thought you knew, sir. Those posts get flooded in a heavy rain. We speculate that the whole cell block area was some kind of reservoir, before. You know, for whoever dug the tunnels in the first place."

Thelyan waved that aside. "You Surveyed the cooks to be sure about the poisoning, I assume?"

"No sir, just questioned them."

"Survey them. Have you discovered yet how the prisoner obtained the drug?"

Warren went fuschia again, deeply embarrassed. "Yes, sir. It was brought in by a guard. A man named Kerr Pastachan. He used the drug as a... a trade item. To obtain a hold over various prisoners from whom he extorted... sexual favors. We have him in lockup now. I thought it best to await your judgment in this matter."

The Director leaned back in his chair, thinking about the implications. Trevarde must have whored himself, and repeatedly, to get a quantity of the drug sufficient to use for mass poisoning. The one Thelyan sought would not do that. That one's arrogance would be intrinsic, even in a mortal incarnation. Allowing himself to be humiliated would be impossible for that one. However, this was balanced by certain evidence on the other side of the equation, sufficient to warrant continued study.

He'd learned all he needed to from this meeting. Thelyan disposed of the rest quickly. "Pastachan must have had confederates. Men who knew what he was doing and didn't report him. Find these men and hang them. Report Pastachan executed and place him with the prisoners. Should his Talent be of interest you may use him as a test subject. If his Talent is not on the list for investigation, let him experience the lot of his former charges for six months -- if they let him live that long. Then shoot him."

Hearing this, Warren went pale, but he made no objection. "Yes, sir."

"You've been insulated, Colonel, here in Research. But you must not allow yourself to forget that justice is the first business of the Watch. Our conduct must be spotless."

"Yes, sir." This speech seemed to give Warren strength.

"I understand."

"I'll remain here as long as I can. The situation in Rainet is under control, pending further developments, so I can guarantee my presence through tomorrow. Barring events that require me elsewhere, I'll supervise the whole of the recapture process. The first item of business is Trevarde. Tell me how you lost him."

"The rain washed out the trace. No doubt he's somewhere in the desert to the west of the compound, if he survived. I have a pair of men out there right now, but I believe I've mentioned I'm understaffed."

"They may as well continue, in case he intends to wander the wilderness, but it seems more likely he'll make for a population center."

"Trestre is closer, sir, but I seem to recall Trevarde had some organized crime connections in Burn River."

Burn River; named for the waterway that drained from the locus of concentrated power that people called the Tama Burn. Thelyan, knowing its source and function, was interested to know whether the connection between Trevarde and the Burn was coincidental. "Send a team there to investigate. There's no permanent Watch office in the town, is there? Authorize them to get assistance from the local police."

He unsealed the room so that Warren could dispatch these orders. Then, satisfied that events were well in train, Thelyan turned to the less interesting business of his office. "Let me see the repair estimates. I'll see what I can do about your funding."

Chapter 13

"There's a trick to it." Kieran was instructing Ash how to jump right, because it was dodgy enough having the northerner tag along without him breaking his leg. "You watch real close when I do it. And for fuck's sake don't jump in any holes or bushes or anything."

"Sure. I can do it."

"Hope so." Kieran leaned out, watching the lights of Burn River spread, flickering, across the horizon. There was still a wash of purply-orange light across the western sky, and they'd have to jump while that still gave them enough to see the ground. Otherwise they'd have to wait for the lights of the city, and someone was sure to notice them. "All right. Flat place coming up. Remember, if you can't hit the ground running, then drop and roll."

He judged the train's speed and the terrain, and leapt; the ground jammed into his feet painfully hard, but he managed a few awkward chicken-steps before falling to his knees, and it didn't feel like anything was actually damaged. Half fearing Ash would just stay on the train, he got up and jogged alongside.

Nope. There went Ash, flailing, tumbling, landing flat on his back. He gave an abortive couple of gasps, then wheezed in a huge breath and started coughing. Kieran went to help him up. "Quiet!" he ordered.

"Sorry. Got the wind knocked out of me."

"Well, keep it down." He gestured around the area they'd landed in: deeply gullied urban-outskirt wasteland, populated by tin-roofed shacks and rusting machinery. More of the latter than the former. "There's bums and whatnot out here. I don't feel like getting in a fight right now."

"I can take 'em." Ash made a few weak punching gestures, grinning to show it was a joke.

Kieran shook his head. "Come on." He set out down the railbed, fatigue keeping his pace down to a weary trudge.

He was having trouble thinking straight. It was the hunger. Fortunately, he'd planned out this part while his brain was still working, and all he had to do was follow the program. He just prayed certain people still remembered him, and others didn't learn he was in town. And that Ash didn't screw things up. The kid was way too nice for this kind of thing. Too idealistic. Obviously thought his deprivation-fired crush on Kieran was True Love and meant to hang around until hanging around got him shot.

Kieran had tried again to explain, in the boxcar, though he'd known it was useless; evidence that his mind was gimping from lack of food. *You should have gone back north,* Kieran had told him. *You've got friends there. They would've hidden you.*

I wouldn't have made it there, Ash had replied. *I'm not as good at surviving as you are.*

I'm not sticking my neck out to save yours, if we get in trouble, Kieran had warned. From the martyr face Ash had put on, he'd believed it. Not thinking straight either, apparently, not putting two and two together. He's surely seen Kieran's agony of relief at when he'd rolled into that boxcar. Kieran figured, if he hadn't been on magic-wrecking rails at the time, sensitives from coast to coast would've sat up at the same moment and thought: *oh thank you fate -- never let me leave you again.*

But Kieran was damned if he'd admit it. His intention to split up had been the correct one. Their chances of survival had gone down the crapper. He really shouldn't be so happy about it.

They walked through the dusk, and as full night fell the city's glow began to brighten overhead. Burn River was a major shipping nexus, point of departure for loads of ore from the mountains, point of arrival for everything heading inland to Canyon and Trestre; produce, dry goods, the raw materials for manufacturing, and people fleeing the overcrowded north to strike it rich on the frontier. What these arrivals usually found instead of wealth was drunkenness and social diseases, drugs and robbery, all indulged by an underfunded, understaffed police force, half of whom were on the take. It was a sick town, a canker, a giant bird dropping on the clean surface of the desert. It was also busy, vital, interesting, and a very good place to get lost.

To Kieran's surprise, coming home felt like coming home. He breathed in the scent of the factory smoke, horse, and fried food, and some knot in him loosened. He was on his own ground now. An animal response to territory. As they drew near the switching yard, the deep mourning howl of a freight sounded; soon the heavily laden beast was grinding past them at a snail's pace, three engines pulling some fifty or sixty cars of taconite.

Kieran remembered playing games with those rusty, slightly squashed pellets of raw iron; they made inferior marbles, but excellent slingshot bullets. He remembered climbing the sand piles behind the glass factory. Remembered lying on his cot in his mother's room, looking at the brown square of city glow on the wall opposite the window, the mottled piece of wall that always seemed frescoed with dancing figures when he was half-asleep, listening to the sound of trains hauling.

The sense of peace brought by coming home loosened his tongue so far that he even told Ash about it. "I've always loved trains. They're freedom, you know? I would have liked to drive one. But natives are banned from those jobs. The only way to get on a train is as a porter, and that's all yessir-nosir."

"Not your style," Ash said quietly, with a smile in his voice.

"At all," Kieran agreed. "I invented jumping boxcars all by myself. Didn't know anyone else did it until I hopped a Canyon local and found four old guys already in the car." He chuckled. "Hopped right out again."

"Probably wise."

"I was a skittish kid. Makes sense, I guess. I was in the way. Kind of extraneous. And you get to the point pretty early on of saying, all right, there's no place for me, I'll just *dig* a place. Kind of under and between. That was why I loved the trains. I can't explain."

"No, I understand," Ash said. "They're ignored space. Temporary, mobile -- they don't seem to belong to anyone. That empty boxcar was like a safe little burrow, all the safer because it was moving."

"Exactly." Kieran looked at Ash in surprise. "Yeah."

Ash smiled slightly. "For me, in Ladygate, it was libraries and schools and churches. They're full of extra rooms no one ever goes into. And you can find the most marvelous things in there. I once found a sapphire earring. Just one, stuck between the boards of the attic floor, in the South Bank Library. I kept it in a box with all this other junk -- I'm kind of a magpie, actually. I've been feeling naked for a while now, not having any possessions."

"Well, they'd be a pain in the ass while you're running."

"Oh, I know. But I need worthless gewgaws or I'm not happy. You wait. As soon as I have pockets I'll start accumulating junk. Keys and pebbles and broken jewelry and that kind of crap."

"Huh." Kieran considered this, a way of being that seemed similar to the hoarding habits of whores, but different in that it seemed to have no reference to wealth nor impact on status. Maybe it was just Ash's way of being nuts. Everybody, Kieran was certain, was nuts in one way or another. "Never trusted *stuff*, myself. Can't rely on it. Gets lost, broken, taken away, et cetera."

"Ah." A long pause. "My aunt never took my stuff away. She even brought me things. A whole ring of numbered key tags, once -- that was my favorite. Gold pen nibs, beach glass, a crystal stopper from a broken decanter --"

"She was as crazy as you are."

"Absolutely."

Kieran laughed, and Ash joined him. It was a moment of friendship, laughing together in the sharp, dry night air, just as Kieran recognized the row of dark warehouses they were passing and got another dose of homecoming. It was pleasant. It was a little marred, though, by his uncertainty about the reception they'd get when they reached their destination. He'd been away a long time. He wasn't sure the same people would be there, or if they were, how they'd feel about seeing him.

He was so tired and hungry that he had no idea what he'd do if they wouldn't let him in.

This was Andel Street, he knew, though there were no signs this far from the city's center. They were in the right part of town, but if they stayed on this road they'd be seen. Andel turned into pubs and boardinghouses five or six blocks up from here, and while prison clothes didn't look that different from an ordinary worker's outfit, he himself was kind of conspicuous, big as he was, and their filthy, barefoot condition would draw interest. He peered down each cross street they came to until he recognized Caire and turned them north on it.

This took them even deeper into industrial territory, but Ash never questioned him. The northerner was reeling, stumbling, with a fixed smile on his face, but still he trusted Kieran absolutely.

Quit trusting me, Kieran thought. *I don't want that kind of power over you.*

But that wasn't the sort of thing you could say out loud, not even to an Empath. He supposed Ash would be disillusioned soon enough. Kieran couldn't go on protecting him forever, after all. Though he meant to try. He'd made his effort to make Ash go home, and that was it, he'd shot his bolt, he didn't have the strength to try again. It was a surprise to realize this, and a relief. He'd gotten used to watching over Ash in Churchrock, he guessed, and now it was just the only way he could be comfortable.

Past the factories -- not the only industrial district in town, but the cheapest -- came an area of long, low houses, all perfectly dark: worker barracks. Curfew was strictly enforced in those places, at least so far as lights went, but that didn't keep the men from slipping out to visit the one house in the neighborhood that had a light showing.

It had been three years since his last visit, and while he still remembered how to sneak around back, the gap in the fence that had been a tight fit for a rangy sixteen-year-old was impossible for him now. He found a bit of rusted barrel hoop in the alley, smashed it flat on the ground, and slipped it through the back gate to pop the latch. To his relief, it was still the simple affair it had been before; if they'd put in a real lock, he supposed he'd have had to climb the fence, and in his present state he wasn't sure he could have done it.

Muffled laughter came from the house, the artificial kind he remembered hearing so often. Fortunately, no one was using the back yard. Paper lanterns hung forlorn from the half-dead trees; rusted iron furniture was scattered about, and some wooden tables, one with an assortment of empty bottles on it, labels warped by water; there had not been a party here since before the rain.

"Where are we?" Ash whispered.

Kieran shushed him. He closed the gate and discarded his impromptu breaking-and entering tool. "Just look harmless."

"My specialty."

It felt strange to climb the three steps to the back porch. Stranger to do it with longer legs, bigger feet. To hear the boards that had once chirped at his bird-boned weight now groan under his heavier step. To have to bend to look into the kitchen window; to tap on the glass and see a total stranger start and squeak in surprise.

The girl at the kitchen table sat staring at him for a long time, hand to chest, cup forgotten in her hand. She was wearing a ratty yellow robe over some kind of frothy underwear, her hair frizzled and her makeup smeared. She was white, blond, a bit pasty. She was probably frightened to see a big, filthy, tattooed native staring in at her, unsettled that it should occur in the one room in the house that clients never saw.

Kieran mouthed his question at her, aware that she would not hear it unless he yelled, and unwilling to yell. When this failed to conquer her fear with curiosity, he turned to his companion.

"Ash, look pitiful."

"Not hard," Ash said with a rueful grin. He waved at the girl, waggling his fingers like a child. "Hello? Miss? Could you open the window?"

Either Ash's waifish face did the trick, or she realized that they could go around the front if all they wanted was to come in. She crossed to the window and bent to open it a crack. "What do you want?"

Kieran tried to sound friendly. "Is Shou-Shou still here?"

"What do you mean, still here? She supposed to go somewhere?"

"It's been a while since I was in town. Could you get her to come talk to me?"

The girl looked suspicious. "Depends on what you want."

Kieran sighed his exasperation. "Girl, if I wanted to make trouble I'd just do it. Go get her. I'll wait here. Oh -- and not that you would, but if you tell anyone else about me, Shou-Shou will pull out your neck hairs with tweezers."

The girl raised an eyebrow, but shrugged her acquiescence as she shut the window. Maybe his knowledge of the way Shou-Shou punished girls who annoyed her convinced this one that he knew what he was talking about.

"This," Ash said abruptly, "is a bordello."

"That would be dignifying it."

To his credit, Ash accepted this and let the subject drop.

A few moments later, a far shorter time than he had expected, he heard the click of the kitchen door's deadbolt. It opened to reveal a plump, sagging native woman of middle years, clothed in purple, her hair bleached an unnatural orange, a grin spreading across her face as she looked at him.

"Well," she said. Then, sounding more pleased with every word, "Well! Fuck me blue. Little Kieran. Little Kieran has come home to roost. I was sure they couldn't kill you."

"Little Kieran," Ash whispered, grinning.

"Who's your friend?" she continued. "No, let me guess.

This must be that Shanin Dyer they talked about."

Kieran felt a wince go across his face, and saw it echoed in Shou-Shou's as she realized she'd blundered. "No," he said simply. "Shan didn't make it. This is Ash Trine."

Ash made a deep, theatrical bow. "At your service, ma'am. I hesitate to cut short the reunion, stranger that I am, but any minute you're going to let us in and I'd like it to be now. I promise I'm housebroken, declawed, and I barely shed at all." He put on his most pathetic face. "Feed me?"

Shou-Shou laughed. "Get your skinny asses in here. There's a pile of leftovers, some customers ordered a banquet and then got too impatient to eat it. You can sleep in the attic -- good god, boy, you look like you been the cat's dinner, and you ain't had no dinner yourself for a *long* time."

This as they came inside, into the light. Kieran looked down at himself, then at his reflection on the inside of the window glass.

It was a shock. He'd known in the abstract that he was thinner, that he was dirty and bedraggled. But it was still unpleasant to *see* it. His eyes were hollow, as were his cheeks, and all the roundness had gone from his muscles until he looked like a sculpture of wire and bone. Mud and blood crusted his skin, matted his hair into clumps. His lips were chapped and cracked. His eyes looked huge and strange in his face, luminous, feral, like those of an injured animal.

This inspired him to take a closer look at Ash. The white boy was, if that were possible, even thinner, even dirtier, all his exposed skin crisscrossed with scratches. His hair stood out in snaggles all over his head, so dirty it looked dark brown instead of red. He needed rest and food. Kieran was prepared to grovel to get it for them, but knew that Shou-Shou was proof against histrionics. He spoke calmly instead.

"I'll tell you the truth, Shou-Shou. We've escaped from prison. They'll be hunting us."

She looked skeptical. The blonde hovering at the other end of the kitchen just looked confused.

"There was a storm," Ash put in. "Broke the place open. We're not the only ones who got out."

"We covered our trail pretty well," said Kieran, "but they *will* be looking for us. If they find out you've sheltered us, you'll be in trouble. It's up to you. If you tell us to go, Shou-Shou, we'll go."

For a long second, she considered the risks. Then she

snorted. "Looking like that? I don't think so. Sit down, both of you, and stop talking noble bullshit. Ami, get the boys something to eat." She glanced over her shoulder at the door that led to the public part of the house. "I've got customers." She swept out, closing the door firmly behind her.

Kieran turned to Ash, ready to fish for praise at this satisfactory solution. The northerner had his head down on the table. He was sleeping like a child.

The blonde burnt some beans and rice and scraped it onto a plate for them, unspeaking, then fled the kitchen. Kieran nudged Ash awake and shoved a fork at him. They both ate with heads drooping, chewing slowly, like cows. The cheap, greasy leftovers were delicious.

Shou-Shou poked her head into the room when they were almost done. "No one's in the bath, and you're not sleeping on any bed of mine all filthy like that. Use the plain soap." She waited for the beginning of Kieran's nod, then vanished again. Despite how late it felt, it was really only mid-evening, and she had business to conduct.

"Bath," Ash said in a stunned tone.

"This way." Kieran stumbled back out onto the porch, with Ash reeling after. He led the way to the most sheltered side of the house, where a lattice of wooden slats screened the bath pool from the world.

It was a social space for the girls, not a working one, and it was a mess with their special towels and scents and brushes scattered all over. The water was well cooled, edged with floral-smelling scum. Kieran stripped off his dirt-stiff prison clothes and threw them aside; they'd probably have to be burned.

Climbing into the water, he instantly started shivering. It was freezing. He looked up to warn Ash, and found that the northerner had made no move toward the pool, but was staring with glazed eyes, swaying slightly.

"Ash. Snap out of it. Gotta wash or Shou-Shou won't give us beds."

"Hnf. Oh. Uh-huh." Ash shucked his clothes with movements as creaky as an old man's. His emaciated body was livid with scratches and sunburn. Though once Kieran might have been aroused or embarrassed by Ash's nakedness, now he could only pity. He reached up a steadying hand to Ash's wrist, fearing a tumble and a broken neck.

The water seemed to wake Ash up, though it made his teeth chatter. Kieran located the cheap soap, used it, and gave it to Ash. He had to keep reminding the white boy of missed spots. "Duck your hair again." "You planning to wash your other arm too?" After he'd rinsed the desert off himself, he took the soap away and scrubbed Ash's back for him, then finished off washing his hair, since he seemed to be having trouble holding his arms up long enough.

He could barely climb out. Then he had to clasp Ash by the wrists and drag him out by main force. Ash couldn't stand; he knelt on the wet boards of the porch, wracked with shivers. Kieran, nearly as exhausted, made an abortive attempt to towel them both dry, then gave up and stole a couple of bathrobes off the row of hooks on the wall. Shrugged into the largest one himself. It was still far too small. Wrapped the next-largest around Ash, and wrapped himself around Ash as well, and stayed like that until they'd both stopped shivering.

After a time, he moved to stand, but Ash had buried his face in Kieran's chest and refused to budge. Kieran sighed. "Are you asleep again?"

"No," Ash murmured.

"Do you want to be?"

A pause. "Yes."

"Then we gotta get up. Come on, you can do it. I'll help you."

He coaxed Ash to his feet, but the northerner was still refusing to look at him. At last he took Ash by the shoulders and pushed him off. Ash turned his head, but not fast enough.

"You're crying? Ash, of all the stupid..."

"I'm just tired. I'm sorry."

"Well, after everything... look, it's all right. Let's just deal with stairs now. Okay?"

A sniffle. "Okay."

Getting up the back stairs to the attic was less of a chore than he'd feared it would be. Ash steadily put one foot in front of another, and though he occasionally reeled backwards, he did it slowly enough that Kieran could catch him. The attic door was standing open. By murky streetlamp light reflected off the sloped ceiling, Kieran could see that a mattress had been laid out for them between rows of steamer trunks and hat boxes, with clean bedding on it.

Ash let out a weak chuckle. "Only one bed. They must think we're..."

Not bothering to answer, Kieran shut the door and helped Ash to the bed. He separated sheet from blanket and tucked the blanket around Ash. Rolled himself in the sheet and lay down.

Suddenly the silence was deafening. When Ash's breath shuddered and hitched, the sound ran across Kieran's skin like a wind.

"Please stop crying," Kieran murmured.

"I'm s-sorry." Another whispered sob. "It's nothing, I'm just so tired."

"Then sleep. That's what you do when you're tired. Not cry. Sleep."

No answer.

Kieran sighed exasperation. He raised himself on one elbow and took Ash's shoulder, made him turn over and show his face. Ash did look exhausted, so fragile and sunken-eyed, but he was also clearly miserable. He rubbed a chapped-knuckled hand across his nose, stared wet-eyed at Kieran, and said nothing.

"Spit it out," Kieran demanded.

"I'm... I'm so --"

"Sorry, I know, I heard you. Now what's really wrong?"

Ash stared hopelessly for another long moment, then surrendered with a sigh. "There's nothing I can do about it. All right."

"About *what*, for fuck's sake?"

"I'm afraid to sleep because I know you'll ditch me. You don't want me around. But I'm just embarrassing us both. I'm sorry, I'd be stronger if I weren't so damned tired."

Kieran blinked, amazed. "You really think I'd do that? Sneak out? Leave while you're sleeping?"

"You're saying you won't?"

"It never crossed my mind."

"Okay." Not completely convinced.

"You win, Ash. You were right, I didn't want to split up. Figured we *should*, but we didn't, and I don't want to fight about it anymore. I can't stand it when you cry. It's not goddamn fair."

"And I can come with you? Wherever we go from here?"

"If you wake up and I'm not here, I'm just taking a piss or getting coffee or something. Swear I won't ditch you. Cross my heart and hope --"

"Don't." Ash's fingers stilled his lips. Kieran smiled and kissed them, took the hand's wrist and kissed the palm. Ash's eyes went round. "Kieran..."

Feeling half like a liar and half in love, Kieran kissed his mouth lightly, then burrowed in behind him and snaked an arm around his waist. "Sleep," he commanded. "I cannot *believe* how fucking tired I am. Sleep now."

One last shuddering exhalation, and Ash relaxed all at once. Leaning back against Kieran's chest, his damp hair cold in the hollow of Kieran's throat, his thin body feverishly warm. Precious. Perishable. Kieran thought distantly, *Maybe we'll be lucky. Maybe I can keep him alive long enough to dump me. Because once the novelty wears off he'll get tired of me real fast. Wonder if saying I-told-you-so will make it sting me less when he changes his mind.* Oblivion killed the thought and dragged him under.

Chapter 14

Slowly, luxuriously, Ash floated through layers of dream to gentle wakefulness. The knowledge of where he was filtered into him bit by bit. A smell of food and soap and cosmetics. Mildew and chemicals. A mattress beneath him that was wide and soft, though a ridge where a rip had been repaired dug into his hip. Golden light and a growing warmth, approaching the threshold of unpleasantly hot but not quite there yet. He was clean, wrapped in cotton sheets worn soft with age. Under the sheets he was wearing only a too-small robe of yellow silk with frayed cuffs.

He was alone. For the first time since his trip in the jail car, he had a space entirely to himself. It was a narrow, peaked room, painted white with thick, gloppy paint. There was a small window at one end, admitting bright sunlight. His bed was a mattress on the floor, hemmed in by battered trunks and crates overflowing with dusty clothing. A fly beat itself against the upper part of the window. The lower part was open. Midday, from the way the light lay on the floor.

He remembered Kieran's assurance of last night, and was able, for the moment, to believe it; that though he'd been left alone in this room, he was not alone in the world. He wanted to think that his sense of Kieran's presence was Empathic power rather than wishful thinking.

He threw off the covers and examined his body. He was thin, his hipbones standing out like knives. All the little cuts and scrapes that had annoyed him so much yesterday were scabbed over now, and no longer felt like anything. His feet were a mess, cracked and blistered. There were streaks and patches of sunburn on his arms and hands, pink but not painful or itchy, just a bit warm. He knew from experience that these would fade in a day or two back to his usual whiteness, their only lasting effect to increase the general profusion of freckles.

Adjusting his borrowed robe for maximum modesty, he cautiously opened the door. A smell of food and faint sound of conversation drifted up from the stairway at the end of the hall. He followed it.

Downstairs, the soothing white walls gave way to garish

flowered wallpaper, the whole decor pink and gold like a girl's bedroom. Which was probably the point. There was a hallway lined with doors, each door labeled with a flowered plaque: Kitta, Darcy, Jeri-Lou. The hall was L-shaped, and at the corner of the L was an open room furnished like a sort of parlor; he put his head in and saw a piano, several couches, a cheap rug, a lot of dirty dishes and empty bottles. The occupants of the house had not yet cleaned up last night's debris. Not early risers. Understandable, he supposed.

Overlaying the perfume and spilled beer he smelled a delicious waft of coffee. He let it lead him to another stairway, this one opening out into a large area a bit like a shabby gentlemen's club, with deep chairs and bare wood floors, a bar occupying one corner, brass-bound kegs gleaming. This, he supposed, was how the house pretended to be a legal operation -- though he guessed that there were a few bottles of bootleg hard liquor around here somewhere. A door beside the bar stood open; the streak of light that fell from it was eclipsed by a moving shadow, and he heard a clank of dishes and a grumbling female voice.

When he appeared at the kitchen doorway, the three women in the room stopped what they were doing and stared at him. Kieran wasn't there, just these women. One, a handsome woman with skin so black it looked almost dusty, like a plum, burst out in loud laughter.

"What are *you* supposed to be?" she said. One of the others, a plain brunette, gave a chuckle. The third woman was Ami, who looked a bit sulky, and didn't smile.

The brunette gestured to his bare legs with a coffee spoon. "You look like a chicken," she said in a lovely, smooth voice. "Is Shou-Shou hiring boys now? Is that the deal? I thought she had an agreement with that place. What's it called."

"Cat and Peaches," the black woman filled in. "They're going to make a stink." She had a faint Prandhari accent, though her skin marked her as Paiwaar. A world traveler. "Isn't that one of Ami's robes?"

"Er." Ash didn't know whether to challenge their misunderstanding or not. "Can I have some of that coffee?"

The black woman shrugged. "Help yourself."

While Ash was busy with finding a cup and wrestling the huge kettle, Ami spoke, sounding more apprehensive than sullen, though she still looked pouty. "Where's Kieran?"

"I don't know."

"Are you his boyfriend?"

"I don't know." It didn't seem odd to be asked that question so bluntly here. Maybe rooming with whores wasn't such a bad prospect. He sat down next to her, giving her a crooked smile. "You sound like you know him. But last night you didn't look like you did."

"Didn't recognize him." Ami looked like she was going to say more, but thought better of it.

The brunette leaned over the table, looking eager. "This sounds like gossip. Who's Kieran?"

The black woman, checking something on the stove, turned with a gunky spoon in her hand. "Before your time, love. You ever hear Shou-Shou talk about a girl named Rasa?"

"The one who died in Pinkie's room?"

"That's the one. This wasn't such a nice house then. It was before Shou-Shou took over. Run by a man at the time, and you can guess what *that* was like."

The two white girls wrinkled their noses. Ash did arithmetic in his head and realized the black woman must be a lot older than she looked.

"Anyway, she had a kid already when she came here. Boyfriend ditched her or something. Most of the girls liked the kid, but the owner didn't want him around. Kept bugging Rasa to get rid of him or put him to work. Finally just pimped him out without telling her. She found out and tried to leave. There was a big scene, and the owner kicked her in the stomach, and she died the next night. That was what made Shou-Shou take over the business, but by then the kid was already gone."

Ash drank coffee to cover his discomfort; it burned his tongue. "How old was he when this happened?"

"Nine or ten, I guess." She looked at him more closely. "I bet you *are* his boyfriend. You're just his type."

"I am?"

"You sure are. You got eyes like big blue china plates. Bet he couldn't tell you 'no' if his life depended on it."

In light of yesterday's events, that was almost literally true. Ash wasn't sure that was a good thing. "I don't think he's happy about it, though."

She chuckled. "Typical." Then, to the brunette, "Anyway, he used to come around sometimes. When he got too beat up or hungry. Never stayed long, though. He's like one of those cats, you know, come around to eat but never let you pet them. He was turning tricks, of course, and Shou-Shou would've let him do it here but he wouldn't. Never liked to have a closed door between him and the desert. After a while he stopped coming around."

"I know where he was," Ami blurted. "He was killing people." Then she looked past Ash at the door and blanched.

"We don't need to talk about that," said Kieran's voice.

Ash turned with a slightly pained smile. The pain went out of it when he saw Kieran smiling back. And not his public smile, either, but something a little bit wry and hopeful, for Ash alone. The rest of the world seemed to gray out. *That's it, I'm definitely in love with him, no question anymore. It's him, not just his looks. Though -- fiery* hell *he's gorgeous.*

A robe was apparently beneath his dignity; he'd constructed some kind of kilt out of a dark blue bedsheet. His hair was freshly brushed, gleaming smooth as black water over his shoulders and past his waist. Unbearable glory. Ash considered testing the theoretical utility of blue eyes in the ordering about of Kierans by commanding him straight up the stairs to bed, but it looked like he was in taking-care-of-business mode. In one big, knuckly hand he held a cup with a brush and razor sticking out of it.

"Found this lying around," he explained, offering it. "You might want to use it pretty quick here. You're starting to look like a grownup."

Ash made sure to touch Kieran's fingers when he took the shaving mug. Despite his calculation, he still felt his face go pink. Kieran looked amused, but his eyes were burning darkly, and their green fire promised that it wouldn't be long before the last distance between them was erased. Ash had to turn away quickly.

The brunette at the table raked her eyes up and down Kieran's body. "Now *that's* more *like* it," she purred.

Kieran grinned. "Sorry, sweetheart. You've got the wrong equipment." To the black woman he said, "Jindallie, wasn't it? You remember me, right?"

"Mm, not so big or smiley, but sure I do. I guess you want some of this." She waved the spoon.

"I don't want to piss off Shou-Shou. We need some clothes, and she might not give 'em to us if we've been eating up all her food." But he was joking; as he spoke he was getting bowls down from a cupboard, going right to them as if he knew where they were kept.

They didn't speak while they ate. Ash gloried in the food and the sunlight, in the rays of contentment that beamed out from Kieran's smile and warmed him from the inside. He had never seen Kieran so peaceful -- so beautiful, when he was happy, that it made Ash's heart ache.

Over the next couple hours, different women filtered in and out of the kitchen; some sampled Jindallie's cooking, others pronounced themselves too hung-over to eat. Most were white and had Rainet or Eskard accents. Ash guessed that they had come south to seek their fortune just as so many men had, but found as little honest work available here as there. According to the wisdom of the Church, a woman existed to be a wife; those who couldn't or wouldn't marry were beneath its notice, as much in the south as in the capitols of the Commonwealth.

They didn't seem unhappy. Rather, no less happy than the women who sold hot pork buns on the streets of Ladygate, or the ones who mended clothes or nets, or most of the wives either. Ash was beginning to think that people's happiness had very little to do with their lot in life. It was annoying to find such a smarmy truism borne out in experience.

The whores sat at the table or leaned in the doorway, went out into the yard to squint at the sun, praised the food or complained of their hangovers, yawned and scratched. Ash went looking for a mirror and shaved, then came back for more coffee. The women teased him about how young he looked without stubble. He found himself becoming more and more at ease in their company. Kieran interjected the occasional dry comment in an amused rumble, and every word he spoke reached out and wrapped Ash in a sense of belonging.

The older ones remembered Kieran, and had to talk about how ridiculously tall he'd become, criticize his tattoos, and cluck over his scars. The younger ones seemed at first apprehensive of him, but were reassured by the others' acceptance. Ash got his fair share of attention too; praise for his pretty hair, laughter for his knobby knees.

Everyone wanted to know how long they were going to stay. Only Ami asked as if hoping to hurry them away. Ash supposed these women didn't see a lot of men who weren't interested in their physical charms, which probably made Kieran and Ash the ideal guests. All talk of the duration of their stay was met by the statement that it was up to Shou-Shou. They were all waiting for her.

When at last she arrived, she was wearing a walking

dress of modest construction, carrying a pair of canvas shopping bags. These she thumped down on the table, saying, "Nothing's going to really fit you, Carrots. You wouldn't wake up when I wanted to ask your size. As for *you*, my boy, we're going to make you *so* handsome --" She paused, noticing what Kieran was wearing. "Tell me you didn't go outside like that."

"Why would I? It's not a political statement, Shou-Shou. It's just a bedsheet."

"Am I missing something?" Ash said tentatively.

Kieran explained, "Traditional dress. Forbidden, like the braids. Have to wear pants." To Shou-Shou, "Tell me you found something long enough."

"Not nearly, but the boots will cover it." She upended one of the bags. Its contents occasioned oohs and aahs from the women. Most prominent were a pair of tall black boots, used but not used hard, with steel toes and half a dozen square steel buckles running up the calf of each. There was a pair of black leather trousers, a bit worn at the knees and seat but otherwise in good shape, also fastened with buckles. There was a black shirt of what looked like raw silk; not all its buttons matched. There was a long coat of gray leather that had probably once been black, and a large black kerchief embroidered with small red squares along the hem.

"I remember you always wore black whenever you could," said Shou-Shou. "Theatrical little monster that you are. Go on, see if it fits." When Kieran hesitated, she laughed and added, "Child, what do you think you have that we ain't seen a million times?"

Kieran smiled back. "It's for your sakes, dears. The little ones would swoon." He collected the clothing and took it out of the room.

Ash reached for the other bag. "Is this for me?"

"Like I said, it might not fit." Shou-Shou scattered out a bunch of brown and blue. "It's your own fault for sleeping so hard."

"I don't remember you trying to wake me."

"Exactly."

What she'd brought for Ash didn't get much of a reaction from the women. He didn't blame them. Tan canvas trousers, a white shirt, a medium-blue sweater unraveling at the hem, brown workman's boots, and a coat of brown sheepskin lined with its own fleece. It all looked functional, durable, and drab.

"Perfect," said Ash. "I just wish you'd got me a hat. My

hair's kind of obvious."

"There's lots of Yelorreans around here," one of the women said.

"And you boys won't be wandering around town," Shou-Shou added. "That would be idiotic."

"That's a point."

Ash reached to gather the whole pile, at which Shou-Shou sighed exaggerated annoyance. "All this modesty. Just put the clothes on."

Ash opened his mouth to protest, then hit on a solution: he put the pants on underneath his robe. There were groans, then laughter.

He had to borrow a belt to cinch in the trousers, which were too big in the waist, though the length was good. The shirt, similarly, billowed around his chest but was the right length in the arms. Putting socks on was luxurious after weeks of bare feet; the women laughed at the way he wriggled his toes and sighed. The boots were a bit too big, but they stayed on. "Marvelous," he said with a big smile.

"Put on the sweater," Shou-Shou ordered. "I got it to match your eyes."

"It's too hot." He held it up to his neck instead, batting his eyes to make them laugh.

Then Kieran came in and turned his knees to water.

It didn't matter that the clothes were secondhand; Kieran looked like a bandit king. All that black made his skin look more gold than brown, made his eyes glow like a cat's. Made his teeth flash startlingly when he smiled. "You're a miracle, Shou-Shou. I owe you."

"Good," she said briskly. "Because I have a job for you. And some for you too, Red. Put away what you're not going to wear and get Jindallie to show you the holes in the fence."

This made the women laugh more, but Ash was content to be put to work. He let himself be handed a hammer and some nails and pointed at the front yard.

It was only fair, after all. Even secondhand, those clothes would not have been free; more to the point, by being here, he and Kieran had endangered the house. The local police might overlook the brothel's existence, especially if they got free service now and then, but they couldn't ignore the harboring of fugitives. Ash wondered what work Shou-Shou had found for Kieran. Something in the house; cleaning, maybe. The thought of Kieran in an apron with a dust mop made him laugh.

Chapter 15

"A couple things have changed around here since you've been gone."

"Well, yeah."

"I mean, in relation to your arrest, your supposed death."

"Tell me."

They were speaking Iavaian now, sitting in Shou-Shou's private office. She'd told him only a couple of the girls had any Iavaian, and that just pidgin, but she'd still closed the door. Kieran guessed that the job she had planned for him was a bit less wholesome than fixing fences.

Shou-Shou located a bottle of smuggled single-malt and two glasses before speaking again. She threw her whiskey back in one practiced motion. Kieran sipped his; he'd never liked being drunk.

"When you left the White Rose boys for the Dyers, it weakened them. You were so public about it. Everybody knew they didn't have their big threat anymore. And if they could let you go, maybe others could break loose. So there was chaos. A lot of splinter gangs. The Rose couldn't punish them all."

"I know that, Shou-Shou. I was there."

"I'm just explaining. You were down in it. This is what it looked like from outside."

"Okay. Go on."

"You know that the Rose was after you and the Dyer brothers. What maybe you don't know is that Kinter was obsessed with you. He let a lot of smaller fish get away."

Kieran nodded. He'd noticed that the old halfblood who ran the Rose had seemed especially stubborn about trying to have the Dyer gang destroyed. There'd been a period of several months when Kieran hadn't had to buy ammunition, getting all he needed off the corpses of the Rose boys sent against him. He hadn't known that Kinter was neglecting his other business.

"Sounds like him," he said.

"When the Watch got you, and the papers said they'd shot you, the Rose started gathering in its strays. They didn't like the way you turned into a martyr, but -- did you know someone wrote a song about you?"

"What?" Kieran laughed.

"It was pretty lame. Made you look like a hero, though, so of course the guy who wrote it got arrested. Anyway, after you 'died,' there was a bloody time, bodies turning up everywhere, the cops were afraid to go out. Now I'll come to the point: I guess Kinter wanted to make sure he had the whole town under his thumb, because he started expanding his interests. Now you can't find a bar, gambling house, or brothel that isn't paying protection to him. Including this one."

Kieran blinked, seeing the implications. "Oh."

"We're paying off the Rose *and* the police. It's cutting into our operating expenses. I want you to take care of it."

"Shou-Shou..." He shook his head slowly. "I can't stay. I have to disappear. You don't seem to understand, having me and Ash here could bring the whole Watch down on you. They won't just shut you down, they'll put you all in work camps. Do you know what those women's work camps are really *for*?"

"Hell, we're just about doing that already. Cops and Rose boys scare our paying customers away -- we're like their little private harem, only we have to pay our own rent and water bill. I'll take the risk."

"Well, I won't. What are you asking? You want me to stand at the door and pitch them out?"

"No." Her eyes glittered. "I want you to kill them all."

Kieran opened his mouth for another protest, and forgot to shut it as understanding hit him. He laughed in admiration. "Shou-Shou. You are an amazing woman. You don't just want this house, do you? You want the whole poppy trade."

She smiled. "It's about time I took a hand in this town. You know I'd do a better job. Kinter's old. And he's a man -- they get too emotional. Present company excepted, of course."

"You can't afford me," Kieran said, though he felt like he was backpedalling. "All I really owe you is a meal and clothes and one night's lodging. What, twenty, thirty signets? I used to charge fifteen hundred *thrones* for a job."

"How often did you see it, though?"

He couldn't reply to that.

"Kinter held your fees. He just kept you smoked up. You only got cash when you worked for some out-of-town colleague of his."

"How do you know that?"

"Ami."

"What's she know?"

"Don't you recognize her? She used to be one of Kinter's little pets, until she started looking like a grown woman. Then he fobbed her off on me. This was while you were still a Rose boy. But I guess you didn't see those girls much, did you?"

Kieran was suddenly tired. He wanted to take Ash and go; get away from all this sordidness into the clean emptiness outside. "Shou-Shou, I'm grateful to you. I owe you. But I don't owe you that much."

She poured another brace of whiskeys and waited for him to drink. Then she said, "You've got no choice. Ami will have gone to them already. They'll be here as soon as they can load their guns and tie their shoes."

He stood, overturning his chair. "You bitch!"

"You should thank me. I'm handing you your revenge."

"You think I need that from you?"

"Kinter was the one who told the cops where you and Shan were hiding. He sacrificed that Burdock creature, that Pyrokinetic of his, to make sure they believed it and knew to call in the Watch." She watched calmly as he clenched his jaw. "Still want to leave your hometown in Kinter's hands?"

Through his teeth, Kieran said, "I don't give half a rat shit what Kinter does. And I'm not going to risk my ass just so you can turn into him."

"I saved something for you." She reached beneath the desk and brought out a bundle wrapped in a towel. It made a heavy thump when she set it on the desk.

Kieran brushed the towel aside; his hand eagerly grasped the thing this revealed before his eyes had quite seen it. His own gun. The one he'd had custom-made when he joined the Dyers. Hart & Sons' brand-new design, an auto-loading pistol that carried a magazine of nine bullets, his little advantage over his adversaries' five- and six-shot revolvers. He ran his thumb across its lapis-inlaid ebony grip, and the familiar weight and texture weakened his knees. He felt whole again. He hadn't realized how weak and cornered he'd been without it.

Closing his eyes, he deliberately slowed his breathing until it was normal again. Then he took the time to examine the gun carefully. Shou-Shou had kept it in good shape. All four of its magazines were nestled in a further curl of the towel, and they were all loaded. Shou-Shou dug in her purse and produced two yellow pasteboard boxes, more familiar to him than the label of the whiskey bottle or the names of trains -- how many times had he said those words at various tack-and-saddle shops all over Iavaiah? Hart's Standard .40-Gauge Rimfire, Fifty Rounds. He snatched them into his pockets, scowling.

"You're overestimating me, you know. A lot. I'm not sure how many men I can handle at once. I hope you put Ash somewhere safe, this isn't his fight."

"Isn't it? Looks to me like he'd walk through hell for you."

"I don't want him to. I'm telling you, Shou-Shou, this is not going to work. You're just going to get a lot of *your* people killed."

She sniffed. Stood, put away the bottle, rolled her shoulders. "Probably about time to get ready. Now, don't get stupid just to prove me wrong. You know you can do this, Kai."

"Don't call me that," he snapped, and slammed out of the room.

As he stormed to the front door, he heard Shou-Shou in the kitchen telling the girls to go upstairs. Kieran grabbed Ash's bundled coat and sweater off the hooks by the front door. He hated to walk out on a debt like this, but Shou-Shou was asking too much. What she wanted was impossible.

Maybe she'd fed him a few times over the years. It might even have kept him alive once or twice when he wouldn't have made it otherwise. But she hadn't kept his mother from getting killed. She'd waited just a little too long before taking over. Now she wanted to be Kinter. Let her. But not with Kieran's help. He threw open the front door.

They were standing in the yard. Three of them, and Ash, looking wild-eyed with a pistol pressed to his throat.

Kieran's options flashed before his eyes, and every single one of them was unacceptable. The fear on Ash's face was unacceptable. The sudden flame of fury rising in him was unacceptable. He couldn't act, couldn't not act; his mind was reduced to a single glyph of refusal. Half a second later, he was a passenger, and something else had the reins.

He ducked back inside and slammed the door. In the same motion he dropped to the floor and rolled aside. A rifle bullet splintered a hole in the door. Missed him by a mile. He heard a startled sound from the direction of the stairs, someone frightened by the gunshot, but that wasn't his problem. Drawing as he dashed across the room, he put his other hand in his pocket and came out with all his spare clips arrayed between his fingers.

He darted for the back door, dropping to one knee as it began to open. He put himself in the shadow of the stove, where his dark shape would blend with the black iron and confuse the eye. He didn't wait to see the man's face. As soon as the door was out of his way, he opened fire.

Luck was with him; his first adversary had pushed at the door, rather than holding it, so when he fell backwards he didn't close it. There were a few scattered thumps and clangs as the Rose boys beyond the dead man tried to find a target, drowned by the thunder of the Hart. Kieran felt their deaths, one after another, like hot breaths on his skin, and then there was no one alive out there. He dropped his clip and slammed another home as he dove back into the front room, making for the shadow of the stairs.

He wasn't quite there when two of the three from the front yard burst in, firing at random. They were using a tactic common in gang warfare -- the usual human urge when bullets are flying is to freeze or run, self-preservation conquering any urge to fight. Those who could return fire would do so wildly, accelerated heartbeat shaking their aim. But all Kieran saw was a pair of targets; everything else was simply gone, the hammer of gunfire just so much background noise. He put holes in the two Rose boys until they stopped being people. There was still a round left in the clip, but he dropped it anyway, not certain what he'd find outside. Not a conscious thought, just the way it was done; conscious thought was gone now.

Kieran knew that the man outside would most likely shoot anything that came out, but there was a good chance his trigger finger would be a little slow, anticipation messing up his sense of time. He took the door at a run, leaping over the crumpled bodies that held the bullet-pocked wood open, not even listening for gunfire -- he'd be hit or he wouldn't. Without pausing to look for his target, he vaulted the porch railing, hit the ground and rolled to his feet.

The last man's gun was following his path; in the heartbeat before that man could correct his aim, Kieran whipped his remaining clip at the guy left-handed. The man's eyes followed the blocky black object flipping toward him, and then red blossoms thumped across his chest and up his face, and he fell.

Kieran looked around for more targets, but there were none. He heard nothing but his own ragged breathing, his own heartbeat, slowing. The rattlesnake mind that had moved him suddenly dropped him back into control, and terror for Ash overwhelmed all else. The last man Kieran had killed was the one who'd held the gun to Ash's throat; had he relinquished his hostage, or killed him?

He heard a whimper: Ash, hurt -- dying hurt, from the sound of it. Kieran was charging for the source of that whimper before he even saw where he was going, tearing out dead rosebushes by the roots to get at the pale shape huddled under the corner of the porch. He didn't feel the thorns lacerating his hands. He wrapped those bleeding hands around Ash's bowed head and raised it to look into his eyes. Blank eyes, like blue paper; he'd seen those before.

"Look at me! Where'd they get you, Ashes? Show me!"

Ash replied by fainting.

Only then did Kieran see that there wasn't a mark on him.

The only blood was smeared on his face from Kieran's hands. His light-colored clothing would have showed any injury, and though Kieran searched for something hidden, a graze across his back or on his inner thigh, felt his boots for holes and checked through his hair for bumps or soft spots on his skull, there was nothing. Terror peaked, tightening Kieran's chest, and then all at once let go. Panic wasn't helping. There was *something* wrong; Kieran knew the difference between some girly swoon and a real loss of consciousness, and this was the latter. He hauled Ash out into the yard and checked him over again.

Ash was pale, his pulse slow and hard, as if his heart were laboring. His skin felt clammy. His white shirt was half translucent from sweat and more still poured from his skin, chill and reeking of fear. Something had happened to him, but damned if Kieran knew what it was. He wished there was someone left to kill.

Well, there will be, if I hang around here any longer. The cops'll take their time, they don't care what happens on this end of town, but Kinter's not going to give up. Dumbshit doesn't know when he's beat. It was hard to leave Ash lying there, but dragging him inside didn't make sense, not when Kieran would just have to drag him out again a minute later. He dashed in, jumping the bodies again, to gather his spent magazines.

Shou-Shou was coming down the stairs as he finished. "You're getting sloppy, hon," she said. "Was a time you wouldn't have let them get a single shot off."

"I oughtta charge you full price for every one of these assholes," he growled. "Would, too, if I thought you had the money." He bent over the meat that used to be an enemy, digging through its pockets. Cash; ammunition; running out of time.

"You're not good enough anymore to charge what you used to. But I guess you'll get plenty of practice in the next few days, won't you?"

"Do it yourself, Shou-Shou." He stuffed the best of the dead men's guns into the deep pockets of his new coat and stood up. "I'm out of this game. I'm out of this town."

She didn't look as if she believed him. "Kai, honey --"

"I told you not to fucking call me that. You are not my mother, Shou-Shou. You're just a crook like the rest of these guys, and I'm done. Thanks for everything." Turning away, he gave a wave that was more dismissal than farewell. He heard her sigh annoyance as he left. She would go on expecting him to come back as long as she thought he might be alive. He'd always come back before. But this time she was wrong. This fight had reminded him how easy killing was, how much he hated how easy it was, like putting your hand through a rotten board. These men had barely been able to fight him, and it made him sick how soft they were. How thoroughly he'd destroyed them. The whole shootout had lasted fifteen seconds, tops.

Still strong with his anger, he lifted Ash easily, settling the northerner over his shoulder. He left the brothel without looking back.

The street was deserted now; people had fled inside the worker barracks at the sound of gunfire. Faces peeked through windows, around the edges of open doors, and there was a current of muttering coming out of the gray clapboard shacks, the occasional child's squalling quickly hushed. Here and there, evidence of a task interrupted sat out on a doorstep; baskets of tobacco leaves, bags of calico squares. The wives and children of factory workers made a few extra moons a day doing piecework, rolling cigarettes or sewing patchwork, and they were waiting to see whether it was safe to return to their tasks. They'd talk about him to anyone who would listen. They'd exaggerate, they'd change things, but he would still be recognized. He had to get out of town.

But he couldn't carry Ash much farther. Now that he was no longer in a huff, he was starting to feel the white boy's weight. Checking up and down the street, he ran through a mental list of hiding places. It was a long list. It seemed, when he thought about it, that he'd spent ninety percent of his life hiding from something or other. Not all of those places would still be there, though, and some that had been ideal for a solitary child made no sense for two grown men.

Two boys the size of grown men, Kieran thought with a sudden pang of self-pity. *I wish Shou-Shou hadn't called me by that name. It's weakened me, going home. I should probably never go home again.*

Turning down a narrow alley between sets of row houses, Kieran began to take random turnings among the maze of shacks and dumps and wire-fenced machine yards that occupied the backside of the factory row. Police trying to find him by asking witnesses would be scattered and slowed by the complexity of the route, most of which was unobserved. If they had Watchmen with them, though, the deserted alleys would show his trail to their magical senses as if it were written in ink on white paper. He knew three ways to shake off a Watch tracker: running water, railroad tracks, or heavy traffic. None of them were absolutely certain. The riverbank was probably his best bet for now. He'd have to get out of town pretty quick though.

Breathing hard now, he hitched Ash's limp form higher on his shoulder as he went. It was something like three quarters of a mile from Shou-Shou's to the river. He came out just upstream of a coal-oil plant -- upstream and downwind. The eye-watering chemical reek should have awakened Ash if anything could have, but the redhead just went on hanging useless over Kieran's shoulder. Kieran even dropped him once, skidding down a weed-choked bank, but Ash only flopped like a doll. Kieran swore, sighed, rolled his shoulders to ease the ache, and scooped him up again.

He emerged onto the riverbank beside a rocky backwater, divided from the main stream by a whitehead, a spit covered with wild cotton plants. The shore here was flat, pebbled, pocked with muddy sinks -- and occupied by bums. He hadn't smelled their cookfire, masked as it was by the oil plant's stink. There were four vagrants staring at him as he trudged toward the flat ground. One held a half-tame coyote by a leash made of braided twine. They were all Iavaian, or else he supposed they would have run when they got a look at him. Working natives might not have been doing well under the

Commonwealth, but it was the whites who didn't last long down on the riverbank. These folks weren't scared of him, though maybe they should have been.

One of the bums, the biggest one, stood up as Kieran arrived. "This is our spot," he said in Iavaian. From among the grayish layers of his many coats, he produced a kitchen knife sharpened to a sliver.

Kieran ignored him. He knelt to lay Ash gently on the pebbled strand, with the sheepskin coat rolled up for a pillow. Still pale and clammy, still out cold.

"Did you hear me, stranger?"

"Yeah." Kieran glanced up, judging whether the man would be stupid enough to attack. The bum was a little pudgy, probably stayed that way by extorting food from the others. Casting an eye over the rest, Kieran decided that one of the remaining two adults might also be considering starting something. The other adult was clearly too bombed to care. And the little one, an adolescent of unguessable gender, was grinning a gaptoothed, lackwit grin. Shifting his attention back to the standing one, Kieran took his gun out from the back of his waistband and stuck it in the front. "Pretend I'm a bear," he said. "Ignore me, and I won't have to kill you."

Kitchen-knife stared a moment longer, then made his blade disappear and sat back down. None of them sat with their back to Kieran, of course, and they all watched him in their ways, but that didn't matter.

Slapping Ash's cheeks didn't do anything. Kieran hadn't expected it to, but it made him feel a little better. "Wake up, you chickenshit. I can't believe you made me carry you all this way." He checked again for injuries, reassured himself that Ash's heart was still beating, slapped him again for good measure. Supposed there'd be a better chance of that working if he could bring himself to slap hard enough to sting. Took off his headscarf and soaked it in the river to bathe the pale boy's clammy face.

While he was doing this, the smallest of the bums blurted out something incomprehensible. The middle grownup reached across the fire to smack the creature upside the head, but it just burbled and started in again.

"I know you," the child said brightly. "You're Death."

Kieran replied, just to pass the time, "That doesn't scare you?"

"Not anymore." The child giggled.

The big bum explained, with the back of his hand, what had happened to the rest of the kid's teeth. Knocked over backwards, the creature started bawling, which started the tame coyote yapping in excitement.

Ash twitched and whimpered.

Kieran put a hand to the redhead's chest and found his heart racing. He was still unconscious, but the occurrence of violence near him had gotten a reaction anyway. Of course -- he was an Empath. What if his state was the result of the deaths of Kinter's men? It would make a kind of sense. Which meant that if he was going to come out of it, he wasn't going to do it while there was any hostility near him. It was a little like the thing Kieran did sometimes, that vacating of himself, except that Kieran walked and talked and killed while he was blacked out, and Ash just sweated and whimpered.

The little bum was babbling while he bawled, and though Kieran couldn't understand much of it, what he did get sounded like bits of old myth-poems. How the kid had come across enough of the stuff to quote, when any mention of the native gods was punishable by death, was a mystery Kieran didn't feel like delving into just now. He said, "You folks need to settle down. You're bothering my friend here."

"Yeah, shut up," said the big guy, raising his hand again.

"Stop!" Kieran ordered. "No hitting."

"You telling me how to raise my own kid, mister?"

"I don't give a shit what you do, but don't do it here. Let the kid talk. Just settle down. If you can't relax, leave."

The kitchen knife came out again. "I don't like your attitude, boy. You think you're some kinda badass cuz you got a gun, I'm sposedta be scared a you? We ain't scared a you. We're Tama, boy, we ain't scared a nothing, specially not some clean-hand whitey-loving punk gangster."

Kieran stared for a moment, then laughed. "You're Tama?"

"That funny?" the man growled.

"Yeah. Sick funny. What clan?"

"Konoku." He named the largest of the Tama clans, the one that was usually translated as Standtall, though the word actually meant lodgepole pine. In the war, the Konoku had led a few other clans, like the Sweetcloud and the Speakingwater, deep into the mountains to hide, believing that the gods would send disasters to punish the foreigners who violated the holy land.

Which the gods had indeed sent -- in the form of the Suneater clan. Kieran gave another chilly laugh. "Your idiot knows who I am. Stand down, buddy."

A growl from the knife man was swallowed in the babbling of the child, who made a sudden emergence into clear-voiced song, among his tears and snot. "He is coming down from the high places today, the death you asked for, the one you called to, he is coming down. His body is a black cloud, his hair is a black cloud, his eyes are poisonous to look upon, he is coming down --"

Knife man made half a move to shut the kid up, but stopped at the click of Kieran's pistol cocking. "Lemme listen," Kieran muttered. He'd heard fragments of this before, enough to recognize it as a battle song from the war. Even whistling the tune of it would get a man killed these days, but there were always those who would sing anyway when they thought they were about to die. Kieran had never let anyone finish. Now he was curious.

The child went on singing, oblivious. "We are in the mood to kill today, our rifles are hungry, our swords are hungry, today there will be blood. His madness fills us like green wine, he is black and green, he is full of death power, he is full of storm power! Above us in the wind, Ka'an! In the smoke of our guns, Ka'an! Dark angry god, it is your time now!" The battle hymn trailed off into giggles.

The three adults were studying Kieran now, with odd expressions. The big one still seemed a little angry. The drunkard, or opium-eater or whatever he was, simply gazed, his look almost adoring. It was the middle adult who spoke up. "These days, that wouldn't surprise me at all."

"What wouldn't, Vei?" the big man said warily.

"If the gods came back. And Ka'an came first."

Big man clenched a fist. "Shut up. Somebody'll hear."

"Well, look at him." The one called Vei stood up, slapping sand from his tattered trousers. He stepped across the fire toward Kieran, who moved the gun to cover him but didn't bother standing. "Looks just like I figured the Prince of Pain would look. What do you say, son? You got a god in you?"

Kieran shrugged, amused by this turn in the conversation. "Not that I know of. But if I did, I guess it would be that one, wouldn't it? Least, my mom always said Tama'ankan was his special favorite." Kieran raised an eyebrow. "You look real impressed by that. What, are all of you

Tama'konoku? Still waiting for the world to end?"

"It will," the drunk chimed in cheerfully. "You gonna make it happen. Kid says so. Kid's a *harai*."

Kieran nodded. That would explain the babbling, and the fact that it was impossible to guess the kid's sex, if it was a real *harai*. A holy androgyne, one who lived on the borders of gender, sanity, life and death. Only among the vagrants and squatters of Burn River's banks could such a creature still exist. Probably had some congenital defect from its mother drinking river water, but that didn't make it any less creepy. Though he doubted its prophesies really had anything to do with him, he still felt a little uneasy. He lifted Ash's head into his lap and began dragging his fingers through the sweat-damp curls. "So," he said. "What are you doing with this *harai* of yours? Besides smacking him around whenever he starts to prophesy."

Big man cringed at the rebuke. "Kid thinks everybody's a god. Sees 'em everywhere."

Vei put in, "You're the best bet so far, though. Only I can't figure why you're dragging around a sharn." At least, that was what the word sounded like.

"A what?"

"A sharn. It's something the kid talks about. The kid likes to talk about foreigners when he ain't seeing gods. He says in Yelorre they got these ghosts, kinda like our bear-people only they come outta the water instead of caves. They call 'em sharn. And that --" he pointed at Ash -- "is just what they look like. Right, kid?"

On cue, the *harai* chirped out, in Eskaran, off key, "O daughters of the Nerrin, don't go walking by the sea, when the wind is high and the moon is high and the land too dark to see, for the siorin boys will come for you and pull you to the deep, to dwell beneath the greeny waves in Medur's briny keep! O their skin is as white as the foam on the sand, but don't go following down the strand, o their hair is bright as the reddest gold, and they'll say if you go that you'll never grow old, but all they'll do is drown you deep, and bury your bones at Medur's keep!"

That song went on for a while, but it was drowned in the chugging of a barge passing on the river. That reminded Kieran that he had to get moving pretty soon, whether Ash woke up or not. It would be easier if Ash woke, though. The theory that it was Empathy that had knocked him out was the best one so far, so he'd operate on the expectation that Ash would come around when things felt safe. He hitched the lolling body higher, so that Ash's head rolled on his shoulder, and wrapped the pale boy tightly in his arms. "Come on out, Ashes," he whispered, knowing that the barge's engine covered it. "I've got you. You're safe now. I'll keep you safe. I won't let anyone hurt you."

After the chugging engine had faded away upriver, the child's song rambled to a close. Something about falling for that Medur character and being turned into one of those sharn things. It wasn't clear whether Medur was supposed to be a goddess or a monster or what, but the water ghost things were the souls of handsome men she'd taken with her into the sea. It was kind of funny that the bum thought Ash looked like one of those. Sure, he was pale and red-haired, but the song didn't say anything about being covered with freckles, and his hair was more rust-colored than 'bright as reddest gold' -- and as for handsome, well, most people wouldn't call Ash good-looking.

Sure, which is why you've got a hard-on from cuddling him like this, right? You're a sick critter, Kai. It's easier for you to kill six men in fifteen seconds than fuck a boy who's gagging for it. Like it's going to hurt any less to watch him leave or die if you stay frustrated.

Not that there was any reason to expect that Ash would still want him, since he went back in the house and left the kid as a hostage. An Empath would know that Kieran hadn't been the least bit torn up about it. He didn't think Ash would understand how he'd gone away and left the reptile in charge.

"Whatcha doing?" The bum named Vei talked into the silence that had fallen after the end of the *harai*'s song. "Looks like you might be a bit *harai* yourself."

"He's a homo, you mean," said big man. He spat. "So much for Suneater."

Kieran was tired of their weirdness. "I think you need to leave now," he said. "I think if you don't get the fuck out of here now I'm going to shoot you."

The biggest bum met Kieran's stare for one moment, then went gray-faced. He grabbed his still mumbling and singing child by the arm and shoved it down the beach, away. The other two caught on quickly. With many glances back, they made their way slowly off along the riverbank, and eventually disappeared into some cut or side channel. When they were out of sight, he put the gun away. He gave Ash all his attention, trying to will some color back into that waxy face.

Most people, he thought again, wouldn't describe Ash as

handsome. Because they associated rusty curls and freckles with some image of awkward childhood, or because he was so frail-looking. It had taken Kieran a while to see. But now -- the delicate lines of him, the colors, the shape of his lips, the sound of his breath -- he was a pearl, a thread of gold, a ruby. To expect for one moment to be allowed to keep this treasure, Kieran was certain, would be insane.

"Those were some pretty strange people, huh?" He made his voice soft. He supposed it didn't matter what he said as long as he said it quietly. "You know, it's weird to think there are all these places in the world, all with their own different stories. You'd think that would kinda prove that they're all wrong. But I know some of ours are true. So maybe theirs are true too, and things are just different all over. Like if there actually were all these different gods before the Dalanists chased 'em out. Where do you figure a god goes when it gets evicted?" He used his kerchief to wipe Ash's face again, though the cloth had dried out and wasn't doing much good. It would have been awkward to get up and go wet it. Besides, he didn't feel like letting go, just now.

"I really need you to wake up, Ashes. We can't stay here. We shoulda been gone already. This fainting shit has to stop, too. If you don't wake up pretty quick here..." Kieran didn't finish the threat. *The hell you're gonna leave him, Trevarde. You can't even take your hands off him.*

Well, if trouble came, he'd deal with it then. He wrapped his arms more tightly around Ash's narrow shoulders and rocked him slowly. Hummed in the back of his throat, songs with no purpose, starting in the middle and not finishing. Little by little, his posture bent so his face was pressed into Ash's hair. He put his lips to Ash's clammy forehead. Tasted his eyelids, feeling the eyeballs twitch and jerk beneath. Picked up Ash's hand, ran his thumb across the palm. Doing this hurt a little, somewhere under his ribs.

"Ashes, please. We have to get moving. Wake up. Please. For me. I'm asking as a favor, all right?" Kieran took Ash's chin in his hand. He looked older than eighteen, now, with his eyes closed. It was his eyes that made him look so young. "Open up those pretty blue eyes of yours, now. Look, the sky's the same color. Don't you want to see?"

When this had no effect, Kieran began to think it didn't matter what he did or said. Nothing would work. He kissed Ash's slack lips. It was like kissing a corpse. He gave a groan of frustration.

"Damn it, boy, what are you *doing* in there that's so much more interesting than being in the world with me? You still scared? Didn't I tell you I'd keep you safe?"

Ash's adam's-apple bobbed. His brows drew in and his lips pressed thin.

Kieran nearly choked on hope. "That's right. Wake up now."

With a small, helpless sound in the back of his throat, Ash opened his eyes a sliver, frowning. He swallowed a few times. "No," he whispered.

"Yeah," Kieran contradicted. "You have to wake up."

"No, you --" More swallowing. "You never said you'd keep me safe."

Suddenly embarrassed, Kieran shifted his grip to help Ash sit up. "Well." Kieran cleared his throat. "I guess I said it while you were out cold. Come on, get up now, my leg's gone to sleep."

"Oh." Ash shifted awkwardly, climbing off Kieran's lap. He was wobbly, as if he'd been down with a fever for weeks. Still frowning, he looked around, then turned back to Kieran questioningly.

"You collapsed during the shootout. You've been out maybe an hour."

"I'm sorry."

"Uh. Yeah. It's okay." Kieran busied himself with his hair, getting it all behind his shoulders and retying the kerchief to keep it back.

"I'm... I'm glad you weren't hurt."

"What?"

"In the fight. I'm glad you won."

"You sure about that? Thought you'd be mad I let 'em keep hold of you."

Ash shook his head. He sniffled, scrubbed at his eyes and nose, then lifted his chin with new calm. "They meant to kill us both. You did the right thing."

"Wasn't sure you'd see it that way."

"You didn't care how I saw it. I'm not sure why you bothered bringing me along. Did you carry me? You must have. Why didn't you just leave me?"

Kieran shrugged, looking away. He stood up and dusted off his coat. "Guess I got used to having you around." He offered a hand.

Ash stared at Kieran's hand for a moment before he grabbed it and let himself be pulled to his feet. He stumbled forward -- no, it was deliberate, he flung himself at Kieran's chest, throwing his arms around, buried his face in the dusty leather of Kieran's coat. His voice was muffled: "Thank you."

"Huh. All right." Kieran returned the embrace reluctantly, afraid that if he didn't pull himself out of this sentimental mood quickly, he'd get stupid and nail Ash right here on the riverbank, and they'd be arrested naked.

After a minute, Ash drew back and let go, giving a wry little laugh. "I scared you. Just now."

"Nah, you surprised me is all. We should get moving."

"No, I scared you. But I could hear, a little bit, when I was coming to -- you were being so sweet to me, and now you get scared if I hug you. I don't get you. I'm going to figure you out, though."

"This Empath shit is getting to be a real pain in the ass. Look, this is me leaving. You coming or not?"

"Okay, hold your horses, I'm coming." Ash grinned.

"And quit grinning at me. You look like a monkey."

"Sure I do."

"You do. Big red grinning monkey."

"You've never seen a monkey, I bet."

"Have too. Saw a circus once. In Trestre. They had monkeys looked just like you."

"You win. I'm secretly really a monkey."

Kieran gave in and laughed. He felt like his chest was full of birds, all rustling and battering to get out. He didn't know what to call the feeling, but he was pretty certain it was one of the ones that turns horrible when thwarted.

Chapter 16

A sense of weary well-being carried Ash along as he followed Kieran down the beach. He could barely remember what had happened after the men with the guns had grabbed him. Later, he'd think about it.

For now, he'd think about how Kieran seemed to like him better today. That was a little odd, not at all what he would have expected. He would have thought going catatonic would be the worst thing he could do. It was exactly the kind of thing Kieran had been afraid of when he'd tried to make Ash head east. He should have awakened in the clutches of the mob or the police or worse, or never woken up at all. Instead, he'd been drawn up by Kieran's heartbeat in his ear, the smell of gunsmoke and leather, and the kind of soft, sweet words he'd never imagined hearing from Kieran's lips, even in his most self-indulgent fantasies.

They still echoed in his head: *those pretty blue eyes of yours... didn't I tell you I'd keep you safe?* And then for all his grumpiness and bantering, Kieran had treated him gently. His reaction to Ash's sudden embrace had contained no anger, no disgust. Just mild alarm, and perhaps a flicker of desire.

Ash felt light, floating, as if nothing were quite real. A little bit head-blind on his left side; the effect of the river? Kieran was leading him along the riverbank, picking a path through tumbled slabs of building stone and fragments of rusted oil barrel. It wasn't at all clear where they were going except that it was upriver. Ash remembered reading that the town of Burn River was the point where the river became navigable, that upstream of the town the water was shallow and fraught with hazards. Maybe it would be cleaner there too, maybe that was why Kieran was taking him this way -- no, what was he thinking, the river was full of chaotic charge even before the factories dumped their phosphors and coal byproducts into it. That was why it was called Burn River.

In fact, now that he was looking, he could see that the vegetation along the bank was a little strange. He didn't recognize most of it, so he couldn't be sure whether it was right, but there were a few plants he knew were wrong. He stepped carefully around a clump of daisies that were bowed over by the too-long petals of their flowers, avoided a cottonwood sapling with white growths on its trunk.

"How can anyone live here?" he murmured.

"Hm?" Kieran turned back to look at him. "Quit dawdling. Look -- here." He stopped to let Ash catch up, and while he waited he dug in the pockets of his coat. "Got a present for you."

"You're kidding."

"Nope. This is for you." He tugged something free of the pocket and held it out.

Ash froze. It was a gun. A fat-bodied revolver. It looked big, even in Kieran's hand. "I -- ah --"

"Take it, you baby. And put your coat on, it's about to get cold."

Glancing at the sky, Ash saw that it was later than he'd thought. The yellowing of the light had just seemed part of his mood, but it was nearly evening. Shrugging into his sheepskin jacket, he gingerly reached out and took the revolver. It was heavy, the metal warm from being in Kieran's pocket. He began to put it in his own pocket, but Kieran stopped him.

"Hang on, it's not loaded."

"I don't want it loaded."

"Tough. I want you to be able to defend yourself. This takes forty standard, same as mine, it's a pretty common caliber. Here's where you break it, see? Just pop 'em in like this -- hold it steady, idiot!"

"Kieran, the only firearm I've ever touched was a bird gun, years ago. I don't know how to use one of these."

"Neither do half the homicidal dumbshits running around out here. Pay attention. Pop it back in like that and it locks. You wanna fire it, you have to cock it first. It's single-action. That means you gotta cock it each time. Just pull it -- no, you do it." He used both his hands to wrap Ash's fingers around the grip, put Ash's thumb on the hammer. "Pull back. Yeah, it's hard."

"It's going to go off."

"Not by itself. What, you think it's an animal, it's gonna bite you? It's a machine, Ashes. Be the boss."

Wincing, ready for the noise of a shot, Ash pulled back the hammer. It hurt his thumb. When it clicked into place, he prayed he was done. Kieran wouldn't risk alerting people that they were down here, would he?

No such luck. Shifting behind Ash, he reached his long arms around and moved Ash's hand, making him aim the gun at the middle of the river. "Get your finger on that trigger, now. You need to feel what it's like or you'll drop it when there's a fight on. Just squeeze down on it."

Breathless both from fear of the gun and from Kieran's voice in his ear, Ash tried to pull away. "Someone's going to hear it and come --"

"No they ain't. People are always shooting off their guns for the hell of it around here. You're not getting out of this."

Ash took a deep breath. "What am I aiming at?"

"Nothing. Just the water. I just want you to feel it kick once."

"It's going to hurt, isn't it?"

"Not if you don't tighten up your wrist. Keep it loose. Not limp, dumbass, just loose." His hands wrapped Ash's wrist, giving it a shake. "That's better. Now don't jerk the trigger. Just haul down on it real slow."

Ash felt the weight of the gun, the heat of Kieran's body at his back, his own anxiety and arousal, the chemical reek of the river, the last rays of sun on his cheek; it all melded into one thing. Frighteningly real and beautiful. *I always pick the strangest times to be happy*, he thought, and tightened his finger.

The gun roared, sending a shock up his arm, more like a sound than a sensation. He realized he'd closed his eyes, and opened them. He couldn't see where his shot had gone, and Kieran was letting go of him. He wanted to start over and do it again, wanted to ask Kieran to show him again, to whisper in his ear the finer points of marksmanship -- *is this why people become so irrational when they get hold of guns? Or am I sick, that it turns me on?* Frightened of his reaction, Ash held still and didn't try to stop Kieran from moving away.

"Still scared?" said Kieran.

"Yeah." It came out a whisper. Ash gulped and tried again. "More scared than I was before. I'm afraid I'm going to fire it again."

Kieran gave a satisfied nod. "Good. You respect it. Put it away now. It won't go off if you don't cock it. Later on I'll show you how to clean it, maybe have you shoot some targets."

"Okay."

"You still think it's gonna bite you, don't you?"

"I think it already did."

Kieran laughed, slapping Ash's shoulder. "You're an

outlaw, kid. Did you forget that? We're outlaws. Now let's get the hell out of town before somebody finds us."

"This came off a dead man, didn't it?"

"Yeah."

"Someone you shot."

"You have a problem with that?" Kieran watched his face, as if his answer mattered.

Ash gave it some thought, for that reason. At last he said, "No." He took one last look at the gun, then set it carefully in his pocket. "It seems appropriate, somehow. I'm just wondering how long I can travel with you before I end up killing someone. Or getting shot because I won't kill someone. You saw what it did to me, just having people die near me."

"Guess we'll cross that one when we come to it."

"It was just -- they were so scared of you. I wanted to tell you that, when they had me --" He pantomimed the gun to his throat.

"Wouldn't have changed anything." Kieran set off down the beach again.

"I suppose you're right," he said, trying to match Kieran's pace. "And it's not as if I'd never felt anyone die before. I lived in Ladygate. People dying and being born all the time. I just didn't know what it was I was feeling. It's worse, knowing. There's this, this blinding fog of fear, and then it just *pops*, and there's *nothing*."

"You figure it was you being scared, or them getting mixed up with you?"

"I'm not sure I can tell the difference. Just like now, I feel full of butterflies, like something good's about to happen, and I don't know if it's me or you."

Kieran turned his head, but his smile was apparent in his voice. "That's me, I guess. Sorry 'bout that."

"Why --?"

"You know damn well. Quit trying to make me say pretty things to you."

Ash smiled to himself, and managed not to answer.

Gradually, the riverbank became less cluttered and less steep. There began to be shacks perched on the shore, sad little things made of sheet metal and scrap wood. Thin, hard-eyed Iavaians in dull-colored clothes watched them pass. Even the children looked wary. Smells of cooking mixed with smells of rot, smoke, and human waste. Ash tried not to stare. Kieran didn't even bother looking.

"It's sad," Ash whispered. "I knew, intellectually, that people lived like this. But I never understood. I wish there was something I could do."

"Pick one."

Ash frowned in puzzlement. "What?"

"Pick one. One family." Kieran swung his coat back to get at his trouser pocket.

"But -- I get it. You can't pick one."

"I'm not being a wiseass. Just point."

"Um. All right." Not certain what Kieran meant to do, Ash peered into the shantytown, intending to choose the nearest house. If you could call them houses. But the nearest one seemed deserted. Just past it, though, was one in front of which two little girls stared at him, frozen in the act of digging a hole with sticks. Their mother, enormously pregnant, stood half-hidden in the doorway of the shack, glaring. The mother looked younger than Ash was. She couldn't have been more than four and a half feet tall, and there was something wrong with her face; her cheeks and chin looked red. She was far enough away to be a blurred to his imperfect sight, so he couldn't tell what exactly was wrong, but it wasn't nice. "That one," said Ash quietly, feeling sick.

"All right. I'm going to teach you some Iavaian. Say it after me: *nahia aberu inamat.*"

"Na -- nay --"

"*Nahia.*"

"*Nahia* --"

"*Nahia. Aberu. Inamat.*"

"*Nahia aberu inamat.*"

"Good. Means 'well water please.' See how she's got a jug by the door? Here." He pressed a bank note into Ash's hand and gave him a little shove. "I'll be right behind you."

"Uh -- okay --" Ash's feeling of floating intensified with everything Kieran did, and he was beginning to wonder if he'd ever wake up. The pregnant girl and the two kids watched him approach. They didn't move. He smiled at the children as he passed them, but they didn't smile back. He stopped in front of the girl and cleared his throat. Now he could see that the skin of her face was flaking off in pink, shiny patches, some disease of the river. "Ah -- um. Nahisa -- I mean -- nahia aberu ina --"

The girl's mouth opened and closed once. Then she burst out laughing.

Ash felt his ears getting red. He turned to see if Kieran

was right behind, as he'd said he would be, but he was too far away to help. Taking his time strolling up to the shack. Smiling sheepishly, Ash tried again. "Nahia aberu inamat." He pointed at the jug. "Inamat."

This only made the girl laugh harder. Now the children were joining in, and a couple neighbors were wandering over to see what was so funny. Ash sent Kieran a pleading look. "Kieran, help! I think I said it wrong!"

"No, no." That was the pregnant girl talking. Her accent was strong, but her Eskaran was understandable. "You say right. But that --" she pointed to the jug -- "is *wizgi*. You see? You ask water. Point to *wizgi*."

"Oh." Ash chuckled a little. "Sorry. Yeah, that's funny."

"I give water, okay. You tell me, *kinatta*, what you want with talk *Iavai'ai*. You white."

He pointed at Kieran. "He's teaching me."

"Why?"

Ash shrugged. "Because he feels like it? I was just doing what he told me."

The girl narrowed her eyes suspiciously, but there was an amused glint in them. "So who is he, eh, get a white man do what he say?"

It was Kieran who answered, with a rapid-fire string of Iavaian that made all the gathered natives burst out laughing. Then he grinned at Ash. "You should see yourself, Ashes. You're bright red."

"That's not fair! What did you say?"

"I just said not all whites are too dumb to take good advice."

Ash turned to the girl. "Is that *all* he said?"

"Oh, he say so all right." She giggled. "You want water? Pay for bottle."

"Right. Here." He pushed the bank note at her.

She examined it, eyes widening. "Too much!"

"Really? How much is it?"

"Too much." She made it disappear anyway. "Rich man, eh?"

Kieran said something else in Iavaian and made them laugh again. The girl ignored Ash's queries this time, ducking into the shack to emerge with a green glass jug mostly full. She thrust it into his arms.

"Thank you, miss. Um -- Kieran?"

"*Inai ou kii an'na*," Kieran prompted.

"Oh ki anna," Ash repeated dutifully. He wasn't much surprised when they burst into laughter again.

Grinning broadly, the pregnant girl, babbling in her own language, gave Ash a series of short shoves until he moved away, back to Kieran's side. Kieran gave him an unreadable smile, taking him briefly by the back of the neck and giving him a little shake before leading him away again. Ash looked back once, to see that most of the shantytown neighbors were clustered round the girl who'd given him the water, but the little ones were smiling at him. One waved her muddy stick. He waggled his fingers at her.

"Here." Ash offered Kieran the jug. Kieran took it, still smiling, and drank a little, then gave it back. Ash drank as well. It was clean water, with only a slight mineral taste. "So what was all that about?"

"You did good."

"I see. You were testing me."

"Nope."

"Yes, you were. You were seeing how I'd act with them."

"Okay, I was a bit curious about that. But mostly we needed the jug. I gotta teach you more of the language -- the farther west we go, the less people are gonna speak Eskaran."

"Sure, and speaking of languages, what was all that about? What did you say to make them laugh so much?"

Kieran grinned. "Nothing."

"Oh, come on. What did you tell them?"

"Nothing."

"I want to know!"

"What I told you I said."

"And when she said I was rich?"

"I said you were just a rich man's friend."

"And what did she say?"

"She told you to get back to your husband."

"*What*?" Ash gaped. "She did not."

"That's what she said."

"What the hell made her think -- Kieran, what did you *really* say?"

"Well, we Iavaians have a lot of words for friend." He looked at Ash, and his grin turned into a laugh. "You look like a fish."

"I -- uh -- well. I'm glad I could amuse you."

"Oh, come on. It's funny."

Ash tried for a little longer to be mad, but it was no use,

he just couldn't be angry. He turned away to hide his smile. "When will it be *your* turn to be the source of humor?"

"Never. That's your job."

There wasn't anything to say after that, but Ash didn't mind. Had Kieran really told those people that Ash was his boyfriend? His lover? It was undignified, a shade belittling, to have it made into a joke like that, and yet -- visions of the possible future filled his head, and despite the chill of impending night his face felt far too warm. *Don't count on it,* he told himself. *He's changed his mind before. It's not safe to assume, with him.* But that was part of Kieran's -- well, charm was a very wrong word. His draw, the truth of him, a component of the thing that made him the only possible destination. *All right, I'm not expecting anything. But I'm not giving up, either.*

They climbed the bank in blue twilight, and found a gravel road at the top, running beside a set of railroad tracks. Kieran led the way parallel to the tracks, back toward the river, where Ash could make out a bridge. It looked like the bridge was just rails and ties over open water, with no road bed to walk on; Ash didn't look forward to crossing it in the dark. But when Kieran stepped onto the tracks, he caught Ash's arm and turned him the other way, away from the water, walking between the rails this time.

Obscuring our trail. I get it. It was a deeper layer of thinking than Ash had expected from Kieran: knowing that Watch trackers would expect them to hide their trace in rail interference, Kieran was making the trail disappear in such a way that the trackers would think they'd crossed the river. *Why can't I get used to how smart he is? I keep thinking he's not quite as intelligent as I am. Is it just the way he talks? In the present circumstances, he's effectively much smarter than I.* The thought made him a little dizzy, a kind of awe. *God, I'm really crazy about him, aren't' I?*

"Hey. Kieran."

"Yep."

"What you told those people, I mean, which of these many words for friend did you use?"

"Tiv'haan."

"What's it mean exactly?"

"Kinda like 'little brother.' Guess that woman assumed I wouldn't call a white boy that unless I was getting some."

"Oh." Disappointed, Ash was prepared to drop the subject.

Kieran wasn't. "The word you're looking for is *ediya'haan*. Unless we're not a couple but we have sex for ritual purposes, and then it's *kaitinan*. Or if one of us was pretending to be female, then it would be *chikeru*, but that's an insult."

"What was the first one again?"

"*Ediya'haan*."

"Which means, exactly?"

"Dear friend. Beloved friend." Kieran shrugged, as if to make it sound less important.

"Beloved friend."

"Yeah."

"Are we?"

"Hell, you're my *only* friend, Ashes. Now you're trying to make me say pretty things again. You know I'm not gonna do that."

"I'm just trying to figure out..." He trailed off, realizing he was digging a hole. Making Kieran uncomfortable and annoyed. "Sorry. I shouldn't push you."

"Yeah. Look, I know I'm jerking you around. Not doing it on purpose. I'm just not... good at this."

"At what?" Ash asked softly.

"At... at being... you know. I don't know. It's just. Whatever."

Of all possible responses, getting incoherent was the last thing Ash had expected Kieran to do. He dared to ask, "Is it because of Shan Dyer?"

A sharp headshake. "I'm not being faithful to his memory or any maudlin shit like that, if that's what you're asking. We weren't like that. We were just good friends who screwed a lot."

"But you liked him."

"Is this going somewhere?"

"I gather you haven't had a lot of people that you've cared about, and so far they've all died horribly."

"Two for two," Kieran said with a nod. "Okay, you might have a point. You do have a point. Hope you don't think talking is gonna fix it."

"Not talking, no." He slipped his hand into Kieran's, meaning it as a gesture of support, reassurance.

Kieran jumped and jerked away as if it had been an attack. "Fucking Empath. Leave my head alone."

Ash stumbled on a rotted tie and stubbed his toe. "Ow. Shit." He was glad of the excuse to swear, because he couldn't quite bring himself to direct it at Kieran. Not yet. Any minute, though. *At least he's being more honest with me.* "So do you still think I'm deluded for -- for liking you?"

"Yep. Just walk for a while, all right? I'm tired of talking."

"Sorry."

"And quit apologizing."

"Oh -- fuck you."

Kieran laughed. "There you go. You're getting it."

"Getting what, for god's sake?"

"Another week and I'll have you drinking corn liquor *wizgi* and smoking cheap cigars."

"And then I'll be bad enough for you? Is that it?"

"Shit, don't get so worked up. It was a joke."

"Go to hell."

"Working on it." He flashed Ash a smile, and all Ash's irritation melted into a little puddle of soppy longing.

I'm such a sucker. He's playing me like an automatic piano. Just push the button and watch it spin. I bet he thinks it's funny. No, it is funny. I wonder where we're sleeping tonight. I hope it's somewhere cold so he'll have to let me hold him.

Soon, though, desire was drowned by exhaustion. The tracks seemed to go on forever. There was a pair of them, and once Kieran pulled Ash across to the other set to let a freight go by, making sure they didn't leave the railbed. Ash didn't like to think what would happen if two trains happened to come at once.

Ash was plodding in a daze of weariness when Kieran finally called a halt. The city's lights had been left behind long ago. Now the stars were blocked on either side by walls of rippled stone. Ash could barely see, but Kieran seemed to have no trouble. He took Ash's hands to help him down a slope of loose gravel, but Ash lost his footing anyway and knocked them both down. Kieran didn't say anything; just helped him up again and led him away.

Kieran seemed to know where he was going, as he hauled Ash through a twisting channel between the stone walls, sometimes so narrow that they had to flatten themselves sideways. It was so dark now that they were navigating by Talent sight alone. Ash just wanted to lean against the wall and rest. But Kieran pulled him onward. The channel widened out, and then they were climbing rounded steps of water-cut stone to a darker shadow in the cliff wall. When they reached the place, so dark Ash couldn't tell if it was a cave or just a dip, Kieran stopped him with a hand on his chest. Rooting in his pockets, Kieran snatched up something from the ground, then made a sudden sharp noise and a blinding light. Ash was so tired it took him a long moment to realize Kieran had struck a match.

Wincing against the light, Ash watched while Kieran lit a handful of dry weeds and used this makeshift torch to explore what seemed to be a shallow cave or deep overhang, not quite high enough for him to stand upright. Kieran bent to peer into a crevice, waved his burning weeds at it, stomped and made a crunching sound. Scraped something off his boot and kicked the befouled sand into the crevice. Then he dropped the torch, which had burned down to his fingers, and stepped on it.

Now doubly blinded, Ash flinched when Kieran's hand brushed his arm and crawled down to his hand. Relaxed and let himself be led. He groped in front of his face to avoid hitting his head on the overhang. When Kieran pulled him down, he folded.

Kieran's voice was something between a rumble and a whisper, and ran over his skin like steam. "Don't bother taking your boots off. We won't sleep long."

Unable to see even where Kieran's face was, Ash used the one hand he held as a reference. Explored up the arm, across the chest; found throat and jaw and mouth; holding his breath. Lips rough with dryness curved under his fingers, and a wave of weakness ran through him at the idea that his touch made Kieran smile. Then a large hand caught his and pushed it away.

"I'm tired," Kieran said. He placed Ash's hand on his side, and both his own hands went around Ash's waist under the jacket. There was some awkward shifting and accidental shin-kicking until they lay pressed together, arms inside each other's coats. "Warm enough?" Kieran whispered.

Ash tried to explain that he wasn't sleepy at all, it would be impossible to sleep with all the marvelous country of Kieran's body yet to be explored, but it came out as: "Mn." His last waking thought was that it wasn't fair that he should feel so safe, when he couldn't make Kieran feel safe in return.

Before the sun was up, they were moving again. They found a place to fill their water jug, a thin trickle sheening a rock face, but they had nothing to eat. They walked the tracks until midmorning, when Kieran chose a dry streambed and followed it to the river. Without explaining himself, he started stripping off his clothes. When he stood stark-naked, he turned to see Ash still clothed and staring, and he laughed.

"We're going across," he said.

"Oh." Ash shook himself, looking away. *You've seen it all before in the bath, haven't you? You're acting like a child.* "Right." Face flaming, he stripped as well, and rolled everything into a bundle. Holding their clothes atop their heads, they forged in. Ash expected the charged river to feel different, but it was just warmish slow-flowing water. He slipped a little, ducking himself, and got part of his bundle wet.

On the other side, Kieran set his bundle down, then glanced back. He flashed a grin: "What the hell." He ran back toward the river, hopped up on a bit of flat stone, and took a flying leap. For a split second he was silhouetted against the sun, wet hair splayed behind, long legs curled up and arms outstretched, like some crazy bird. Then he hit the water with a gigantic splash.

Ash had to do the same thing, of course. And of course he botched it, slipping on Kieran's wet footprints on the stone, hitting the water hands-first where it was only about a foot deep. He came up yelping and popped a scraped finger into his mouth. Kieran, damn him, laughed. Then he turned thoughtful.

"Hey Ash. Does a river count?"

"What?"

"Remember what you said once? How when we got out we should find a lake and swim around until we get pruney?"

"Oh. Yeah, I guess this counts."

Kieran gathered up his hair behind his head, stretching, twisting to look downstream. Rivulets ran glittering down his skin, spattered off him in showers of diamonds. Ash aborted his motion to get out of the shallows, and knew he was staring saucer-eyed. The rushing in his ears prevented him from hearing the words when Kieran's mouth moved, though he fully appreciated the glint of teeth behind finely shaped lips. Kieran glanced at him, arching an eyebrow.

"Um. What?"

"I said, we don't have time to make raisins of ourselves. Which means we don't have time for what you're thinking about, either."

Ash gulped and tore his eyes away. "You're cruel."

Kieran laughed. *"I'm* cruel? You're the one *reclining* with your ass half out of the water. Get in deeper, get cooled off, it'll revive you. Then we gotta go."

Ash obeyed, hoping it would also cool the embarrassment, disappointment, relief, and blind searing horniness that were warring right beneath his skin. And that bastard Kieran was just laughing and splashing like it didn't matter. Infuriating and lovable. He was really enjoying himself. Was this the real Kieran, this whirl of energy and sparkling eyes and flashing teeth? Had the dour killer he'd first known been as much a mask as his own meekness? Probably exactly like that, he decided. He had that meekness in him, could play the mouse when threatened because it was part of him; similarly, Kieran had made a wall of the cruelty that was already in his soul, but could play in the river like an overgrown otter when he didn't need to defend.

Ash was warmed by the understanding. Kieran trusted him enough to cut loose. That was wonderful. But it didn't make it much easier to put his clothes on and leave the river behind only a few minutes later.

Up another twisting path through the rocks, they reached a dirt road, and started walking roughly west. Northwest, Ash thought, but he wasn't sure. The terrain was so confusing. They were really in the badlands now, and nothing was flat or straight.

"Where are we going?"

"There." Kieran pointed at a space between melting castles of sandstone which looked much like every other direction.

"I don't see anything."

"You don't see that smoke?"

"Nearsighted, remember?"

"Oh, yeah. I forgot. You'll see soon enough, I guess."

About an hour later, they rounded a bend to see a dozen buildings clustered around a shallow creek. The road went right through the creek, without even a bridge. Two of the buildings were large, square, and wooden, with signs over their doors. Most of the others were those little adobe beehives the natives built. At the end of the village, on higher ground, stood a small temple in very poor repair. Beside the road where it crossed the creek was a fenced area with horses in it. They looked tired. The whole town looked tired. Kieran led Ash down the road as if they weren't wanted men. He hopped the creek as lightly as if they hadn't been walking all morning.

Kieran stopped to lean on the fence, looking at the horses. Just past the corral was a shack built against the side of the stable, and on the side of the shack was a misspelled sign indicating that these horses could be rented.

"Can you ride, Ash?"

"Yes, please."

Kieran considered for a moment, then slapped the fence post. "Okay. Riding it is."

"Thank you," said Ash as they made for the shack. "I was afraid we'd have to walk the whole way. To wherever."

"Doubt you could," Kieran said, and pushed the door open. Inside was dark and surprisingly cool. The only furnishings were a small table and a chair; an old white man sat in the latter with his feet up on the former, head back, asleep. The rest of the single room was crowded with stacked barrels; one near the door was open, revealing dry oats and a scoop. A sign proclaimed it eight moons a bag.

Kieran knocked on the table. The man continued to snore. With a nasty smile, Kieran grasped the table by a leg and yanked it out from under the fellow's feet. Coming awake with a snort, the man flailed and fell off his chair.

"Ouch! Dammit!" Scowling and rubbing his backside, the man climbed to his feet. "You didn't have to do that."

"We did try knocking," Ash said sheepishly.

Kieran replaced the table with a businesslike thump. "Two horses and feed for a week."

"Right. Um." The man fumbled in his shirt pocket, producing a pair of spectacles. "Two. A week, you say?"

"Now."

"No manners, you natives." He continued to fiddle with his glasses, putting them on and adjusting their fit meticulously. Kieran reached across and plucked them off his face, startling an indignant "Hey!" from the old man.

"Ash, try these on."

Half guilty and half amused, Ash put the glasses on. He blinked a bit as things struggled into focus. He'd nearly forgotten what it was like to be able to see fine details. He peered out the open door, checking his long sight. "Better than without. Not as good as the ones that got broken."

"Fine. We'll take those too."

"The hell you will, you thieving --" The man stopped with a gulp as he found himself talking up the barrel of Kieran's gun.

"We'll pay for them, of course," Kieran smiled.

"Um." The old man swallowed hard. "Yes. Thank you. I appreciate that." Afraid to take his eyes off the gun, he scrambled blindly for a pencil and ledger book perched on a barrel behind him. "Um. Two horses. One week. Standard fee is one throne, plus one-five a week, five throne deposit or kind, that's per horse, and you'll need feed, two sacks per horse, that comes to, um --"

"Fifteen three and two," Ash finished for him. "And a throne for the specs."

In a moment of insane and pointless courage, the man drew himself up and said, "They cost me one-nine."

"You got ripped off," Kieran said. He put his gun away and pulled out a wad of paper money, thrusting it into Ash's hands. "Ash, pay the man. I'll pick out the animals." He shouldered through the side door into the corral.

Shaking his head and smiling, Ash peeled off banknotes. A ten-throne note, six ones, four signets. When he looked up, it was down the length of a rifle. Where had the old man had that hiding?

While his mind froze, his body went on moving. He put the counted money down on the table, and slipped the rest into his pocket. The one that had the revolver in it. He saw a speck of rust on the end of the rifle barrel, saw his own left hand coming up to catch the rifle's end and thrust it upwards. He thumped it against the low ceiling of the shack, locking his arm straight, while his right hand seemed to remember how to cock the pistol without his intervention. He stopped short of aiming it at the old man.

"I believe my change is eight moons," he said, and the calm in his own voice astonished him.

"You're those escapees," the old man said. "The ones the Watch was asking about."

"We've done you no harm. Let's not start, okay? Let go of the rifle. Let go. Thank you." Ash slung the rifle over his shoulder on its grimy strap.

"You're not bringing my horses back, I'll bet."

"Probably not. I think you should get that feed ready." Ash looked at his pistol and sighed. He took his finger off the trigger and eased the hammer up. "Hell, I'm not going to shoot you. But my friend gets impatient." When the man still hesitated, Ash added, "He kills people. In batches, to save time."

Nodding so his jowls shook, the old man snatched a stack of bags off a shelf.

When Kieran came back in, he looked from the sacks of feed on the table to the cowering proprietor to the rifle that had appeared across Ash's back. "What happened?"

With a wry smile, Ash unslung the rifle. "This kind gentleman gave us a present."

Kieran took it, examined it, tossed it at the old man's feet. "Rusted out piece of shit's more likely to blow up in your hands than shoot straight. We'll get you a better one in Canyon." He pointed at the old man. "We were never here, understand?"

The man nodded, looking down at his rifle as if it were a poisonous snake.

Outside, two horses were saddled and waiting. There was a dark-gray gelding who danced and nodded in excitement, and a bay mare who regarded the gray's antics with cool scorn.

"You get the bay," Kieran said.

"Why am I not surprised?" Ash patted the mare's neck, let her whuffle his hair, getting to know him. "I'm going to have the last laugh, you know. Look at this lady's big feet. Look at her big fat butt. We hit a patch of soft ground and she'll leave your jumpy gray way behind."

Kieran smiled. "Could be."

"The old man said the Watch had been 'asking about' us, by the way. Which doesn't sound like some printed notice. They were here."

"Already? That's not so good." Taking the gray's bridle, Kieran set off toward one of the two large buildings, the one with a sign that read 'Hengist's Dry Goods.' "You hungry?"

"Yeah, but shouldn't we get out of town? That man --"

"Won't do anything. I know him. Course, he doesn't remember me 'cause he's a racist dipshit and we all look alike to him, but I pulled that once on him already. Pay for a week, they can't report the horses stolen until the week's up. By which time you're in West Mauraine for all he knows."

"But he knew who we are. He said 'You're those escapees.' What if he --"

"Suddenly decides to risk his life to do his civic duty? He'll wait until we're gone."

"*Immediately* after we're gone. So why pay for the horses?"

"I didn't know the Watch was here," Kieran said patiently. "You want to go take the money back?" He threw the gray's reins over the rail in front of the store, looping them in a one-handed half-knot as if he'd done it a thousand times. Which he probably had. Ash was a little slower about tying up his own horse; he'd never owned one, and it had been a couple years since he'd ridden.

Kieran waited for him, with no sign of impatience. *It's like he doesn't want to risk letting me out of his sight. Does he even know he's doing it?* Ash hurried to join him, not wanting to test this new attitude too far.

A plump middle-aged woman behind the counter glared at them suspiciously as they came in. Her suspicion only deepened when Ash handed Kieran what was left of the money. She leaned back when Kieran came and put his hands flat on the counter.

"Hafta wait outside," she belched out.

Kieran tilted his head. "What was that?"

The woman found a bit more space behind her, and occupied it. She pointed at Kieran and spoke with exaggerated slowness. "You. Hafta wait. Outside. No darkie, see? No *wizgi*."

Ash darted forward just in time to catch Kieran's hand before he could draw his weapon. "Let me talk to her, okay? Please?"

"Like hell I'm gonna let some pea-brained sow push me around. What happened to the old lady used to run this place? How do you expect to make any money around here if --"

"You ain't nothing but trouble, you people. Now git outta my store."

"Kieran, please. Please. Just take a step back, okay?"

Kieran turned his glare on Ash; if he'd been giving the shopkeeper that look this whole time, Ash was surprised she was still standing. His green eyes were like glowing pools of poison. But Ash stared him down, and after a long breath, he relaxed into a bitter smile. "Sure. Since you asked so nicely." He put his hands up in surrender and stepped back.

Ash turned to the shopkeeper. "Ma'am, you've offended us both by talking to my friend that way. We'd really like an apology from you."

"Like hell. You can both get outta my store, you and your sand-rat pal."

"I see." Ash shrugged and put his hand in his pocket. *I can't believe I'm doing this.* He drew his gun and aimed it at the woman's face, deliberately cocked it. "Open your till, please."

Behind him, he heard Kieran give a small, surprised

laugh. "Oh, Ashes."

"Well, she wouldn't apologize. The till, ma'am."

The woman stared at him a moment longer. Then, with shaking fingers, she got a key from her pocket and unlocked the drawer. She stood back, hands up by her ears.

"Very good," Ash said soothingly. "Thank you. Now I'd like you to pack us some picnic lunches. How about, what, ten pounds of flour? Couple pounds of coffee, couple pounds of sugar -- what else, Kieran?"

With a smile in his voice, Kieran rattled off a long list as if reading it from a page. While the woman got what Kieran asked for, including a pair of prospector's knapsacks and some saddlebags to load it all in, Ash moved around behind the counter and cleaned out the till. There wasn't much in it, maybe twenty thrones in paper and coin. All the time, the thought kept going through his head: *I can't believe I'm doing this. I can't believe I'm doing this.*

"Thank you *so* much," Kieran drawled as he slung a pack over each shoulder. "You've been a great help to us, ma'am."

"And so polite and friendly," Ash added. "We'll be sure to visit again next time we're in town."

Still with her hands raised, the woman spat. "The Watch'll get you. They know where you are."

"Oh? And do you know where *they* are?" Ash smiled sweetly.

Too quickly: "No, no."

"Please don't lie to us, ma'am. It makes us sad."

"I -- I ain't --"

Ash leveled the revolver, wondering if he was about to pull the trigger. The heel of his hand was already anticipating the kick. Lying to an Empath; she was too stupid to live.

"They're next door!" the woman blurted, eyes going round. "They're at Bee's, asleep! They came in this morning, asked around, then got rooms! I have three children, please don't, please don't kill me." Her fear was so intense, it was like a kind of amazement, around her in a cloud, blinding her.

Kieran chuckled. "Don't kill the lady, Ash. Don't want to deprive those poor kiddies of the chance to grow up bigoted and rude, right?"

"It would sure be a shame." Grinning, Ash saluted her with his gun and backed out of the store.

Outside, he put the gun away and took one of the packs from Kieran, tried to hide the way his hands shook as he untied his horse. Kieran was already in the saddle by the time he got the loop undone. The Iavaian was staring up the street at the building marked 'Bee's Tavern -- Rooms to Let.'

"I'm tempted to go see if they're really in there."

"For god's sake, Kieran, can we get out of here?"

"Lost your nerve?"

"I'm about to lose my lunch." Ash was thankful for the placid temper of the mare, because his pack nearly overbalanced him as he mounted. "I just *robbed* someone. At gunpoint!"

"And it was *beautiful*." Kieran grinned. He bent over the gray's neck and kicked its flanks hard. "Yah!"

"Wait! Oh, hell." Ash tried to follow, but the mare wouldn't do better than trot. He left the nameless village in a cloud of Kieran's dust.

All the way out of town, he kept feeling eyes on his back. Each time he turned, though, the road was empty. The feeling persisted even after he was out of sight of the village. At the top of a rising loop where the eroded ground opened out into a high plain, he found Kieran waiting for him, still looking delighted. Only then did the sensation of being watched go away.

"Please stop looking so happy," Ash said as they began riding side by side at a calmer pace.

"What, you don't want me to be happy?"

"*Be* happy, yes, but --"

"But don't *look* happy? Maybe I'm prettier when I sulk?" Kieran pulled a long face, sticking out his lip and batting his eyes comically.

Shaking his head, trying to clear it, Ash rubbed his dust-stung eyes. "Be serious. I didn't mean -- I like to see you smile, Kieran, you have the most beautiful smile in the world, but --"

"Don't get sappy on me."

"-- but that's the problem, don't you see? It makes me proud of what I did, and that's not something I want to be proud of."

Kieran raised an eyebrow at him, and said nothing for a while. The silence stretched long enough that Ash was startled when Kieran reached out and flicked his sleeve. "Tell you what, Ashes. You go ahead and feel bad for what you did. But be proud of how well you did it. That was one of the sweetest robberies I've ever been in. Just calm and clear, you told the bitch what to do and gave her room to do it, enough threat to get the job done and not enough that she freaked out and did something desperate. And you have to admit she deserved it."

"Kieran --"

"Go on. Admit it."

Ash found a smile on his face, wiped it off, felt it come back. "Okay. She deserved it."

"How much did you get?"

"Chump change. About twenty thrones."

"Hang onto it. Just in case we get separated."

The bay sidled and snorted as Ash tensed in alarm. "Separated? You're planning something that could split us up? Kieran --"

"No. I said I wouldn't ditch you." Annoyed. "I'm just covering all the angles. Let's pick it up now -- wouldn't be surprised if those Watchmen are half an hour behind us." Kieran sighed at the way Ash twisted in the saddle to look behind. "On tired horses. And I took the only decent ones at the livery. Plus they'll be lazy, 'cause they can track us."

"Oh god. They can. Horses can't walk on the rails, Kieran, they'll lame themselves."

"I know. It's covered. Trust me. You trust me?"

"Yes."

"Shit, I was afraid you'd say that." Kieran grinned, and nudged his mount to a faster walk.

Chapter 17

The road swung between north and west, paralleling the river in long, slow sweeps, though usually so far from the water that hills blocked the view. To the left, the broken land ran raggedly alongside, sometimes so far that the golden stone had a gray tint, sometimes so close that the road had been blasted through a cliff. As the sun began to sink before them, they came to a crossroads.

Back was Smith 12 and Burn River 28. Ahead were the Carver, Blackrock, and Harden mines, 21, 40, and 86 respectively, making Ash wonder if anyone bothered to take the road that far when there must be rails laid to those places to get the ore out. To the right, a small track was labeled Leyden Farm. To the left, the sign said Canyon Township was 24 miles away. Kieran turned left.

"Wait a second," Ash said, and Kieran obligingly reined in.

"Problem?"

"We're actually *going* to Canyon? I thought you were saying that in front of that old man as a kind of misdirection."

"What good would that do? They can track us, remember?" Kieran started down the Canyon road. "Never leave a live enemy behind you. I know this area better than just about anybody. Me and Shan had a shack upstairs of Canyon, up on Blind Horse Hill. I wonder if it's still there." He shook his head, frowning. "What am I thinking? It hasn't been half a year since I saw it last. Of course it's still there."

Ash sensed the sadness behind the words, and decided to do Kieran a favor by ignoring the digression. "So you're planning an ambush."

"Yep. There's a great place for it, up this way a stretch. Used it a few times before. Nice high rock, good campsite behind it, and you can see about a mile back down the road. We'll just pick them off. Wish I had a decent rifle, I can't do anything at range with a short barrel."

"Do we have to kill them?"

"How long do you want to be running?" Kieran retorted.

"I don't think I can help. I won't try to stop you, but you'll have to do it by yourself."

"You were about to shoot that stupid woman, I could tell by her reaction. She saw it in your face."

Ashamed, Ash looked away. "Maybe. I don't know. Just -- don't plan on me killing anyone."

"Your conscience is going to land us back in Churchrock."

"Would you rather I let you count on me and then found I couldn't pull the trigger? Is that a good plan?"

Kieran's lips thinned, and he didn't answer for so long that Ash thought he wasn't going to. After several minutes, though, he said suddenly, "I'm an unforgivable asshole for making it sound like I'm mad you don't want to kill folks. I wouldn't even ask if I didn't think two shooters would near double our chances. But you're right about not planning on it. Fact is, I hope you don't have to kill anybody. I hope to -- fuck it, I can't 'hope to god' like people do, I don't believe in that shit. I hope to the *old* gods, they were right bastards but I know they were real. Be a damn shame for you to get twisted like me. That's part of why I didn't want you to come with me. I guess it's pretty unlikely we'll survive without doing some nasty shit."

He turned his green gaze on Ash, who was staring in surprise at this uncharacteristically long speech, and for once he didn't smile even a little at Ash's expression. Shortly he looked away again and continued. "That little robbery was a tiny tykes' birthday party compared to pretty much everything we'll have to do from here on in. We barely inconvenienced that bigoted old twat, and the fact is if you hadn't taken the lead, I would've just shot her. Just shot her in the face without giving a damn one way or another.

"I know I'm warped as all hell. Didn't feel nice getting this way. To keep that from happening to you, I'd have done anything, even send you away and let you think I was okay with it. Too late for that. Now I ask you to shoot somebody. Fucked in the head, me. Look, Ash, do you have the faintest concept what the hell kind of disgusting heartless broke-brained *thug* I am?"

Fighting the urge to smother Kieran with stupid reassurance, Ash forced himself to answer honestly. "You're a criminal, yes, a murderer, and that doesn't go away. You're badly damaged. Sometimes I'm a little frightened of what you might do. But heartless? Listen to yourself. And I'm sad, but not disgusted."

Kieran chewed his lip and watched the road for a while. A sad smile slowly grew across his face. "You're really a good guy, Ash. I mean really a stand-up guy. There aren't enough apologies or thanks, and that shit never changes anything, but I want you to know I'm glad you're around."

"Thank you," Ash said, a little stunned. "That matters."

"Yeah, it does, doesn't it?" Smile going bright, Kieran reached out and ruffled Ash's hair. He sat straighter in the saddle for hours after that.

The sky was still light when Kieran turned off the road into a narrow wash, but the sun had been behind the mountains for an hour. It was a rotten path, so choked with brush and boulders that they had to dismount and coax the horses along. After about half a mile, though, it opened up, curving back the way they'd come, and ended at a bit of sandy, gently sloping ground surrounded by flat-topped rocks the size of four-story tenements. Kieran handed Ash his reins.

"Should be water down there, you might have to dig for it. Don't make a fire unless you're sure it won't smoke." Before Ash could reply, Kieran was halfway up one of the cliffs, climbing a nearly vertical face of broken stone as if it were a hotel staircase.

Being busy keeps you from worrying -- Ash had heard that lots of times. It didn't seem to work very well, though. He gave the horses and camp chores his full attention, but he was still sick to his stomach.

Building a good fire was easy. He found quite a bit of wood caught in a dry jam in a narrow tributary canyon, and it was all completely desiccated. A single match, a brief flare of high flame, and it was burning quietly and steadily, giving off no more smoke than a cigar. Where Kieran had pointed him for water, he was pleased to find a tiny stream. Just a thin trickle, like something poured out of a teacup, but clear and steady.

He reorganized the packs and saddlebags. There was a shaving kit among the items from the dry goods store, including a little round mirror; he propped it against a stone and cleaned up his face. He didn't really need it yet, only started to get obviously scruffy after four or five days, but he had the time so he guessed he might as well. Then he stared up for a while at the rock that had swallowed Kieran. Waiting for shots.

There were fat felted blankets rolled up and tied to the packs, and an oilcloth, so he made a bed. There were also a skillet and a saucepan. Using the saucepan as a mixing bowl, he had a go at flatbread, certain that Kieran would laugh at him for it. Then he put some water in the floury saucepan and boiled it until it thickened. Handful of beans, some rice -- there wasn't much of either -- and the contents of a can of stewed tomatoes. It took some doing to find the can opener, but in the process he located a string of chilies and a box of salt. Amazing that all this food had been crammed into their packs.

And what if they didn't live to eat it? And what if the Watchmen had snuck up on Kieran and used some quiet magic to abduct him? The thought made Ash's chest tighten up so he couldn't breathe. Night's chill suddenly seemed more severe. He thought of Kieran up there on that rock alone, in the dark, waiting for his chance to do murder. It wasn't right. He didn't know what he could do to change it, but it wasn't right. Leaving the stew simmering at the edge of the fire, he went to the place where Kieran had climbed up.

There was a scuffing sound above, and a shower of dust. "You want me to fall on your head?" said Kieran's voice. "Get back from there."

Feeling foolish, Ash went back to the fire. Kieran descended in a patter of gravel, slapped dust from his pants. Ash said, "You don't think they're coming?"

"They won't move in the dark. They're not in a hurry. Besides, I couldn't hit jack shit -- it's pitch black down on the road. What are you making? Smells almost like real food."

"I'm not sure. I just sort of threw together some stuff I found. I wasn't really paying attention when you said what you were getting -- thanks for the shaving kit, by the way."

"Don't need your chin wearing a hole in my shirt at night." He picked up a slab of bread, took a thoughtful bite. "You made flatbread?"

"Is it okay?"

"It's just like my mom made."

"Thanks."

"She made shitty flatbread. She was a terrible cook." Nevertheless he went on eating it, tearing off big bites and gulping them down, barely chewing. Then he reached for another. Ash had to grab his own and hold it for fear Kieran would eat his share too. After a while he tasted the stew, and was surprised how good it was. He set it between them and they ate out of the pot with tin spoons. Kieran made sounds of approval. "Stick to this stuff. This is good."

"Total accident, I swear."

"Nah, you have an instinct for it. I think you have a cooking Talent."

Ash beamed. "Thank you!"

"Yeah." Kieran gave a wry grin. "You'll make someone a wonderful wife someday."

"Oh, go to hell. See if I ever do anything nice for you again."

"You will. I have no idea why, but I bet you'll go on being nice to me until it lands you in a pine box."

"You want me to tell you why?"

Kieran's smile faltered, came back forced. "Hell no."

Ash dropped his spoon into the empty pan. "You get to wash up."

After a moment's dismay, Kieran laughed. "I guess that's fair. Even if the flatbread was pretty bad."

"If you'd pretended it was good, I would have washed up as well," Ash retorted. He stood and stretched with a jaw-popping yawn. He went and lay down on the bed he'd made. Got up, moved a rock he'd missed, lay down again.

He wanted to be sleepy and content, listening to Kieran moving around the camp. Sleep was lurking; all his muscles ached with tiredness. But something in him was too tense. Knowing that there would be a fight tomorrow, knowing almost for sure that someone would die, it was different from the vague knowledge that their chances weren't so good. He lay on his side and watched the last red embers of the fire collapse on themselves, seeing Kieran as a mobile shadow beyond.

He was jolted out of a doze by his glasses shifting on his face. He'd forgotten he was wearing them. Now Kieran gently removed them and set them aside. Ash could see his smile by golden light; he'd built the fire up. "You gonna sleep with your boots on?" said Kieran quietly.

"Should I?"

"I'm not."

Ash groaned a little as he sat up, stretching muscles that had begun to tighten up from being at rest. His fingers were clumsy on his bootlaces. Meanwhile, Kieran flipped the buckles of his own boots one after another as if he weren't tired at all.

"You just made the one bed," Kieran said accusingly. "You're trying to get into my pants again."

"What do you mean, again? I've never been there."

"I mean you're trying again."

"But --" Ash finally got his boots off. "But we always..."

"You figure everybody always sleeps all cuddled up, around here? Now we have blankets, we don't have to do that anymore."

"Oh." *We're back to this stage again? I could kick him, the tease. Or am I being selfish?* "Well then. I guess I should, um, I'll just..."

"You'll take your damn coat off in bed, you rude bastard. Were you raised in a barn? Give it here."

Ash saw the glint of teeth, and realized Kieran was just playing with him again. He relinquished his coat, shivering, the fire's warmth just a stripe down his side. Wished he hadn't lost that blue sweater. Kieran draped Ash's jacket across their feet and spread his own long coat atop the blankets. Then he lay down in such a way that there was nowhere for Ash's head but on his shoulder.

Gratitude robbed Ash of all his strength. He took the offered embrace, and the sweetness of it made his eyes sting; he didn't trust himself to speak for a long time. And when he was finally about to talk, Kieran's hand began stroking his hair, and that stripped him of words again. In the end, he wasn't the one who broke the quiet.

"You remember once, you asked me about my real name?"

"Yes," Ash whispered.

"It's Kai."

"That's beautiful."

"It's a plain word. Spirit, courage, ghost, soul. Not sure which one my mother meant when she named me. She never said, I never asked."

"Can I call you Kai?"

"Not in front of people."

"I understand." Gathering his courage, Ash raised himself on one elbow, resting his other hand on Kieran's heartbeat, searching for clues in eyes that the firelight had turned black. He found only mild worry and calm affection. Now he couldn't remember how he'd meant to say it, and the sound of Kieran's real name closed his throat. "Kai."

"Now, don't you get sentimental on me." There was a smile in Kieran's voice.

"It's not sentiment, really. I just -- knowing that tomorrow --"

"I'm going to win, you idiot. Don't start talking like this is the last time you'll see me. I'm going to drag you across half this desert before I'm through."

"Promise?"

A low laugh. "I don't like to make promises. But that's the plan."

"When you say things like that, I believe you really like me. But sometimes you act like I'm a bother. And I -- I just really need to know. How you feel about me."

"Oh hell." Kieran's brow furrowed, and he bit his lip. The warmth between them passed on his sudden anxiety. "Ashes, I do like you. I do." The hovering 'but' was louder for being unsaid.

So it's my turn to be reasonable. I suppose it's about time. "I won't get mad or whiny if you don't say what want to hear. I'm asking so we can be clear with each other. I think we can do that."

"You can't just -- *Empath* it out of my head, then."

"No. I can feel that you're discouraged, that's all."

"Discouraged? I'm scared shitless. You probably think I'm just gun-shy."

"You have reason."

"But holding you off won't change our chance of surviving."

"True."

Kieran reached up and tucked a strand of Ash's hair back, watching his eyes. "The way you trust me, and how you act small and young, and you need me, and then I see the steel under all that cream and sugar -- it's confusing. And scary. And sexy as dammitall. I don't know what to do about it."

Ash swallowed down a reply that he knew he would have phrased wrong, not sure he could find a line between crude and stilted. Instead, going slowly to give Kieran time to refuse, he bent close enough that he could feel Kieran's breath on his lips. Their noses bumped, and Kieran gave a whisper of a laugh but didn't push him away. Kieran's hand found the gap between shirt and trousers and wrapped warm around Ash's side, the other hand still in his hair, not pressing. Waiting. Delicious agony. By tiny fractions of inches, Ash followed the trail of Kieran's breath. Lips brushed, dry, tentative, touched again and stayed. Kieran's hand slid suddenly up his back, between his shoulderblades, and pulled him down hard.

With a groan in his throat, Ash melted like wax, forgot

himself in the realness of Kieran's body all along the length of him. And this time Kieran was making sounds too, crushing him, bruising his lips, and it was better than anything, worth anything.

The first time they'd kissed, back in the prison cell, it had been tainted with hopelessness and fear, a tiny flame of comfort in smothering darkness. Now, though tomorrow promised danger, they were free, alone under stars thick as paint. Nothing to distract or interrupt. Ash gave his whole attention, knew nothing but this kiss, the heat and strength of Kieran's arms around him, the unbearable sweetness of his mouth, heavy coolness of his hair falling down around them when he rolled Ash under him.

Their legs twined together, and Ash was unprepared for the lightning jitters caused by Kieran's thigh grinding into his crotch. He couldn't get enough air, had to break the kiss to gasp, groan out his need, fumbling at the buttons of Kieran's trousers, biting at Kieran's neck and ear, tasting salt. He could feel Kieran's arousal, both by Empathy and by the obvious and rather frighteningly large erection just one thin layer of leather away from his hand. He didn't know what he was going to do once he got these pants undone, only that he needed them the hell out of the way. Quick, before Kieran changed his mind.

Suddenly Kieran's arms tightened so he couldn't breathe, making his ribs creak. The sand-and-syrup voice that was his greatest weakness murmured his private nickname into his ear: "Oh Ashes, my Ashes." There was no bearing that; he was whimpering, arching against Kieran's hip, pulling his hair; gone.

As he subsided into himself among whirling sparks and warm dizziness, he realized what he had done, and was horrified. Kieran drew back to look down at him, expression unreadable. "I'm sorry," Ash whispered.

"It's all right."

"Are you... mad at me?"

Kieran suddenly grinned, chuckling low in his throat. "Mad? Because you're so hot for me that you lost it just because I said your name? Hell no, I'm not mad." He moved aside. "You might want to go clean up, though."

Though Ash was still embarrassed as he went to the stream to wash, he began to be able to see the humor in it. He heard Kieran rustling around, probably smoothing the bedding disrupted by their rolling. Without turning, he said, "This raises an ambiguity."

"Yeah?"

"Am I still a virgin?"

"Huh. Hard question. Is it coming in company or actual boning that trips the virgin meter?" From the laugh in his voice, he was more amused than Ash was by this turn of events.

Finished, Ash got up to come back -- then stopped, and stood swaying beside the fire in shock. That rustling had been Kieran disrobing. He was sitting up, his hair spilling over his bare chest, the blanket riding low enough on his hips to prove that it was the only thing covering him. He gave Ash a wicked grin.

"Figure we better make sure," Kieran said.

Ash trembled as he knelt on the edge of the bedroll. He picked at his shirt buttons, unable to take his eyes off Kieran. Kieran laughed and pushed his hands away, began methodically undressing him. Not a speck of embarrassment.

Of course he hasn't any shame. He's done this for money. I might fear it meant as little now, if not for the way he said my name -- the way he's looking at me -- Ash swallowed hard as Kieran pushed the shirt from his shoulders with warm, scratchy hands. "When you say -- make sure -- do you mean --?" Ash gulped, unable to finish.

"Do I mean what, treasure?"

Nearly undone by this new term of endearment, Ash could hardly force himself to speak. "Do you mean, um. You know. Intercourse."

Kieran looked startled, then flashed a grin. "Only if you want to."

"It sounds rather unhygienic."

"It isn't really. But it's up to you."

"And possibly painful."

The laughter stopped. Kieran blinked at him, hands frozen on the second button of his trousers.

Terrified that he'd ruined everything, Ash begged, "Forgive me if I said something wrong. What did I say?"

Thoughtfully, Kieran let go and sat back, watched him with tilted head, eyes clear and mild under thick black lashes. For a long, still moment he stared. Then his lips quirked in an ironic smile. "It never occurred to me that you might want *me* to fuck *you*. No one -- they all -- I guess they wanted to see me on my knees. Pretend they tamed me."

"It would be a lie."

"Yeah. It would."

"I'm not everyone."

"Ashes, I will do whatever you want, or if you want to stop we can, I just want your first time to be what you hoped for. Damn it, I sound fucking moronic. What I'm trying to say is, this is for *you*, okay?"

"What I hoped for," Ash echoed. He set a hand on Kieran's chest, felt the pounding of his heart. Made a decision: he was afraid, but he needed to be *connected*. "It doesn't sound crude when you say it, but it feels... weird... in my mind. In my voice in my head." He sighed as Kieran's arms scooped him in closer, then took a sharp breath at what he felt beneath the covers.

"Go ahead and be weird then," Kieran murmured.

His voice came out as a tiny whisper, but he said it: "Please fuck me."

Kieran replied by drowning him in a kiss. Finished stripping him with a few efficient movements. Rolled them both in the blanket, nothing between them, skin on skin, amazing -- all tenderness now -- long slow kisses, warm dry friction of hands exploring. After sweet ages of this, when Ash was gasping hoarse breaths and could hardly see for the spinning in his head, Kieran let go and rolled away to dig in one of the packs. Came back with the tin of cooking oil. Chuckled at the look on Ash's face.

"You look like you're changing your mind."

"No," Ash said, though his voice shook. "Still want it."

And he did, he knew he did, but he still wasn't quite ready for the sensation of oiled fingers teasing at him. He felt his eyes go big as saucers, locked onto Kieran's steady gaze and slight smile. Kieran didn't seem to think this was disgusting, or in any way shameful. It felt weird, definitely, but not bad, and it didn't hurt. Ash began to think he might rather enjoy the physical part of this connection -- and then Kieran touched something inside him that sent a scalding wave through him, and his cry was as much shock as pleasure.

Kieran whispered against his cheek: "You didn't think it would feel this good, did you?"

"Ah god -- no, I didn't expect it to -- to feel good at all."

The whisper moved to his ear. "You thought you were making a sacrifice?" Teeth in his earlobe, steely arm around his waist, and the red wave came again, forcing a wild groan out of him. He couldn't answer. Words were gone. When the fingers were withdrawn, he whimpered a protest, distantly shocked at how wanton he sounded. As Kieran lifted his knees, a tiny remnant of his civilized sensibilities chattered at him in horror, just for a moment, knowing the disgust society had for this. But the rest of him was unanimous: *This is exactly right. It's everyone else that's wrong.*

More whispers. "Relax as much as you can. This might sting a little." Breath from the words vibrated his skin, and he couldn't explain that he didn't give half a damn for 'sting a little', he wanted it *now* dammit, every atom in his body was hungry for it. When Kieran pushed at him, too tentative, too careful, he pushed back. Grabbed handfuls of Kieran's yard-long hair and pulled. He felt Kieran's pleased surprise. Then a shudder of hot sweetness, a hundred times better than before. He felt stretched, but that small twinge couldn't compete. Kieran overwhelmed him. His Empathy opened to a new level, all at once, and he could no longer tell which feelings were Kieran's and which his own, marvelous confusion, a flood of fire and diamonds.

Holding him tightly, Kieran began a tide-slow rhythm, shaking from the effort of being so gentle. Ash's incoherent cries begged him to stop holding back, *just go, harder faster, pound me to powder, I can't take this* -- but Kieran refused. Almost-kissing, lips just touching, he breathed shudderingly into Ash's mouth, eyes half open, feasting on Ash's desperation.

Ash finally managed to sob out his name. "Kai, ah Kai please --"

"My Ashes, treasure, precious, wonder -- *ediyana, kii aveh, kini, inai* --"

The string of endearments was too much, and when Kieran lapsed into Iavaian, Ash could no longer bear it. This time was far more intense; started deeper, peaked higher, blew every nerve like a blasting charge, destroyed him utterly. And just as the white fire began to recede, Kieran let go restraint and thumped hard into him with a groaning cry, which brought Ash, impossibly, to a second peak. Mind ended. Self was gone.

The world slowly reassembled. They moved apart a little to lie side by side, only half embracing, heads leaning together with foreheads touching, as if they could pass thoughts back and forth that way. Damp skin cooled. Kieran pulled up the blanket with clumsy movements. Ash finally found a word:

"Sticky. Ek."

A breathless chuckle from Kieran. "Yeah, that happens." Several seconds later, he went on, "Was that what you wanted?"

"How could I have known to want that?" Squirming closer, Ash pushed his fingers into the heavy mass of Kieran's hair, scratching lightly. This brought a happy noise from Kieran, so he went on doing it. "I had no idea anything could be so good."

"Mm. Glad."

"I just wanted to be as close to you as possible."

"Heh. That was about it."

"Yeah." There didn't seem to be much else to say. Despite stickiness, Ash was nodding off. He was too happy to move. He just barely managed to keep his hand going through Kieran's hair, since he could feel how much Kieran liked that. Just before he lost even that volition, he remembered one more thing he wanted to say. "I love you. I love you so much."

Kieran's answer was a faint snore. He hadn't heard.

That's all right, Ash thought. *Next time I'll say it before he falls asleep.* Content in this resolution, he let go of consciousness as well.

Chapter 18

His temple was in a deep cave from which a spring ran, and there the leaders of the people came to dream prophetic dreams. They brought sacrifice of smoke and song; or, if their need was great, blood and bone. Sometimes he gave them oracles. Sometimes he ignored them. They were his to do with as he pleased.

Ka'an, they called to him, *Dreamer, king of storm and darkness, bright-eyed, keeper of secrets, hear us, answer our prayers.*

They brought forth the offering. The sacrifice stumbled dazed to the spring and lay himself down, staring, eyes like circles of blue paper. Drugged, or drunk with lust. His cheeks were flushed, breath shallow, and when the knife went in his cry was one of ecstasy.

And the prophecy came, and it was this:

All we know is a lie, and the time of liars is ending.
All we know is fear, and the time for cruelty has come.
All we know is a dream, and it is time to wake.

They backed away, shaking their heads. They did not want this oracle. But the eyes of the sacrifice shone, and his blood-filled mouth moved with words:

"Kieran, wake up now."

Colors smeared; meaning fled.

"Kieran. Come on. I'm not going to shake you, you'd probably punch me, but I really don't fancy the idea of those Watch bastards sneaking up on us while you snore."

The images sank into the darkness behind his eyes; he opened them to predawn indigo. Ash was squatting a few feet away, dressed, hands dangling over his knees, talking in a near-whisper.

"Yes, it's early, but for all we know they're early risers, and we probably want the camp packed up just in case, right? I made coffee. Do I need to wave it under your nose?"

"I'm awake," Kieran said, which made Ash start a bit. "Didn't you see my eyes are open?"

"I can't see a damn thing," Ash admitted.

Kieran sat up, knuckling his eyes. "Since when do you get up before me?"

"Since I slept like a stone for maybe four hours and then popped awake. I feel pretty rested, actually. Found a snake in my boot."

"Really? I didn't hear you screaming." Kieran grinned as he got the sand out of his clothes and himself into them.

"Jackass," Ash said affectionately.

"Oh, *before* you put it on." Yawning, Kieran shook out his own boots, but discovered no interesting creatures. "Did you say I was snoring?"

"Like a sawmill."

"You're a big fat liar." Joking around. Suddenly wondered if Ash maybe couldn't tell, would be offended; but the redhead -- sweet boy, *edeime* to him now and oh it was good to remember -- gave an easy laugh.

"There was a sound coming out of you. For lack of a better word --"

"Do I always do that?"

"No, just sometimes. It's cute."

Kieran chuckled as he finished buckling his boots. "I've been called a lot of things, but -- I can't believe you said cute."

"It is. You are. I have the courage to speak the truth."

"Well, imagine that. All these years folks been shitting their britches 'cause I looked at 'em funny, and the whole time I was cute as a bug. They just failed to *recognize* it." He snapped his coat like a flag, dislodging a large spider and several beetles, and put it on. "Where's my scarf thing? Thanks." Not bothering with a comb, though he knew he'd pay for it in matted tangles later, he tied his hair back under the kerchief. He was too nervous now to spend time combing his hair, knowing what was coming. "You coming upstairs with me? You can wait here if you want. Safer down here."

Ash had begun rolling up the blankets, but now he sat back on his heels and shoved his hands through his hair. Looked like he'd combed his. The blood-ochre mop was brushing his shoulders, Kieran noticed, long enough to tie back. "No, I'll come with you. I don't really feel like wondering what's going on."

"Suit yourself." Trying not to show his relief.

By the time they'd eaten breakfast and packed up camp, the sky was flushed yellow-white with dawn. Kieran insisted on leaving the horses saddled and loaded, just in case. Then he pointed Ash at the cliff. "You go first."

"Ha ha very funny."

"Fine. You want rocks falling on your head and nobody to catch you, that's your business."

"Hang on. Okay, I'll go first. But no laughing." Ash went to the rock wall and craned his neck up at it, rubbing his hands together. "Right. Climbing."

"You got up that wall at Churchrock."

"I have no clue how I did that."

"Time's a-wasting, kid."

"Keep your knickers on, I'm going." Ash picked a handhold low enough that Kieran wouldn't have bothered with it, spidered his pale fingers around it, and began hauling himself up. Kieran watched with arms crossed, biting back unhelpful comments. When Ash was about fifteen feet up, Kieran started his own climb. It was a chore to go slow enough that he didn't end up climbing right past Ash. He wasn't sure he could be any use if Ash fell. Pebbles bounced off his head.

Halfway up, he realized he was in a better mood than he'd been in for just about as long as he could remember.

Above him, Ash had stalled out. Kieran moved up beside him to point out a hold. Ash smiled thanks before moving on, and Kieran smiled back without reservation. *You're not enjoying yourself, are you?* his inner voice mocked. *If you're not careful, he's going to make you happy. Quick, find something to be bitter about!*

Well, he answered himself, *there's the fact that I'm probably not good enough to keep him alive much longer. I dreamed him dead again, even if it wasn't me who killed him this time. If we hit serious trouble, and he can't fight, I'm going to have a hard time protecting him.*

What happened to 'I'm not going to stick my neck out for you,' then? Oh, you're a hardass all right, Trevarde. You just can't wait for a chance to play big strong hero. Has it crossed your mind that picking these guys off from cover might not impress him? Maybe you should go down and stand in the road, give them a little morality speech before you kill them.

Even this only made him grin at himself. He was just plain happy, and he couldn't wreck it for trying.

At the top, Ash was sitting around picking pebbles out of his palms, but he jumped up gamely enough when Kieran beckoned. It was about a quarter mile to the place Kieran was thinking of. The way was rough; ground that looked flat from a distance but up close turned out to be made up of cracks, wobbly rocks, and ankle-twisting holes full of deceptively solid-looking sand. Ash started to crouch as they neared the edge, but Kieran walked upright and stood looking down on the road.

"No need to sneak," he said. "We'll see their dust half an hour before we see them."

"What if they don't come?"

"What else are they going to do? Go home and say they had a lead but didn't feel like following it?"

"No, I mean, what if they're doing something different? Took a train to Canyon to wait for us, maybe. Or maybe they have some other options. I'm just trying not to get stuck on the one plan."

"Huh." Kieran sat crosslegged near the edge, still looking down the road toward where he expected the enemy to come from. "Well, you think about it. But I don't think they're scared of us. We might have Talents, but mine's untrained and yours is useless in a fight, so I don't see the Watch being real nervous about us. Them knowing pattern magic and so forth. I'm betting they'll come straight at us."

Ash didn't speak for a while; he made himself comfortable on a bit of hard-packed dirt, watching Kieran set out boxes of bullets and begin loading magazines. After a few minutes, he picked up a loaded clip and examined it, popped the top bullet out and pushed it back in. "You have strong thumbs," he commented as he put the clip down.

"You got your gun?"

"You realize I probably couldn't hit the broad side of a barn. For one thing, these glasses are a bit weak." Nevertheless he produced the revolver Kieran had given him, acting a lot less nervous about it than before he'd robbed someone with it. He turned it over thoughtfully in his hands, then surprised Kieran by taking a bullet from the box and loading it into the cylinder's one empty slot almost as smoothly as Kieran would have.

"Hey. You've been practicing while I was sleeping."

"Nope."

"Day before yesterday you were all --" Kieran dangled his own gun from two fingers, pretending to be afraid of it. "Oh help me, it's a deadly weapon!"

"I've been thinking about what you said. It's a machine. I get machines. Hell, I've studied diagrams of various different types of guns, I know how to make gunpowder, so it's --"

"Seriously?"

"Yeah."

"You know how to make gunpowder?"

"Black powder's not difficult. The modern stuff, what's in these, you need some chemicals that are hard to get legally. But yeah."

"I'm impressed."

Ash glowed. "Well, thank you. But I was saying -- if I know how something works, there's no point me being scared of it. Right?"

"There are probably exceptions."

"This isn't one of them." Ash stripped off his coat and folded it into a pillow. He put his gun close to his right hand when he lay down. "I can't promise I won't black out when the fight starts," he said with his eyes closed. "I'll try not to, though."

"Well, if you do, I know how to wake you up."

Ash opened one eye. "You do? How?"

"I'll just roll you off the cliff. That should get your attention."

"Bastard." Ash smiled. A few moments later, the smile faded into the slack face of sleep.

Kieran sat watching him for a time. He looked like he had in the dream. When he was dead in the dream. Something about the shape of his wrist and hand where it rested across his flat stomach, the length and paleness of his neck, the bit of collarbone and freckled shoulder visible where his shirt was pulled askew. Fragile. Yet Kieran remembered the surprising strength of those slender arms; hanging on for dear life as Kieran banged him into oblivion. Not at all what Kieran had expected, that request. Nor the unflinching eagerness with which Ash had taken it, or the abandon with which he'd enjoyed it.

A new experience for both of them; Kieran had only been on the giving side once before, when he'd pestered Shan to let him try it, and Shan hadn't liked it much. Had wanted him to get done and get out, had not come that way, and certainly hadn't begged for it with writhings and groanings and snapping teeth. Ash's reaction made him feel like a god. Addictive. He was hooked.

It was an effort to pull his eyes away to watch the road. *Mind on your business, Trevarde. You're gonna look like an idiot if you let the Watch sneak up on you while you're supposed to be ambushing them.*

So he scanned the distance, the way he'd learned to do when he and Shan were highwaymen: don't stare, don't strain your eyes, just let 'em wander around in that direction and catch on anything interesting. It felt strange to be using those habits again. How everything was changing, but some of it was familiar. He was different now from how he'd been the last time he'd used this ambush spot, but somehow more like that person than like the one he'd been a couple weeks ago, in prison. Had it only been days? It felt like months. And years since he'd last been the way he was today.

He couldn't go back to who he'd been before. Time had marked him. But apparently some of him was still salvageable. He could still feel things beginning, still be glad about it, even if he didn't trust beginnings at all.

So what was it that was starting? Not just the fact that he was now properly *edeimos* with Ash, nothing so simple or immediate. Something was lurking just under the horizon of the future, sending out rays, hints, pretending to be all bright and perfect, but the future always lied. It was something bigger than running and fighting, something that had his dreams in it, and something maybe about his Talent, a partial answer to the big question that had been hovering over him all his life, the question that was too big to put into words.

Which was ridiculous. Everyone had that same question, he was sure, and he'd long ago decided there was no answer to it. But the thought put an idea in his head about where to go next.

He had hiding places all over the western part of the province. Some he'd found with Shan, but Shan had never wanted to go too far from the roads that brought them their money or the towns they spent it in. Shan hadn't seen the point of wandering, hadn't liked solitude. The best spots were the ones Kieran had found alone. As a child, when he'd felt himself dug too deep into the hustler's life, crowded by pains and needs, sometimes he'd launched out into the desert to wander. Mostly he'd gone just far enough to get some solitude, a day or two, but in his early teens he'd started taking weeks and months of silence and sun to earn his sanity back. After he'd learned well enough how to find water and what he could eat, he'd gone out several times with the intention of living out there and never going back, or dying out there if that was his fate. He'd always thought he could defeat loneliness. In the end, loneliness had always won.

But if he had Ash with him...

He shook his head ruefully. No way was Ash going to

want to live off the land, fifty miles from the nearest plumbing. And even if he were crazy about the idea, it wouldn't change the fact that they were cornered, in purely reactive mode. But the idea of having Ash around pretty much indefinitely was looking better every day. And more plausible as well, so that he felt like a self-defeating idiot for assuming there was no chance Ash would survive. Ash had guts, he'd make it. *How come I'm getting optimistic all of a sudden? Did I just need to get laid?*

Before he could examine it too deeply, a drifting twist of dust to the northeast caught his attention.

Relieved to have something simple to deal with, even if it might kill him, he studied it to see if it could just be a dust devil. After a few seconds he was sure it was not. He gathered up his loaded clips and stretched out a leg to kick Ash's foot. "Wake up. They're coming."

Ash tensed and snorted in confusion as he woke. His hand went immediately to the revolver beside him. Without sitting up, he scooted back from the edge, wriggling into his jacket as he went. He whispered, "What do you want me to do?"

"First, come here."

Too slowly, as if his reluctance could postpone the fight, Ash obeyed. His response to Kieran's kiss was lukewarm at first, so that Kieran began to worry that he'd misjudged everything, but after a moment's hesitation Ash grabbed him tightly and kissed back hard. Then released him with decisive suddenness. "And now what do I do?"

"Hide." Kieran stretched out on the rock, forcing his attention back to the dust plume. He aimed his thumb over his shoulder. "There's some brush and stuff back there, right? Get behind it and stay down. And if something goes wrong, you run. Get to the horses and go."

Ash gave an incredulous snort. "Go *where*, Kieran?"

"Anywhere." He waited, but got no answer, heard no movement. "You hear me? If I buy it you better run like hell."

"Somehow I don't see that doing any good. Just concentrate on your shooting." Ash slapped the side of Kieran's boot as he went past.

"Ash -- Ash -- Ashleigh Trine, I'm talking to you!" He twisted around to see that Ash had stopped in a half-kneeling crouch, looking back at him with a sad little smile.

"Be serious," Ash said. "If they beat you, I don't have a chance. But don't worry, I'm not going back to Churchrock."

He pressed the revolver's muzzle under his chin briefly, then put it away. "So if you, um, buy it, hold up a minute on the other side and wait for me." He turned and dashed off toward the clump of brush, and Kieran couldn't yell after him for fear of the enemy hearing it.

Fuming, Kieran scowled out at the gray-brown plume growing nearer. *Thanks a lot, Ash, like I needed more pressure.* But something warm and sweetly painful snaked through his guts and made him feel more awake than he'd ever been before. He was irrationally certain, all of a sudden, that he couldn't possibly lose, because Ash was counting on him.

These few minutes of waiting were always the worst. Knowing that if he'd overlooked anything it was too late now. And these were White Watch, they could have any Talents and god-knows-what else prepped by ritual beforehand. It was a relief when he actually saw them come around the bend, small pale figures on dark horses, so that he could begin judging range and taking aim. He wished he could've gotten a rifle somehow. The Hart was a nice gun, but a short barrel just couldn't do what he needed right now.

A breath of wind stirred the dust that cloaked the Watchmen, and Kieran caught his breath in dismay. There was a third rider coming around the curve. He had his rifle over his arm, not slung across his back like the other two, and he was far enough behind them that they'd be past Kieran's position before he came into good range. As if they were anticipating an ambush.

"Shit," Kieran whispered. All right, if they wanted to play clever bastards, let them. He'd take the last man first. He shifted slightly, covering a piece of ground behind the two lead men. *Here we go,* he thought. It was as close to a prayer as he was willing to get.

The first two were almost under the rock.

The third rode into Kieran's sights.

Three shots smashed the silence, echoing, clattering like a rockfall. The third man began to raise his rifle, but he was falling from his horse at the same time. Kieran, ears still ringing, thrust himself half over the edge to empty the rest of the clip at the startled faces below. Everything was in motion down there, and the angle was bad; he heard ricochets and a horse's scream, saw one man starting to raise his hand in a looping gesture, flung himself back and rolled away.

Not fast enough. Something invisible punched him in the

left arm, jarring his elbow so that he threw his full clip up in the air instead of getting it into the gun. Chunks of rock and earth sprayed up, then pattered down around him where he lay sprawled on his back, knocked breathless.

There were a few words from below, but he was too deafened and suffocated to make sense of them. He forced his left hand to get another clip into the gun despite the buzzing numbness spreading up from his elbow. His fingers wouldn't grip hard enough to pull the slide back. He switched hands, managed to get a bullet into the chamber just as a tingle rushed across his skin. The air's temperature dropped sharply; his stomach lurched; instinctively, he lashed out at nothing with his heart's hand, and felt it turn away some kind of groping energy.

A figure in dusty white suddenly rose above the lip of the cliff, as if jerked by strings. He had a rifle aimed in Kieran's general vicinity.

Kieran was faster, but the Watchman was more ready. They fired at the same time. Kieran felt his right shoulder slammed against the ground, felt his fingers open and loose his gun, while the Watchman's head snapped back and then rocked forward in a cloud of scarlet. The rifle dropped from its flopping hands, but the corpse continued to hang in air. It was a second or two before it fell out of sight.

So the last man was the Kinetic. He could pop up anywhere. Kieran tried to lift his pistol, but his hand wouldn't close. He sent the orders, but his body ignored them. Goosebumps ran over his skin. Under the hot morning sun, he started to shiver. The only warmth on him came in the form of trickles that ran into his armpit and pooled in the hollows of his collarbone.

"Oh, fuck, I'm shot," he said quietly. His words were mushy, drunken-mouthed. His back felt wet now too.

It's only shock. You aren't hit anywhere vital. Just broke your shoulder, is all. Pick up that gun. His silent railing at himself didn't do any good. He still hadn't managed to get his finger on the trigger when a pale shape appeared beside him.

The man had come up somewhere other than the front of the rock. Kieran hadn't seen him, hadn't heard his footsteps. Still couldn't hear properly; the man's mouth moved, but it was just noise. He understood the smile that came next, though. They'd won. Kieran had lost.

Kieran's eyes jammed shut for a moment against a

sudden sting. *Ash is going to watch me get caught, and then he's going to blow his head off.* The fatalism in his thoughts sickened him. He forced his eyes open to the too-bright sky again. *Not fucking acceptable. I will do something, somehow.*

The Watchman spoke again, and this time his words made a sort of sense. "Where's the other one? I was told there were two of you."

Kieran tried to answer, but had to spit out something metallic before he could talk. *Great. It hit my lung. How many sucking chest wounds is a man entitled to in one lifetime?* "He's dead," Kieran gurgled. "I killed him and ate him." As he spoke, he began to feel his gun's grip resting on his fingers, and sent all his strength into that hand. But as he finally got a proper hold on it, the Watchman casually stepped on his wrist.

Pain ripped up his arm and across his chest; bile rose in his throat, and the world went all red and white. A helpless, broken animal noise came out of him. He hated the whimpering even as he couldn't stop. The man was doing it some more, grinding with his heel, trying to break Kieran's wrist. He felt the pain loosening the weld between mind and body, knew he was about to leap free -- and for the first time in his life, he fought it. He would not leave Ash behind.

Clenching his teeth, Kieran raised his head, sweeping with his left hand for a rock or a chunk of wood or anything, finding nothing, his only clear thought sent in Ash's direction: *Don't do yourself in yet, I'm not done.*

Then came the bellow of the revolver. He recognized it, cried out in dismay, his determination burst like a bubble -- until he saw the red rose that had opened in the Watchman's thigh.

"Get off him! Fucker, get the fuck off him!"

Another boom of thunder called a fine, dark spray from the man's gut, a slop of almost black blood drooling down the front of his white uniform. Only then did the man recall himself enough to raise his rifle. Too late. The third shot removed his face and sent him tumbling off the cliff's edge.

Kieran whispered, "Ash. Oh god. Thank you."

Scrambling footsteps, and Ash flung himself into Kieran's field of view, dropping to his knees. He was white as chalk, eyes too wide, but he held his gun as if ready to destroy anything that came near. "Is that all of them? Kieran, was that all of them? I can't feel anything, I think I blinded myself."

"That's all." Kieran's voice was thick, and he had to spit again. "I was so scared you'd -- thank you."

Ash forced a smile. The light tone of his words sounded a little strained: "Since I can't live without you, call it self-defense. Let's have a look at this." With infinite gentleness, he began unbuttoning Kieran's shirt, peeling it back from the wound. He was taking deep breaths to calm himself. It looked like it was only half working.

"How's it look?"

"Ugly. I can see bone. You'll have that arm in a sling for a while. There's a lot of blood, too, but I'm pretty sure you won't bleed to death. It's not spurting or anything, just trickling. The bullet went in just above the top of your ribs."

"Come out the back?"

"I can't tell yet. I'm going to cut your shirt off, I don't think we can get it off the normal way."

"With what? You have a knife?"

"Oh. Damn. Okay, look, I'll be back in two seconds, all right? God, I hate to leave you here."

"I'll live." Kieran mustered a grin. "Glad I left my coat off. Can't patch leather."

Ash stayed a moment longer, biting his lip. Blinking fast, he bent to drop a kiss on Kieran's forehead. Then he dashed away.

"Wait," Kieran croaked, but not loud enough and too late. He was glad Ash hadn't heard; it had been a reflex. He closed his eyes again; the sky was too bright. Waves of needing to cough ran through his chest, but the least tension of his diaphragm pulled so painfully on his shoulder that he couldn't complete the motion. He could feel the blood trickling in, tickling him inside, imagined it filling him up until he drowned. Suffocation was a hell of a way to go.

He rescued me. There's one for the books. That was some damn fine shooting, too, for a beginner. A nearsighted beginner. I wonder what the range was? See if I can stay alive long enough to ask.

Something cold touched his hand; he flinched, eyes popping open to the blinding sky.

"Damn it! Hold still, Kieran, I'm using the razor."

Kieran chuckled. "Trying to save me and you slit my wrists. How dumb would *that* be." Talking broke his resolution not to cough; he managed to croak out "Wait," before he convulsed. He couldn't quite spit right this time. It drooled down his chin. "Aw, yuck."

"Oh dear," Ash said in a small voice. His eyes were anguished as he tenderly mopped the blood from Kieran's lips with his sleeve. Then he went back to work with the razor.

Time broke down after that. Events occurred with no connection to each other. Kieran felt horrible and fine by turns; sometimes there was no pain, sometimes it was overwhelming. Sometimes he babbled, and sometimes Ash checked to make sure he was still alive. It was forever before he had to sit up so Ash could look at his back and inform him that there was an exit wound just above his shoulderblade, but then the world flickered and he was under a blanket while Ash made him drink water, his arm was bound tightly to his side, and Ash was shirtless and starting to sunburn.

"Where'd your shirt go?" Kieran mumbled.

"I used it for bandages," Ash answered patiently, as if he'd said it a number of times before.

"You have a lot of freckles."

"I think you're right that we can't stay up here, but I'm still not letting you climb down, considering the state you're in."

"Did I say that?"

Ash put his hands over his face. "Oh god. I don't know what to do."

Alarmed, Kieran walked his good hand out from under the blanket to touch Ash's knee. "Hey. Ashes. Don't cry."

"I'm not." Ash lifted his head to show a fake smile. "At least you stopped spitting blood. It stopped bubbling even before I got the bandage on. Maybe that part of your lung collapsed. Which would normally not be good, but in this case... hell, what am I talking about, I don't know anything about this. I didn't even study anatomy in school, I just read a couple books my aunt had. Kieran, we really need to get you down to the horses. Just hang on a bit and I'll think of something."

There was a lull during which Ash held Kieran's hand and periodically kissed the knuckles, even though they were smeared with dried blood. Kieran thought for a while that he might be falling asleep, but as the tickling in his lungs settled down to a dull feeling of stiffness, unreality began to fade. The blanket was way too warm, his shoulder hurt like hellfire, and his thoughts began to string together properly.

"Tell you what," he said, and something in his voice made Ash look up suddenly with an expression of relief. "You climb next to me, and we'll sort of leapfrog it. I mean, you find a hold, grab on good, and then kind of push on my back while I move my hand."

"It's a long climb. Do you have the strength for it?"

"Think so. If I rest once we get there, before we start down."

"Maybe you should rest here a while longer first."

"Won't help." Wincing and groaning, Kieran sat up and pushed the blanket aside. When he tried to get his legs under him, Ash grabbed his left arm and helped. He leaned on Ash while dizziness coursed through him and then faded. "God *damn* that hurts. Okay, let's do this."

Ash ducked under Kieran's arm, and together they wobbled across the broken ground. The walk made him tired, but it didn't exhaust him; he rested sitting, didn't have to lie down. While he rested, Ash ran back and got the blanket and canteen, scooted down the cliff like a lizard to get more water, came back up nearly as fast as Kieran would have. Between them, they drained the canteen. Ash tossed it down to the spot where they'd slept last night. The mark of the bedroll was clear on the dust. Kieran wished fiercely he could turn the clock back and be there again, live last night again a few more times before coming to this. He wasn't afraid of dying, but leaving Ash -- *You'll live, you bastard, because if you break that boy's heart by croaking, that's your only chance at redemption down the shitter. Your next life, you'll be a damn rattlesnake or something.* He wasn't sure where that thought came from -- he'd never been much of a believer -- but it still gave him strength.

"You ready?"

"Ashes, listen, I'm really sorry about -- you know. Everything."

"No, no, no. You say that kind of thing when you're dying. And even then it's kind of trite. Tell you what, if you ever get a good chance for last words, how about you just tell a long joke and leave off the punchline?"

"Okay." His smile was thin, but genuine.

"You really think you can handle this right now? We could camp up here tonight."

"Nah. We have to get moving. You can bet those whitecoats' officers know they're dead. No, I got it. It's not really vertical here, so if I slip I'll just kind of bounce and roll."

"And break your head open. Let's try to avoid that." Ash backed over the edge, then beckoned.

What followed was the hardest half hour of Kieran's life, at least in a physical sense. Going up and down had tired Ash out, so he sometimes couldn't quite hold Kieran up while he shifted holds; they both had near-misses, flailing and scrabbling one-armed at the rocks. With one hand having to do all the work, they tore up their fingers something awful. Kieran's left arm started shaking almost immediately, followed by his legs, and then his whole body was quivering like custard. Sweat poured off him. The wound hurt, of course, and his broken collarbone sometimes jarred and made him want to puke. Despite the water he'd had before starting, his head was pounding with dehydration before they were halfway down.

But Ash kept murmuring encouragement, even when his fingers were bleeding. The boy who'd been unsure whether he could climb at all now did the whole thing with one hand, hanging on less-than-certain bits of the slope to leave Kieran the easy path, and all the time he was saying, "I've got you, you're doing fine, left foot about six inches farther down, ready? You're doing great, we're almost there." Eyes so calm and kind that they seemed to numb away the pain like a pipe of poppy.

When Kieran finally reached the bottom and sank to his knees, Ash left him there and wobbled away. It was an effort not to call after him. Weariness warred with frustration in Kieran's mind; he hated being so helpless. His exhaustion kept him from expressing his anger, while the anger kept him from collapsing, but it was something else that snuck up and won the war: *So much for fragile. I didn't think he had it in him, not any of this, killing a man or dealing with a messy wound or climbing like that -- but he does have it, in spades. There's no telling how tough he really is. Steel under the meringue and cherries -- enough steel to arm a battalion.*

"This is going to seem stupid," Ash said behind him, "but it makes sense when you think about it. Are you all right sitting like that?"

"Yeah. What's going to be stupid?"

As an answer, cool hands gathered up his sweat-damp hair and pulled his kerchief off his head. It felt nice, but he was puzzled when it felt like Ash was combing his hair.

"I'm thinking about it, and it's still stupid."

It sounded like Ash had something in his teeth when he replied. "Just a second... I had the damnedest time keeping your hair out of the bandages, so..." The sensation of tugging changed from combing to braiding. "Otherwise we'll maybe end up having to cut it off. And I get the feeling you wouldn't enjoy that." Another minute, and the rope of a braid slapped against his spine. Then a damp cloth spread blessed coolness across his neck and back, washing off the itchy grit.

Kieran sighed happily. "Okay. Good idea after all."

"Still feeling all right?"

"Little tired. Sore. But the shock's over. I'm coping."

"Good. I think it would be easier if you rode and I led the horse. I mean, through that twisty little path. You want help getting up?"

"No." Kieran started, wobbled, stopped. "Yes."

Getting into the mare's saddle was easier than he'd expected. It was staying there that was hard. He was starting to be really sick to his stomach, very dizzy and tired. He nearly fell asleep while Ash attached the gray's lead to the mare's saddle, though it couldn't have taken more than a moment. It seemed to take forever to get back to the road.

When they reached it, Ash tried to turn back the way they'd come. Kieran said, "Whoa, where are you going?"

"You really need medical attention."

"I'm not going to get it in Smith. Not after we robbed the store."

"Smith? You mean that place had a name? Look, never mind, at least we can find some shelter. It can't be good for you to be out in the sun like this, and when night comes --"

"No no. Go the other way. That way."

"To Canyon? Kieran, we can't -- ohshit." This last was because Kieran had begun to topple off the horse. Ash managed to catch him in time and prop him back up, but he couldn't sit up straight anymore. He clutched the saddle horn in a white-knuckled grip, shivering. Some time went away; Ash moved around and did things, and Kieran studied the mare's brown mane. Light in the coarse hairs made strange shapes, pulled him in and lost him, and whenever the horse impatiently shook her head, he felt as if he'd been thrown across a room.

When Ash pried his foot from the stirrup, he thought at first he was supposed to get down, and voiced an incoherent protest. But instead, Ash climbed up behind him.

"Lucky we're both skinny," Ash said as his arm circled Kieran's waist. "No way would this work if we were fat. You can lean back, I've got you -- ow! Careful!"

"What? What'd I do?"

"Smacked me in the nose with your head, is all. Just relax and try to rest. I won't let you fall."

A pale hand reached past to pick up the reins. White fingers, pink knuckles, all spattered with freckles. As if someone had dipped a brush in liquid bronze and flicked a spray across silk. Kieran sagged back; their skin immediately stuck together with sweat where it touched, and his shoulder was aching even more now. But it felt good to rest. Good to know he was being supported and wouldn't pitch out of the saddle.

"Now." Ash's voice was soft in his ear. "You wanted to go to Canyon? Why?"

"No. Just before it. There's a crossing. Unmarked. It's hard to see... first flat place you come to, big open space... sometimes you can't see the road, it gets washed out. West. From there."

"And what's down that road? Shelter? A healer? You need a healer, or at least a doctor."

"Yeah. Show you when we get there. M gonna sleep now."

A kiss landed on the side of his neck. "Okay. You sleep."

Kieran's eyes were falling shut as the horse began to walk. He wanted to say: *Keep talking, it helps when you talk*. But his mouth wouldn't move. He sank into a strange, paralyzed state between sleep and waking, suspended between pain and comfort.

After a stretch of time he couldn't measure, full of whirling thoughts and windy silences, Ash's voice started up again. The sound was so near it vibrated his skin; the meaning so distant it took ages to filter down.

"I should have shot sooner. I guess I froze up -- not that that's an excuse. If I'd been helping all along, from the start, then maybe that, that *fucker* wouldn't have got you. Does it ever scare you how good it feels to shoot someone? No, I don't suppose it does; you're not afraid of anything. Except maybe me, sometimes. I suppose because I'm a thing that can be taken away from you, and you're scared that if one more scrap of happiness is stolen from you, you'll break. So the more you like me, the more I scare you. Maybe I shouldn't have said that, though." A slight shifting, as if Ash tried to see Kieran's face. Kieran could feel a smile lurking in his throat, but it didn't reach his lips, and Ash went on talking.

"You know what's funny? I felt the death when I killed that guy, but it didn't hit as hard as when you were shooting people at Shou-Shou's. It just numbed me. Sort of blinded me, like looking at the sun. That's fading now. Enough that I can tell you're sleeping better because I'm here. Don't worry. You couldn't get rid of me if you tried. I'm not going to leave you alone.

"I love you, Kieran. I'm not deluded, and I wish you could see yourself the way I see you. I'm not going to give up on you. You can't even get rid of me by dying, I'd follow you. Kai. My beautiful Kai. I'd follow you."

Kieran didn't like the implication of that, but was too far down to protest. Eventually, the meaning of the words Ash was murmuring fled entirely, leaving only a tenor lullaby to assure him that someone was watching over him while he slept.

Chapter 19

He'd run out of things to talk about and was mumbling nonsense by the time he found the turnoff Kieran had told him to look for. He babbled about that for a while, then recited some poetry he'd had to memorize in grammar school. It was terrible, stupid, self-righteous poetry, but it was all he could think of right now. And he had to keep talking, because whenever he fell silent, Kieran started to have nightmares. He could feel them through the place where their skin touched.

Throat-sore and thirsty, he could barely keep Kieran in the saddle. He rode straight at the setting sun now. From her plodding pace, the mare was just as tired as he was. The skin of his face felt tight with sunburn. Even Kieran was a little burned, despite his dark skin; some red was showing under the brown in places. They'd left the canyonlands behind, or at least that particular stretch of them. This faint track crossed a flat pan of featureless yellow-gray dirt. He prayed they reached something before dark, because it would be easy to get lost here, and they were almost out of water.

As the sun went behind the mountains, chill descended like a wall. He stopped long enough to get their coats from the bundle behind the gray's saddle, but he did it without dismounting; he was fairly sure he wouldn't be able to get up again. Careful not to let Kieran fall, he put on his sheepskin jacket, wincing as the dirty fleece scraped his sunburn. Then he arranged Kieran's leather coat like a blanket before coaxing the mare to walk again.

All this should have made Kieran wake up, at least a little. It didn't.

Now that the sun's heat was gone, Ash could tell that the warmth he was feeling from Kieran's skin was too much. Fever. Between that and the stupor in which Kieran seemed caught, which was even now pitching toward nightmare again, Ash began to worry that things were rather more severe than he'd thought.

But what could he do about it? Stop and make camp? Here, where there was no water he could find, and Kieran unable to perform his near-magical water-finding act? The horses were exhausted, Ash was exhausted, and Kieran was more passed out than sleeping, spiraling down into a fever dream.

"It's all right," Ash tried to say, but his voice scraped out like rusty nails. He couldn't talk anymore. So he tightened his arm around Kieran's waist and thought at him. *I'm here, I have you, I love you, I won't let you fall. Everything is going to be all right. Lean on me, stay with me, I'll take care of you.*

And the rising spin of fear broke; Kieran relaxed into more restful slumber as if Ash had spoken.

What was that? No one ever told me Empathy goes both ways. Well, no one ever told me anything useful about it, I guess. But if it can give Kieran any comfort... For the first time since he'd learned he was an Empath, Ash was glad of his Talent. He went on sending love and calm, while the light faded.

Just when it had become so dark that he thought he would have to stop, he made out a yellow speck of light in the distance.

So there was something out here, after all. He rode toward it, expecting more lights to join it at any moment, but none did. If it wasn't a town, what was it? A lone farmhouse? That might be easier to deal with, though he might have to sit awake and guard Kieran all night if it looked like the occupants planned to inform on them. Or god forbid, try to capture them. His weariness spiked at the thought, reminding him that he hadn't slept enough last night. Then up before dawn, a fight, lots of climbing, then riding all day -- on an empty stomach, he realized. He'd forgotten to eat. Kieran hadn't eaten either. Nor had the horses.

But there was this light. Coming closer. A window, a lamp in a window. A shape moving in front of it, alerted by the sound of the horses; window in a pale wall, square building, shaped funny on top... a dome. It had a dome. It was a temple. Of all the rotten luck. But there was no choice. What was a temple doing way out here?

A rectangle of dim brownish gold opened in the middle of the wall. There was a man-shape silhouetted in it, black against the light spilling from another room. A moment's hesitation, and the man came out into the night, head forward as if he were squinting, trying to see in the dark. He was wearing the long robe of a priest, open over more normal clothing.

"Hello?" A soft voice, uncertain. "Do you need shelter?"

Ash stopped the mare. The gelding tugged at the lead a bit, then stopped as well. Ash croaked, "Help?"

"Oh my. Miyan! Miyan, come quick!" The priest rushed to Ash's side, reaching up as if to take Kieran.

"No," Ash croaked. "Other side. Left... left side." He moved the coat they'd been using as a blanket, so the priest could see the way Kieran's right side was all bandaged up.

Another shape came out of the door, a smaller one in a skirt. There was a feminine gasp, then a burst of Iavaian.

The priest, to Ash's astonishment, replied in the same language.

Working together, the priest and the native girl managed to take Kieran's weight as Ash eased him down. He didn't wake. Then Ash dismounted, and immediately crumbled to his knees.

"Are you hurt as well, son?" said the priest.

"No. Just tired. Take care of him, please, please. Do you have any medicine? Bandages? Even clean water --"

The girl reached out to pat Ash's hand. "You no worry. We fix. You good man, bring him to help. We help." She bent over Kieran, examining the bandages. "What happen? You shoot him?"

"No!" Ash struggled to his feet. He tried to pick Kieran up, but his shaking arms couldn't even begin to lift the tall Iavaian. The priest motioned him away and, with a grunt of effort, picked Kieran up all by himself.

"Oh god -- careful --" Ash followed, reaching helplessly, but the girl caught his arm.

"He strong. You no worry. You worry?"

"Yes."

"Why? He good servant?"

"*Servant?*" Ash gasped. Then he flung up a hand to shade his face as they went inside; the lamplight was blinding after the dark outside. The girl tugged his other hand, leading him after the priest who staggered under Kieran's weight.

"Not servant?"

"Not even close," Ash said absently, far more interested in following Kieran than answering the child's questions. Squinting against the light, he saw that they'd gone through the temple part of the building and into a smaller room that contained a bed and table.

The priest set Kieran on the bed, then stood up with his hands to his back. "Whew. That is one large young man. Now, you --" The priest stopped, staring at Ash in sudden recognition.

Not knowing what else to do, Ash stared back, trying to show all the pleading he felt. He didn't say what he was thinking, for fear that he was misinterpreting the priest's look, but it was only a small doubt. Their descriptions had made it here ahead of them. The Watch must have spread the word to every tiny town and outpost as soon as the jailbreak occurred.

"You stay here," the priest finished. "I'll get the medical kit. I have a medical kit." He rushed away.

Sick with helplessness, Ash knelt beside the bed and took up Kieran's hand. Bowed his forehead to it. "It's going to be all right," he whispered. A shadow fell over him, and he looked up to see the girl peering curiously at Kieran's tattoos. She was probably about fourteen years old, round-faced, wearing a modest Eskaran dress of dark gray enlivened by a yellow sash. He wondered if he ought to take her hostage, in case the priest came back with a rifle. He couldn't bring himself to seriously consider it.

"*Kai'adiin*," the girl breathed.

Confused, Ash studied her face. "You said Kai. What was the other word?"

"One word. Holy man." She glanced over her shoulder, then turned back with a conspiratorial smile. "You no tell priest. Okay? Here, look. *Auanit*." She reached as if to poke the big tattoo on Kieran's chest, but found herself blocked by Ash's hand.

"Please don't touch him."

"I no hurt. Not servant, eh? You all --" she made a strange flapping gesture. "Like mother. Good friend, eh?"

Now it was Ash's turn to make sure the priest was out of earshot. "*Ediya'haan*," he said.

The girl's eyes went round. "Oh!" She glanced between the prone Iavaian and the white boy clutching his hand. "Too bad. I hope maybe marry him. Have big huge babies. Joke! No be mad. *Iavai'ai sheishu*?"

"No, I don't speak Iavaian. Sorry."

"Okay. Hungry?"

"Um. Sure, yeah. Thank you."

She dashed away, leaving Ash to wonder if she was simpleminded, or if it was just the language barrier that made her sound that way. The thought was drowned by a wave of anxiety from Kieran. Ash bent to soothing him, brushing back the wisps that had escaped his braid, forcing down the

241

nightmare. He was deep enough in this that he forgot to watch for the priest's return. It was a metallic click that got his attention.

He turned to see the priest standing in the doorway, aiming a shotgun at him.

Ash was too tired to be angry. The only emotion he could muster was sadness. "Don't do this," he murmured.

"I'm terribly sorry," the priest said. He looked tired as well, though it was probably how he looked all the time. Deep creases worn by sun and dry air made his face look older than he probably was; his bald head was sunburned. His eyes were as dark as a native's, and looked gentle despite the shotgun. "It's just that the notice said you two are violent, and I have my little Miyan to think about."

"You think I'd hurt her? What did they say we did? No, it doesn't matter." Ash let his head sag, made no attempt to stop his eyes from spilling over. "I suppose if I make a wrong move you'll shoot me."

"That seems to be the way it's done."

"Then all I can do is beg." He looked up, facing the uncertainty and dawning guilt in the priest's heart. "Save him. He's got a high fever, he won't wake up, his collarbone's broken and I think the wound might be infected, he won't survive without proper care." His vision, already blurry, unfocused entirely, and he sagged against the edge of the bed. He took off his glasses and rubbed his eyes. "I wish I could offer a trade, save him and you can take me out back and shoot me, but what good would that do you?"

"Well, you see, my duty to the Church means I have to assist the Watch however I can. Granted, you don't *seem* dangerous, but that's not for me to judge, is it?"

"You're the one with the shotgun."

"I suppose you're armed? The notice said you were armed."

Ash groaned. "Yes, look, I'm taking off my coat, both our guns are in my coat." He threw the jacket on the floor and shoved it away. "And money and everything, take it, just stop dithering and either help or fire!"

The priest stood there a few seconds longer. Then, with a sigh, he put up the shotgun, scooped up Ash's jacket, and walked away. A moment later he came back carrying a wooden crate. The girl, Miyan, was right behind with a kettle and a bowl.

"Thank you," Ash whispered.

"Yes, well, I still haven't decided what to do with you. But I can't very well let this young man die, can I?" Rooting around in his crate, the priest produced a roll of gauze and a cork full of needles. "How did this happen? Was he shot?"

"Yes. A rifle at close range. The bullet went through, but it broke some bones on the way, and it hit his lung a little. I don't think he's bleeding into his lungs anymore, though."

"How long ago was this?"

"Early this morning."

"Well, if he were going to die from a punctured lung, he would have done it already. Why don't you have a seat? Stay out of my light."

Ash stood, wobbled as dizziness overcame him. Looked at the chair the priest had indicated, and realized that he didn't dare be out of contact with Kieran. As if the only thing keeping Kieran alive was Ash's presence -- self-centered thought, that, but he couldn't shake it. So he moved around to the head of the bed and rested his hand on Kieran's brow.

"What's this? You think I'm going to make him vanish if you don't keep an eye on me?"

"He needs me," Ash said simply.

He tried to watch as the priest undid the makeshift bandages. It was getting harder and harder to hold his head up, though. He rested it on the pillow beside Kieran's, just for a moment. Just to catch his breath.

The next thing he knew, Miyan was tugging at him, chattering in his ear. Groggily raising his head, he saw that the crusted shreds of his and Kieran's shirts that he'd used for bandages were gone, replaced by clean white gauze. There were only a few flecks of blood spotting over the wound. Kieran looked cleaner, too, and his feet were bare. The girl was babbling something about eating.

"I'm not -- I'm not hungry, I'm too tired -- thank you, stop pulling."

"Up, up! Silly boy, you sleep on floor?"

He managed to get upright, but resisted when she tried to move him away, even when he saw bread and cheese and water set out on the table she was shoving him towards. "He needs me, he'll have nightmares if I'm not there."

"Eat!" she insisted.

With a last glance to Kieran, he surrendered. His stomach demanded it. While he was wolfing down the food, the priest returned, holding a lantern and wearing a nightshirt.

"When you're finished, son, let me show you where you'll be sleeping."

"Thank you, no." Ash washed the last of the bread down with the last of the water, pushed himself up on the edge of the table. He nearly knocked it over.

"I'm afraid I can't let you leave."

"Huh?" Ash blinked at him. "Leave?" He staggered back to the bed and sat down beside Kieran.

Miyan bustled around picking up the dishes, then pushed them at the priest, chattering. They had a little exchange in Iavaian. The priest cleared his throat. "You do realize," he said stiffly, "that what you boys do is a sin against God."

Of course he shouldn't have blurted *ediya'haan* at the girl, she was just a child, and had no reason to keep his secrets anyway. Ash gave the priest a weary smile. "Can we discuss that later? I just need to know if he's going to be all right. Is there anything I can do for him?"

"Let him rest. It's in God's hands now."

"God owes him a lot of favors; let's hope He decides to pay up."

The priest made a hand sign against blasphemy. Ash lay down along the edge of the bed, wrapping his hands around Kieran's good arm. Miyan rushed over and slapped at his leg, crying, "Boots! Boots!"

"Sorry," Ash mumbled. He couldn't move. He barely felt the girl taking his boots off. By the time a thin blanket settled over him, he was too sleepy even to thank her. He reached for Kieran's dream, twined himself around it, and let go of the world.

They rose slowly out of sleep together, simultaneously losing the thread of the same dream; Ash realized that just before he came awake. He opened his eyes just in time to see Kieran open his. They looked at each other for a while, gradually becoming separate, becoming real. Kieran glanced around, lost, frowning, then looked back to Ash and smiled.

"I dreamed you were here," he rasped.

"Every moment," Ash answered in a voice almost as ruined. His arm had gone numb; he'd slept in the same position all night. He sat up and tried to rub some feeling back into it.

"Where are we?"

"A little temple in the middle of nowhere. I took the road you told me to, and this was all I found. I'm afraid the priest wants to turn us over to the Watch, but I had to do *something*. You were in bad shape."

"I feel like shit. How do I look?"

"Better than last night." He felt Kieran's forehead. "And your fever went down. I'll see if I can find you some water."

Kieran's hand moved to catch Ash's wrist. "Not yet."

"Aren't you thirsty?"

"I'm -- yeah. But I'm just a little lost, still. Let me wake up. I'll come with you."

Ash tried not to show his concern. This was downright clingy by Kieran standards, and Ash wasn't sure how to interpret it. "I don't know if you should get up yet."

"I'm tired of being helpless. What if this priest..."

"He's got our guns. I don't know yet whether I could take them back; you're in no shape to try. I don't think he'll do us any harm, though, not after he patched you up so nicely. And there's this girl, seems to be a kind of foster daughter or something, and she's quite taken with you. She won't let him do anything wrong."

Kieran held his wrist for a moment longer, then let go with a sigh. "Yeah. Okay. I don't know why I'm being such a chickenshit."

"I guess being tough for so long wears you out. Take a vacation. I'll be the mean one for a couple days, all right? Just until you're back on your feet."

As he'd hoped, that made Kieran smile.

His boots were gone. No doubt the priest had hidden them, intending to keep the fugitives from leaving. That was all right if the Watch wasn't too close behind them. As long as they had a couple days, Ash guessed that he could manage. At the worst, he could clobber the priest with a chair or something and search the premises.

In daylight, the temple looked shabby. He stood in the sanctuary for a moment, noting that the benches had all been stacked against the wall, and the altar was dusty. There was a wooden eye-of-Dalan hanging on the wall above it, the gilding mostly flaked off, and a rank of candles that were so furred with dust he guessed they hadn't been lit in a year. What the hell kind of temple was this, anyway?

There were two other doors off the sanctuary. The first one he checked was locked. The other led into a kitchen, where the priest sat at a roughly made table with a book in front of him, half-round spectacles perched on his nose. He looked blankly at Ash, eyes bloodshot. A door stood open to the outside, showing a yard with a well, where the horses were tied near a trough. With a start of guilt, Ash realized he'd forgotten all about them. Fortunately someone had unloaded them, and they looked happy enough. Beyond the horses, all he could see was flat desert, all the way to the purple-gray line of the mountains.

"Good morning," Ash said.

"Um. Good morning. How is, uh, Mr. Trevarde? Still alive?"

"Awake and thirsty."

"Good, good. There's the water barrel. Cups on the hook there. We have nothing to drink but water, before you ask."

"No coffee?"

"Oh. Coffee. A little. I meant, uh, we don't..."

"Have any liquor. Wouldn't expect it. This is a temple, after all. Can I take this pitcher?"

"That's a vase."

"Can I take it?"

"Well, yes, I suppose. As for this being a temple, it's a mission actually." The priest marked his place in the book and closed it. "A failed mission. At least so far. I'm making a little progress with Miyan, I think. The rest of them, well, I was too late."

Ash turned with water dripping off his chin. "What are you talking about?"

As a reply, the priest got up and opened a shuttered window behind him. Ash went to look through it, and froze halfway through wiping his mouth. In that direction, there was a village, or the remains of one. The rounded huts were fallen in on themselves, like broken eggs. Some still showed scorch marks.

"What happened?"

The priest gave a weary shrug. "They refused to convert. I hid Miyan, but the rest, well, I couldn't do anything about it."

"The Watch did this?"

"Yes, they did. It's the law, you see, there's really no alternative."

"And how did the Watch learn that this village refused to convert?" He met the priest's eyes for a moment; then the priest looked away. For a long moment, Ash fought the urge to slug the man in the face. In the end he just went back to the water barrel, then back to Kieran.

He found the room full of Miyan. She was fluttering around, chattering like a squirrel while she did things that looked vaguely like cleaning. Kieran gave Ash a grin, then croaked a reply to the girl in Iavaian.

"Miyan," Ash said, "don't wear him out."

"She's entertaining me, Ashes. Let her stay. Damn, I'm thirsty, gimme that."

Ash sat on the edge of the bed while Kieran worked his way through the large tin pitcher that was actually a vase. "So what are you two talking about?"

"Tattoos. She likes my wind knot. Says there's a big one back in the hills a ways. Wants to show it to me."

"So pretty," Miyan put in, with a large hand gesture that scattered a cloud of dust from the rag she was using. "Big cave, so big *auanit* made all -- *haya*? -- all little rocks."

"A mosaic?" Ash said.

"All little rocks," Miyan repeated, and went back to her dusting.

Kieran finished the water and gave the pitcher back. He let his head fall back on the pillow as if raising it to drink had exhausted him. "I kinda heard you talking in the other room. What was that about?"

"I don't know. Nothing. There used to be a village here but the Watch burned it out. I think we should leave as soon as you can ride. The priest hid our boots, but I can probably find them."

"No no." Miyan gestured with the rag again. "Miyan hide boots. Hide coat, hide all guns. Miyan keep one gun, okay?"

"Like hell," Kieran said, but Ash contradicted him.

"You can have one of the rifles, if you want. We have a spare."

"Rifles?" Kieran raised an eyebrow.

"You didn't notice me taking them? No point letting the Watch have them. We don't have a lot of ammunition for them, though."

Kieran gave a laugh that was half cough. "You're all right."

"I bet you're hungry."

"Starving."

"Back in a minute." He stood to go, but found his way

blocked by a suddenly stern-looking Miyan.

"You no get food. Miyan get food. Man no cook."

"Why not?"

"Man no cook. Dalan say. Woman cook."

"Yes, well, I happen to be quite good at cooking, thank you very much."

Miyan put a fist on her hip, looking skeptical. "Dalan say. Man no cook."

"Kieran, would you tell her to let me through?"

"What makes you think I can change her mind? She's just as opinionated in her native language."

Ash sighed. "Look -- Miyan -- you can help me. Okay? Show me where you put our food supply. We have a big bag of coffee, you want some coffee?"

The girl blocked his way a moment longer before breaking into giggles. She punched his arm. "Joke. You cook. Come on."

In the kitchen, the priest watched sourly while Miyan and Ash ran in and out, stoking up the stove, fetching water. When Ash rolled up his sleeves and started chopping garlic, the priest cleared his throat.

"You do realize that the scriptures say that the work of the home is woman's. 'It is hers to make bread, and to see that the mouths of her family are not hungry.' You're going to corrupt my little girl with your invert ways."

"You're insane." Ash scooped the garlic into the pot and started in on some dried peppers. "Bachelors are supposed to starve?"

"Bachelor is a very kind word for what you are."

"Your moral high ground is pretty shaky, priest. I'd say your 'duty to the church' has probably killed more people than we ever did. Were there children in that village?"

Miyan blurted something in her own language and stormed out the door.

"I was wrong about you," the priest told Ash. "You're a demon." Then he followed Miyan.

"I'm sorry," Ash said, too late. He felt awful. He didn't have a lot of sympathy for the priest, but he hadn't wanted to hurt the girl. He went and looked out the window, and saw the two of them talking among the remains of the village. He turned his attention to the book the priest had left on the table. It didn't have a title printed on the cover; when he opened it, he saw why. It was a journal, and written in some kind of code.

Interesting. He flipped to the front, then the back, and laughed when he saw that the last page had been ripped out. So the fellow had developed his cipher in the back of the book and got rid of it once he memorized it. That implied a fairly simple code, maybe even a straight substitution cipher, if he could keep it in his head. What was he writing about, that he had to keep it in code?

Another glance out the window assured him that the conversation was nowhere near over. Ash snatched up the book and took it to the room where Kieran lay.

Kieran was asleep. He jerked and gasped when Ash woke him, staring in momentary alarm.

"I'm sorry," Ash said.

"What? What is it?"

"Calm down. Nothing really urgent, I just want to hide this."

Kieran frowned at the book. "Why?"

"Might be able to trade it for our stuff, I don't know." He lifted the blanket and slid the book under Kieran's knees. "I'll think of a better place later."

"You better. That feels weird."

"I will. Go back to sleep now. Food's going to be about half an hour."

"Sleep. Hell. Fuck sleep. I was having nightmares. Don't leave me here, I'm bored, I think I'm gonna puke and what if I choke on it --"

"Okay," he agreed immediately, feeling as if he were sliced open by the fear in Kieran's eyes. It didn't look right there.

But as Ash started to sit down, Kieran scowled and waved him off. "No, don't listen to me. I don't know what my fucking problem is."

"If you're sure... I'll just be in the next room."

"Go. Get out of here."

The priest still wasn't back when he returned to the kitchen. He could no longer see either of them out the window or the door. After a quick check of the cupboards, just in case Miyan had hidden their things there, he went back to work.

If I ever manage to stop being a fugitive, I think I'll be a cook. It's the only thing I'm halfway decent at besides writing inflammatory prose, and a lot less likely to get me in trouble. Wonder if there's a market for Yelorrean food in Prandhar?

A shadow crossed the doorway, paused a moment

before the priest came slouching in. He avoided Ash's eyes. When he saw the empty table, he stood still for a long time. Ash just went on working as if nothing was unusual.

"What did you do with it?" the priest said at last.

"What did you do with our boots and guns?"

"It won't do you any good. It's not a fair trade. If the Watch find out I had you and let you go --"

"What I find myself wondering," Ash interrupted, "is what they'd think of the contents of that book. Wouldn't take them long to crack a simple substitution cipher. I'm guessing I could do it myself in less than a day." The look of shocked dismay on the priest's face confirmed his guess. Ash grinned and went on, "Didn't the notice say? I was a bit of an encryption expert when I was with the Resistance. Kieran's got sort of a talent for it, too. Hell, he cracked one of *my* ciphers, which is damn near impossible. Granted he just guessed the key, but -- oh, were we done talking?" This to the priest's back as the man dashed into the sanctuary.

Ash followed and watched as the poor bastard upended his bench pile, looked behind the altar, growing more and more frantic.

"Damn you!" The priest rounded on him. "I should have let you have both barrels, you sneaky godless faggot! You're going to bring them down on us, and poor Miyan -- after everything I did to save her --"

"They're going to get you anyway. That hadn't occurred to you?"

The priest stomped into the room with the bed, aiming a scowl at Kieran before beginning his search. "If I turn you two in, they'll take you and go. But you'll tell them I have a book in code, won't you? Just for spite! And they'll take my little girl away and wreck her beautiful mind!"

"Why would -- her mind?" Understanding dawned. "Oh, you poor stupid trusting son of a bitch."

From the bed, Kieran made a sound of annoyance. "Ash, would you just break this fucker's neck for me? He's making way too much noise."

"Only if he doesn't settle down." Ash cracked his knuckles, which got the priest to stop searching. "Look, I don't know what kind of happy world you've been living in, but in the real one, the Watch don't give a damn for you or anyone. They have no respect. What did you think, you were going to get a medal? They'll rape your mind to find out if we told you anything interesting -- which is not fun, believe me, they did it to us a bunch of times. Then they'll probably kill you for knowing too much. And I'm guessing from what you said that you suspect Miyan's got a Talent, and you've been putting off giving her up to have it burned out. That's big trouble for you right there. You're screwed either way. So much for your duty to the Church."

"I wish you'd never come here," the priest said tightly.

"I'd be sorry, but I saw the village."

"Miyan's done nothing to deserve any of this."

"You're right, we owe her an apology. You, though... well, I just don't like you. Come on back to the kitchen, priest. We've kept Kieran awake long enough."

With a final glare, the priest stomped out of the room. Kieran chuckled and said, "You're gonna be the mean one, huh?"

"How am I doing?"

"Not half bad."

"I better go keep the pressure on."

He went back into the kitchen, just in time to meet the priest coming in from the yard, shotgun at the ready. The end of it was shaking a little, but at this range he couldn't miss. Sweat beaded on the priest's forehead as he nerved himself to shoot.

"That's one solution," Ash said, his voice level even as his stomach dropped through the floor. "Going to make Miyan help clean my intestines off the wall?"

Slowly, by inches, the priest lowered the gun. "God help me, I can't." He leaned in the doorway, weariness dragging down every line of his frame. "You can't understand. Life is cheap for you, you outlaws. You kill and leave. And I have to live with the evidence every day... it's like having a corpse in your bed. You just don't understand. I had to send reports, I had to report my progress, I never thought it would condemn them..."

Ash sighed, bowing his head. He was suddenly very sorry for everything he'd said to this man. "I shouldn't have thrown it in your face. You have no excuse to be naive again, though. If I were you, I'd watch for riders, and if you see dust on the horizon, take Miyan and run like hell. Or if you can stand our company, we could all leave together *before* they come for us. I don't agree with that 'life is cheap' comment, but we can defend you two better than you can defend yourselves."

"Oh, certainly, I give you those guns and you immediately murder us."

"Don't be ridiculous."

"You killed women, why not a child and a priest?"

"Women?" Ash shook his head slightly. "Can I see that notice you mentioned?"

"I -- I suppose." Warily, keeping a close grip on the shotgun, the priest edged past. He went to the locked room, and came out a moment later, locking it behind him. He'd exchanged his weapon for a sheet of cheap cardstock, which he held out to Ash at arm's length.

Ash's first reaction was a smile at the portraits. There must have been a sketch artist at the prison, because whoever drew these had obviously seen them in person. The pictures made them look much meaner than Ash thought they did in real life, and showed Ash with his old squarish specs instead of the round ones he had on now. Nevertheless they were quite recognizable.

Then he read the text. No charge of practicing unlicensed magic was listed, nor was concealing a Talent. The Watch were apparently keeping a lid on that one, which meant the priest didn't know. But they were wanted for the murder of eight people. Eight. Six of the names were male, and looked like the names of city-bred natives -- names like Addy Tallgrass and Laine Breakrocks. Probably the gangsters Kieran had shot in Shou-Shou's yard. But two were female: Jinnie Harkes and Amica Welard. His teeth creaked, and he had to force himself to stop grinding them. "Those -- those liars, those unimaginable *shits!*"

Despite a flinch, the priest said bravely, "You expect me to believe you didn't kill those people?"

"Not the girls! Those men attacked us, Kieran shot them, but not the girls! The Watch must have taken them or killed them in questioning. Oh god. Amica Welard; I think that's Ami. She lent me her bathrobe. Oh god."

"I see. You killed those women simply by existing. Now you know how I feel."

Ash stared at him in astonishment. "Are you going to stand there and feel sorry for yourself? I pity Miyan for having to live with you. Look, there's only one way out of this. Go find her, get our weapons, and let's all get the hell out of here. The sooner we go, the colder our trail gets."

"If I do -- imagine for a moment that I do -- is your...

friend in any shape to ride?"

"I don't know. We can ride double again, or rig a litter."

The priest dragged his hands down his face. Then he nodded. "I'm afraid you're right."

Ash folded the notice and put it in his pants pocket; Kieran might want to see it, later. "Hurry, now. We should go right after we eat."

"It's very strange to be taking orders from a boy half my age."

"Oh for -- would you climb out of your rut already? Get moving!"

Chapter 20

He cried out as he woke, and was immediately ashamed. Pain surged in waves through his arm and neck and back, a tight feeling in his lungs, a headache, shivers. The sound of Ash's voice made him angry; the smell of food nauseated him.

No stranger to pain, he knew he could conquer it if he could only concentrate. If he could only find that place in his mind again, the one where he stood alone on top of things and looked down on his own suffering from a great height. This was Ash's fault. No, it was Kieran's own. He'd let himself sink for a while into dependance, and now he had to fight with himself to win back his heart's solitude. Because no one else could ride this pain for him. No one else could still his shivers and relax the tenseness they brought, keep from breaking his stitches, hold his rising stomach down when bone ends grated. Comfort was an illusion; but it had looked so real yesterday.

"Get that away from me," he growled, slapping at the bowl Ash thrust at him. "I can't eat. I feel sick."

"You feel sick because you haven't eaten."

"I feel sick because I *am* sick, you idiot."

"And you'll get sicker if you don't get something in your stomach." The patience in Ash's eyes was infuriating.

"Piss off, will you? Why can't you let me sleep? I need sleep."

"You can't, I'm afraid. We're leaving as soon as you've eaten. I persuaded the priest to give our things back and leave with us."

Scowling, Kieran tried to see if Ash was serious, if he was bragging, if he was still wearing that sappy expression of forbearance, but all he could see were the owl-like circles of reflected light on Ash's glasses. "You *persuaded* him?"

"He's resistant to logic, but not fully immune. Unlike a certain someone, whom I will have to force-feed if he doesn't cooperate."

"The hell you will."

"I will. I said I'd be the mean one and I meant it. I'm going to keep you alive whether you help or not, you overgrown adolescent, so stop wasting time."

The effort to keep frowning was too much. Kieran closed his eyes with a sigh. "Fine. It'll come right back up, but fine."

"Fine." A hand that felt chill by contrast wrapped the back of Kieran's neck, lifting his head so something could be placed behind it. Rougher and stiffer than a pillow, maybe a rolled rug. The sound of metal against crockery. Something touched Kieran's lips; he allowed the spoon, swallowed something warm and salty with chunks in it, coughed. There was pain. Once his face relaxed from grimacing, the spoon came back.

It tasted wrong. Too salty, not salty enough, metallic, he wasn't sure. There was a slight burn of peppers growing in the back of his throat as he ate. Good for the head, bad for the stomach. Whatever it was had a canned taste to it. He remembered taking a stack of tinned goods at the store in Smith without looking what was on the labels. For all he knew he was eating dog food.

"What's in this?" he asked between swallows.

"Rice, corn, sausage, stuff like that. We have one can of beans left and a couple cans of olives. Why'd you get olives?"

"Dunno. Wait..." He turned his head away from the spoon and coughed again. A gob of something thick and nasty-tasting came up, and he swallowed it rather than make Ash deal with it. "Stuff doesn't taste right."

"That's because your fever's back, but you won't get over it if you don't eat. Come on now, you're halfway through."

After a few more bites, he heard light footsteps, the rustle of Miyan's skirt. "All ready. You come now."

"We'll be a few more minutes," Ash said. "Did you and the priest eat the rest?"

"Yes, all gone." Then she added in Iavaian, to Kieran, "You don't look in any shape to ride. What are you going to do?"

Kieran opened his eyes. That damn silly cheerful girl was gawking at him while he let himself be fed like an infant. He was gearing up for an angry reply when the humor of the situation struck him. "Whatever my nursemaid tells me to, I guess."

"That's good. He's strong, for all he looks like a baby chickenhawk. He made Father Ilder agree to run away before the white coats come."

"What are you two talking about?" Ash asked.

Kieran ignored him. "Any idea where we're going? I doubt I can make it very far. It might be better to stay and get my strength back so I can fight."

Miyan shook her head, serious-faced for once. "Your *edeime* is a smart man, and the only thing in the world he cares about is you. If you don't listen to someone like that, everything will go wrong."

"I'm very sorry to interrupt," Ash said, "but this is the last hot meal he'll get for I don't know how long, and I'd like him to eat it while it *is* hot."

"Okay," Miyan chirped, and dashed off.

Resigned, Kieran looked to Ash, waiting for the next spoon of wrong-tasting glop, and noticed something he hadn't before. "Where'd you get a shirt?"

"Bummed it from the priest. I have one for you too, but first you have to finish eating."

"I want my gun."

"I'm going to smack you in a second here. Then I'm going to hold your nose and pour this down your throat."

Kieran gave up and let himself be fed.

When he'd swallowed the last spoonful and washed it down with warm water, he let himself be pulled to a sitting position, though the pain of it nearly brought all that corn and rice back up, and he managed to stay sitting while Ash helped him dress. Because of the sling, the shirt had to be draped around his right shoulder, he couldn't put his arm in the sleeve. His leather trousers smelled of horse and stale Kieran, so he didn't want to wear them, but was just cogent enough to stop himself from complaining.

Ash took the book he'd hidden earlier and slipped it into a pack already full of food and ammunition. Then he knelt and started stuffing Kieran's feet into his boots. "My god, you have enormous feet. I've never seen such gigantic feet in my life. How on earth did Shou-Shou ever find boots to fit you?"

"She's a clever woman. And *you* have a big nose," he added in a surly tone.

"I didn't mean it as an insult. I was just observing."

"So was I. You just have a big nose. Maybe it looks bigger because it's red."

"You think my face is red, you should see my back. It's coming off in patches."

"Oh, *that's* attractive."

"Yeah, I'm thinking I'll start a new fashion. The flayed look. Tell me if I'm buckling these too tight."

"Pull it all the way, they're a bit loose."

"Better?" Ash finished fastening the last buckle. He stood and put his pack on his back. Then he bent to lift Kieran's left arm around his neck.

"What, now?" Kieran froze in alarm, then made himself relax. Of course it was going to hurt. Fearing the pain just made it worse. "Okay. Let's go."

It hurt. It hurt enough to make his head spin. But he got his legs under him somehow, and walked, albeit with a drunkard's slithering gait.

They went outside. The priest and Miyan waited with the horses. There were bundles tied behind each saddle, and rifles tied to the bundles. Three rifles and a shotgun.

"Where's my gun? I want my gun."

"Hold onto the saddle then." Ash left Kieran leaning against the bay mare and rummaged in his pack. He produced the Hart and offered it. "I didn't reload it or anything; you only used one round out of that magazine, right?"

"Wish I'd got hold of a holster somehow." In the process of putting the gun in his waistband left-handed, he nearly fell, but recovered. "Where's yours?"

As an answer, Ash pulled up the back of his shirt. He'd stuck the revolver down along the furrow of his spine, the way Kieran carried his. "Holsters would be nice," he agreed. "This chafes. Ready to mount up?"

"Hell no, but I'm gonna do it anyway."

While Kieran was struggling into the saddle, the priest got up on the gray, then bent to lift Miyan up in front of himself. So both horses would be carrying double, then. It would be slow going. Ash got up behind him. This time there was no fascination in Ash's hand on the reins, no comfort in the practical embrace that would keep him from falling. It was just business.

"Where are we going?" That was the priest. "Have you given any thought to where we're going? I hope it's somewhere suitable for a young lady, and not some bandit's encampment or something."

"Thought we'd start off with a little tour of historic sites," Ash answered. "Miyan, would you like to show us where you found that mosaic?"

She didn't understand. "Show what?"

"*Auanit ikarae'ena sadi,*" Kieran clarified.

"Oh! Yes." She pointed; due south, toward a shade of darker color on the horizon that implied hills.

"Is there water on the way? Take us by a route that passes somewhere we can get water."

"Yes." She slapped at her guardian's leg and flapped her bare heels against the horse's sides. "Go, go now." As they began moving, she lifted her face with a smile. She was glad to be leaving.

Well, considering what Ash had said about the Watch burning out the village, it must have worn on her living beside its ruins. Kieran sure wasn't feeling brokenhearted about leaving that mission. Probably the priest wasn't too happy about it, though. Which reminded him -- if they were going to be traveling with the guy, it might be better to be on good terms. "Hey, priest." What had the girl called him? "Ilder."

"Yes?" He sounded wary.

"Thanks for stitching me up. I owe you one."

The priest sniffed. "You owe us more than that. If you hadn't come, we wouldn't have to leave our home."

Ash said, "Isn't there something in the scriptures about God moving you where he wants you? Maybe it was time for you to leave."

"In the company of a pair of murderous perverts? Somehow I doubt that's the divine plan."

"Perverts?" Kieran said dryly.

"He's got that on the brain," Ash said with a laugh in his voice. "We're really very nice once you get to know us. Aren't we, Kieran?"

"No."

"No, I guess you're right. We're jerks. Well, *I* like us, anyway." He chuckled in Kieran's ear, and no more was said for a long time.

As the day progressed, Kieran began to feel less sick, though he got more tired at the same time. Mid-afternoon, he dozed off leaning back against Ash. This time, though, he didn't feel quite so safe doing it as he had right after he'd been hurt. Then, he'd been a rope's end snapping in the wind, grateful for any touch that might still his helpless whirling. Now he was only himself, weakened.

There was still plenty of light in the sky when they reached water, a tiny trickle of a stream that could be dammed with one hand, but Ash declared that they would camp beside it. Cold camp, since this plain was so open that someone might see a campfire from the road, though they must have gone ten miles today. When Kieran touched the ground, his legs went out from under him, and he couldn't stand even to move to the bed Ash made for him. So Ash moved the bed, and lifted him onto it by bits; feet, hips, shoulders. Moving hurt so much that he couldn't keep from making noises, and the sounds of his pain called a flood of soothing talk from Ash, which was annoying.

The especially irritating part was that it worked; the pain backed off a few steps, and he fell asleep. Woke long enough to drink some water, and again later to force down some food he didn't remember taking from the store: anise biscuits, raisins, and dried apples. Maybe supplies from the mission. Then he drifted in an aching stupor that wasn't sleep, shivering, listening to the others talking but unable to understand their words. Half-dreams came, twisting bitter dreams in which Father Ilder lectured him about Dalan's holy law against carnal contact between man and man, while dropping his pants and waving a five-throne note. Kieran tried to explain that he wasn't a whore anymore, he was big enough that he didn't need to do this, but realized all his life had been a dream and he was still a scrawny twelve-year-old on his knees in an alley behind the transients' hotel.

When something touched him, he came awake with a start.

"Hush, it's all right." Ash's hand over his hammering heart; blankets shifted.

Relief; he'd only dreamed that he'd dreamed growing up. He measured himself by Ash as the redhead climbed under the blankets with him, noting that their faces were side by side but Ash's toes were nudging his ankles. "I'm about four inches taller than you," he said happily.

"And about six degrees hotter. If your fever gets any higher, maybe I should be trying to cool you down instead of keeping you warm. I wish I'd paid more attention to this kind of thing. I'm sure I read a book about it somewhere."

"You and your books." Kieran smiled. A cough tightened his chest, but didn't make it out his throat. "Say, we're the tallest people we know. We're tall."

A sigh. "Yes, Kieran, we're tall. Go back to sleep now."

"Can't. Bad dreams."

"I'll make sure you don't have bad dreams."

"How?"

"I'll dream with you."

"You don't want my dreams."

A murmur in his ear. "Sleep, my Kai."

"*Ki edei ou'ena ki,*" he commanded; "*Ou'ena minoun,*" then remembered that Ash couldn't understand. He had closed his eyes, at some point, and when he tried to translate, his voice wouldn't cooperate. *Tell me you love me. Say it again.* That would have helped. His awareness of Ash beside him followed him into sleep, and in his dreams he was strong. Lost and confused, but strong.

Morning hit him between the eyes like a hammer. His headache astonished him. He couldn't move, it was so bad. Had to open his eyes by tiny increments; he could feel his irises struggling to contract. His nose was numb. Summer night's cold; the humidity of spring that kept the nights tolerable had ended.

I have a birthday coming up, he thought, and remembered when he'd been certain he wouldn't live to see twenty. Well, maybe he would and maybe he wouldn't.

There was a repetitive scraping sound happening near his head. It would go *scratcha-scratcha-scratch* for a while and then pause. Some kind of rodent? Digging? When he got his eyes opened, he rolled them without turning his head, and saw Ash sitting crosslegged beside him, bent over a pad of paper, writing things and then crossing them out. His shoulders were hunched high; he was in his shirtsleeves, neck and wrists rough with goosebumps. Both their coats were piled on top of the blankets that were tucked up around Kieran's chin.

When Kieran swallowed, preparatory to speaking, Ash instantly looked to him in concern. It was a pain to have to reassure him, but Kieran forced a smile to forestall questions about how he felt. "Whatcha doing?" he whispered.

"Breaking code. Thirsty?"

"Some."

Reaching behind him, Ash brought out a canteen. The chill water made Kieran's headache spike. "Rest a little longer. Those lazy people are still fast asleep. I want to get this before that priest wakes up; I don't have any excuse to keep it anymore. He'll get up his nerve to ask about it pretty soon."

"So tell him to fuck off."

"Well, it's *his* journal. It's really none of my business. I just took it to get some leverage. Turns out I didn't need it."

"Maybe it helped."

"Maybe." Ash bent over his notebook again; Kieran wondered where he'd got it. The book he'd stolen from the priest was laid out flat on the ground in front of him, and every few seconds he'd lean over to squint at it, lips moving. Then he'd scribble some more.

Several minutes later, Kieran gave a quiet groan of exasperation. "I have to piss like a racehorse. No," he added when Ash started to set his book aside, "let me see if I can..." He threw the blankets and coats aside, grimacing as the chill struck him.

"Stop," Ash snapped. He pointed between Kieran's feet.

Raising his head, Kieran saw that there was a snake coiled there, tasting the air in sluggish alarm. It was just a cricket snake, though. "Harmless," he said.

"Not poisonous?"

"No."

"Okay." Ash matter-of-factly grabbed the snake and tossed it away. "Want some help?"

"I think I'm all right." By aching stages, he got to his feet, rode out the rush of dizziness that resulted, and stumbled away.

Dealing with his pants one-handed took a long time. Getting them undone was hard; doing them up again was impossible. He dreaded asking Ash to do it for him, but in the end had to come back holding them closed with his hand.

"Um..."

Ash glanced up. "Oh." Without a hint of embarrassment, he held his pencil in his teeth, did up the buttons, then went back to his scribbling. He was no longer crossing things out. Now he was just writing, glancing back and forth between notebook and journal.

Easing back down into what was left of his warmth, Kieran pulled the blanket over himself. "Looks like you got it. What's it say?"

"It's fascinating."

"And?"

"It took me longer than I thought. I'd hoped he was using a straight rotation, but he's a little smarter than that, and I had to do some trial-and-error. But he didn't make any effort to disguise the length of words, so --"

"Ash, what's it *say*?"

"Oh." Ash looked up, blinking as if coming awake. "He's been making a study of the native religion and spiritual system. This is a collection of legends and stories he got out of the villagers before the Watch came. No wonder they wouldn't convert; he was reminding them of their own faith while he was pushing the new one. But as an anthropological record, this thing is priceless."

"Nah, I bet I have all that same old-religion bullshit in my head."

"Bullshit? Kieran, this is your heritage."

"Huh. I don't have a heritage."

"If you don't have a heritage, then why have you got a wind knot tattooed on your chest? What were you and Miyan calling it -- *auanit*? It says here that that's the symbol of a rather scary god called Kan."

"Ka'an," Kieran corrected. "Yeah. He's a real asshole of a god. Kind you don't want to meet in a dark alley, you know?" He crawled his left hand up under his shirt to touch the tattoo, feeling the slight ridge of the inked skin there. "It's a Tama'ankan thing. My mom had a little one on her ankle, but her pimp burned it off. I guess I got this one to kind of spit on that guy's grave."

"So your tribe worshipped this god?"

"You don't worship Ka'an. You try to get on his good side or you stay the hell out of his way. Not my whole tribe, anyway, just the Ankan. The Suneater clan. He's supposed to like us specially, I guess because we're all nuts."

"Do you believe that Ka'an actually exists? I mean you personally?" Ash didn't seem concerned by the possibility; he asked with scholarly detachment.

"Not really. I have dreams about him sometimes, but that doesn't mean anything." He remembered the bums back in Burn River identifying him with Ka'an, and smiled. "We do kinda need a god like him, though. We Iavaians. Dalan's just not doing the trick for us."

Ash studied the book some more. "Let's see -- 'This god was considered responsible for certain types of dreams, especially true or prophetic dreams. Iyula claims that several times this god has mated with her in her visions, but as she is an inveterate opium-eater I did not bother recording her statements. He was also thought to bring storms, being the deity responsible for the severe thunderstorms of spring. Most of all, however, he was the god of violent death, and thus not to be invoked lightly.' And this is your clan's special friend?"

Kieran grinned. "You bet."

"Hey, what tribe is Miyan?"

"Beats me. I didn't ask. Miyan's a fairly common name; means cornflower."

"When she first saw that tattoo, she called you a holy man. At first I thought she must know you from somewhere, because the word had 'Kai' in it."

"Oh, *kai'adiin*. Yeah. Literally, that would be 'spirit horse'. Not really a priest, more like a medium."

"Why would she think that, if the wind knot is just a Suneater thing?"

"Dunno."

"I think I'll keep this book for a while after all." He put it and his writing materials away, his movements neat and precise, reminding Kieran of the way he'd been when they'd first met. He'd been so careful, then. So polite and nervous. He'd relaxed a lot, but some things were intrinsic, apparently. The way his pale fingers flicked through the contents of his pack to make room, worked the pack's buckle, tucked his pencil in his shirt pocket; the same tidy efficiency with which he'd handled his revolver when he'd surprised Kieran by reloading it on his own.

Kieran wanted to see more of that. Wanted to watch Ash repair clockwork or do surgery or something. The way Ash's hands worked soothed his eyes. In this moment the bird-boned narrowness of Ash's body didn't seem fragile; it was part of the design, streamlined, modern, a state-of-the-art machine. A very clever automaton powered by something quieter than steam, you could see the gas flames in his eyes...

"Damn," Kieran muttered. "I'm going delirious again."

Ash checked Kieran's temperature, made an unhappy face. "I don't know what it means when the fever keeps breaking and then rising again. I think it's better than if it's constant, though. You don't have to do anything, so just rest. You want your coat?"

"Yeah."

Ash arranged Kieran's coat around him, then packed up the bed. Kieran sat crosslegged and watched him put away the camp. He'd only done it once or twice before, but he was now doing it faster than Kieran would have. Quick learner. He woke Miyan and Ilder with sharp taps on their shoulders, made them get up before they were quite awake, had their blankets packed up before they'd finished blinking and scratching. While they drank water and ate handfuls of dried fruit, Ash saddled the horses. Kieran calculated that from the time Ash put the book away to the time when they were ready to leave took ten minutes at most.

He doesn't repeat his mistakes; now that I think about it, he's never had to be taught anything twice. I admire him. This is what it means to admire someone.

"Come on now, people," Ash was saying, gently but insistently. "You don't have to be coherent, just vertical. Mount up now, go on." He came back to get Kieran, helped him onto the horse, and got the mare moving before the others were quite ready.

"You needn't be in such a hurry all the time," the priest complained.

"Imagine that the White Watch are after us," Ash retorted. "Because they are."

They entered the hills a few hours later, and Kieran recognized where they were. The place he'd intended to go to was northwest of here, so they were sort of heading away from it, but he knew a route that followed the curve of these hills around and would probably be a better path than the road. Much slower and more difficult, but no one who didn't know this area better than his own face would ever be able to find it.

For now, though, they followed Miyan's instructions. Feeling a little better now that the day's heat had replaced night's cold, Kieran chatted with her a bit. The priest joined in sometimes, mostly to instruct or chastise her. His accent was pretty good, and his grasp of the grammar excellent. His attitude stank, though. He was always monitoring Miyan for unladylike language or concepts, and wouldn't let her talk too much about what had happened to the village. He seemed to think it would distress her. Since she shuttled off immediately to other things, as if the subject couldn't hold her, Kieran didn't try to interfere.

Ash didn't demand a translation; he seemed lost in his own thoughts. Kieran told him a few of the things that seemed to matter most: that Miyan's village had been composed of Tallgrass people, mostly a clan called Dogtooth that Kieran had never heard of, with a few families that were Valley Blue-Eye. That latter name referred to a flower, not the coloring of the inhabitants; Highland Blue-Eye came from south of Canyon and had been moved into town after the Assimilation to work the mines. There was a silver mine in that area called Dogtooth, so maybe that was the other clan's original turf. It was a little odd to find a village of Tallgrass down here, when Tallgrass were mostly sheep-farming hill people, but Miyan lost interest before explaining it, and went on to talk about how she wanted a dress made out of a yellow calico she'd seen on a trip to Trestre. The priest didn't like that idea; he considered bright colors immodest. Kieran laughed at him, then had a coughing fit and brought up something so nasty he expected it to wilt the sawgrass where he spit it.

He was feeling pretty foul when they reached their destination. Nevertheless a sense of homecoming eased his mood a little when he saw it. He'd been here before.

At the end of a shallow-sloped canyon, a slab of yellow sandstone made a porch in front of a natural cave mouth that had been widened at the bottom by human hands. It was a sort of bottle shape, maybe twenty feet high.

"I camped out here once," Kieran said, ignoring the gurgle in his voice. "Maybe five, six years ago? I don't remember any *auanit*, though."

"It's in the floor," Miyan answered. "I found it when I swept out the dirt. I bet you didn't clean it at all, even though it's a shrine. Boys are so dirty."

The priest leapt in, speaking Iavaian as well. "I'm not comfortable with this. Evil gods were worshipped here, and I won't have you treating it as a holy place, Miyan. Remember, Dalan is the True God."

"Okay," she agreed easily, and hopped down off the horse before Ilder reined in. "I'll make it all nice for us. Be good to the horses!" She dashed into the cave.

Ash, left out of the conversation, said, "I take it this is the place she mentioned."

"Yeah. It's an okay place to camp, I guess, but --" Kieran broke off to clamp his teeth together against a cry of pain as he dismounted. It felt like a red-hot awl was being jammed into his right lung. Ash held him upright while he took short breaths through his nose until the feeling subsided. Then he did his best to resume as if nothing had happened, though his voice was weaker. "I'm not sure why you wanted to come here. You know something I don't?"

"Just a hunch. Father Ilder, would you please see to the

horses? I'll be back shortly to help you carry things inside." Supporting Kieran with one arm, he picked apart knots behind the mare's saddle, letting everything fall on the ground except the blanket he was trying to get. "I'm going to let you set your pace. Take your time. I've got you."

Inside the shrine, the cool, still air smelled of water. That was why Kieran had camped here when he'd come this way, years ago, and he supposed why the shrine was here at all. Springs in caves tended to end up being revered as holy places. This one was just a tiny drip, barely enough to make a puddle in the basin that had been carved out around it. Lime deposits on the floor below the basin's lip testified to the times when the spring ran faster than evaporation, but at the moment its flow was nearly lost among the clots of minerals it had coated the basin with.

Miyan was using a handful of weeds to sweep the floor. There wasn't enough dust to hide the mosaic, though. Rounded stones ranging in color from dark jade to pale sage were set into channels cut in the floor, making a mottled green wind knot the length of a man. It was on one side of the spring; on the other was a scooped out area of floor, as if another symbol had been there and someone had tried to erase it.

Kieran wanted to go look at the scoured floor, try to see what had been there, but couldn't even stand up on his own. He had to let Ash lay him down on the blanket, had to lie there helpless and wait.

When Ash went outside, Miyan glanced out the door and then gave Kieran a conspiratorial smile. "Don't tell them, okay?" She dipped her bundle of weeds in the spring and scattered water across the wind knot. "Don't be angry with us, Ka'an. We're only little, and we're not hurting anything." Then she dipped it again and spattered Kieran. "Watch over this man, your *heriye*, and send misfortune to his enemies."

At her ritual, a strange feeling rose in Kieran, a pressure behind his eyes, a charge over his skin. There was power here. Yet he felt no awe; instead, he almost laughed at the futility of her action. If Ka'an really existed, he was weak, beaten back by the Dalanists. And what a silly thing she was, to call Kieran a *heriye*, when that term was supposed to apply only to the noblest and most upright warriors of the people. Kieran wasn't even a warrior of the people at all, just a criminal. And -- "Since when does Ka'an have *heriye*, Miyan? You're gonna piss him off, getting him confused with Viha and Urotu and those guys."

"I wasn't," she said indignantly. "Anyway, Sun and Bear are dead. Ka'an's the only one who's still alive."

He decided to humor her instead of arguing with her. "How do you know that? Priestess, are you?"

"I have to be, since the rest of my folks are dead. Somebody has to do the rites here. But don't tell Father Ilder, please, he'd make me stop. Anyway, I know it because the good gods couldn't stand the way things are now. They must have died in battle, or they would be helping us. The only one who helps us is the Dreamer, because he doesn't care who has power, only who has guts. I bet he likes you a lot, Kieran."

Smiling, he didn't answer. He liked the idea she'd come up with, and wondered if it were her own invention, or something she'd heard from her people before they'd died. Kieran had heard old folks bemoaning the fact that there were no *heriye* left, but it would sure be interesting if the term could be applied to a different kind of person. It wasn't that Iavaians had lost their fighting spirit. They'd just been soiled by circumstance, gone hard and bitter, used their strength however they could to survive. And if any god was going to give power to that sort of coyote soul, it would be the Prince of Pain.

Maybe that was why he kept dreaming he *was* Ka'an. A little message to tell him the road he was on had a patron. That there was a power in tune with him.

What the hell good that would do, he had no idea.

Chapter 21

Worry was wearing Ash down. He didn't think he'd ever been this tired before in his life. Tired in quite this way, at least. He wasn't as physically worn out as when he'd brought Kieran to the mission, but resting his body didn't seem to be erasing the weariness in his mind. He was tired of running, tired of fear, tired of hunger and saddle sores and thinking about horses and water. Tired of Kieran being hurt. Tired of the priest's sourness and Miyan's mindless cheer.

He didn't listen to the talk in Iavaian between Ilder and Miyan while he stowed their belongings with the military neatness that could no longer soothe him. When Miyan wanted to take over the food-related chores, he let her. He changed Kieran's bandage, sniffing at it for a hint of rot as he'd seen doctors do, trying to be relieved that he didn't smell any despite the fact that the wound was leaking pale fluid and looked angrily red. Kept his temper when Kieran grumbled at him about having to eat, about having to drink water, reminded himself that it was easy to be angry about everything when you were in constant pain. Maybe Kieran's anger was infecting him; maybe if he stayed calm it would ease the pain a little; but it was getting harder. There was a feeling within the cave like a thunderstorm building, which made the hairs on his arms stand up. Maybe that was why he'd wanted to come here. He didn't know, and hoped no one demanded an explanation.

At last, when the light began to fade and the air's heat to dissipate, he couldn't stand it anymore. Kieran was sleeping and there was no work left to do. He took the priest's book and one of the rifles and walked out. Father Ilder watched him go and didn't say anything about the book. Scared of him, now that he was armed again.

Outside, the sky was still bright, but everything down in the little valley was in shadow. Sunlight yellow as beer still poured across the high ground, and his impulse was to go up there and open his mouth, let it pour into him. Half-walking and half-climbing, he scrambled up the easiest part of the slope.

A view opened before him, a view of such hugeness that it seemed to snatch him away from himself, spread him out so thin he was intangible. To the north, beyond the gullied land they'd traveled today, featureless yellow-gray plain spread out to the limits of distance. East, it curved around farther out, then swallowed the hills as it did to the north. South, the eroded squareness of these hills smoothed out into rounder, higher land, each progressively more enormous mound identically bald on top. A few sported twisted trees on their flanks. And to the west, the workings of time grew more apparent, the land redder, until the horizon was made up of chops and slices that he supposed were buttes and canyonland, but which in the low-slanting sun looked just like the cracked mud plates of the flat where he'd awakened the morning after their escape.

He counted back. That had been only nine days ago. Only nine days. It was inconceivable how much had happened in nine days. No wonder he was exhausted.

From below, he could still hear the priest's voice, faintly. He walked south until he couldn't hear it anymore, and then a little farther, until he couldn't have heard anyone from camp even if they yelled. It was irresponsible of him, he knew. And part of him cried out against leaving Kieran with those people, who didn't care enough. But it was a small part, drowned out by the need to be alone, just for a few minutes, to have no one looking at him or judging him. He found a knob of reddish clay earth about his own height, climbed it, and sat down facing north, toward the most open of his views.

Feeling a little self-conscious, he looked the rifle over, thinking about the dead man from whom it had come. Had that man left some trace of his nature on his weapon? It didn't feel charged in any way; didn't even feel like a weapon, just some metal and wood that happened to be made in this shape. He worked the bolt, and his hands wanted to follow that by firing. Instead, he set it across his knees. Opened Ilder's journal. Read a little, but it made that trapped-irritated-weary feeling start to rise up again; Ilder's tone was so condescending, so convinced that the people he studied were misguided, backwards and wrong. So Ash left the book alone and just stared at the place where the sky met the world.

Homesickness crept up on him. It was too dry here, far too open, the trees were sick and the grass angry, the animals hostile and the people lost. He wanted to water the whole desert and make green spring up with a wave of his hand. He wondered what Kieran would think of Ladygate, where the passage of a million feet couldn't keep moss out of the sidewalks, where the drainpipe of every tenement had a wisp of ivy climbing it, and rain was a lullaby all summer. And in the winter, snow, turning the night sky yellow with the reflection of streetlights, smothering sound, making every conversation an exchange of secrets; had Kieran ever seen snow? Ash wanted to take him north and show it to him. Show him the Shale River gray as its namesake under a sky clotted with cloud; show him Tenkist Park in the spring, a blizzard of pink petals from the cherry trees swirling through burgeoning green; take him to the top floor of the South Bank Library, to the little corner window at the back of the science section that looked down on a landscape of moss-splotched roof tiles and haphazard chimney pots almost as strange as the desert. Feed him the library's thick silence, the smell of leather and dust there. Lie with him among the sound of bees up on the bluffs at midsummer, when the air was wet enough that you drank it instead of breathing it.

And after that, why not farther north? All the way to Yelorre, to fogbound shores Ash barely remembered. He wasn't even certain whether the views he recalled were real, or whether he'd invented them. He could never see his parents' faces, though sometimes a voice would flood him with a memory of wonder and a warm sweetish smell and the color blue, so that he thought his mother's must have sounded similar. Of the house where he'd been born, and where his parents had died, all he recalled was a flash here and there: a brick-edged step where a hole in the mortar contained an anthill, a brown carpet on a shiny wooden floor, a green caterpillar hanging from a thread in spring rain. The only really clear image he retained was of a stretch of jagged shore, red-black granite standing against a heaving sea, the wet beach sharply dark at his feet and graduating into soft paleness with distance. It was so clear a picture that he felt he must have constructed it in later life, because a four-year-old's mind could not have been so observant, could it?

But now he wanted to find that beach. He wanted that coolness in his throat, that fine mist against his skin. His soul felt parched. The beauty of Iavaiah was one that battered and scoured. He couldn't rest here.

What tired him was the sense that every single thing he touched was hostile. Nothing accepted him; land, people, air, everything abraded him. Everything but Kieran, and even he, being as precious and endangered as he was, caused an anxiety

Ash had no idea how to work past. He'd never been so lonely in his life as he was now, not even after his arrest when he'd occupied a solitary disinfectant-smelling cell beneath the courthouse wondering whether his aunt would be arrested as well. Then, he hadn't had any options. Now he had too many, and they all looked bad. He wanted to go home.

And he knew that if he had to leave Kieran behind to do it, he'd never see Aunt Isobel or Ladygate again.

I'm going to die here in the dust and heat, it's foolish to think there's any other possible outcome. Kieran will die and then I'll die. Because I can't take care of him, because there's no one to help me help him, no one to save him. How can this be happening to us? We're not even old enough to join the army! So unfair...

He let his self-pity run that far, and no farther. His own illogical whining was starting to make him angry; he certainly wasn't going to give those pointless thoughts any more time.

I should be thinking about staying alive. The Watch isn't going to give up on us, not if they sent three men after us on the Canyon road. Unless we have a serious storm or come up with some other way to hide our trail, we're going to have more of them to deal with. And they'll be readier this time, and we won't know their movements to ambush them. With Kieran basically useless, I'm the only one here who can shoot, and I can't shoot that well.

So think, Ashleigh. What washes out the kind of trail Watch trackers follow? Lots of other people -- should we be heading for a city? Rails; don't know where any are, from here. Water -- hah. Weather; no control. Time. That's about it, as far as I know. My hunch that something in a place like this might help, well, there's kind of a power feeling inside the cave, but how the hell would I know if it was doing anything? And this is a damn bad place for them to find us, we'd be cornered.

We should never have come out here. We should have laid low in Burn River until we could get on a train going to the coast, Gevarne or somewhere big like that, and then we should have left the country.

He turned his head to look wistfully at the mountains, beyond which Prandhar declined to comply with the extradition treaty. Realized that he'd heard no news for so long that for all he knew the Commonwealth was at war with Prandhar now. Saw a flicker of movement and froze, tightening his grip on the rifle.

Just a dozen yards away, a small hoofed animal was picking its way along the shoulder of another mound of dirt. He thought at first it was a goat, from the size, but as it came into better light he saw that it was a deer. It stopped every few feet to nose at the ground, but didn't seem to be actually eating what it found. He didn't blame it; nothing here looked really edible. All dry and thorny. That something as rounded and graceful as that little deer could live here was strange, beautiful and wrong.

He set the rifle against his shoulder. There wasn't much in the way of decision behind the action. Regret warred with what he could only think of as the spirit of the desert seeping into him. He didn't really try to put the deer's neck in the notch of the sight, it just ended up there.

The gun cracked and punched his shoulder, and the deer half-leapt and fell.

When he came skidding down into the valley with the deer across his back, Miyan and the priest were waiting for him. The priest looked anxious, but the girl was smiling broadly. She had a kitchen knife in one hand and a folded oilcloth tarp in the other.

Ash dumped the dead animal before her. He looked pointedly at the knife. "How'd you know?"

She darted a wary glance at Ilder, then smiled and shrugged, and didn't answer.

"Okay. You butcher it. I'm done." He went from evening blue to the grainy almost-black of the cave. When his eyes had adjusted enough that he could find Kieran without stepping on him, he knelt down beside him. Tested the temperature of Kieran's face -- still too hot. Listened to the thick sound of Kieran's breathing.

Bent over his knees until his forehead rested on the blanket over Kieran's stomach, and gave in to silent weeping.

When Kieran moved, Ash froze. He was about to sit up when Kieran's hand landed on the back of his neck.

"What did you kill?" Kieran whispered.

"A deer," Ash answered just as quietly.

"I dreamed you killed a ghost." Then, a little while later, "I trust you, Ashes. Did I say that before? I think I really trust you."

Ash couldn't answer. Could only squeeze his eyes shut and bite his lip, hoping Kieran wouldn't see he'd been crying. He was afraid evidence of his weakness might cause that statement to be retracted, and he couldn't have borne it.

"I don't trust those people at all," Kieran went on in the

same phlegmy whisper. "Let's get out of here. Let's ditch them, okay?"

"You need rest," Ash murmured.

"I won't get it with them around. I want to leave."

Ash nodded slightly, knowing Kieran would feel it if he couldn't see it.

"Do you... like the desert, Ash? Do you think you could stand living out here for a while? Not in this --" The beginning of a cough, swallowed down. "Not here. A better place I know about. It's... pretty lonely. I should warn you."

Swallowing down the lump in his throat, Ash managed to keep the quaver out of his voice. "We'd have each other to talk to, right?"

"Right. So tell me. Yes or no."

"Yes. Of course yes. I'd live on the moon, if that's where you are." He could no longer hold his weeping in check. Kieran's hand tightened on the nape of his neck, then slid down to his shaking shoulder.

"Why are you crying, Ashes?"

"I'm scared. I'm tired."

"One of us hurting is enough, *edeime*, you don't have to hurt with me. Can't you see -- feel -- *kii aveh*, you're the blood that my heart beats, you're in my veins. *Yena ma kii aveh*. Please don't cry." Kieran's voice was failing, barely audible, and his hand slid weakly down Ash's arm. Tangled in his hair; tugged at a curl, a sad mockery of playfulness. They were both exhausted, no longer able to protect each other, and Ash was terrified.

He reached out with his mind, groping with his Empathic sense at the frustrating divide between himself and Kieran, the distance which made them separate. It seemed impossible to breach at first -- then suddenly his mind relaxed into the right shape, and warmth came welling up, concern, love, weary joy at the simple fact of his presence. Feelings enough like his own that they might have been hard to distinguish, but he had learned the flavor of Kieran's emotions now, the particular cornered hopefulness of them. There was a haven of kindness in the world after all. Just a little one. Just Kieran-sized. Not enough light to find his way, perhaps, but enough that he knew he wasn't blind. Not enough to solve any problems, but enough to remind him why he couldn't give up trying.

"I'm done crying now," Ash promised. "I'll be stronger in the morning."

"Come sleep, then. I'm cold."

Ash took his boots off and eased under the blanket. He couldn't put his head on Kieran's shoulder, because weight on the uninjured one would pull at the injured one, but he could curl up with his arm draped over Kieran's waist. "Warmer?"

"Yeah. Thanks." A gurgle of a laugh. "You know it's going to give that priest the screaming creepies, that we sleep like this."

"Who cares what he thinks?"

"Well, I never cared what anyone thought, but I didn't know if you might."

"Nope."

"Good." A long sigh, and Kieran was asleep.

Ash lay awake a little longer, listening to the sounds of the priest and Miyan working by lamplight outside. Feeling his heart swell up until it threatened to choke him. *I love you*, he thought at Kieran, *you have to fight this off and get well, because if you die the whole world will end.* He knew that in theory people survived grief and were even happy later, but somehow couldn't believe it would apply to him. If he lost Kieran, his heart would simply stop; he was certain of it.

When he slept, he dreamed a barren wasteland of sun and stone with a tiny pool of water at the center. Beside the water, he had built a little box and was growing a flower in it. He kept telling Kieran to wait a few minutes longer for his birthday present, the flower would bloom any moment. But Kieran got impatient and walked away, and no matter how Ash ran, he couldn't catch up.

Pain and distress woke him; he panicked for a moment when he found the blankets empty, his mind full of the agony that spiked in time with the sound of coughing from outside. As he scrambled up to go to Kieran's rescue, though, the sensation grew less acute, and the distress faded to mere disgust, punctuated by a spitting noise.

He went out into light so near the color he'd last left that only the sharp cold told him it was just before dawn instead of just after sunset. Kieran was leaning on the edge of the stone porch, taking shallow breaths.

Ash sensed his annoyance, and decided it would be a bad idea to be too solicitous. "Want a hand there?"

"Yeah, with my pants." Kieran backed away from the edge; he was holding his fly closed again. "Damn embarrassing.

Don't step in the spit, I just hocked up something that looks like a raw egg."

"Charming." Ash hopped down next to him and did up his trousers for him. "It's generally considered impolite to describe what you spit up."

"Yeah, but this one's so interesting. I think I'll name it, and drag it around on a leash."

Grinning despite himself, Ash tested Kieran's forehead, found it sweaty and warm instead of dry and burning. "You sound like you're feeling better."

"Yeah. A lot. So I'm thinking we should just go. Before they wake up."

"Oh." Ash frowned. "That seems a bit dishonest."

"We didn't promise to babysit them."

"True, but... all right, but we'll only take one of the horses, and leave them most of the deer. And some of the other supplies. I promised Miyan one of the rifles."

"Fine, whatever." Kieran's hand closed hard around Ash's arm, and his look was as close to pleading as he ever got. "I just want to get away from them."

Puzzled, Ash nodded. "What's wrong, what's bothering you so much? You seem really --"

"I heard them talking, when you went out yesterday. That priest was telling his innocent little girl all about the various tortures and punishments that God has planned for 'perverts and sodomites' both on earth and in Hell. Really filthy stuff -- red-hot iron up the ass kind of stuff. And she was just listening and nodding, like none of it mattered to her." He paused to breathe, looked as if he might cough but managed not to. "And then you came in and you were like clean air all of a sudden, and I just want to go, all right? Things will never be simple with people like that around."

Ash couldn't refuse him. "Let's go where things are simpler."

As quietly as he could, he brought the packs outside and sorted them. He took all the food that he and Kieran had brought with them except for the canned goods and the can opener. In exchange, he took a bag of raisins, which he thought was a fair trade. He took the notepad and pencils he'd grabbed from the priest's private room, but left the coded journal. Kept one of the two kitchen knives they'd brought from the mission, left one of the rifles and a handful of ammunition. He carved a flank from the deer hanging up outside and rolled it in salt in the bloodstained tarp, packed up saddlebags and backpack and bedroll, filled canteens and divided the remaining horse feed. While he worked, Kieran watched him with silent interest, slightly smiling.

He chose the mare, as he'd done for the past few days, because her sturdier frame was better able to stand their riding double. He didn't mount behind Kieran yet, though, wanting to spare the animal's strength as long as Kieran was able to ride without help. The gelding whickered plaintively as they left him behind.

Kieran directed him by a meandering route that had a general westward trend, and was never straight or level. As the sun climbed higher, as they crept across the pale-yellow hugeness of the desert, Ash began to feel *free* in a way he never had before. It was a little frightening, this freedom, knowing in his bones that no one could judge him or change him. Not even the tiniest pretense could survive out here in this emptiness. He was only himself. Kieran was only Kieran. The sky was emptier than he'd ever seen it.

They talked a little, from time to time, about small things. Ash talked more than Kieran did. Kieran would ask a question, then sit back and listen while Ash babbled. He said he liked listening. Contentment radiated from him; tainted though it was with pain and the constant current of wary anger that always ran beneath the surface of Kieran's mind, it was nevertheless a good feeling. And for all his worry and weariness, Ash was filled with quiet joy to know that Kieran was happier for his presence.

They saw no sign of pursuit, nor in fact any indication that human beings had been here within the past thousand years. Kieran sometimes pointed out small carvings on solitary stones, sigils so weathered that Ash would not have known they were made by human hands unless Kieran had told him so.

Several times during the day they halted to rest. Though Kieran was more alert than he had been most of the time since he'd been shot, he was nevertheless bone-tired and hurting. They found water mid-afternoon, just a seep where Ash had to dig for it; Ash had Kieran drink off all that was left in their canteens, then took his time filling them again. Kieran took a nap while he did this. Insects shrilled and rustled, a wandering breeze stirred the dust along the ground without raising it into the air, and overhead an eagle circled on an updraft as if it were out for pleasure rather than business. Ash let Kieran sleep for about an hour; watched over him, listened to the thick sound of his breathing, thought kisses at his pain-pinched face but did not touch him. Then they moved on, to where the hillsides grew rockier and steeper, more often cut to the bone by wind and water, and at last became canyonlands indistinguishable from the others they'd walked or ridden through in the past days.

Kieran was able to dismount without help when they stopped for the night. He even helped a little with the cooking, stirring the pot of venison stew so it wouldn't burn while Ash took care of everything else. Ash fried thick slabs of flatbread, and dusted them with sugar this time, contrary to custom. Kieran protested the weirdness of putting sugar on flatbread, but ate five pieces anyway.

When it came time to change the bandage, he helped, using his good arm to ease the injured one out of the sling, holding it carefully in his lap. His chest looked lopsided. Ash worried about how to get the pad of gauze unstuck from the wound, but when he undid the strips of stronger fabric that held the pad in place, the stained square of bandaging fell off into his hand. It was so wet it felt heavy, and he nearly dropped it in disgust. The stain was brown at the edges and pale at the center, and it smelled. Not like rotting meat, thank god, but still not pleasant.

Kieran's shoulders were uneven. The left one showed clearly the angular structure of bone and muscle that Ash found so delicious; the right was smoothly swollen, all shape drowned in a fatness of engorged flesh. The wrongness of the sight made him want to gag. Something watery was leaking out around the stitches.

"That's pretty damn disgusting," Kieran said mildly.

"It's... it's part of the healing process."

"Don't bullshit me. I might not be an Empath, but I can see the look on your face."

Ash sighed. "Okay. Yeah. I guess I know better than to try to tell you pretty lies. It's obviously seriously infected, and the infection's gotten into your lungs. You should be in a nice clean hospital bed somewhere, not riding all day and sleeping on the ground at night."

"Huh. They don't let folks my color into nice clean hospitals."

"They do in Prandhar."

"How'd you plan on getting there? Fly?"

"Wish really hard, maybe," Ash returned, forcing a wry smile. "Let's get this cleaned up. You're the toughest person I've ever heard of, let alone met, and if anyone can fight this off it's you."

Kieran started to say something, coughed, spat a mottled brownish string into the dust. "Damn straight," he croaked, but with his head lolling back and his eyes narrow in pain.

Ash had boiled a pan of water before starting, and now he dipped a cloth in the pan and started dabbing away the crusted pus that had been under the bandage. Father Ilder's neat stitches had all held; the priest had known better than to pull them too tight, so the swelling hadn't forced them. But the bullet's entry hole was a ragged star shape, and the exit wound above Kieran's shoulderblade was a rough half-moon as long as Ash's palm, hard to heal. If the bone hadn't deflected it upwards, the bullet would have torn a plum-sized hole on its way out. Ash had seen what the same caliber did to the deer's neck.

Thinking about that led by a meandering path to the more general thought of Watch weaponry, and thence to other things they could do, and from there to the idea of pattern-magic, the closely guarded secrets of ritual thaumaturgy that only government-sanctioned mages were allowed to know. Ash had once proposed, in one of his rare face-to-face meetings with a Resistance contact, that they gather what they could of thaumaturgic secrets and disseminate them as widely as possible. Even a list of which superstitions and kitchen-spells seemed to work the best would be a blow against the government monopoly, if it was spread widely enough. The contact had admitted that it would be a good idea, except that no one had been able to get hold of one book, one single page from any Watch collegium in the Commonwealth.

As for foreign material, there was a certain quantity of the stuff which could potentially be translated, though smuggling it into the country was difficult work. And it was primitive, for the most part, relying more on Talents than on pattern. Only in the Commonwealth had magic been advanced to a science. Ash's contact had also suspected the Theocracy of planting agents in foreign countries to disseminate misinformation, write books and articles that clouded the subject and advanced plausible but incorrect theories. None of it was reliable.

Now he found himself wondering how any of that could

possibly matter. Magic was all sense and force; he knew this when he could feel it working. How could there possibly be a finite set of words and pictures and gestures that worked, among an infinite stretch of possibilities? Someone who really understood the way energy flowed should be able to make up his own ritual.

He set the pan back on the fire and dropped the bandage in to boil. Then he got his rifle and ejected the magazine. It took a moment to find the catch that released it; it was in a different place from the one on a hunting rifle, and the magazine was rectangular, hidden in the stock.

"Lockeart bolt-action repeater," Kieran creaked, sounding dazed. "Always wanted one of those. Army issue. Only way to get it's off a dead soldier."

"Or a dead Watchman," Ash said while he thumbed a round out of the open-sided clip.

"One of those rifles is mine, right?"

"Of course."

"Who you gonna shoot? Not time to put me out of my misery yet."

Having put the magazine back in, now two rounds short of its load of six, Ash set the rifle aside. "I just wanted a bullet. Look at the size of this bastard. Can you believe one of these actually went through you?" He held up the thing where Kieran could see it, fully two inches long and pointier than an ordinary bullet, its brass casing stamped with the letters *ECT-LS* in tiny print. Eskarne Theocratic Commonwealth, Long Standard. Ash started combing the dust around him for a likely-looking rock.

"Whatcha doing?"

"Something stupid, probably."

"I said that to you once. Remember? Got my head kicked in."

"Different kind of stupid." Finding a pebble with the right kind of surface, Ash bent to filing the letters off the casing.

Kieran watched him for a while, then let his head sink back, smiling a little. "You're a weird kid."

"Ever heard of having a bullet with your name on it?"

"Yeah, so?"

"I got to wondering if anybody ever really did that. I mean, when they set out to hunt somebody, did anyone ever actually scratch that person's name into the bullet?"

"I never did." He coughed, sat up halfway to spit. "Wish

you'd picked up the one that got me. Now that would be *chalhia*."

"Translation?"

"Lucky metal. It's usually a coin -- something you had in your pocket on a day when everything went right, drill a hole in it and hang it around your neck. I got shot point blank with -- what is that, forty-six cal? And I'm still breathing, and the fucker who shot me isn't. I call that lucky."

"Well, it looks like we're thinking in tandem this evening. Because lucky metal is exactly what I'm making here. I hope. To tell the truth I have no idea what I'm doing, but I've begun to suspect that no one else does either." He thumbed dust off the bullet, held it up to the light, and nodded. Then he got the knife from his pack.

"Wait." Kieran raised himself on his elbow. "You gonna draw on it? Draw this." He smoothed the ground beside him, then doodled a simple little design, a chevron shape with a dot in it. "Don't know the whole old alphabet, there's about four thousand symbols in it, but people still use a few of 'em. That one's *iku*, and also *at'ta*. Means 'fly straight' or 'do it right' -- I got it written on my gun, dunno if you saw that." He let himself fall with a grunt. "Who's that bullet for?"

"Me." Then, "Relax!" he added as Kieran growled with trying to sit up again. "I'm not suicidal. Relax."

Frowning, Kieran stayed lying down, but rolled his head to watch what Ash was doing. With the knife's point, Ash scratched carefully at the brass. Thumbed the filings off and popped the bullet into his mouth. The metallic flavor of it flooded his throat and sinuses, and he began to feel flutters rising in his stomach, tightness in his head. Kieran felt it too, his scowl turning to puzzlement as Ash worked. A length of brown twine from the neck of the coffee bag was the best string he could come up with; he untwisted the center section slightly, plucked a few of the fine hairs from the back of his neck and laid them in the untwisted part, let it twist itself back up to hold them. His eyes had watered a little when he'd pulled out the hairs; taking the bullet from his mouth, he dabbed tears on it along with the spit. Finally, he nicked his left middle finger, which he'd heard carried the vein that ran straightest from the heart, and dabbed a drop of blood on as well.

"What the fuck are you doing, Ash?"

"I'm not quite certain." He held the bullet up, waiting for it to dry. "I'm not sure it's going to do anything. I'm not sure we could tell if it did."

"Think I felt magic, a minute ago."

"Me too."

"But *what* --"

"I put my true name on it, so to speak. Here's my initials, and your fly-straight rune. Blood, spit and tears. Hairs in the string. It's a piece of me now, or at least that's the theory. But it's also a bullet, still. So it wants to *go* -- it wants to bury itself somewhere." Judging it sufficiently dry, he knotted the string around it. He bent to put it around Kieran's neck; when the bullet settled in the hollow of Kieran's throat, the Iavian gave a small gasp of startlement. His green eyes went wide, and a flush spread across his cheeks bright enough to be visible under his dark pigmentation.

"It's a compass," he said wonderingly.

"That's the idea," Ash nodded. "Did it hurt you? Are you okay?"

"I'm fine. I'm -- I'm not going to tell you what that felt like. Oh, it's definitely working. That's creative as hell, how did you think of it? What I don't get is why you think I need it. We playing hide and seek?"

"I noticed that you sleep more easily and wake up less ill if I'm with you, that you have nightmares if I'm not. Now I'm with you every second; you always know where I am. So if I have to scout ahead, or go hunting, anything like that, you'll still be able to rest. And also..." he trailed off.

"Also?"

"Aw, it's morbid. Forget it."

"You figure morbid's gonna bother *me*?" Kieran laughed a little.

Ash shrugged noncommittally. "I can't afford to get hurt, not while you still need me. I guess I thought if there was already a bullet around with my name on it, maybe the others couldn't get a fix on me."

"That's a good idea. Maybe I should make one too."

"Kai, every long-standard round in the territory is already sniffing after you."

Kieran grinned as if that were a compliment.

Chapter 22

In the morning Kieran said he felt better again, but Ash noticed his movements were slower, accompanied by more wincing, and he coughed more often. The skin around the wound was hot; his forehead was clammy. He stumbled when he tried to get up on the horse alone. He turned it into a joke, complaining that he was seasick and would stay in his cabin until the storm was over, but he couldn't hide his frustration and growing fear. Sometimes his directions were confusing; he'd say things wrong, telling Ash to go round the left side of that tree, when there were no trees to be seen, or up a slope when the slope led down. Sometimes he lapsed into Iavaian, and had to be reminded that Ash didn't speak that language. Throughout the day's travel he dozed more than he had the day before. Even with Ash pouring oil on the waters of his dreams, he wandered into nightmare more easily than before, grunting and mumbling in his sleep.

The mare was getting thinner. Ash could see every tendon and bone in his own hands, and as for Kieran, there was nothing left of him but rope and girders. To pass the time, and to give himself something to settle Kieran's dreams with, Ash fantasized about where he'd rather be, and how he'd rather nurse Kieran -- an ivy-cloaked house on Helermont Bay, windows thrown open to the salt wind, sunlight blue and gold with the sparkling sea. There would be a stone-tiled stove to drive off the damp at night, and blankets of soft red wool, and clean white sheets and towels to cool Kieran's fever. Shelves on the walls would be full of old familiar books, so that he could entertain Kieran by reading to him; there would be plenty of warm, filling food, and fruit, and tea, and silly urchin children singing for spare change and sweets under the window. There would be days when gentle rain fell, when the only sound would be the creaking of fishing boats along the docks, and there would be lots of windy bright days when the gulls would yelp and holler overhead. Ash sometimes let himself fall so deeply into this fantasy that the next thing to bring him back to reality hit him with an almost physical shock. After that happened a few times, he decided the daydream's escape wasn't worth the dismay of returning from it.

That night, neither slept well. Kieran kept them both awake coughing. His lungs were making noise constantly now. His pain overflowed into Ash, his fear showed in his eyes, his weariness had reached the bone. He said nothing about it, but gripped Ash's hand desperately all night.

When it was light enough to travel, a potential problem occurred to Ash. He'd been following Kieran's instructions, but what if Kieran became unable to give them? He had no idea where they were. He doubted he could even retrace their circuitous path, let alone find the river or the road or any landmark from here. As for their destination, Kieran had been vague about it, and what if there was no help for them when they got there?

He addressed this concern tentatively once they were underway, but he must have been leaking emotion, because Kieran went off on a delirious streak of apologizing. He meandered between Eskarne and Iavaian, incoherent in both languages, and seemed to be talking to a lot of people who weren't there. Ash could only try to soothe and quiet him, and got no answer to his question. A sickness of a different kind was growing in Ash's heart. To see someone so strong broken down so badly was hard enough. But Kieran wasn't getting any better. He just kept getting worse.

At midday, they rested. In trying to dismount, Kieran took a disastrous spill, falling on his injured side, which dragged out of him a high scream like a dying animal's. It made Ash's scalp crawl to hear it, and to see Kieran panting and whimpering and coughing in the wake of the fall was unbearable. In addition, this accident broke several stitches; or, rather, ripped the loops of thread through weakened skin, and a rivulet of stinking yellow-and-red liquid ran out from under the bandage.

Trying to stay calm, Ash built a small fire, boiled water, and cleaned the wound as best he could. Kieran was conscious through this, but couldn't seem to keep his eyes open for more than a few seconds at a time. His breathing was shallow, full of clicks and whistles. He seemed to have nodded off by the time Ash tied on a clean bandage, but stirred when Ash tried to move away.

When he spoke, his voice was so weak that Ash had to ask him to repeat himself. "You'll like it there," Kieran wheezed. "It's like a garden. There's a pond... and pictures... I found a wild rose with... all those little thorns... looks like hairy legs... like a bug..."

"You don't have to talk," Ash said gently. He tried not to share his fear.

"Not delirious," Kieran said a moment later.

"Okay. You should sleep a bit. We could call it a day --"

"No. Listen." Kieran opened his eyes long enough to find Ash's face, closed them again with a smile. "I want to think about you being... being there... in the garden. You need green. Flowers. Love you. God I love you. I'm picturing... you there by the pond."

Ash thought he could actually hear a crack run through his heart, like lake ice breaking. He couldn't speak.

"I won't make it. You go, though. Down... from here take any... anything looks like water... cut it running down. Hit a dry stream... bed..." Pause to cough, wracking, fiery agony all across his chest echoing in Ash's mind. "Upstream there. Find a wet... a stream... wet sand, maybe mud... upstream. Got it?"

"Yes." Ash's voice betrayed him; the word came out as a sob, making Kieran open his eyes again.

"Don't be sad. Giving you a present. Listen. Not far now, nobody... knows about it and it... it's got power still. It might. Hide you. Oh god --" A convulsion of a cough, which left him gray and shaking.

Moving to the uninjured side, Ash helped him sit up to spit. Wiped his lips and chin, smoothed back the sweaty tendrils of hair that had escaped his braid. Kieran leaned into Ash's shoulder, walking his hand clumsily up to grip a handful of Ash's shirt. Ash said, "You're not going to die. I won't let you."

"I'm scared," Kieran whispered.

"Don't you dare give up."

"Not. Go down swinging."

"Don't go down at all! Damn it, Kai, are you listening to me? I refuse to live without you!"

Kieran made a sound that might have been a laugh. "You're such... a kid... but I do love to hear... hear you talk."

"Fuck this. Get up." Ash levered Kieran's arm around his shoulders. "Help me. You know you can. Come on, for god's sake get your legs under you --"

"Oh shit. Ow." But Kieran managed not to be completely limp, even if Ash had to take most of his weight.

"Good. Just a couple steps. Lean on me and I'm going to put your foot in the stirrup, now grab -- good --" It wasn't as hard as it should have been to boost Kieran into the saddle. For someone so tall, he didn't weigh nearly enough.

"What's the damn hurry?" Kieran wheezed.

Ash took his place and the reins, holding tight to keep Kieran from falling, for the Iavaian was entirely strengthless now, too weak even to sit up. "You're going to see your garden with the wild roses." He forced the weary horse to walk. Only after they were well underway did he realize he'd left the saucepan behind. It didn't matter. Nothing mattered. The world was flat, unreal, composed of only three things: *I love him; he loves me; he is dying.* It seemed to Ash that there was nothing more painful than those three statements together.

"Gonna sleep a little bit," Kieran said. "If I die... wake me up... so I can watch."

"If you die I'll follow you and beat you up, you jerk. *Fight.*"

"Yeah. Okay. Bury me... in the garden. Write... my name on the... wall." A slight laugh. "Big heart around it. Like kids do."

"Look, stop thinking about death things. Think about life things. What do you want to do while you're recovering, in this garden?" This got no response, but Ash could sense that Kieran was awake. "What's our day going to be like? You want to teach me things? I'll teach you Hanite if you want, I'll teach you to swear in Prandhari --"

"Tattoo." Kieran raised his good hand weakly, then dropped it. "Need eight dots. You too -- you want one?"

"Sure. You can show me how. Then what? There's a pond, you said; Maybe we could go fishing?"

A faint nod was all Kieran could manage.

"And then when you're well, what do you want to do?"

"Fuck your brains out." Kieran's laugh started strongly, but ended in another gurgling cough.

With a painful smile, blinking too fast, Ash managed to return a bit of a chuckle. "There, now, you wouldn't want to miss out on that, would you? You're just going to have to stay alive."

"I'll see... what I can do."

A few minutes later Kieran sank into unconsciousness, and this time he fell quickly below the strata where dreams occurred, down into the trenches of his mind where Ash couldn't find him. To the Empathic sense, he gave out nothing but pain and sickness; his emotions dropped off the map.

This left Ash free to weep as much as he wanted, and so, ironically, the tears wouldn't come. *Maybe I'm starting to believe my own talk about there being a future. Such a sweet future. I could never have imagined a world so perfect, even an hour ago. This garden he was talking about, I wonder... no, it does exist, it has to be real, and he will live to see it, and he'll get better, and we'll live there together and we'll be happy...*

If he dies, I'll bury him under that rosebush he mentioned. Then I'll put his gun in my mouth and blow my head off.

Ash tried not to think so much, after that. He concentrated hard on figuring out which way was downhill, discerning the marks cut by water long-dried, guessing which way it had flowed.

Hours crawled. The sun was sinking when he found the dry streambed Kieran had mentioned; he cursed the slow pace, but even if the horse had been capable of a better gait, anything faster would have jolted Kieran unbearably. Then he wasted an hour going the wrong way before he found some patterns in the sand that corrected his guess about which direction was downstream. This area was wind-whipped and bare, a plain of scattered boulders and mean, straggling weeds, with far-apart buttes standing out of it like rotten teeth. Eventually a line of stunted cottonwoods resolved into view; he deduced this must be the waterway Kieran had described, and impatience made him urge the mare to go faster. She ignored him. The animal was exhausted. Kieran was still comatose, breath bubbling in his lungs.

Evening fell purple across the land. The moon was already up, and by its growing light Ash was able to keep the trees in sight, and eventually to turn upstream on the buried creek; little more than a wet place in the sand, with occasional deposits of thick mud that sucked at the mare's hooves and made her prone to stopping. He feared she'd refuse to start walking again, but he always managed to convince her.

At a stretch of open water, he let the horse drink, and lowered a canteen on its strap to fill itself. He dribbled some into Kieran's mouth. Kieran didn't even swallow.

Time went even stranger. The moon hung still for what felt like years, and then moved a handsbreadth in the sky when he blinked. Eventually the stream became continuous, and he had to urge the horse up out of it, onto the dry land beside. He didn't remember when he'd left the open plain, but somehow he'd gone beyond the scattered outcroppings that had made a horizon at sunset, and was in a valley. Sometimes it was so narrow that he had to move back into the water, praying that the horse wouldn't step on a buried rock and break a leg. Sometimes it was as wide and gently sloped as he thought a valley ought to be, and he imagined it carpeted with green grass. From time to time the stream spread out so that it was just a wet spot on the ground, but that happened less often as the night wore on. Trees grew here, and the way was sometimes choked with brush and weeds.

All this time, Kieran was sinking deeper. Little by little his pain stopped transmitting itself to Ash; it was not that the wound hurt less, but that Kieran was subsiding below it. Ash had the feeling his own heartbeat was driving Kieran's, felt that somehow his own life was being drained away to keep Kieran alive. He hoped it was true.

When the hills faded away to either side, he thought at first it was just another valley. Not until the stream began to swing into a series of oxbow loops did he realize he was crossing a wide plain.

Riding with his head bowed for so long, he'd missed the point where the near and narrow horizon fell away, but now he was seeing some distance ahead. In the dark it was hard to tell just how far. Stands of trees punctuated this flat area, and the horse began to balk every few minutes to grab at a patch of grass or snatch a clump of leaves from some low-growing bush. *Let this be it,* he prayed, *please let this be the garden, and shelter not far ahead...* A sparkle off to the left proved to be the moon reflected in water, and as he saw it, Ash sat up straighter in a frail burst of new energy. Kieran had said something about there being power here. Was it this water, was the water sacred? But as he skirted the pond, he felt a greater energy beyond, like a fire's warmth on his face. The black horizon rose as he drew nearer to the power's source. He'd found the far edge of the plain, apparently a sheer cliff, its height impossible to judge, and in the cliff wall some kind of regular shapes were emerging.

All at once it came clear, and a thrill of awe ran through him at the size of the thing, at the mere fact of its existence in this country where so many ancient temples had been thrown down. An opening in the stone, twenty feet tall and a hundred wide, lay before him. This open mouth was toothed with thick pillars. Broad, shallow steps led up into the place. From between the center pair of pillars the stream flowed out, guided by a paved channel into a reflecting pool that was crossed by two flat bridges. These bridges were each a single slab of stone a foot thick; one had cracked and fallen into the pool, but the other was intact. Grasses, vines and flowers twined and choked these structures. The air was full of the smells of water, blossoms, and rot.

Ash guided the horse across the intact bridge and up the steps. Echoes of each hoof's fall clattered loudly inside, giving the impression of a vast space, but Ash didn't bother going in much past the rank of pillars.

There's something here. Or someone. Some old god, some lingering scent of sanctity, and I've just ridden a muddy-hoofed animal into the temple. That's probably blasphemy. Well, let your curse fall on me, whoever you are, but don't blame Kieran for it.

Gathering what strength he had -- a little more than he really had, it seemed, borrowing on credit -- he dismounted and pulled Kieran down with him. He couldn't stand; catching Kieran knocked him down, and it was all he could do to gentle Kieran's fall a little. Then there was no way he could get up again to unpack blankets and things, even if the mare weren't wandering away in search of the vegetation he hadn't let her explore on the way in. So he stayed where he fell. Sprawled, cradling Kieran in aching arms.

I'll just rest a moment. Just until I'm strong enough to go catch that stupid horse. He could hardly find any sign of life in Kieran's mind at all now. As for Kieran's body, it was utterly limp, skin chilled and greasy, heartbeat weak, breath labored and loud. With each breath, liquid gurgled and clicked in Kieran's lungs. The sound was dreamily horrifying. Too terrible to be real.

Through the remnant of the night, Ash lay listening to that sound. Through the blues and grays and purples of daybreak, through the gold and white of dawn, he listened to the wet rattle of Kieran's breathing.

Until, just as sunlight flooded the western mountains, the sound stopped.

The next few minutes were a chaos of frantic action in denial; trying to make Kieran take just one more breath, trying to turn back time just a few moments, to that last breath he'd allowed to slip by, as if he could have caught it with both hands and held it, shoved life back in; trying to trade anything, everything of himself to turn the broken body in his arms from a corpse to a person again.

No use. No hope. Everything wrecked. Every second of his life in vain, all leading up to this second of understanding that Kieran was destroyed, that there was no more of him in the world anywhere. All that strength and striving, all that brilliance and cruelty and sweetness and fear and love, vanished like a voice in still air.

He opened his throat and let the grief rush out; he couldn't stop howling, even though howling didn't help. If he could have smashed the world to powder, in that moment, he would have.

Chapter 23

Like snapping out of a daydream, pattern where there had been chaos: he was suddenly whole and real. All the smallness of mortality, gone in an instant. Pain shed like an ill-fitting garment. The confining walls of a twisted, damaged mind, an injured body full of limitations and riddled with needs and fears like wormy wood, shucked aside. Free.

Alone. Cut off. Amputated...

No; not quite free. He could stretch, yes, unfurl, but there were still limits, only farther and less solid. These senses were not as precise as those of the body, either. There were reasons for mortality. Yes. Memory was stored in the brain more than in the mind. His recollections were vague. This pattern was weak, this pattern was missing things, contained new whorls and new colors, he didn't know himself now. What did these patterns mean? Whole spiral arms of himself were unfamiliar. Creations of the last life lived. Had this happened before? Had he ever made himself new before, just by living as flesh?

More power. More power would be needed for thinking and knowing and being. There was power here -- stale, small. He drew it, and drew with it a sense of outside, of farther, deeper, higher, elsewhere. Prayers needled him immediately. Stinging rain of small entreaties. No proper offering, only begging and cursing.

Then, right inside, heartfire, a pure black flame of lamentation. Rare, sweet, mind-stinging perfume of anguish, offered directly to him as --

For me? -- no one could possibly hurt so much for me --

-- a sense of place and form began to resolve. More appropriate in every moment, the sacrifice. Beauty of shape and color; beauty of broken heart, involved in him entirely. A song of screams, a kneeling dance of rocking and ground-punching and hair-tearing, an incense of tears.

I didn't mean to hurt you so much, I'm sorry, I'm sorry --

He might bless this mourner with a gift of madness. It would be a short gift; the line of that life was veering sharply toward the border. The intention was clear; he'd never seen an imminent suicide so free from blurring doubt.

-- you idiot, you overdramatic stupid precious thoughtless wonderful selfish --

Patterns within his pattern moved against him. Perspectives smaller and sharper than his own threatened to become him. He perceived a kinship with the corpse now, remembered what he should not have retained, images and qualities from that life. Only one life, out of so many. But new. There had not been anything new for so very long. There had not been a reason for anything. And this pattern, semi-self, rather than fading to feed his power, sank tiny barbs into his older substance and tore him.

It was a sick thing, a broken thing, steely and smoldering and rusty and splintered; full of calcified, encysted passions, it was angry with a child's ill-aimed despairing anger, it was a child, he had been a child, he had been very nearly a man and *then this stupid thing happened and it's never fair, it's like the world hates me, everything I touch turns to shit* as a nearly direct result of actions taken centuries ago in order to eradicate him, propagating through the economy of history to include all his people in suffering *like this, he doesn't deserve it, maybe I do but he's a really good person and this is just wrong* as so many things had been wrong for such a long time.

With a sight that needed no eyes, he perceived the body of the boy he'd briefly been. Its death was growing more final by the second; soon it would cool. Then rot. Then dry to dust. And he? Burdened with the part of self he'd grown while in it, would he crack? Rot from the inside? Would he -- unbelievable! -- ache forever for that dirty, skinny mortal who was even now hunched wailing beside the corpse? A creature that lived in a flicker, fragile, a life too short for learning, even if this particular life weren't planning to end itself before sunset anyway. Was it possible that even one moment -- face tear-glazed and blotchy raised howling, bloodshot blue eyes sightless to the sightless sky -- was now indelibly part of his pattern? Unacceptable. Unacceptable. Horrible. It could not happen like this. It might fragment him. It could destroy him. Already the colors of the newer, lesser self were beating back the true equations of his power, eating at them like a cancer.

What am I, a ghost? If that were all, I'd say it was all right, at least I died free, but he -- how can I abandon him like this? I won't leave him, I won't!

That suddenly, the lesser pattern overwhelmed the greater, and he was reaching for more power than he'd meant to draw. Sudden wind stirred the mourner's hair as the temperature inside the temple dropped; plumes of vapor now carried the mourner's keening sobs, leaking between clenched teeth. There would be nothing left, all would go into this effort. He feared that fighting with himself at this point would break him up like smoke. He would truly be a ghost, then. So there was only one option. But still the power wasn't big enough. To push, to kill, took only a little; all life was under tension, reeling steadily toward its end, and a sharp shock in the right place could break it loose. Forcing those parted strands back together, on the other hand...

Trees in the garden stirred, then tossed, then thrashed and shed branches. Farther and farther he ranged, looking for anything he could use. Over the pool, down the stream, fog rolled. Within the temple, a skin of ice formed on the water in the channel. Even in the madness of grief, the mourner paused to wonder at the cold. From the depths of the earth, he tapped the groaning pressure of opposing stone, and the ground shuddered. Thunder rose up; dust sifted down.

Almost. Almost. Now.

Pain so intense was a thing like ecstasy; he couldn't even scream for it, while his body wrenched with the effort of expelling the stuff that had drowned him. His state was something more than consciousness, and less -- all sensation, no volition. He was nothing but a giant swollen throat, splitting open with agony, heaving and heaving and heaving.

Blocked, suffocating. Couldn't force it all out, lungs hitching, trying to inhale, choked, the stuff was reeling back in --

Then hands on him, fingers in his throat, gagging him, but the blockage was going out again, these hands were -- someone was -- Ash was reaching down his throat and hauling out fistfuls of the stuff.

And he was breathing. Searing, hot-cold air, more coughing, more pain. Then vomiting, and all the time his eyes and nose were running, and he could hear the sounds he was making, broken-backed-dog sounds... but he was alive. He had been dead. He was alive. Blind with pain, barely strong enough to breathe, but breathing. Heart stuttering like a string of firecrackers. Would have thought he was dying if he hadn't just been dead.

Did I dream that?

Does it matter?

"Oh thank you oh thank you thank you." Ash was sobbing the words as if he couldn't hear himself, over and over like an incantation.

Gradually he calmed; Kieran heard sanity return in his voice as it trailed away. Eventually Ash got up and moved around a bit, sometimes more or less near but always near enough. The compass around Kieran's neck knew where Ash was. Near enough. Talking, crying, cleaning with wet cloths, making a soft place for Kieran's head, petting and soothing. Warmth was returning. Fragmented thought began to pull together.

When water dribbled between his lips, Kieran found swallowing a terrible effort. Nevertheless he had to make a further effort after that, to pry his eyes open and to smile.

He was pillowed on Ash's lap. Above him, Ash's face was pale as dust, eyes black-circled as if he'd been punched twice. Dirty-haired, sunburned, tear-tracked, hollow-cheeked; beautiful, precious.

"Oh Kai, I was sure I'd lost you. I felt you go."

With great concentration, Kieran forced his lips to move. "Came back."

"Please stay with me now. Please get better. You're going to get better, right?"

He couldn't keep his eyes open anymore, but he managed one more word. "Yes."

As pain seeped away, back to being bearable, a sleepy contentment came over him. Something very strange had happened, but he could think about it later. There was going to be a later. Ash's voice followed him down, a whisper: "Don't go too far."

I won't, he thought gratefully. *I don't have to, now.*

Brilliant dreams came then. Dreams of pure color and meaning, without faces or time. He slept shallowly, dreamed close to the surface, half-lucidly, and never lost his sense of Ash's nearness. Sometimes he woke enough to perceive the real world outside his dreaming. There was birdsong and a smell of green. He heard Ash talking to the horse. For a while Ash lay beside him, and they dreamed together, and then he saw things he'd never seen before: snow sifting through a streetlamp's glow of yellow gaslight; the smell of wet leaves and gunpowder and dog, cramped legs and cold hands, ducks rising from among rushes in a whirring, yapping cloud; a woman's face, lined and smiling, pencils stuck in the coil of russet braids that crowned her; a whispering, mist-covered sea.

Best of all, when he woke in the dark, shivering, Ash woke as well and talked to soothe him. The words came with pictures, sounds, even smells. *I've smelled the sea. Never been within a hundred miles of it, but I know now what it smells like.* He could feel his strength returning, drop by drop. He could be patient until he was well. It was all going to be okay now.

There came, inevitably, a time when he woke with a full bladder and a rumbling stomach. Morning was near, he could smell it in the air, and somehow the smell was lonely. The sound of predawn birdsong was lonely. Ash still slept, hadn't woken with him; that perfect connection was gone.

He was cold, weak, and dizzy. For several minutes he weighed the warmth of the blankets against the pressure of his bladder. At last he surrendered to necessity and moved.

Inch by inch. Every movement took concentration. His attempt to stand was nearly a disaster, and he went quickly back to his knees. Settling on a halting motion on his knees and one hand, like a three-legged cat, he made it as far as the edge of the top step, between a pillar and a stone-lined groove carrying a stream of smooth water. But one look at the stairs told him that there was no way he could make it down. So he pulled himself upright against the pillar and, leaning on it, pissed in the stream.

Then he laughed. He'd befouled the temple. And he remembered dreaming that it was *his own* temple. A temple to him. In which case, using the sacred spring as a toilet was permitted.

Now he had the problem of his trouser buttons again. Which, he realized, was not a problem at all. He didn't have to sleep with his pants on. There wouldn't be an early-morning scramble for departure; this was their destination, and he could lie around until he was entirely recovered. Sitting on the edge of the blanket, he methodically removed his boots, socks, and pants, smiling a little to see how yellow-pale his legs looked compared to his arms. Then he slid back into the warmth he'd left, and relaxed, and was ambushed by weariness. Surprised he'd gotten up at all.

The next time he woke, Ash wasn't present. Kieran's boots were standing neatly together by the nearest pillar, but the rest of his clothes were gone. His compass told him that Ash wasn't far, though. He was out there, would probably be visible if Kieran sat up. Kieran didn't feel like sitting up. All he could do was lie here and wait for Ash to come back, but that was okay now. He was surprised to discover that he was completely certain Ash *would* come back, and would have been doing something good and necessary, and would go on doing good and necessary things. He hadn't ever known that kind of certainty before.

Which left one unanswered question: *What the hell does he see in me?*

By the time Ash returned, he'd wandered a long way from that train of thought. He'd dozed a little more, but hunger kept him from really sleeping. So it was with great pleasure that he watched the redhead kneel and lay out his bundled shirt, spilling a pile of ripe vegetables.

"Where'd you get those?" Kieran said. His voice was painfully hoarse, but he could achieve a conversational volume now.

Ash gave a grin that seemed to light him up like a beam of sunshine. "You were right, it's just like a garden! There are garden plants running wild all over the place! I found tomatoes, peppers, eggplants, squash, there's corn but it's not ripe, everything's a little on the small side -- how are you feeling?"

"Hungry."

"I figured. Besides that?"

"Tired. Bit sore. Uh... how are *you* holding up, Ashes? You looked pretty beat the other day."

Ash came closer, and when he was no longer half-eclipsed by the bright day behind him, Kieran could see that he was much cleaner than before. His clothes looked cleaner too, and a little damp along the seams. His face was still too thin, but his color was healthier. Sunburn nearly gone, eyes no longer bruised. He said, "How am I? Better than I've ever been in my life." A bright fragment of laughter spun out of him. "Can you believe how much has happened in just a few days? Not even three weeks since we left Churchrock. At the moment, I'm in serious danger of starvation, and so are you. That would have really scared me a little while ago. Now I'm just thinking -- so we feast on fresh veggies today, and *something's* bound to turn up tomorrow. What the hell does tomorrow matter?"

"Sounds like you've gone off your head a little." Kieran smiled to soften it.

"Most likely. I don't have clue one what I'm going to do with this stuff -- I can't stew it, I forgot the saucepan where you had that fall." Ash had to roll his eyes up and think: "Day before yesterday." Kieran didn't blame him for hesitating; it seemed they'd been here much longer.

"I'll eat it raw."

"Can you eat eggplant raw? You can't eat squash raw. Just a second." He brought over a tomato -- smallish, as he'd said, but it gave off a dusty savor even before he cut it into quarters. He bit into a slice and chewed thoughtfully. "It's all right. Probably wouldn't like it if I paid for it, but for free, with hunger sauce, it's good. Here, I'll help you sit -- oh!" He said this last syllable in a tone of mixed pleasure and apprehension, because Kieran had managed to sit up all by himself. "You sure you're up to that? Want something to lean on?"

"Nope." Kieran was as surprised as Ash was. "This isn't hard at all."

They ate the tomatoes raw; there were just enough of the small, tough, intensely-flavored fruits to take the edge off their hunger. The one bell pepper Ash had found tasted bitter and woody, but they managed to get that down as well. For dessert, they had the remains of a bag of raisins Ash had lifted off the priest.

"I'll bake the squash for supper. I think I can manage something involving stones and coals, but it might turn out a little burnt. There isn't much of anywhere to build a fire, though."

"What are you talking about?" With a gesture of his good hand, Kieran indicated the expanse of stone around them.

"You mean, in here? But this is some kind of temple. I don't want to make any... thing... angry."

Kieran grinned. "Hell, I pissed in the stream last night 'cause I couldn't get down the steps. I don't seem to be cursed."

"You did what?" Ash looked horrified for a second, but he couldn't keep it up. He let out a giggle. "You have no respect for anything, do you?"

"Almost."

"But still -- I didn't tell you this before because I didn't want to alarm you, but when you... when you died, for a minute, then just before you came back, the air got really cold in here. I mean, I could see my breath. And then the ground gave this little shimmy, almost like an earthquake."

"I know. I saw it."

"You... *saw* it?" Ash leaned closer, fascinated and frightened. "Tell me."

Kieran shook his head. "I don't understand, really. Or remember very well. But I was here... all over the place, I sort of occupied this whole space. And I wasn't really me. I was something else, or part of something else, and... you realize I wasn't in any shape to remember anything, I didn't have a brain to remember with... I got the impression that I -- this other me, this bigger me -- I'd been around for a long time. A *long* time. I mean, hundreds of years, maybe thousands." He looked down, and realized his hand had started trembling. "Help me lie down?"

Ash lowered him gently onto the pillow that was actually his rolled coat, then rested a hand on his forehead, smoothing back the strands of hair that tickled his face. "So you were really outside your body?"

"I was outside my *mind*, Ashes. I could almost *see* it. All these twisty swirly -- ideas, fibers of ideas, symbols? I can't, there are just no words, but it was intense, the bigger part of me wasn't real happy with the part that belonged to the body. Like it had been a big waste of time or something. This big part scared the living shit out of me, it was like an animal's mind, like some big meat-eating animal, it had no conscience. It was primitive. It was disgusted by me, like I was a bug crawling on it. But at the same time, I *was* that big mind, and I could see so far into the past I was nearly blind with it..." He bit his lip, as something seemed to stir in his memory, something nauseatingly large and powerful. A sea monster in tar. "I think it *was* a carnivore. Not literally. I mean, I think it was a thing -- I was a thing -- that ate other minds. Or had done, in the past. And I was scared that I couldn't eat the -- *this* me -- because it was too prickly.

"That all went by really fast, but then I could sort of see, only it wasn't in pictures, not like with eyes, more like that sense of space you get with having a Talent, when you kind of know where stuff is even in the dark. But this was really clear. I could see things -- heat, I could see *sounds* -- and you were just off your head, yelling and crying, and I could taste the craziness in you. The fucked-up thing is that it tasted good. Not good exactly -- good like pepper. Like liquor, how it burns, and I really liked it, and at the same time I couldn't stand it, and I was so sorry to be doing that to you... there was something else in you, Ash. I don't know if I was seeing your soul, or your magic, or what, but it looked all scrunched down and knotted. Then... somehow I *decided* to come back. I couldn't leave you. So I grabbed all the energy I could find, and I kind of knocked the sickness out of my body to make room, and --" He waved vaguely. "I think it was partly a dream. Maybe anyone with a death Talent can do that -- come back, if there's anything to come back to. But I just have this really vivid image of you looking up, and your eyes are so bloodshot that the blue part seems to be glowing..."

"It's all right now. It's over now."

"I know. The worst part was being cut off from you. No, the worst part was that I was sure you were planning to kill yourself. Were you?"

Ash looked away. "Yeah," he whispered.

"That's not okay, Ash! What if you'd done it before I could make it back, and I came back for nothing?"

"For nothing?" Ash echoed in quiet disbelief.

"And even if you could somehow be sure, before you did it -- I won't ask why you'd want to but -- but I wouldn't want you to, I'd want you to keep going, maybe then there'd be somebody in the world that remembered me as something besides a waste of skin." He grabbed Ash's hand and squeezed it as hard as he could, which wasn't very hard. "Promise you'll put all that suicidal bullshit out of your head. Promise, if something else happens to me, you won't --"

"I'm not sure I can." Ash tried a smile, but it didn't look right. "I was really not in control of my faculties. Sorry. This is a burden on you, I know. Maybe we should talk about something else."

"Okay. For now. Later, I'm going to make you promise."

Ash scrubbed his hands down his face. "Are you up to having your bandage changed? Or do you want to rest a bit first?"

"Go ahead."

It was difficult not to keep talking about the subject he'd agreed to drop. Not that he planned on getting killed, but the world was a dangerous place, and the thought of Ash following him into the grave -- especially now that he had an idea how strange and lonely death would be -- he couldn't stand it. But a minute later, Ash found something that distracted them both.

"This is unbelievable."

"What is?" Kieran ducked his chin as far as it would go, but couldn't see the wound.

"It's closed. It's completely healed over. Does this hurt?" Ash touched the place, gently. Then, when Kieran shook his head no, poked it a little harder.

"Ow. That one hurt."

"Okay, then this will hurt some too, but I have to test it." Hands walked along his collarbone, testing the join.

"Weird," Kieran said. "You know what it feels like? It feels like there's no break at all. It just feels bruised."

"All I can find is a little bump. I want to leave your arm in the sling for a while longer so you don't rebreak it. But I think you're healing incredibly fast, all of a sudden. I'd better get these stitches out before they turn into a novel form of tattoo."

"Do you think maybe *you're* healing me?"

"Me?" Ash looked up from snipping the loops of thread. "But I don't have a healing Talent."

"Maybe you do. Maybe that was what I saw balled up inside you."

Ash shook his head. "I wish. I think you're doing it yourself. This is going to feel weird, now -- I don't have a tweezers and I can't get a grip with my fingers, so I'm going to have to use my teeth."

"Whatever works."

Patiently, he sat still while Ash pulled the stitches out. The sensation was actually rather pleasant, for all it hurt a little. Everything seemed more vivid today. When he'd first discovered this place, it had been during a rare cold snap, one of those times that came along every two or three winters when night's frost stayed on the ground all day, and high clouds grayed the world. Hard pellets of snow had been spitting down on and off. He'd been up on the high ground, trying to find something to eat, and had stumbled on this place from above. A small herd of deer, and the shelter the temple provided, had kept him alive until the cold broke.

He hadn't explored the temple much. He knew the part he could see from here -- a warehouse-like space supported by fat pillars every twenty feet or so, with a mouth-shaped hole in the back wall that poured out water. There were paintings on the walls, but only toward the back were any of them even recognizable as human figures, and it was impossible to guess what they were doing or who they were meant to be. He hadn't explored the two side passages, having lacked a lantern. His most vivid recollection of the four or five days he'd spent in the place was of running into a thicket of wild rose, rich with the glossy red ovals of rose hips, which he had eaten. It was off to the left, he thought, the south end of the valley. He'd made a circuit of the area, and judged the valley to be an oblong about a mile wide and a bit less than two miles long.

Now, instead of a browned landscape salted with dirty white at the roots, he saw a green paradise. Grass and wildflowers spread the open places; beneath tall pines and cottonwoods, thicker vegetation grew, viny tangles and thorny shrubs. Here and there a lone acacia stood. On the north side, where the slope was gentle, irregular swathes of other plants made strange textures of green; he couldn't see, at this distance, what they were, but he guessed that was where Ash had found the vegetables. Someone had planted a kitchen garden there, once upon a time. And in the rockier places, the wild roses grew. As he watched, half distracted by the sensation of Ash's lips and teeth nudging the new scar on his back, he saw a dark speck appear on the crest of the hill.

Apprehension made him tense enough that Ash sensed it, and stopped. But it wasn't a man, he realized when the speck started down the slope, two others coming up and over behind it. "I think," he said slowly, "that our dinner has arrived."

"Where?" Ash peered along Kieran's pointing finger, but shook his head.

"Those brown things. I think those are deer."

"I can't tell. These glasses aren't quite right. I'll get one for you, though, if they are. You'll have to give me some pointers -- that one I got the other day was a lucky shot."

"Huh. They'll see you coming a long way off. Might be better to wait until they get closer."

"But they'll eat all the veggies!"

Kieran laughed. "Wouldn't you rather have venison than eggplant?"

"We'll need both, if we're going to get our strength back."

"Okay. All I can tell you is, go really slow, and stop whenever they notice you. Hold still until they forget about you, then move again. Deer have really short memories. Oh, and stay downwind."

"I knew *that* much already. I'll finish with the stitches

later." He took his rifle and trotted away.

Kieran quickly lost interest in watching him stalk the deer. It would take him quite a while to get close enough. To pass the time, Kieran had a go at standing up, and discovered that he was barely dizzy at all. Much of his earlier shakiness must have been due to hunger. He wrapped one of the blankets around his waist as a kilt -- it hardly hurt at all to use his right hand now, as long as he didn't try to hold any weight with it -- and went exploring.

First he explored the packs and saddlebags. Ash had done his usual neat-freak job of things, and Kieran was pleased to see that this included laying out all their weapons in plain view and easy reach, fully loaded, with spare ammunition nearby. He'd also done some laundry. Kieran found his leather pants turned inside out and laid flat in a patch of sunlight, his shirt and an extra blanket and all the spare bandaging materials washed and drying. What food they had was carefully stowed. There was nothing left in quantity but coffee, sugar, salt, and flour; only about one meal's worth of beans and rice remained.

Kieran set the remaining beans soaking in the skillet. If Ash didn't bag a critter, they could at least fill their stomachs tonight.

One of the knapsacks contained bullets and soap and the like. Complimenting himself on his foresight, Kieran took a candle out of one of the two bundles of a dozen he'd gotten from the store in Smith. He lit it, tucked the remaining matches in the waist of his kilt, and went to have a look around.

The spring wasn't as interesting as it should have been. It was just a hole in the wall where water fell out. Some painted shapes above it looked like they were meant to be stormclouds. The water ran in a sheet down the wall to fill a basin paved with pale limestone, which narrowed down into the channel that crossed the temple and went outside. He felt there should have been some carvings or something around it, but there weren't. The central two files of pillars had carvings, but they were just geometric designs. It was like the place had been left unfinished; no, more like the builders had cut corners. Rushed? Broke? Didn't care?

Passages led out from the back two corners. Doorless openings, on a more human scale than the rest of the place, they led into utter darkness. He tried the left-hand one first. Trying to summon up a sense of awe at his ancestors' engineering greatness, he could only manage a feeling that he was sneaking around in somebody's house while the owner was on vacation.

The hallway dead-ended about thirty feet in. Disappointed, he tried the other one, expecting it to do the same. But here, he found a wonder. Colors glittered and danced in the light of his candle. Not faded parades of figures, like the ones in the main room, but dense blocks of text interspersed with jewel-like scenes of frenetic detail. The text was in the old symbol-script that he couldn't read. That was all right, though, because just looking at these pictures would occupy him indefinitely.

The first one he brought his candle close to depicted a city in a valley. The artist had simplified it to a few buildings, but they way they were jammed together on top of each other made it clear they symbolized a great metropolis. Water, painted deep lapis blue, lapped at the city's foot. Bright flags flew from its heights. The sun still had some gold leaf clinging to it.

Another picture showed a leopard killing a rabbit. The leopard wore a jeweled collar. In the background, a smiling woman in an elaborately draped and girdled gown directed the leopard with a gesture of her hand.

Another was full of tiny human figures, each one wearing a conical helmet and carrying a spear, each spear decorated by intricately drawn lacings and wrappings, all different.

He could make out no sense of narrative flow, no matter which direction he read the pictures. Some seemed to show important people, kings or gods, because certain figures were drawn larger than others. Many showed only animals or vegetation; a few were filled with abstract geometric shapes. He recognized one of these geometrics as being a stylized wind knot, which implied the others had symbols hidden in them as well. There was an entire book's worth of writing in this place, which piqued his curiosity, got him thinking about hunting up some old guy who could still read this stuff.

At the end of the hall was a closed door. It had once been lacquered red, but it was faded now, cracked in many places; when he touched it the whole thing came apart. Jumping back to get out of the way extinguished his candle. He groped out another match, stopped himself from striking it on the wall lest he harm the paint, struck it on the floor instead and relit the candle. And let his jaw fall open in wonder.

Gold. There was gold in there. Great masses of it.

Stepping carefully over the splintered remnants of the door, he entered a glittering vault of color and shine. Vases, boxes, candleholders, incense burners, and all manner of smooth-polished objects stood in ranks from wall to painted wall, and all of them shone with the same buttery gleam. The colors of these walls' paintings were even brighter, and the human figures they depicted were not marching straitly through history, but celebrating and fighting and dancing and fucking and dying in ornate profusion.

But the centerpiece of the room, which it was hard to look away from, was a life-sized statue of a young man reclining on a couch piled with cushions. It seemed to be carved of limestone, but beneath all the paint and ornament it was hard to tell. Even more than the gold things, this seemed to be a lost treasure. The subject's body was posed realistically, his kilt draped in such a way that Kieran could guess it was linen edged with cloth-of-gold rather than some other fabric, the tiny braids of his long hair were each individually carved; it was almost as if a real boy had been frozen in stone. If so, he seemed to have enjoyed the process. The unnaturally beautiful face held a serene expression, tinged with just a hint of a sardonic smile. He was crowned with a wreath of poppies. Kieran wondered how the sculptor had managed to get their petals so paper-thin without breaking the stone, until he worked up the courage to step closer and saw that the flowers were actually, of all things, glass.

Kieran closed his weak right hand around the bullet hanging at his throat. He wanted Ash to come see this, and wondered if it was possible to send a message. He didn't want to turn his back on the statue for fear it would -- he wasn't sure what. Disappear, or wake... it disturbed him. It made him think of the spiritual predator he had halfway been in the moments of his death.

How long he looked at it, he didn't know. Eventually he heard Ash say his name and muttered some reply; he couldn't bring himself to yell.

Some time later Ash stood beside him, caught by the statue into ignoring the gold just as Kieran had been. The carving looked new; none of the paint had worn or chipped, not one gem had fallen from the golden armbands and anklets the reclining figure wore. The skin had been painted reddish-brown, the hair black, the eyes darkly outlined. The ends of the tiny braids had been crosshatched to make them look like bundled hair. Someone had adored the subject of this statue, to spend such effort on detail. It must have been a king, or a god... Kieran was afraid he knew which god it was meant to be.

At last, Ash spoke. "It's you," he said quietly.

Chapter 24

Kieran turned slowly to look at him, unwilling to understand. He saw that there was a streak of fresh blood on Ash's sleeve. So he'd got his deer after all. "What do you mean, it's me?"

"Look at it." Ash pointed at the statue's face. "Right down to the expression. I know it doesn't make sense, but that's you. I half expect the thing to open its mouth and say, *You done staring yet?*"

Kieran smiled a little at Ash's imitation of his voice, but an uncomfortable sense of recognition was stealing over him. "Maybe it's an ancestor of mine. That would be ironic, huh? If this -- king, or whatever -- was my gazillion-times-great grandfather."

"Ironic? It would be *spooky*. It *is* spooky. Look, he's even got your hands, I think he's even as tall as you are. And I think... move the candle a little." Ash nudged his hand, and as the light moved, a reflection started up eerily in the statue's eyes. They weren't painted, as Kieran had assumed. They were inlaid. And they were not black, but dark green.

"Well. That's... that's pretty fucking odd. Because, I mean, obviously it's not me, so I guess..."

"It's a portrait. Look at the details. Look -- oh, there's a difference. His nose is a little crooked."

"It is?" Kieran ducked to get a better look, head-on, face-to-face with the statue.

When he found himself at the same level, head tilted at the same angle, he had the sudden impression he was looking in a mirror. And his reflection was laughing at him. He straightened suddenly and turned his back on it.

"That is creepy as fuck," he said quietly.

As he walked away, he could feel it staring at his back. He didn't realize he'd tensed up his injured shoulder until he was back in the big room and was surprised at a sudden lessening of the ache.

He went all the way outside, down the steps to the grass. He didn't feel quite clear of it until he was standing in the sunshine, listening to the buzzing of flies over the carcass of the deer that Ash had shot. The sun was over the mountains. The air was hot and still. The wound that had nearly killed him was healing practically overnight, Ash was turning out to be a damn good hunter, there had been that thing about being outside himself and the crushing sense of history he'd seen there, and now he'd found an unbelievable fortune in ancient gold, with which he could do nothing on account of being a fugitive, and a statue that looked way too much like him. Minus scars, plus a crooked nose. He was tired.

Ash came silently down behind him and put a hand on the small of his back. "You can blow out your candle now, if you want."

"Oh." With a startled laugh, Kieran pinched the wick. "What happened to the horse? I don't see it."

"She wandered off as soon as I unsaddled her. She's out there somewhere."

"Won't be hard to find, I guess."

"What do you suppose this place is? How come the people who put all that gold in there never came back for it? And why's it never been looted?"

"How should I know?"

Ash shrugged. "I'm just making noise, I guess. It's funny -- we've found this humongous pile of treasure, and we can't touch it."

"Yeah. We try to sell it, we'd get caught."

"*Sell* it? I was thinking about studying it. There's almost no Iavaian temple art left in the world, and here we've found all the lost altar furniture or something. How could you think about selling it?"

"How could I not? That stuff was made of solid gold!"

"But it's your --"

"Heritage. Huh." Kieran spat into the reflecting pool. "Lemme tell you something about heritage."

Ash took the candle and matches from him and set them on the bottom step. "Tell me while I butcher this deer. You can stop me if I'm about to do a bad job, because I've seen it done but I never did it myself."

"You're pretty good at killing 'em, for someone who's never done it before."

"I've hunted before, but it was a bit too civilized. My aunt and I always hired a couple of guys to come with us and do the icky stuff. I didn't even have to carry the raw meat. I watched them, though." He'd apparently watched closely enough, because he started with the right sort of cut. Although he worked so slowly and meticulously that he seemed to be dissecting the thing for science rather than butchering it for food.

Kieran sat down on the lower step to watch. It was a relief to be off his feet. He had no stamina. Still, he thought he was doing pretty well for someone who'd been dead the previous morning. He held his right arm across his lap to rest the shoulder. "What do you know about the war?" he said.

"Guess I don't have to ask which war you mean. Well, I know the official version, which goes something like: after about three hundred years of missionary work, Dalanists had gained a small number of converts in Iavaian territory. The rest of the people continued to worship devils and live sinfully. Then came the Nine Days' War, in which tribal leaders tried to abolish Dalanism. The Iavaian Dalanists, fearing for their lives, petitioned the Commonwealth for assistance. Commonwealth troops occupied and annexed the territory and imposed law and order, to the great benefit of the inhabitants, who are lazy benighted savages and should be grateful. Oh, I forgot to throw in the phrase 'minimal bloodshed' -- the histories always have to put that in somewhere. And then I know a bit of the unofficial version, which is that the reason the death tolls are so low is that the Commonwealth only counted armed enemies killed in organized conflict. Guerilla fighters are counted as bandits. Noncombatants aren't counted at all, even though -- I gather -- they died in droves."

"Ever talk with somebody who was there?"

"No. Never really got a chance to talk with any Iavaians but you, and I studiously avoided soldiers and Watchmen back home." He lifted his wrist as if to wipe his brow, but stopped, wrinkling his nose at the sheen of jelly-like deer blood that clung to it. He stripped off his shirt and tossed it in the reflecting pool, where it immediately became the center of a comet-shaped red cloud.

Kieran watched the thread of blood being swept down the stream, until Ash bent to his task again. Then he watched the working of bone and muscle under freckled skin. Remembered how Ash had splayed a hand across his back a moment ago, how good it had been to feel that. The illusion of fragility was fading the more he watched Ash's body. Abruptly he was glad he was wearing a makeshift kilt instead of his tight leather pants.

"Well." Kieran cleared his throat, trying to get back on topic. "What they call the Nine Days War, that was actually about three years long. Only, it was the Dalanists who started it. Bands of 'em were knocking down temples and stealing stuff from them. These weren't really religious people, see, they were mercenaries. Mostly poppy farmers who got put out of work when the *Tiwa'hanaka* outlawed opium growing. Which they did because the Commonwealth made them do it."

"Yeah, with trade sanctions and stuff, I read about that. The Tiwawhatsit, that's the tribal ruling body, right?"

"The Five Tribes' Brotherhood, yeah. So these farmers were wrecking temples and holy sites, and any kind of religious or historical thing they could find. Which the Commonwealth was paying them to do. They found a lot more of 'em than the Eskaran army would've found, too, because they grew up being shown those places and told to be reverent. Also they were assassinating priests and holy people. Now, before the Annexation, most Iavaians with a Talent didn't do anything with it, but the ones who did were mostly priests. What I hear is that the Eskarans were offering a bounty for heads with shaved scalps. Because priests shaved their heads, male and female both. Five *ya* for a woman and eight for a man."

"Which is?"

"I dunno how much a *ya* was worth. I've seen the coins, people collect them and melt them down for the silver. I'd guess about half a throne."

"Okay. Go on. Presumably people got fed up with this."

"Right. And there were little skirmishes, and attempts to arrest the temple-burners, and so forth. But the way things were set up, each of the five tribes had its own army, and those were raised by levy from each clan, so they weren't real organized. And a couple tribes that didn't have a member on council, like the *Riaha*, the High Pass tribe, were represented at the clan level, but they resented that, so their troop levies weren't real cooperative."

"I'm impressed. You know a lot about this."

"It only happened thirty years ago. The Eskarans couldn't kill *everybody* who remembered. And arresting them for talking about it only works if they talk in public. Anyway, as soon as the *Tiwa'hanaka* started making some progress against the temple-burners, in jumps the Eskarne Theocratic Commonwealth, claiming its converts are being persecuted. On that basis they rounded up and imprisoned whole villages, and when they ran out of room in their prison camps, they just started killing everyone they found who wasn't for sure on their side. But like you said, they didn't count those, because they were noncombatants. By the time the *Tiwa'hanaka* got it through their thick heads that they couldn't make the invasion stop by lodging diplomatic protests, the Eskarans were dug in. And then the different tribes had different ideas about how to fight, and they argued, and some of 'em went off half-cocked, and some of 'em sat around blabbing until it was too late.

"When they finally did get right down to fighting, the ones who took any serious casualties fled or surrendered. The only ones who ran a decent war were the Tama, and even then, most of them bugged out when the going got too tough. I want to be proud of my clan because they stuck it out to the end, but all they managed to do was get a whole generation wiped out. Men and women were both fighting by then, so only kids and old folks were left. My mom was raised by her grandma. She told me she had two brothers and a sister, but they died of cholera when they were moved into the cities."

"That's... that's really sad, Kieran. It's horrible."

"Sad? It's stupid! My point is that they brought it on themselves! It was their own fucking fault! What were they thinking? There wasn't even a real border between them and the Commonwealth, just a river partway and an imaginary line. The biggest military power in the world, which a hundred years ago took a big bite out of Paiwaar and then spent their time taking Yelorre and losing it and retaking it -- my point is, it should have been obvious there was a wolf at the door. A goddamn rabid wolf, camped out on their doorstep. But did they have a coherent political body that could make fast decisions if it had to? No. Did they have any solid diplomatic ties to anyone who could maybe step in on their side if it was needed? No! They pissed off Prandhar arguing over some dumb chunk of land nobody wanted anyway. And did they have a competent military force? No, they had a bunch of village bullies who'd been sent to drill because they were raising hell at home. Untrained, illiterate, narcissistic fuckwits who had more loyalty to their second cousins than to the People as a whole. What I'm saying is, we asked for it."

"You would have done it differently, I take it."

"Hell yeah."

"What's this? Do we eat this?"

"That's the liver. We eat that. We fry it with that eggplant you're so keen on, as soon as you're done there."

Ash gave a half-happy groan. "Never thought I could be so hungry while up to the elbows in lukewarm slithery guts."

"Welcome to the country life."

"Anyway. You were saying?"

"I was done."

"I don't get what brought that on, though. Just felt like ranting about history?"

"Oh. Well, I figure the reason all that treasure is holed up in here is because it was hidden from the temple-burners. And I guess it makes me kinda mad that someone had the presence of mind, and the manpower, to move things like that big heavy statue here to this place nobody knew about, and then keep anyone from knowing about it all this time, but they couldn't get their shit together enough to fight a war. What the hell good does all that gold do anyone? They should've sold it to buy rifles. If they had a hiding place this good, they should've used it as a guerilla base. Staged raids from here."

Ash was picking up speed, slicing off meal-sized strips and laying them out on the grass. Blood was running off his elbows, spattering his pants. The soles of his feet were black with dirt. He looked savage, primitive; his cultured voice was an amusing contrast. "Isn't this place kind of far away from things? I mean, to be any use as a staging area."

"Actually, it's only about fifteen miles to the road, that way. South," he added, as he realized Ash hadn't seen him pointing. "From there, only a couple days' ride to Canyon, and you can do it faster if you're on foot. If I'm not carrying much more than a canteen, a rifle, and a sack of lunch, I can do forty miles in a day, easy. That is, if I'm in top shape. I probably couldn't make it across the valley, right now."

"You'll get your strength back."

"Plus there's a built-in escape route. The way's a bit twisty, but if you go all the way downstream -- you remember that dry riverbed? You must've followed it to get here. Well, you follow that down about fifty more miles, and it runs into the Burn."

Now Ash craned around to look at him, frowning. There was a smudge of blood on one lens of his glasses, where he'd shoved them up his nose with the back of his hand. "Why would you want to do that?"

"Gotta swear you to secrecy." Kieran grinned to show it was a joke, but Ash took him seriously.

"Cross my heart."

"Little known fact, you can spend hours -- maybe days -- in the edge of the Burn and not get hurt. And the power, even on the fringe, will backlash down your trail and blur it out, so nobody can trace you by magic. The rumor is that the more Tama blood you've got in you, the less the Burn hurts you."

"Hence its name?"

"Yep."

"Do you think anyone's ever been to the middle of it?"

"Huh. No way. Thing's thirty-six miles across, and what I heard is that the fringe part ends about two miles in. After that... *bloosh*."

"Bloosh?"

"Your nose bleeds, your ears bleed, and then you have about five minutes to get out before your brain turns to jelly and you die."

"Oh. Well, I should probably avoid the place, since I'm pretty sure I have no Tama blood in me whatsoever. Although I seem to have a great quantity of deer blood *on* me, so if you'll excuse me, I'm going to wash off."

"We should decide where the garbage goes."

"You decide."

"I guess just pitch it in those weeds over there. We really should bury it, but --"

"No shovel." Wrinkling his nose, Ash hoisted the bundle of hide, hooves, and guts, and hauled it into the thicket Kieran had indicated, about a hundred yards away. It still might attract coyotes and wildcats, not to mention flies, but at least the smell wouldn't bother them. Probably.

As Kieran levered himself off the step, he found he was formulating an excuse to join Ash in bathing. Several casual things to say about it ran through his mind. But none of them came out of his mouth. He watched Ash walk away, and stayed where he was. He told himself it was because he was still weak and sore from his injury, however fast it was healing.

So he decided to see what he could do about food. He'd just remembered that their only pan was currently full of beans.

The best way to deal with dried beans was to soak them for an hour, then boil them to mush, then fry the mush. But it was also possible to soak them overnight, then cook them lightly; he'd never liked them that way, but it crossed his mind to tie them up in a square of bandage gauze and hang them in the stream. Then they'd be ready tomorrow. That done, he set to slicing up the deer's liver. He'd never bothered slicing one before, just roasted it whole, so he made a literal hash of it. Oh well, it was meat. Fortunately Ash returned, in wet pants, with an armload of wood, before Kieran could get too far into the eggplant.

"You plan to eat the stem?"

"Oh. Huh. I suck at this. You do it."

"Okay, you make the fire."

"My arm's tired."

"You can do it one-handed, right? Where's your sling? Put your sling back on."

"Cluck, cluck."

"I am *not* being a hen, *you're* being a -- the kind of person who makes everything worse by trying to be tough, I'm sure there's a word for it."

Kieran washed his hands, re-slung his arm, and built the fire. Then he leaned his back against the nearest pillar and dozed off in the afternoon sun.

The next thing he knew Ash was prodding him awake, looking concerned and a bit shaken.

"What's wrong?" Kieran glanced around, half expecting to see a rank of Watchmen charging across the valley.

"Time to eat."

"That's why you look like you found a bone in your applesauce?"

"Uh. No. You were talking in your sleep."

Not sure whether to be embarrassed or amused, Kieran took the bowl of food he was offered and busied himself with eating for a little while. After the first bite, it was no longer a pose. He was pretty sure *he* couldn't have made fried liver and some boring vegetable taste so good. He wolfed down half of it before he was willing to stop long enough to talk. "What was I saying?"

"I don't know, it was Iavaian. The thing that spooked me is you weren't mumbling like people usually do when they talk in their sleep. You sounded like you were lecturing."

"Weird."

"This whole place is weird."

"Yeah, but..." A sudden spike of worry hit him as he realized Ash might want to leave. Where could they go? And what if Ash associated him with the weirdness, wanted to ditch him, he'd been a huge burden lately --

Before he could say anything, Ash reached out to rest a

hand briefly on his knee. "It's all right. It's a friendly weirdness, I think. Look at how fast you're healing. It likes you."

I'm going to have to say something soon, or do something. To make sure he knows how much I want him to stay with me. But can I make that kind of -- it's a demand, really, can I demand that of him? No, I can't ask, because if staying made him unhappy, and my asking made him do it anyway --

"Kai, it's all *right*," Ash insisted. Responding to the feeling, not knowing its source. Kieran resolved to set it aside for now, think it over when Ash was asleep or something.

After they'd finished with the liver and eggplant, Ash juggled the two halves of the squash out of the hot embers. He'd sprinkled sugar on them, but they were still not very good. Kind of dry and stringy.

"You really need butter to do this right," Ash explained. "I thought of using a bit of deer fat, but decided against it."

"Gah. Good call."

"Maybe we'll find a bee tree, get some honey, that would've worked."

"Well, I'm eating mine anyway. I'll have yours if you don't want it. Pass it over." He polished off both portions, right down to the charred skin. Finally, his belly felt full for the first time in -- he couldn't remember how long. "Now this," he said, "is life."

"Don't get too comfy. You've still got some stitches in you."

Kieran moved away from the pillar and took off his sling so Ash could get at his back. Probing at the scar with his fingers to find out how many stitches were left, he found that it didn't hurt unless he really dug in. "This is bizarre. It hurts a lot less now than it did -- what, four hours ago?"

"Not even that. I think it was a bit after noon when I started pulling the stitches, and the sun's still at half-mast. Yeah, something around here is definitely healing you. Oh. Bad thing." He tugged at a stitch with his fingers. "You've totally healed up around the thread."

"Just go ahead and haul it out."

"If you say so." Ash's breath washed across his shoulder, and then he felt a slight scrape of teeth and a sharp needling sensation. This was repeated three times in the same spot before it was followed by a tug, and Ash switched to fingers to pull the loosened thread the rest of the way out.

"That didn't hurt much."

"It didn't bleed much, either. Just little dots. When I did it before, it ripped the scar some. Ready for the next one?"

"Quit asking me. Just do 'em all."

Now that he was full of good food and feeling nearly healthy, he found he was far more bothered by the feeling of Ash's mouth on him than he'd been before. *Definitely getting better. Well enough to --?* He was abruptly unsure how Ash would respond if he turned around and kissed him. They were comfortable together, true, glad together, good friends, there was trust. But for all he knew, Ash had been feeling filthy and regretful about that night -- might not be remembering it as lovemaking, but as a seduction. They hadn't discussed it. *Even if he still wants me, he'd probably rather not do anything right now. He's had to deal with spit and blood and pus and vomit. And I'm not real clean just presently.*

I'm making excuses. I'm scared. This is idiotic. I know he cares for me, loves me -- I know that, right?

The other day, when I said I loved him, he didn't say it back.

Ash paused in the middle of working on a particularly tricky thread. "Are you all right? Is something bothering you?"

"Just because you're an Empath doesn't mean you get to eavesdrop while I'm thinking."

"Oh. Hell. I was, wasn't I? I'm really sorry."

Kieran sighed, wishing he'd phrased that better. "Just get it done, will you?"

That was the last thread on his back. Then Ash came around to work on the front, and that was even more disturbing. Kieran couldn't stop imagining warm breath and grazing teeth moving upwards from there, in along his collarbone, up his throat. His hands made fists to keep from reaching out, and he wondered why he was stopping himself.

Seven stitches later, Ash picked the final bloodstained thread out of his teeth and held it up, and Kieran breathed a sigh of relief that it was over. Relief and regret.

"What a day," Ash said. "I saw a hill of gold, got a history lesson, squidged around in guts, and ate scab."

Uncomfortable as he was, Kieran couldn't help grinning. "That was fun, what do you wanna do now?"

"You should bathe." A hesitation, Ash's smile faltering as he realized he was being rude. "I don't mean you smell, it's just, when you've been ill --"

"No, I do smell, I can smell me."

"And if you wait any longer, you'll have wet hair when

night comes."

"Yeah."

"Sorry, I'm usually more tactful than that. Don't be mad."

"Don't be such a drama hog. Of course I'm not mad." Feigning exasperation, Kieran got up and lurched off toward the pond. When he reached it and looked back, he couldn't see Ash in the entrance of the temple. Ash was making no effort to watch. He really wasn't interested.

Well, naturally. Like you're such a prize, Trevarde. Why would anyone want to look at your skinny yellow ass?

Dropping his blanket-kilt, carefully setting his compass on top of it, he waded in. The water was warmer than he'd expected. Just cool enough to offset the hot sun. His legs looked sickly-pale under the surface. Weeds and mud squished between his toes, making him wonder how he'd get out without ending up with mud shoes.

He was tempted to swim out to the middle, but wasn't sure he had the strength to get back again if he did. Instead, he skirted the edges, beginning to enjoy the water despite his self-pity. About halfway around, he found a place where the mud gave way to sand. This shallow beach, he discovered, ran twenty feet out, then suddenly dropped off. He didn't test the drop-off; he was sure weeds would wrap his ankles and drown him. It was sickening to be so weak.

Sitting crosslegged on the sand so that the water was chest-high, he pulled the string off his braid. A bunch of hairs came with it. Strands kept coming out as he unraveled the braid, wrapping around his fingers, so he imagined that when he got it completely undone the whole thing would fall off, leaving him bald. Of course, that didn't happen. He ducked his head a few times, working his fingers in, and each time had to pick loose hair off his hands.

"Hey."

Ash's voice startled him. He twisted around, shoving his wet hair back. The redhead was standing on the edge of the grass where it met the sand, rifle slung over his shoulder, offering a lump of soap. When he saw he had Kieran's attention, he tossed it underhand.

Kieran caught the soap neatly. "Going hunting again? We've got enough to last us a week."

"Nah, I thought I'd kind of stand watch."

"Oh."

"There might be, you know, various toothy critters. Not that you couldn't take 'em, normally, but --"

"Yeah, okay."

Ash sat down with the rifle across his knees and made a show of gazing off into the distance.

Funny that I didn't sense him coming closer. I'm not wearing that compass charm he made, true, but didn't I used to have a better sense of where he is? I guess we don't have that connection anymore. No, what am I thinking, it's because I'm in water. Why am I hunting reasons to be unhappy? What am I trying to push away?

Turning his back on Ash, more to hide his expression than from modesty, he went to work with the soap. His skin was two shades lighter when he was done scrubbing it. When he washed his hair, the lather turned gray, and grit got caught under his fingernails.

He lay back to rinse off. Watched his hair swirl above him, deep black clouds streaked with milky soap-water. Then he did the whole thing again. As he did, he was aware that he was stalling. Because now would be a very good time to open the subject -- all those difficult subjects -- what sort of relationship they had, whether to stand by confessions made in strange circumstances. Once it was given a label, it could no longer be changed or denied. And if it turned out to be a bad idea, things could get so much worse...

Leaving things unspoken wasn't really an option anymore, though. It was all too obvious. He just knew he was going to botch everything, but if he acted like it didn't matter, that would be a kind of botch as well. It shouldn't have been so confusing. He couldn't figure out why the thought of being the one to reach out seemed so sick. Why he felt he ought to convince Ash that he was -- what, unworthy? Dangerous? Wasn't that a kind of arrogance?

So he wasted time, trying to think of what he wanted to say, finding all his words scrambled and useless.

Eventually he started to get chilled. He tossed the soap up on the bank. Ash set the rifle aside and offered the spare blanket, the one he'd washed earlier. Kieran wrapped the blanket around his waist and wrung out his hair. When he looked up again, Ash had a comb.

"Thanks." Kieran reached for it, but Ash didn't hand it to him.

"I'll do it for you."

"Oh. Okay." For the zillionth time that day, he sat with

his back turned and let Ash mess with him.

It was a beautiful day. They were free. He was miraculously healed, when by rights he should have been dead. It was stupid to brood. So how come he had to drag out memories of almosts and false starts and mull over them like some crippled soldier wearing out his old battles?

If I try to explain, I might drive a wedge between us. I don't really have to say anything now, do I? Maybe it can wait. Maybe it's an insult to him to assume he doesn't understand. Maybe I don't want him to understand.

The comb paused. "Kieran, what on earth is the matter?"

"Eavesdropping again?"

Combing resumed, but stopped again after only a few seconds. "But you seem so unhappy. Can't I help?"

"You *are* helping."

"Then why does it seem like it's me you're unhappy with?"

Kieran studied his oversized, knobby hands where they rested on his oversized, knobby knees. He hated the whole clumsy overgrown body he was stuck in. As he tried to find a way to answer that wouldn't make his decision for him, his stomach began to roil as if it were full of rattlesnakes. His voice came out whispery: "You're not the problem."

"Then what is?" After a moment, Ash's hands touched his sides. Sun-hot arms slid around his waist; a faintly stubbled cheek rested against the sensitive new scar. Lightly, painlessly. Helpless to refuse, Kieran leaned back into the embrace.

And there goes the option of leaving the subject alone. Oh shit, I'm going to blurt and babble, aren't I? Kieran's head started to hurt, right in the middle of his forehead. "It's hard to explain." His own voice sounded strange to him. "I guess I'm just -- I'm confused. That's all."

"Tell me. I'll help you figure it out."

"It's not -- can I use your own words on you? Is that fair?"

"Go ahead. I won't be angry."

"Then... I need to know how you feel about me." He winced when he heard himself say that. *I sound pathetic.*

Slowly, Ash let go. He moved to where he could see Kieran's face. "You don't *know*?" He sounded incredulous. "I love you. I thought you knew. I guess I've been a coward. I should have shown it more. I love you."

The words were like physical blows, with the weight of

quiet intensity Ash put into them. Kieran felt his expression go strange as he met Ash's eyes, was caught by blinding blue. His headache spread all across his forehead, his whole head felt too tight. "Say it again."

Ash's smile was lopsided. "I'm stupidly, helplessly, crazy in love with you. I'd do anything for you. I want to belong to you like a name, I want to be a thing people have to know to know you. I don't understand why that's hurting you."

"I don't... I don't know either." To his shock and dismay, his voice broke.

"Kieran?"

"I'm not -- shit, I'm sorry --" He put his hand wonderingly to his face, disbelieving, as a hot spill of wetness streaked down the side of his nose. Next, to make matters worse, came a hiccuping sound that he realized was a sob.

"*Please* tell me what's wrong. I didn't mean to hurt you."

Kieran could only shake his head. He clamped his hand over his mouth to contain the mounting pressure of this feeling, these noises, but they wouldn't stop. He couldn't see. He couldn't think. He wasn't *ready*. Showing teeth, clenched in a futile attempt to silence himself, he reached blindly and blundered into Ash's arm, wrapped his fingers around it. Reached out with his heart's hand, not to do harm but simply to make contact. *Show me. Show me you know what kind of poisonous animal I am, before you say those things.*

Through that touch a flood of feeling poured. So good it was agonizing. How could anyone stand it? How could Ash ever feel something that pure for someone so wrecked?

"Say it again!" Kieran ordered, hating the way his voice wobbled and fractured.

"I love you, I want to make you happy, I'll do anything."

"Why, Ash? Why -- why *me*? Of all the people in the world -- you couldn't have found someone *worse*, don't you know what I am?"

Ash's voice was low and sweet, trying to calm him. "Yes, I know what you are."

"And what I've done. All the things I've done."

"I see why you did those things. Maybe you had alternatives, maybe in hindsight you can think of what they were, but at the time -- do you need me to forgive you? Would that help?"

"There are things no one can forgive me for."

"Stop. I don't blame you. I don't have the right to judge

you, but I'm the only one who really knows you, and I say you're not a bad person. Sometimes you're a very good person; the rest of the time you're just trying to stay alive. But you're not bad. That's the truth." When that only made Kieran cry harder, he grabbed Kieran's chin and made him look. His eyes were pale and bright as sunlight on water. "You deserve to be loved. I'm going to keep saying so until you believe me. I think you're wonderful. You're strong and smart and funny and brave, and so gorgeous it breaks my heart to look at you. There's no one else in the world remotely like you. Do you know why it drove me out of my mind when I thought you were dead? Not just because I missed you, not just because I wanted you to be alive, but because something totally unique had been destroyed. As if the tallest mountain in the world just one day fell down, or the deepest lake just dried up. I cried because I missed you, but I lost it because the *world* missed you. Missed out on you. That's how important you are."

"I can't believe that." It was easier to talk now, though the tears were still running.

"You don't have to. I'll believe it for you."

"And when you change your mind --"

"I won't."

"You should! I can't be trusted, I don't know why you keep trusting me, it's going to get you killed, what if I get you killed?"

"What if it's worth it?"

Kieran jammed his eyes shut, hiding from the clarity of Ash's stare. He drew a shuddering breath. It was a while before he could speak, and even then he couldn't answer what Ash had said. "This is so embarrassing. After all the times I called you a crybaby." He dragged his wrist across his eyes, examined the wet streak on his skin so he wouldn't have to look up. "I've been such a rotten person. Don't tell me I haven't -- I was a contract killer, for fuck's sake, I murdered people I didn't even hate! I want to atone for it. Don't just forgive me outright, Ashes, let me earn free of it."

"That's fair."

"I'm afraid to touch you. I'm afraid I'll spoil you. You're so pure, and I'm such a fucking cesspit."

"No."

"I'll dirty the one clean thing I ever knew."

With a sad smile, Ash took up his hand and kissed the knuckles. "If that's the case, well, the truth is it goes the other way. The closer you get to me, the cleaner you become. Look back on the time we've known each other. Look at the changes."

Gathering his thoughts, looking honestly at memory, was harder than it had ever been. But he forced himself to see clearly, and it was true. His cynicism had been eroding ever since he'd first seen a gawky nameless white boy staring at him on the train. It had become impossible to lie to himself, shout himself down. "I'm too raw now," he said. "I used to say you care about things too much. I'm starting to do that too."

"It gets easier."

"I've never said anything nice to you, have I?"

Some of the sad went out of Ash's smile. "A few things. One thing especially comes to mind, though you might not remember saying it."

"I remember. I meant it."

"You could say it again, now, if you want."

It stopped in his throat, then came out in a rush. "I love you."

He was astonished by the feeling that ran into him from Ash's hands; he had no point of reference for anything so high and bright. Such joy. It was true, it was all true, somehow it made Ash perfectly happy to hear those words, despite their flawed source. Suddenly he was no longer helpless or confused.

Saying it the next time was easier. "I love you, Ash. I love the way you do things, how you learn so fast, your hands are so fast and clever, it makes me happy to look in my pack just because it's so like you to line everything up neat like that." This could be addictive, how easily he was making Ash flush with pleasure just by talking. "I should have said all this a long time ago. I like your curiosity, the way you listen and ask questions, I like how you see the world, without judging people, I don't understand how you do it but I really admire it. I could go on all day. The way you talk. The way you laugh. I love the way you try to do right without thinking whether it'll hurt. I love the way you curl your hands up by your mouth when you sleep, and the way you scratch your nose when you're thinking -- everything you do leaves trails in my brain, it stays."

Ash was studying his hands, ears scarlet. "You can go on like that as long as you want. Um. Particularly you could tell me -- oh, now I'm going to sound vulgar -- do you remember saying, when you got well, you were going to. Um."

"Fuck your brains out?" Kieran laughed, feeling light

and dizzy.

"Well, yeah." Ash glanced up, then ducked his head again. "I know I'm sort of funny-looking, and you deserve to be with someone as gorgeous as you are, but if you do still... want me..."

"You're *not* funny-looking. You're like gold and ivory, your eyes are diamonds, you're a treasure to me." Kieran took a deep breath, watching Ash's face in profile, waiting until Ash finally straightened to look at him. He bent to place a deliberate single kiss on Ash's lips; when he pulled back, Ash leaned after him just a little, wanting more, and only then was Kieran certain.

With shaking hands, he took Ash's glasses and set them aside, just for the relief of looking away for a moment. The touch of Ash's hand pushing back his damp hair was as strong as burning, but good, far too good.

"Kai," Ash whispered; the shape of his lips moving around the name was unbearable. Kieran barely began the motion to embrace him, and Ash was suddenly all over him, kissing him ravenously. Sun-warmed skin, legs tangling; they couldn't get close enough, sitting up; Ash bore him down and pressed along the length of him, biting his lips, and it didn't hurt, it was perfect, it was the first unshadowed beginning he'd ever tasted.

For aeons they clung together, locked in an alchemy of breath and spit and wondering, gradually realizing that they had lost the barrier between themselves, were mingling now in mind and heart, could no longer be certain which of them originated which sensation. Even groans and sighs could be told apart only by timbre. The blurring of identity abated a little when Ash broke the kiss in order to follow the line of Kieran's jaw to his ear, but every touch was still amplified. With hands and lips they began to explore each other. While he tasted freckled shoulders and narrow wrists, Kieran was aware that Ash had been wanting just as strongly to taste scars and tattoos.

He rolled Ash under him, slid his hand down. "Can I --?"

"Oh please yes --"

Neither of them could stand waiting, but he drew it out anyway, taking his time with the buttons, dragging his palms down Ash's thighs to strip him, savoring. "There are freckles on your knees." Kieran returned to Ash's throat and kissed his way down. He went as slowly as he could, not wanting to rush this, but Ash's hands knotted in his hair, desperately impatient.

He surrendered, opened his throat and gulped Ash down, a skill he'd learned in his sordid former life finally put to a good use; he knew now exactly how good it felt, as he caught an echo through the Empath's skin, following Ash's broken whimpers with muffled sounds of his own. When Ash arched convulsively and let out a moan two octaves lower than his speaking voice, Kieran nearly went off as well.

For a time, Ash lay stunned, round-eyed. His mouth worked several times before he was able to speak. "Kai. You. Oh."

"Yes." Words were silly things now. They had a much better way to communicate. As soon as Ash got his breath back, he was caught in the echo of Kieran's need, hungry to reply in kind. Curious, awkward, his unsure touch lethally sweet. His eagerness seemed so young; there was something kittenish in the way he wouldn't let Kieran do anything but lie there while he methodically worked out what ought to be kissed, bitten, licked -- and what tickled. But then he was done with exploring and invited Kieran to fulfill his promise, and once Kieran was inside him wiry muscle jumped into sharp relief, his eyes burned, his intensity was almost frightening. Flying, falling, Kieran had a moment of terror that he would somehow break Ash if he let himself go, that he might release all his magic along with his tensioned desire and kill them both, but it was too late to make decisions. The sight of their fingers knotted together, brown against white, was the last straw. He called out Ash's name and lost his own. Heard himself sobbing incoherent endearments in two languages, was rolled under the storm of Ash's reaction, surrendered to the Empath's twining of their emotions into a loop that fed on itself until they were both blind and blazing. For a timeless time, the universe consisted entirely of one two-stranded knot of ecstasy.

Returning from that place was like regaining consciousness after being knocked cold. They lay breathlessly twined together for a time, tasting their own flavor in each other's mouths, running hands aimlessly along sated skin, mirroring the awe in each other's eyes.

"Are we..." Kieran found speaking hard for a different reason now. A fierce proprietary joy was welling up, filling him so full there was hardly room for speech anymore. "Is there a word for what we are? What that was? Or should I just say -- *edeime kii*, my lover?"

"Yes. Say it a lot," Ash replied with a dreamy smile. "Say

'mine.' Get all jealous and possessive, and growl at anyone who comes near me. It gives me such a kick when you do that."

A laugh bubbled up in him, coming out strange and jerky. "I've been doing that all along, haven't I?" He pushed his fingers through Ash's hair, viscerally pleased at the way the curls sprang back. Picked a fragment of grass off Ash's neck.

"I wish we could stay like this forever. Right here, in the sun, by the water."

"Why can't we?"

"We'll have to come up with more supplies somehow. And we can't be sure we've lost the Watch. Even if this place masks us, there hasn't been any rain. Our trail hasn't washed out."

"Huh." It was hard to think about anything at all, but that was a valid point. Kieran took his time brushing away grass and leaves that had stuck to Ash's skin, letting the idea roll around in his head. His mind felt clean and empty. There was plenty of room to think. "Well," he said slowly, "I wonder if maybe we can do something about that."

"What do you mean?"

"Just a sec." He got up long enough to spread out the blanket he'd been using for a kilt, and they both lay down on it. Now Ash got into the game of picking off bits of vegetation, so they let themselves be distracted by it, laughing -- giggling. Kieran was fairly sure he'd never giggled before in his life. And now he was like a kid, just playing.

Eventually, when they could no longer find any more twigs in each other's hair, Ash reminded him. "What did you mean, we can do something about it?"

"When I saw that storm, the one that broke us out of prison, I kind of got the feeling that I'd called it. It was there already, but I told it where to go. We're past the season for heavy rain, but maybe I could find something, steer it over."

"That would be really interesting, if you could."

"Yeah. For one thing, it would make me a bit of a stormcaller, as well as a jinx. Which means two Talents."

"But you said 'we' -- what can I do?"

Kieran wasn't sure how to answer. He was distracted by the faint line of tiny, gilded hairs that ran up to Ash's navel. All the gold hidden in the temple was spare change compared to this. "You shine," he murmured, raising his eyes to the copper-speckled alabaster of Ash's face. "I saw you shining like this once in a dream. Have you noticed you're not sunburned anymore?"

"No, I --" Ash blinked and caught his breath as Kieran touched his lips, no longer chapped and cracked as they'd been yesterday.

"There's a lot more power here than I thought. It's healed you too, you just didn't notice because you weren't too beat up. Did you get the feeling there's more of it between us? I mean, do you feel stronger than before? Magically. Because I do."

"Absolutely. I don't have to strain to sense you -- in fact, I have to make an effort to keep from smudging our minds together."

"So I think we can maybe do more than we could alone. Maybe if you sort of ride with me, I could make it rain."

"How do I --"

"How do you think?" He pulled Ash close again.

Without the force of pent-up desire behind it, the mingling of their minds was not so sudden this time, and he could watch it happening. They both watched it, experiencing each other's wonder; sometimes as an echo, sometimes in tandem; the border was in constant motion.

It was a bit of a shock to recognize, suddenly, the same kind of pattern he'd witnessed during the minute or two he'd been dead. The same branching whorls, sigils more idea than picture, the map of a life. He saw, in a rush that made him gasp, how Ash's Empathy worked. The edges of his pattern were open and hungry, fashioned to grasp and explore whatever idea-shapes came near them. Now Kieran's symbol-body was doing the same thing; they were like thousands of clasped hands.

Once, he thought he glimpsed the tight coil of strange matter he'd seen in Ash before, but left it for later exploration. Right now the task was to reach outward. A slight shift of focus, and he saw that everything else had a pattern too, the whole world was full of pattern. The lines of earth were slow and fat, plants and insects a thick mat of repeating forms, water a dense mass of designs so tiny and so interlocked that nothing could penetrate it. Even the blanket had its form. The wire frames of Ash's glasses smeared the pattern of the grass a little where metal touched leaf. Exploring this new level of sight could make up the work of a lifetime. Kieran thought he might have gotten lost in it and never come back to himself if Ash hadn't been, at the same time, reminding him of his skin.

Air was a pattern as well. Hot and cold, wet and dry, its movements were more beautiful than anything solid, such a shame that people couldn't see it -- but Ash could see it, and so the beauty was shared, and didn't have to hurt. Higher, wider, the small shapes made up large ones, which made up even larger ones, until he could see the greatest air-shapes of all.

"What?" Ash pulled away to look at him, and he realized he'd cried out.

"I just --" It was hard to focus on something so small as explaining. "I just understood why there's a desert here."

"Show me."

"No... you have to anchor me, pull me back if I... there's no limit to how much power I could use. I could use myself up."

"I've got you."

Trusting Ash to catch him if he spent too much, he plunged back into the sky. West, toward the sun. He meant to pass the mountains, but something on the ground called to him. A massive dome of roiling energy, a three-dimensional whirlpool of intricate symmetrical pattern. The Burn, he realized. It was the Burn.

It looked, somehow, tasty.

No. Don't touch it. The thought didn't come in words, but Ash's caution reached him, and he left the Burn alone, though it felt like seeing money in the street and just stepping over it. Turned his mind from it and reached out for the wet warmth beyond the mountains' teeth. It was raining over there, on the far slopes. Why couldn't the clouds get over the mountains, stream between them and form on the other side? Maybe... ah, there, a cold river of air out of the northwest, coming down the coast, wringing out all the moisture. He sent a warning to Ash that he was about to begin, then wrapped himself around the cold wind and wrenched --

Suddenly he was trapped in his body, sweat-drenched and shivering, mind numb, exhausted.

"Just breathe," Ash told him. From the places where their skin touched, warmth and life were pouring in. "I think I pulled you back before you could do anything."

"Dunno." He blinked a few times, flexed his hands. Strength was returning. Within a few seconds he felt almost normal, but that was a far cry from the towering dominion he'd had a minute ago.

"It's enough for one day, anyhow. We don't know what we're doing. We need to play with it a while, get the hang of it.

Otherwise we could get hurt."

"Tomorrow, then."

"Okay." Ash gave him a brilliant smile. "Everything started over today. Did you notice that? Every day of my life before this one looks stale and dusty."

Kieran nodded. Ash was right. He felt reborn, remade. "And you know... that thing with the air, with seeing all the twisty shapes, the magic -- it's not half as interesting as you are. If I had to pick between magic and you, magic could go to hell."

"Stay with me always?"

"You couldn't get rid of me." He grinned. "It'll take years just to get used to making love to you. You have no idea how good it can be."

"You mean it gets *better*?"

Rather than answer, Kieran decided to demonstrate.

Chapter 25

Everything all at once; that was how it had always been. Chaiel had never been able to choose what he saw. He could, sometimes, leap from one image to a related one, but even then the images rarely made sense. His clairaudience wasn't nearly as reliable as his clairvoyance, and the occasional bursts of clairsentience were simply confusing. He dimly remembered that it hadn't been like that before he was put in the bubble, but he tried not to think about that time.

So it was a pleasant surprise to be suddenly shown Thelyan boarding a train in a great hurry, and immediately on the heels of the image get a clear sense that the Director was on his way to see Chaiel.

Thelyan's visits were stressful. Nevertheless they provided new fodder for thought. Knowledge came through much more strongly when the bubble was opened to sight and sound. But what could have got the chilly bastard so worked up? That thing his predicting people had seen, a while back? Chaiel's memories of that visit were tangled, but he did remember that he hadn't been able to answer the question. Thelyan didn't understand how Chaiel's abilities worked. There had been, of course, a remote chance that a scrap of clairsentience would have given Chaiel the answer by pure coincidence, but Thelyan always acted like Chaiel could know whatever he wanted.

I used to be a god, Chaiel reminded himself. He said it out loud, to have his voice for company. "I used to be a god."

Then he lost some time. He discovered he'd chewed his nails to bleeding, and bitten his hands and arms raw. This happened sometimes.

He remembered that Thelyan was coming to see him. Nothing by which he could judge time presented itself, so he didn't know whether he'd seen the train-boarding scene a minute ago or a day or a year. Now there were sounds coming to him, so he held his breath, hoping for music. It was so good when music came.

There was a hissing sound. Then a sharp crack, followed by a clank. Then a voice, speaking a language he didn't know;

there were many languages he didn't know, though he heard them all the time; also foreign words the meaning of which came to him, though he didn't know what language they were. Then, suddenly, with a feeling of a dislocated joint snapping into place, a blizzard of clear speech in Eskaran:

very strong surge lasted only eight seconds, though the atmospheric effects

resolved, unfortunately. Yes, sir. Yes, sir. No.

can't get anything from him except this garbage about a green man, even in Survey. Well, the report -- yes. The report I received from Sandwell made mention of a green woman, though they've had minimal loss of personnel there. I can't correlate it with the thunderstorm prophesies, though. Yes, the locus appears to be the same, but it

just realized why there's a desert here.

Drink up, it's the end of the world!

When the talking faded away, Chaiel listened to it all in his head several times again. He made no attempt to draw conclusions; he'd discovered long ago that he only frustrated himself by trying to understand. Only one visual image had come with the speech, just a flicker: six wooden matches and an unlit candle scattered on a rough stone surface. This image was somehow sexual.

He kept coming back to one of the voices. The second to last voice caught in his head more than the others. Something about it frightened him, though the tone hadn't been threatening or angry. It was maybe more familiar than the others, though by now all voices, all images seemed at least a bit familiar.

Flash. More time gone. Now his genitals hurt. Apparently he'd been trying to masturbate again. He hated when he did that. It didn't work -- the same suspension that kept him from aging made it impossible for him to shed tears, sweat, void waste, or ejaculate. All the scraps of hair and fingernail he'd swallowed over the decades still lumped in his stomach, and once he'd vomited an accretion of the stuff and found it still sharp-edged, cemented by sticky clots of ancient blood, completely undigested. But his body sometimes did stupid things without his knowledge.

Something nagged at his mind, he'd forgotten something, something important... But then, when had he not? He'd forgotten more than any mortal ever knew.

Sound came again. Another voice, one he heard often,

the words too routine to comprehend. This one stayed for a while. It repeated. After a time, he began to understand that the voice was Thelyan's, the familiar word his own name.

He opened his eyes, and discovered that he was upside down relative to the rest of the world. That was sort of interesting. Arching his back, he reached out toward the litter on the floor, bits of himself that he had dropped. Most of it gone to dust. Bits of his body, and his body was made out of energy, and the energy was pure thought. Knowledge was his food. He put knowledge inside himself; hair and skin and nails and blood came out and fell and decayed, a pile of decayed knowledge on the ground... suddenly he was afraid that Thelyan would eat the dust, and know things.

"Chaiel, give me your attention. Chaiel. Speak so I know you can hear me."

"You never bring me any presents. I want a puppy." Chaiel laughed at his own joke. He had a shadow. He waved at it.

Thelyan's voice behind him. "I don't have time for your wanderings now. Tell me what you know about the atmospheric disturbance over Paiwaar this afternoon."

So Thelyan didn't have time. Good for Thelyan. "It must be nice to be so busy." He twisted until he could see Thelyan's face right side up. The Director -- the Judge -- eater of gods, shitter-out of laws -- looked like a woman, suddenly. A pretty girl. Chaiel smiled. "Sometimes I see naked ladies. Sometimes I see very old ugly naked ladies. Once I heard a girl teaching a parrot to talk."

"Tell me what you know about the --"

"Atmospheric effects are still developing. Yes, sir, I'll have a copy sent up. They're not sure yet. A storm system of some significant size, at least, possibly a major climatic change. Yes. I'm quite sure. There's absolutely no way this could be natural. High-altitude winds simply don't move like that." Chaiel clamped his hands over his mouth, as he realized he'd inadvertently spoken what he was hearing, possibly told Thelyan something useful. It was almost certain, in fact, because Thelyan was smiling.

"Very good, Chaiel. That's the disturbance I mean. Now tell me who caused it."

"No."

"Come now. There's no one you have any reason to protect."

"No."

Thelyan's smile, though still icy, grew fractionally warmer. "That is, unless the culprit is one of my enemies. You would protect my enemies, wouldn't you?"

Chaiel tried to escape into the stream of images, but it was thin and sporadic even though the bubble was clear. *I'm not going to talk, I'm not going to talk, I don't have to talk. I don't know anyway, I didn't see, nobody ever tells me anything, besides he can work it out for himself, what does he need me for? If Ka'an wants to make rain that's his business.*

"So Ka'an has gained control of his host."

Realizing that he'd spoken out loud, Chaiel howled. He hid his face, willing himself to blank out, but when he opened his eyes again Thelyan was still there. All white and sparkly and mean-looking. "I hate you. I'm so thirsty. I hate everybody."

"Even Ka'an?"

"I don't care. You go find him and I hope you kill each other. I hope you kill everybody." A thought occurred to him, and he hastily added, "Everybody but Medur. If you find her, can I have her?"

An expression of disgust crossed Thelyan's face. "I'm not looking for her. She's no use to me. Tell me where Ka'an is."

"No. I don't know." But a flash, shockingly clear, gave him the answer, and he blurted it out before he could stop himself. "Under the acacia tree with the green man, breathing through his elbows, going to get rained on, yes. Ooh, that's against your law now, dog in the manger, bet you wish you ever had that much fun, guess what? I know something about you."

Even more disgusted now, Thelyan said, "I'm not remotely interested in what you think you know about me. What I want to know is --"

"I know why you hate him," Chaiel interrupted. Before he could go on, though, a deafening clatter of machinery burst through his head, accompanied by a picture of children poking a dead dog with sticks, and when it was finished he woke to silent darkness. Thelyan had blanked the sphere while Chaiel was caught in a fit of seeing.

Frustrated, Chaiel wept with dry eyes. "I know why you hate him," he repeated to the nothingness around him. "Other people get over that, you know. Other people don't have to rule the world just because someone was mean to them once. I know. I know. All the things I know." He screamed, then whispered. "Let me out."

His voice didn't even echo.

༄ ❋ ༅

Ash lay propped on his elbow, watching Kieran sleep by candlelight. He was a little cold, and all his muscles ached, and he'd never been so happy before in his life. It seemed impossible that anything so good could happen to anyone, let alone to him. He didn't want to sleep, for fear everything would be different when he woke up.

Kieran was sprawled on his back, taking up most of the blanket. One hand was curled on his chest, the other stretched out palm-up across the dusty floor. His mouth was slightly open, and his hair spread in loops and slow curves along his outflung arm. The light of the candle's steady flame gilded the planes of his face, brought structures of muscle and bone into sharp relief, showed the twitch of dreaming eyes under eyelids that Ash's lips knew were soft as warm wind.

Ash's heart was sore with too much joy; he was tempted to wake Kieran and talk to him some more, just to take some of the pressure off. That would be unkind, though. They were both exhausted. They'd barely had the energy to drag themselves inside the temple when the sun set, laughingly comparing how shaky their legs were, and then despite that they'd lit the candle and made love a third time while full night fell. Ash was surprised he could stay awake. By rights he should be sleeping like a baby. He knew his dreams would be as sweet as Kieran's were right now; he could sense the slow swells of emotion rolling in his lover's sleeping mind, curiosity and amusement and the occasional bright flash of discovery.

Twining coils of shining black hair around his fingers, Ash considered what Kieran had said before everything had gone beautiful. The objections he had raised. He'd been so frightened; though he wouldn't have admitted it, wouldn't have used the word fear, he'd been terribly afraid. This meant so much to him.

Much as Ash wanted to dismiss those fears as reflexive, he made himself ask: *What could go wrong? What are the ways I might hurt him? I need to think of those things to make sure I never do them.* Well, the obvious one was leaving, and that, he was sure, he would not do. Eventually the shine would wear off, being together would become routine -- Ash couldn't imagine what it would be like to take Kieran for granted, but he knew it was human nature. It wasn't about the newness, though. This wasn't a conquest. The things he loved about Kieran would only grow more precious with time. *I have to find a way to assure him of that.* Ash smoothed stray hairs back from Kieran's brow to make him smile in his sleep. *When he wakes. For now what he needs is rest.*

Just as he made up his mind to blow out the candle and join the dream, a sighing sound began outside. He looked out past the pillars, but saw only blackness. The candle flame ducked, whirling shadows, and a breath of wind stirred his hair. The wind's sound faded, then rose higher, carrying a scent that made him think of home. Summer. A heat wave; lying in bed sweating in the humid air, and then a wind, and this smell, and a great sense of relief...

"Uh-oh."

He nudged Kieran, but got no response. Well, let Kieran sleep a little longer. Probably there was no danger. He got up and found his pants and shirt and glasses. Another gust blew the candle out, so he got dressed by feel. Flickering light to the west caught his attention. He watched, for a moment, eyes adjusted to the dark now enough to see moonlight dusting a curled shape in the sky; under the towering cloud, dim purple bands rippled.

There was time to grope his way back to the bed -- almost entirely by his Talent's spacial sense -- before the mutter of thunder reached his ears. This time he made a more serious effort to wake Kieran, and this time succeeded.

Mumbling and rubbing his eyes, Kieran began an incoherent protest, but a new gust of colder wind brought him fully awake. Lightning just strong enough to limn him in blue caught him beginning a smile. "Oh. Hey." He sounded pleased. "Will you look at that."

"It seems we succeeded after all."

"Guess so. Wanna go up in it? See what it looks like from inside?"

Ash was tempted, but shook his head. "I think we should move the supplies farther in. Could you help?"

"Yep." Kieran didn't seem to feel any sense of urgency, despite the brightening flickers in the cloud and the increasing wind. He scratched and yawned and fumbled with his clothes at great length while Ash gathered the candle and matches and blankets. Well, if Kieran wasn't afraid of the storm, Ash wouldn't be either.

By the time they'd shifted their belongings to the back of the main room, the wind was constant, strong, and cold. Lightning was visible beneath the cloud as well as in it, and thunder cracked rather than rumbling. Ash bundled up the blankets and coats, and began to take them down a side passage.

"Don't you want to watch?" Kieran said.

Ash dropped his bundle. "Why not?" He let Kieran take his hand and lead him out to the temple steps, into the teeth of the wind.

A flash of lightning printed an image on his mind: Kieran standing on the edge of the step, gathering his hair back with one hand as it tried to fly into his face, unbuttoned shirt billowing around his scarred, lean-muscled chest, teeth bared in a feral grin. Then Kieran pulled him close, and they watched with their arms around each other as the storm stalked toward them on long insect-legs of lightning.

The first drops of rain brought a bark of exhilarated laughter from Kieran, which Ash echoed more quietly. It was exciting, the strength and size of the forces at work, though Ash thought he wouldn't enjoy it nearly as much if he were seeing it alone. Rain speckled his glasses, danced along his arms and across his bare feet; then the skies gave a roar and dumped it down in buckets, drenching them. Laughing, they pressed closer for warmth, kissed the rain from each other's faces, burrowed hands into each other's sodden clothes. They were no longer tired; it was as if the thunder's energy was pouring into them through their skin.

"Again? Already?" Ash raised his eyebrows, knowing Kieran could sense that his surprise was feigned, perhaps even sense in echo the interesting texture of wet leather under his hands. But at that moment a blast of rain hit them with enough force to make them stagger, driven by a wind that was rising to a howl.

No discussion was needed. They fled back inside, to the back wall; then, when the cold wind reached them even there, to the side passage with the painted walls. The thunder was sharp and hard now, frighteningly loud.

"Maybe I overdid it." Kieran laughed.

"You think?"

"You're shivering."

"So are you."

Kieran grabbed up a blanket to wrap around them. They sat on the floor, making themselves small, listening to the roar that echoed through the temple. Ash set his useless glasses aside. He lit the candle, setting it on the side of them away from the main room, where it didn't flicker so much.

"I want to go look at it," Kieran said, glancing up to indicate the storm raging overhead. Ash knew he didn't mean physically. He wanted to repeat the wild, high flight of mind he'd performed that afternoon.

Ash remembered what it had been like. The half-glimpsed geometries of force, of life, the mind-wrecking complexity into which Kieran had dived as if born to it. It was frightening, the strength of yearning Kieran emitted when he contemplated that world. Ash feared he'd be lost in it. But it gave him such joy; Ash couldn't deny him. "Be careful. You don't know what it might do."

As before, Kieran's eyes went blank. The wavering light showed him staring past Ash's ear, lips parted, head tilted as if listening. Ash closed his eyes and reached out with his mind, suddenly afraid Kieran's soul would leap entirely free of his body and be lost to the winds.

But what he sensed was no rise -- Kieran's seeking went no farther than the walls around them. Something there had distracted him, fascinated him, so that the din of wind and water outside was brushed aside as an annoyance.

"Tell me." Ash formed the words gently, thinking them before speaking, hoping not to break Kieran's trance. It succeeded; Kieran answered slowly, absently, still mentally groping along the walls.

"The writing. It shows up in this light. These are just... well, I don't get how... how anyone can not be able to read them."

It seemed safe to open his eyes. Kieran was now staring fixedly at the opposite wall, eyes moving from side to side as if reading. "What do they say?"

Kieran was silent for a while, before speaking in Iavaian. Ash caught scraps of meaning in the words, but couldn't really understand. Whatever Kieran was reading, though, seemed to amuse him quite a bit. At last he switched back to Eskaran. "Can you believe they wrote down things like that?"

Suspecting that a request for translation would wreck Kieran's concentration, Ash played along. "Why shouldn't they?"

"Because oracles are only true in the moment." His eyes snapped into focus, an expression of shock leaping across his face as he looked at Ash. "So *that's* where you went." Suddenly a change went through him, an upwelling of unease quickly mounting toward terror.

It was hard not to look, but Ash had to close his eyes to force himself from visual to mental, strengthen his hold on Kieran's -- whatever it was, mind, soul, spirit -- and try to bring him back from whatever was scaring him. Then Ash saw it, and he began to be frightened as well, nearly recoiled but held tighter instead.

Something was surging up through the familiar texture of Kieran's thoughts. Something huge, strange, dark as oil, something so horribly *old* that to find it there sent icy claws scrabbling at the edges of Ash's sanity. And it knew him. It was aware of him. It was observing him, and it wasn't impressed.

It was inside Kieran like a parasite. Rage gave Ash strength; he added himself to the force Kieran was already expending in pushing it back, and together they fought to stop its progress.

You can't have him. He's mine. How dare you dirty him with your greasy night!

A wordless reply raked at him: the outrage of an arrogance so immense that it could not recognize any claim but its own. It weakened, though, bit by bit. Finally, all at once, it was gone. Kieran slumped against him, breathing in hoarse gasps.

Ash was barely able to speak. "What *was* that?" His voice was half drowned by thunder, but Kieran heard him.

"The same thing I saw when I died. The bigger me. That wanted to eat *this* me. Oh god. Oh shit. Ash, it's going to come back."

Panic made his skin prickle. "It's coming back?"

"Not now. But it will."

"But what is it? Why's it in you? Do you have any idea?"

"I'm afraid I might." Kieran swallowed hard, burrowed his face into Ash's hair, and stayed like that for a long time. Ash just held him until his despair subsided, until his usual confidence began to reassert itself. At last he straightened and shook himself, visibly gathering his courage. "You know what's stupid? I was warned. Some crazy bum back in Burn River warned me, but I thought he was just, you know, being a crazy bum."

"What did he say?"

"He thought I was a god. He said I was Ka'an."

Incredulity and alarm collided in Ash's mind. He stammered out a few disconnected syllables, then stopped, realizing he wasn't going to be able to make sense.

"Yeah," Kieran agreed.

"But -- that -- you mean the one --"

"Yeah. That one."

"You mean an actual, literal -- you mean a real --"

"A god."

"But. That would. But. Kai, that --"

Kieran looped a hand in the air angrily. "Yeah, I know! I don't believe in them either! Who knows what it really is? Who gives a fuck? The thing's riding piggyback on my brain, and it's getting stronger! It wants things I don't want! It doesn't care what I want!"

"Like what? What does it want?"

"I don't even remember. I know it recognized you, though. There's something in you -- I told you about it, that thing I saw knotted up in you, I thought it was maybe another Talent, like you've got healing too, or something. But this -- Ka'an -- he recognized it."

Scalp crawling, Ash had to make a couple tries before he got the words out: "Do, do, do you remember saying -- do you remember talking --"

"No."

"You looked at me and you said, 'So that's where you went.'"

"Shit." Kieran shoved his hands up his face, took handfuls of his wet hair, shook his head and growled. Then he dropped his hands with a sigh. "Whatever. We should've expected weirdness; nobody ever told us anything about our magic, right? For all I know, I was just seeing my Talent or something. Putting a face on it, getting paranoid. Anyway, panicking now is useless. We can talk about it in the morning."

"I guess you're right. We're too tired to make sense."

"Yeah. But... ah..." Glancing up at the painted walls, Kieran scooped up their blankets. "Let's sleep in the *other* hallway."

"I was hoping you'd say that."

The storm calmed later, subsiding to steady rain. Having

stripped off their wet clothing, they were soon warm enough to sleep, and weariness conquered the nervous feeling that whatever had been playing with Kieran's mind would return any moment. They dreamed in unison again. This time it was Kieran's dream they occupied; a sickly-sweet vision of opium and incense in a scarlet-veiled pavilion.

In the dream, they fed each other from cups of mixed wine and blood, watching uncaring as floodwaters climbed the hill where the pavilion stood. Soon the flood lapped around their feet. The colors of rugs and gold-threaded cushions under water fascinated them. Then the embroidered veils of the tent walls were lifting and swirling in the flood, and they realized there was nowhere to go. Their hill would be drowned, and them with it. Already, bowls of fruit were drifting away out of the pavilion, like little boats, onto the lake that now stretched all the way to the distant mountains. With a creak and a flapping sound, the tent began to lean. It fell around them and pressed them down into the water.

Ash woke thrashing, fighting free of wet cloth. Beside him, Kieran started up, teeth chattering. They lay in an inch of cold water. Not the brilliantly clear lake of the dream, but mud-milky water scummed with leaves and drowned insects.

"The fuck?" Kieran looked around disbelievingly. He lifted a hand and watched it drip. "What the fuck is this?"

Clutching his arms around him to contain his shivering, Ash got up and splashed out of the short hallway. There he stood -- naked, wet, and confused -- for so long that Kieran gave up asking him questions and came to join him. When Kieran saw what Ash had been looking at, he let out a low whistle.

"Well. That's gonna suck."

It was still raining. But now, instead of veiling a green valley with a stream down the middle, the rain furred the surface of a muddy, swirling lake whose waters were lapping over the top step of the temple and pouring back into it in widening rivulets. The channel down the middle of the temple was brimful and overflowing. The spring no longer sheeted calmly down the wall; now it poured in an arcing stream, chattering and splashing. Outside, debris swirled slowly in currents of inflow. Trees poked up out of the new lake, and in their branches things were caught. Things like the drowned carcass of the bay mare who'd so faithfully brought them here.

Ash made a faint sound of pity for the poor animal,

wishing he'd gone and brought her in when the rain started. Not that he would've been able to find her. Besides, they had bigger problems. "Our supplies."

"Our *clothes*," Kieran retorted. He stomped back into the dead-end where they'd slept, searching with his feet. After a moment he snatched up his pants with a cry of dismay. "You're not supposed to *do* this to leather! Where's my coat? Where's *your* coat, Ashes, you're turning blue! Aw, hell. This stinks."

"We have to get out of here."

"No shit."

"Where are we going to go?"

Kieran waved that off as unimportant. "Wherever. Up. First order of business is to not drown."

"Yeah, I'm with you there."

Grumbling and swearing, they dressed in their wet clothes and gathered the dripping blankets. Ash found a stretch of floor that was still dry and used it to fold the blankets lengthwise and roll them up, pressing streams of water out of them. While he did this, Kieran was hauling their supplies into a different area of dry floor, giving a running commentary.

"Flour's all right. Coffee's all right. Sugar's gone to sludge. Salt's all right, it was on top. Meat's kinda crappy, it's been soaking. What's this? Was this rice? It's everywhere. Aw, shit, half the matches are wrecked. And -- oh, this is great. This is brilliant. Fuck."

Ash turned to see what was the matter. Kieran held out his gun, and with a grimace tipped it so water poured out of the barrel.

"That's not so good," Ash said.

"Both the short guns were lying in a puddle. The rifles were stood up, so they're okay, 'cept all their ammo's under water."

"Modern ammunition's supposed to be watertight, isn't it?"

"Sure, it's okay if it gets rained on or dunked real quick, but this stuff's been stewing. I bet half of it's gone dud. And there's no way to tell which half until you try to fire it. *Shit*."

With a sigh of resignation, Ash went to tie the blankets onto the packs. "Nothing we can do about it now. Let's just worry about getting to higher ground. Even if the rain stopped now the water would still keep getting deeper for a while. And that rain's not stopping."

As if to illustrate his point, a gust of wind sent a wave

across the lake toward them, spilling into the temple in a flat sheet that quickly eliminated what little dry ground was left. Ash finished lacing his boots, wincing at the disgusting way they squelched. Kieran, oddly enough, laughed as he got his own boots on. "What's so damn funny?" Ash growled.

"My boots are dry."

"Well, nice for you."

That made Kieran laugh harder. "I'd let you wear 'em, but you know, I've got these gigantic feet. Or was it humongous?"

"I'm glad you can see the humor of the situation." Then Ash heard his own words, and smiled halfway. "Actually, I mean that. I think we need to have a sense of humor today."

"I'd rather have a boat." Grinning, Kieran hefted his pack; Ash noticed he'd picked the heavier one. "You know, this is so weird I can't even be mad about it. Ten minutes from now we might be drowned or something, but I don't believe it because it's just -- I mean, I've seen flash floods before, but I've never seen standing water like this. I've never seen it rain like this before."

"Got your guns?"

"Yeah. You? Stick the rifle through the pack flap, keep it out of your way."

"Oh, that works. Okay."

"Ready?"

"Guess I'd better be."

They stood in the temple's open mouth, ankle-deep, examining their options. The only way to get out of the valley would be up the least steep slope, the one on the north side where the deer had come down yesterday. To get there, they'd have to wade, and possibly swim. Then they'd have to toil up among the slicked-down grasses and soupy mud to get to the top. That hill was cut by a number of new streams, which implied that the land above was awash. And there was no end to the rain; the sky was thickly gray as far as the eye could see.

Kieran gave Ash an encouraging smile, kissed him lightly. "Think of it like this: there's no way the Watch is going to be tracking us today."

Steadying themselves against each other's shoulders, they forged into the flood.

Ash's glasses were immediately splattered to near uselessness. Following the cliff wall, half climbing and half swimming, they inched around the head of the valley. It would have been easier if this had been normal desert, but here there were clutching branches and swirling grass to snarl their legs, sinks of deep mud to suck at their feet. At one point Ash reached out for a cracked boulder to work his way across a deep place, when his hand jerked back of its own accord, his stranger senses telling him something wasn't right. A closer examination showed him hundreds of light-brown scorpions clinging in the crack. He warned Kieran about it, used a nail-wrenching grip on the outside of the rock to get across, and somehow kept from falling into the rising flood.

Their work wasn't over when they reached the place where the valley's wall wasn't vertical. Here, tumbled slabs of stone were set in ground rapidly going to mud, and they shifted underfoot in dangerous ways. Their Talent sense was no use in telling which ground was solid and which treacherous; the water made everything a blank. Ash found himself thinking that if Kieran hadn't had magical healing -- from whatever source -- neither of them would have made it. Nevertheless he saw Kieran wincing more than once when he had to use his right arm for something. He didn't have the option of favoring that side. This was a two-handed job.

At last they reached the top. Uniformly yellow-brown with sticky mud, scratched and bruised, they stood bent-over and panting for several minutes.

Ash was the first to straighten up and look around. Kieran had had a much harder time of it, not only because he was still weakened from his injury, but because he was bigger. There was more of him to move, which mattered on a climb like that. Ash set a hand on his shoulder to let him know he could rest as long as he wanted. There was no danger up here that he could see.

To the west, he could just make out that the land dropped off in a lacework of cuts and furrows. East, and out to north and south, the high ground stretched in shallow ripples and low hills for what looked like forever. It was hard to make out distant features accurately, because of the rain streaking his glasses, but he thought he saw something that might be a taller rock off to the northeast. Not more than two miles, he guessed, probably a lot less.

He pointed it out to Kieran, got a nod in reply, and they struck out for it.

The going was a lot tougher than it looked like it should have been. Water was everywhere, pouring, seeping, cutting, pooling. Uphill areas were slippery with mud or uneven with broken rock, and the lower places between hills were choked with thorny brush and debris when they weren't impassably flooded.

What should have been a matter of half an hour's walking turned into a three-hour nightmare of climbing and slipping. But they got closer, bit by bit, to the looming rock that Ash prayed would have an overhang they could shelter under. His teeth were chattering now, as much with fatigue as with cold.

Finally they were skirting the slope of debris that had fallen from the rock. It was a squat spire that stood maybe thirty feet taller than the land around it, convoluted and crumbly from aeons of weathering. There wasn't anything that looked like shelter on this side, but they hadn't seen the whole thing yet.

Please, please let there be a cave or something, Ash prayed as they trudged through the rain.

Suddenly Kieran's hand knotted in his collar, yanking him to a halt. Puzzled, Ash glanced back at him, then followed his stare up to the foot of the spire.

Where a man in a white oilcloth rain cape stood staring back at them.

Kieran had his gun out before Ash quite registered what he was looking at, but the weapon only produced a sad click. Ash reached behind him to tug his rifle free of his pack, but two more men in white were coming around a buttress of rock, and Kieran grabbed Ash's wrist to haul him back.

"Just *run*," Kieran said through his teeth.

They turned and bolted. Behind him, Ash heard a shout, then multiple voices yelling. Just ahead of him, the ground bulged and spattered with a *whump* sound, spraying mud out of a crater a yard across. He glanced back, trying to make sense of the scene behind him, but Kieran yanked him onward.

"Dodge. They've got a breaker."

"There's six of them!" Ash yelled back. "With horses!"

They skidded down a slope and pelted across rock-strewn sand. With a frantic look over his shoulder, Kieran shrugged his pack from his shoulders and dropped it. Ash did the same, reaching back in the process to catch out his rifle before letting the pack fall. Kieran was pulling ahead; Ash stumbled as he looped the rifle over his shoulder, then ducked his head and put on a burst of speed to catch up.

Voices were shouting behind. It sounded like they were calling out to the fugitives to stop, most likely making dire threats about what would happen if they didn't. It was impossible to hear words over the sounds of running, and it didn't matter. Magics were cutting the air now, hooves were thudding, gaining.

Ash had no time to dwell on how stupidly unfair it was to run into the Watch by pure chance on a day when rain would have made them invisible to magical senses. There was no time even to be afraid, for himself or for Kieran. Sound and time went strange, took on an eerie clarity. He heard the flat crack of rifle fire, knew by the sound that it had been a warning shot, not meant to hit. Now they'd be trying to wing him. All around, sudden potholes appeared as the Watch group's Entropist broke apart the earth. There was at least one Pyro among them as well, and a Kinetic or two, from the way mud kept bursting into blasts of scalding steam and flying across the path to obscure it.

Ash ran zigzags across the plain, dodging rocks and leaping potholes. Didn't bother wondering how long he could go on doing it. Tried to keep Kieran in sight. Tried to probe the ground ahead for solidity, but was repeatedly thwarted by the complexity of water. Maybe that was why the Watchmen kept missing. Followed Kieran down another slope and through a stream, into more rippled terrain. A horse screamed, somewhere, and he began to think they might have a chance of escaping.

His pulse beat painfully in his temples, his sinuses, his eardrums. His breath rasped his throat raw. Tan water sprayed in arcing sheets from every footstep, squelched in his boots, weighed his legs.

Kieran led him into a maze of tiny hills, strangely rounded and no taller than a house, where the sand-and-clay earth shed water well enough for their senses to work on it. Unfortunately, it also made a heavier mud, which sucked at their boots and slowed them down. Ash guessed that Kieran was hoping it would break the legs of their pursuers' horses. He was trying not to think of how the Watchmen could simply dismount and chase them on foot. The men in white were better rested, better fed, and had dry ammunition. The small hills suddenly gave way to a steep slope, leading to a drop into a gully full of braided water.

Digging in with their heels and hands, they tried to keep

from sliding into it. For a moment it looked like it would work. Then, just as they reached the edge, the ground gave way. Ash yelped as the crumbled mud hauled him down. Kieran reached out to him, but missed. The Iavaian was slowed by his long coat, which dragged above him, catching on rocks; Ash had no such impediment, and had barely time to start to be afraid before he was slammed against the bottom of the gully.

He thrashed and swam to be free of the mud. The runoff stream helped, cutting through the piled mudslide and whisking it away. For a moment his glasses were totally opaque before the downpour started to wash them clean. But as he tried to stand, he felt that his left foot was caught in something, just before a nauseating pain jolted up his leg.

Kieran landed beside him, having had a more controlled slide down the slope. He reached for Ash's arm, but Ash pulled away. "Wait! Ow!"

"Come on!" Kieran grabbed at him again, glancing fearfully up to where their pursuers would appear any second.

"I can't! My -- it's broken --"

"Broken? What is?"

"Foot or ankle." Ash wrapped his hands around his calf and hauled his foot out of the obstruction, letting out a screech like a stepped-on cat as it came free. Then he fell forward on his elbows and retched.

"Broken," Kieran said distantly. "Holy shit, Ash. We're fucked."

Ash drew a ragged breath. "No. Just me. You run. Go."

"Like hell I will!"

"Run, I said." He was surprised how level his voice sounded, even if it was forced through clenched teeth.

"I'll carry you."

"Then we'll both get caught." Ash pulled his rifle around and shook a clump of mud off it. "Listen, damn you! Let them catch me. You get free. Then you can come rescue me. You know where they'll take me."

"Ashleigh!" Kieran whimpered his name, eyes too wide, panicked. Ash had never seen him panic before.

"Fucking *do* it, Kai!" Ash shouted back.

Kieran's eyes squeezed shut for a second; when he opened them, his face was stony. In a whirl of flying water, he spun and pounded off down the wash.

Ash watched him go until a bend in the gully took him out of sight. Only then did he allow his eyes to spill over. They both knew it had been a lie between them. There was no way Kieran was going to be able to bust Ash out of Churchrock. But they had to pretend to believe it, or there was no hope in the world anywhere.

He hoped Kieran was out of earshot when the sobs began, wrung out of him through a painfully tight throat, high and thin behind his teeth. He hoped Kieran couldn't hear him.

I didn't get to tell him those things. About forever, and never hurting him. Damn it, why can't the world leave us alone? All sorts of wretched, horrible people get to live out their lives, but this shining thing we found -- the world can't stop trying to put the light out. At that moment, Ash wanted desperately to kill something. The fact that he would soon have that option didn't escape him.

Gritting his teeth, he sat up. He avoided looking at the way his foot was kinked sideways. Patiently, he picked a gob of muddy grass out of his rifle's bolt, then slid it back just enough to see that there was a round chambered. He settled the stock against his shoulder, aiming upslope, and waited.

The longer it took them to capture him, the farther away Kieran got. That was all that could possibly matter now.

Chapter 26

The tables had turned. Now the raw and thorny part of his pattern was curled in upon itself, and he was whole outside it. And in whole possession of this body, for what that was worth.

Ka'an had to admit that it was a good body. Far better than he was used to. Of course it resembled his first, as all his bodies had. But of those he'd actually experienced since his defeat at the Judge's hands -- the few in which he'd emerged briefly to self-awareness -- most were in some way weakened or damaged. The mortal state was a fragile one. And all his vessels back to the first had been thin, as weak and graceful as reeds, most further atrophied by dreaming, in various stages of succumbing to the poppy that was his gift to the world.

This one, though... he reveled in its strength as he ran. The frame was his own, the long bones, the precarious height. Somehow, though, this version of him had clothed that delicate frame with muscle like braided wire, toughened and hardened itself -- and, he realized, picked up a great number of scars in the process. No matter; those could be repaired once he took back his power.

First, though, he had to win free of those minions of Theylan who chased him. He was lucky the smaller mind had folded when it had, or it would have gotten this fine body killed, and Ka'an wouldn't have had this chance. Even now, the diseased mind was paining him. Like a splinter under a fingernail. Keening and raging within itself, yearning to run back to that weak northern creature he'd left behind. Doubt and contradiction. The body's mind had decided two things at once: simultaneously to obey the northerner's order to run, and to refuse and stay. That break had allowed Ka'an an opening. Now he'd shake off the trouble the mortal mind had gotten him into, and then he'd go take back his power, and then he'd find Thelyan and teach that leprous-pale upstart the consequences of standing against his elders.

All this water was inconvenient. He doubted he had the strength to change the weather just now, though. Some knowledge of this life was available to him, and it informed him that all rain falling in this area would eventually drain into the pattern that mortals called the Tama Burn. Thus all he had to do was follow it downstream. Pleased by the slow heat of well-conditioned muscles, he ran along the ankle-deep stream. There was a possibility, of course, that it would deepen suddenly and drown this body.

The thought brought a twitch from the curled, abrasive lesser mind within him. That mind, which he would crush and absorb as soon as he had the time and power -- call it Kai, one of the body's names, appropriate in its sense of 'ghost' -- was not willing to risk drowning. Apparently the northerner they'd left behind was depending on a rescue.

Ka'an laughed out loud. Such a small life Kai had. The world was full of boys much prettier than that one. Girls, too, once Ka'an altered the body so that it could respond to them. Any of them could be made to adore him. They would surrender themselves utterly, without all the playing at equality that the northerner had done.

Anger from Kai. *He has a name.*

Oh yes. Ashes; a burned thing, worthless. The only interesting thing about him was... there had been something interesting... why, he almost thought that Kai might be denying him access to some of his memories.

Well, there was no time for that now. He'd handle it later. Now the gully he ran along was widening, and he could see that it opened ahead onto flatter ground. Yes; a lip of stone, a short leap, and he ran on bare rock. Something off to the left made a sharp popping noise, and he wondered what it could be. A rockfall?

Gunfire, idiot.

The image this brain threw at him clarified the risk. It would have to be dealt with. He found some solid earth where he could plant his feet. The rain and the thick soles of these boots would interfere with his drawing of power, but he didn't suppose that would matter much. The two men running toward him across the rocky plain were only mortals, after all. Wearing Thelyan's white, they carried things Kai recognized as rifles, and were surrounded by a fine mist of static power. Mages with weapons? What use did a mage have for a weapon? His power should be his only weapon. Ka'an would show them how it was done.

He drew heat from stone, force from the tiny concussions of raindrops. Not much, but it should be enough to teach these ridiculous creatures a lesson. He spun up a ward against projectiles. Ignoring the furious thrashing of Kai inside him, he fashioned a noose of will and cast it into the nearer man's heart.

That man sagged, choking. How irritating; he should have died in an instant. He was somehow fighting off Ka'an's death spell. Ka'an would win, but it would take time, and the other man had dropped to one knee and raised his rifle.

Crack and whine, and chips flew up from between Ka'an's feet. He ignored that, busy forcing aside the shieldings of his victim. These gave way, flinging the man into death, just as another gunshot sounded. Ka'an was startled to feel a slap against his thigh, followed by a stinging sensation. He looked down to see a red rip in his trousers where the bullet had creased him. How had it gotten through his ward?

His flicker of confusion quickly turned to anger as Kai surged up inside him, running along the body's nerves like fire on spilled oil. He pressed back, and a thought struck him like a slap: *Not now, fuckwit.* Then he was moving, and the next bullet buzzed past without striking.

Just below the surface, Ka'an fumed at Kai's actions as the body dashed straight at the enemy. *How dare he. How dare he oppose my will and endanger this body, which I have claimed?* The enemy was throwing aside his gun, standing, raising his hand and opening his mouth to trigger a spell. Ka'an tried to jerk the body aside, and found Kai's will weakly held, but now it was as if the body itself had intentions of its own. The first syllable of the spell was spoken, making air chill and skin prickle; then Ka'an's new body was airborne, heel striking the white-clad man in the center of the chest, knocking him down.

A wash of heat swept over him and was gone: a fire spell cut off before it could catch hold. Kai was in control now, snatching up the fallen rifle and aiming it. His thoughts as he put it to his shoulder were chaotic, spinning vaguely in the direction of picking off these men one by one and rescuing the red-haired boy. He pulled the trigger; the enemy's head splattered red across the ground; the rifle kicked against half-healed bone.

In the pain that followed, Ka'an took charge again.

There would be no more silliness about rescues. And there would most certainly be no more name-calling or disrespect. Ka'an was a god. Kai was just a trace left in the brain, soon to be absorbed. From deep within, Kai growled defiance as Ka'an pushed him down, but Ka'an paid him no attention.

By nightfall, he could not make the body do more than trudge stumblingly along. It was exhausted. He let it lie down, though he was impatient with mortal limitations. Now he had to remember how to fall asleep without being trapped in unconsciousness. He, the Dreamer, afraid of dreams! Yet he could still sense Kai rumbling in him like an undigested meal. It was possible that the mortal might take control when Ka'an relaxed his grip.

And do what? Ka'an smiled. He would be unable to stand, let alone take them anywhere Ka'an didn't want to go.

Nevertheless it was a delicate operation. Ka'an would have to remain lucid if he wished to retain control after the body had rested. Gently, carefully, he let Kai slip past him just enough to inhabit the upper layer, the one that felt cold and tasted grit. Let him deal with the ache of hunger in the body's stomach. Ka'an remained just behind him, lacing tendrils of himself through Kai's perceptions; eavesdropping.

Blinking, Kai flexed his hand before his face, then groaned. He pushed himself up on his hands. Ka'an immediately jerked him back; the body flopped like a rag doll. *You shan't go anywhere, Kai. I simply mean to let you sleep.*

"In a mud puddle?" Kai mumbled when Ka'an let him out again. "Just going upslope a bit. Asshole." This insult got him pulled away once more. The next time Ka'an gave him the body, he crawled on his belly away from the waterway they'd been following. Once on harder ground, he wrapped his coat around him and curled into a ball. Miserably chilled and hungry, he put his arms over his face. He was, Ka'an realized, aware of the same dilemma Ka'an had seen, that of relinquishing control to sleep. Why he was so determined to go blundering back into danger for some white-faced catamite was a mystery.

From Kai's part of their shared pattern came a surge of pity. *You have no idea what anything's worth.*

Sleep, Ghost, Ka'an replied angrily. *Neither of us is served by your maundering.*

Kai's reluctant agreement was followed by a relaxing of muscles, if not of mind. The mortal had to bear the brunt of the body's discomfort; if he hadn't been perfectly exhausted, sleep would have been impossible. Ka'an caught his last waking thought: the determination that, when he had rested, he would certainly force himself to the front, defeat what he saw as an intruding, alien mind. He still didn't understand. He should have been honored to be host to his god. Thelyan's influence had done a great deal of harm. Kai didn't have the faintest idea what Ka'an really was, how impossible it would be to win against him, and thus intended to try. This, as he sank into Ka'an's own realm, carrying Ka'an with him.

Kai's dreams began as planning; he tried to find a method of effecting his intended rescue. Mental maps unrolled. These plans soon skewed out of lucidity, but Ka'an was easily able to retain detachment and observe rather than being involved. Kai ran through nightmare landscapes of looming water-walls, hunting the red-haired boy. He was frantic. Black towers of water crashed on him, and he believed his Ashes had drowned, but went on searching. He believed that if he could find the body, he could follow the departing soul into the land of ghosts.

Several times, Ka'an was nearly drawn into the dream by its intensity. Had people dreamed so forcefully in his days of rulership? The body wasn't getting good rest. With a twist of power he hadn't exercised in centuries, Ka'an washed light over the dreamscape and put dry land before the eye of Kai's thoughts. But it wasn't enough; Kai was still in nightmare, still searching, reeling with despair. So Ka'an gave him an image of his white-faced boy, standing unharmed in a field of poppies. He waited to see if the symbolism of the poppies would reach him, remind him how to surrender his will.

Then something disturbing happened: the image of the white boy changed without Ka'an's permission, and without the intervention of Kai's imagination either. It went into sharp focus, suddenly detached from the fabric of the dream. Ka'an had cleaned the boy up a bit, but abruptly he was just as wet and bedraggled as he'd been when Kai last saw him, one arm of his white shirt soaked thinly red. He reached out to snatch up Kai's hand and press it to his cheek.

"Where were you, I was looking for you," Kai said in a dreamer's babbling voice. His relief was overwhelming, strong enough to disturb Ka'an's concentration; this time he was actually dragged partway into the dream before he shook himself free.

"You got away. You're all right," Ashes replied; his voice was also a dreamer's, and there came with it a thread of trickled power. Ka'an fought for the detachment to trace it.

"You're bleeding."

"They shot me but they healed it. And my ankle."

"They caught you. I'm so sorry, I'm so sorry." Kai's dream-self shimmered with anguish, much stronger than anything that could be expressed while awake. The storm of regret subsided instantly when Ashes kissed his fingers and smiled forgiveness.

"I don't know where I am. Some kind of trance. This is a true dream, isn't it? I can feel your hand."

"Yes."

The boy's blue eyes widened in anxiety. "You'll come for me, won't you? I already miss you."

"I promise. But I have to fight this monster first."

"That one?" He pointed. They both turned to look, and they were staring at Ka'an. Too late, he realized he'd been drawn into the dream.

Very well. He'd show the mortal what a god looked like. Wrapping his aspect around him in full glory, he glared, making his eyes crackle with green fire. Made his voice thrum in Kai's chest like a drum when he spoke: "You are only a small part of me, Ghost. All that is great or bright or true in you comes from me. Don't you want to be united with something higher than yourself?" He held his arms out, changing the tone of the dream to one of lostness, loneliness, presenting himself as the only home.

But instead of longing toward the vision of the god, Kai wrapped his arms protectively around Ashes, meeting Ka'an's glare with a scowl. "Get the hell out of my head!"

"How dare you speak to me that way!" Ka'an reared up, becoming terrible, but Kai wasn't frightened. Even Ashes was just looking on with faintly disapproving curiosity, as if watching someone else's child misbehave.

Disgusted with himself, Ka'an jerked free of Kai's thoughts, leaving the dream in ruins behind him. He shivered awake. He had possession of the body, which seemed on the verge of hypothermia. Inside him, Kai threshed about helplessly, looking for his lost dream, and was easily subdued.

The rain had stopped. Clouds fled in rags, revealing glimpses of thin moonlight. Where there had been a foaming river, there now flowed a quieter stream. Ka'an dragged his sluggish body upright, reflecting that it must be a well-trained body indeed, to be able to go on after only an hour's sleep in such wretched conditions, especially chilled as it was. Fortunate, that the dream had gone badly. He might have died -- *it* might have died of the cold, otherwise, casting him blindly toward his next birth.

Not this time. He was determined that this time, he would rise to his true power again. He would take his rightful place. Forcing the exhausted body onward, he followed the flowing water.

☙ ✻ ❧

Something big was happening out there. Hints and echoes tortured Chaiel, made him twist within his prison. Something big.

He couldn't make sense of it. Couldn't slow it down enough to look at it. The babble of voices beat him, visions bludgeoned him, knowledge stretched his brain and cluttered him until he couldn't think. Memories tore at him, never quite coming clear. He was afraid.

When light burst suddenly in on him, he screamed.

It's only Thelyan, he told himself sternly, and calmed enough to look, though a desperate edge stayed on his thoughts. Why was the Judge bothering him again so soon? And why -- the novelty of this took Chaiel's breath away -- why did he have another person with him? He always came alone. What was happening?

This other person was a hollow-cheeked youth in dirty clothes, whose eyelids sagged as if he were half asleep. He stood with a slumping posture, hands loose at his sides, gazing incuriously at Chaiel. Behind streaked spectacles, his eyes were glassy crescents of watery blue. Thelyan was smiling.

"I don't have any questions for you this time, Chaiel," Thelyan said. "I've found Ka'an, and I'll absorb him soon. Tomorrow or the next day, if all goes well. After that, whether I have a use for you depends on how cooperative you are. With that in mind, I've decided to give you a present." He turned to the slack-faced youth. "Undress and remove your spectacles."

Still hammered by fragmentary visions, Chaiel fought to make sense of this. He felt his lips twisting in a posture between laughing and weeping. "What do I want with that? Bring me a girl."

"You asked me if you could have Medur. The answer is yes."

With dawning horror, Chaiel remembered. He

remembered how he had seen that Medur was housed in male flesh this incarnation, and he remembered asking, as a joke, to be given her if she was found, and had not connected the two conversations. Now he understood what he'd brought on himself. Thelyan was not a prankster. He really meant to throw this mindless body into Chaiel's prison to crowd him, to drool and mumble at him and keep him from ever knowing a moment's peace. Probably the thing would be left in here with him for eternity.

He babbled and whimpered, begging, blustering, warning, promising, but Thelyan paid him no mind. Like a statue carved from salt, the Judge watched until he was certain the blank-faced boy had no material on him that might be used for a tool, then steered the unresisting creature to the wall of the sphere. He touched a seal he'd never released before.

Chaiel gasped as air moved against his skin. The bubble was open, it was open! He could get out, if only he could get to the surface he could reach through, he smelled things and felt a breeze on his face!

Thelyan gestured, and the idiot boy was jerked through the air and into the sphere. He fell limply against Chaiel, who shoved and clawed to be free of the entangling limbs, to get *out* -- but Thelyan touched the seal again, and the sphere went stagnant as before.

"Fuck you, Judge!" Chaiel screeched. "Fuck you! Shit on you! I hope your eyes fall out! I hope bugs eat your bowels!"

"I'll leave you a light," Thelyan replied. "So you can get acquainted." He sent his glowing spot up to cling to the ceiling. He went out of the room, and the door clanged behind him.

Weeping in rage, Chaiel punched and slapped at unresponsive body that sagged all over him. It was drawn to the center of the sphere, as he was, and thus it pressed against him no matter what he did. Briefly he entertained the thought of eating it. When it was dead, he could vomit it out, and it would fall out of the sphere and leave him alone.

Alone. A groan wrung out of him. He didn't want to be alone.

But this flopping doll was no company. He turned it around, held it away from him with his feet against its chest. It looked a little bit familiar -- but then, didn't everything? As he watched it, its eyes slid meaninglessly sideways, clearly not seeing anything.

Bewilderment rushed through him. It was quickly

followed by regret, then longing, then worry for the safety of -- someone.

Chaiel sucked in his breath. Those weren't his own feelings. The floppy boy was sending them. Forcing himself calm, he sorted through what had been said, trying to separate his stuttering visions from actual dialogue.

Medur. In a male body. Given to him. This. The Green Lady who wove the vines between hearts; voices babbling about a Green Man; emotions coming up through the soles of his feet. Chaiel squatted on the stranger's chest, peering at him. Well, he looked like a Yelorrean, and immortals tended to incarnate near where they'd first come to power, and there was something foggy about him, like thick clothing, only underneath his skin. *Remember. You know how to do this. It's been so long... you know how to do this, Chaiel. Look properly.*

It had been so long since there had been any pattern in here but his own. He'd stopped seeing it. Blinded by too much information. Making his sight work on the body in front of him was a long, frustrating chore, exacerbated by the leaking emotions that came out wherever their skin touched. And he could not keep from touching, because the stupid sphere pushed them both toward the center, and stupid Thelyan made them be naked so Chaiel couldn't find a way to kill himself with his clothes. Or make a noose of them and swing out to catch the seals when the sphere was opened -- *I could have used my hair, I could have made a braid and swung it out and caught it on a seal when he put this person in, oh damn me why didn't I do that?* Too late now; he bit himself hard on the forearm, then returned to his task.

Just when he thought he'd forgotten forever, would never remember, pattern bloomed before his eyes in all its brilliant colors of thought.

His own pattern was not pleasant to look at. He was insane, and it showed. Chaotic, jerking and spiking with nauseating randomness. He focused instead on the boy's. It was hard to make out; that fog was still there. Chaiel thought its regularity was a bit reminiscent of Thelyan's style. A spell of passivity, of course. He could shatter it with a word, but stopped himself -- stilled himself, though it was difficult -- and carefully spun off the power in it, instead. Not nearly enough power to break out of the sphere. There might not be enough in the world for that. But more was good anyway. As the last shreds of the spell pulled free, the blue-eyed youth blinked and twitched, distaste and panic spilling out of him.

"Hold still," Chaiel barked. "We'll just get tangled if you move."

Looking from Chaiel's face to his own body to the room beyond the ripple of the sphere, the stranger let out a groan. "What is this?"

"You're in the sphere. Thelyan said Medur's in you. Let me look."

Hands hovering in awkward consideration near Chaiel's feet, the stranger spilled out confusion shading into anger. "Who's Thelyan?"

"The one who brought you here."

"I don't remember that. I don't remember coming here. What's Medur?"

"You're not very bright, are you?"

The boy's brows snapped down. Suddenly he moved, grabbing Chaiel's ankle and thrusting him away. Chaiel began a laugh as he bounced up and began to come down again, but it was cut off when the boy's fist smacked into the side of his jaw, spinning him around. As he yelped in surprise, the stranger reversed their earlier positions, so that he was now kneeling on Chaiel's chest, and he had a fistful of Chaiel's hair.

"Just so you know," the boy said tightly, "I've had one hell of a rotten day, so I advise you to leave off smartassing and answer my goddamned question."

Chaiel gaped at the newcomer. His jaw hurt now. The boy looked so thin, but he'd hit awfully hard. And he was so angry. He was still leaking emotion, which meant he was an Empath like Medur's vessel should be, but the feeling coming out of him was a cold burn of fury. Chaiel whimpered. "Don't hit me anymore."

The emission of anger flickered, but came back almost as strongly. "That's up to you, kid. We can be friends or enemies. Your call."

"Friends!" Chaiel tugged to get his hair out of the stranger's fist. The stranger let go with a sigh, anger fading to weary irritation.

"Good. My name's Ashleigh Trine. Call me Ash if you like." He offered his hand, and Chaiel shook it, though the angle was awkward.

"My name is Chaiel," he said, and waited for a reaction. Got none. Sniffed. "So Thelyan really has erased me from history."

"What is this place? This *thing*? How come we're all sideways and sticky?"

"It's called a null sphere. It suspends me so that Thelyan can try to make me answer questions. It stops aging. Mostly. Hair and nails still grow. But I hope you don't need to piss, because you can't."

"Yeah, I can see your hair. Do they feed us? I'm hungry as hell, and thirsty."

"Eventually, you'll bite yourself and suck your own blood, trying to stop the thirst. It doesn't work, but you'll do it anyway."

"So that would be a no," the boy named Ash said calmly, but there had been a spike of fear in him. "Who's this Thelyan character, then?"

Chaiel's lips quirked. "Say the name a lot of times very quickly."

"No thanks."

"Thelyan Thelan Telan Delan Dalan."

"So? What's that supposed to mean?"

"Are you a Dalanist?"

"You're smartassing again." Ash cracked his knuckles.

"I'm not. I swear. He's an immortal, a theophage like I am, like Ka'an and Medur -- gods. We were all mortal once, but he's forgotten that. He's eaten all the rest, and made the world think he's the only one. Now he's going to go eat Ka'an, and then he'll eat us. He's incarnated right now, made himself Director of the Watch. That's who put you in here, because you have Medur in you, though I can't see her, I don't know how he knew --"

"Calm down. Shy -- what was your name?"

"Chaiel."

"Okay. Look, I happen to think you're nuts, but let's see if it hangs together. I've heard of Ka'an. Tell me about him."

"You should know. You've been fucking him."

The newcomer's already pale face blanched gray. "Oh god."

"Precisely."

"So Kieran really -- how did you know that?"

"It's my function. I know things. Just as it's Thelyan's function to divide things, and yours to bring things together, and your evil sweetheart's to do all sorts of things no one wants done."

"What?"

355

"Oh, he's a scary one, Ka'an. I can remember when he ruled the rest of us. He was horrible. He must've been buried awfully deep in your Kieran person, if you can regard him with anything but loathing. Just like Medur's buried so far down in you I can't find her."

Ash shook his head rapidly. "Damn it -- this is all crazy. Okay, who's Medur, and what's this crap about... *her*... being inside me?"

"Let me see if I can find her. Draw her out. Then I won't have to explain things."

"No. I saw that -- Ka'an -- coming up in Kieran, and it scared the hell out of me. I don't think I want to go through something like that."

"With Medur?" Chaiel laughed. "She's harmless."

"Nope. Don't try," he added warningly, cocking a fist.

"And she has the answers you want."

"Didn't I just tell you no?"

"And I miss her."

"Tough. I don't want some girl taking over my mind."

"Don't you want to know all about the god that's running your starving, hypothermic boyfriend to death right about now?"

Immediately after he'd said it -- after it had leapt from his lips as things sometimes did if he had a clairsentient moment while he was talking -- he wished he'd somehow kept his mouth shut. The emotion that spilled into him from Ash was more sharply painful than anything he'd felt in a very long time. Its aftereffects were even worse; Ash was just gnawing a knuckle, afraid because something bad was happening to someone he loved, but Chaiel was forced to see how dulled and numb he'd become over the centuries, and was in danger of losing his numbness because of it.

They remained like that for a time, throwing pain back and forth, until Ash steeled himself and shut down the circuit. His magic was clumsy -- he slammed himself closed far harder than he had to. Still, it was a relief.

Ash covered his face with his hands for a moment, then took a deep breath and met Chaiel's eyes. "All right. Do it."

"It's easier if you open up again," Chaiel said reluctantly.

"If I get scared, it'll distract you."

"Never mind that. You just startled me. You're no good at this. You never had any training, I suppose."

"No."

"Just open."

Scowling, Ash closed his eyes. After a few breaths, his face relaxed, and his mind's barriers relaxed as well. All he was leaking now was a faint anxiety, which was a sensation Chaiel was well accustomed to.

There was the fellow's pattern, a pleasingly even one, almost floral in its unfurled receptiveness. Shapes of open-minded reason repeated within it. The mind of a scholar. Of course it contained the uneven glyphs of hot-blooded tendencies that were to be expected in someone so young, and the whole was currently underlaid by a deep sense of loss and anger, but on the whole it was a very sane mind. The certain shape of magic which Thelyan's minions had been taught to call a Talent was there, a little stretched and scarred as if he'd been trying to get it to do things it couldn't. Or, Chaiel realized, as if it had recently been caught against a will like Thelyan's. Ash had certainly been interrogated before being brought here, but he didn't seem much changed by it.

Chaiel resented him for that.

After much careful sorting and delving, he saw what he'd been looking for. Scented the faintest hint of someone he knew. Following the hint, he found it tightly knotted, incurved in such a way that it could not, of its own action, break free. A touch from outside was needed to release it. Medur had made herself a seed that could only germinate when conditions were just right.

That was so like her. Chaiel smiled as he touched the intricately tiny glyph, teased free a burr of semi-awareness and saw the whole thing start to unfold.

He drew back into himself and opened his eyes. Ash looked puzzled at him.

"I thought it would be like a Survey," Ash said. "But that didn't hurt."

"Doing it right takes finesse. Creativity. Thelyan's people don't have that. He pounds it out of them."

"Well, I appreciate it. I can sort of see what you were looking at, but I don't feel any different. Should I?"

"Give it time."

"I don't *have* time, not if what you said about Kieran is true!"

"Oh, Ka'an won't break his body while it's still useful. Probably."

"*Probably?*" Ash bared his teeth, about to have a tantrum.

Then he stopped. His look turned inward. He drew a sharp breath. "Oh."

Chaiel waited, half fearful and half pleased, while Medur unfurled.

༄ ✹ ༅

Thelyan studied the map. He could get a team into the Burn area within four hours. Faster, if the Splitwood Mine spur was clear, or the engineers handy about shunting traffic off it. But he had to assume the worst, and in the worst case he'd only be throwing those men away. Well, he could withdraw them if the situation changed.

Interrogating Ashleigh Trine had yielded some interesting results. He'd done it himself, not trusting the information to any of his officers. He hadn't made any special effort to leave the recaptured fugitive sane or alive at the end of the session; giving the boy to Chaiel had been an afterthought. The combination of Survey, Compulsion, and physical stressing had broken Trine wide open. Thelyan now knew that Kieran Trevarde was Ka'an's current host, that Ka'an had nearly awakened at least once, that the two fugitives' homosexual relationship might provide a hold on Trevarde if Ka'an didn't emerge, and that Ka'an had apparently seen something in Trine to startle him. A deeper probe of Trine had told Thelyan what it was: Medur, dormant.

One of his two enemies had fallen into his hand without any effort on his part. He had a fairly clear idea of the location and plans of the other. And the weather was clearing, which would allow tracking.

Either Ka'an had emerged, or he had not. If he had emerged, he would make straight for the Burn as quickly as possible. If he hadn't, he might do so at any point, or he might remain buried. If he remained buried, the motivation would be Trevarde's; either to hide himself, or to attempt to free Trine. That last possibility seemed unlikely, as things stood; some people actually were that suicidally noble, but Thelyan doubted that the multiple murderer Trevarde was one of them. It was also unlikely that Ka'an would remain buried long.

Therefore it made sense to plan for two contingencies: Ka'an in fresh possession of his power, or Trevarde fleeing for the border.

Ways to leave the country were limited, and already

closely monitored. It wouldn't hurt to have a search team combing the area where Trevarde had last been sighted, in case he tried to find a bolthole within the country. But Thelyan considered it far more likely that Ka'an had awakened.

In which case, his first action after reassuming his power would be to strike at Thelyan. The evil one wasn't stupid; he knew that planning and preparing were Thelyan's skills, not his own, and would try not to give Thelyan time to be ready. He would not understand that Thelyan had always been ready. Coming fresh from reabsorbing his greater pattern, wearing a body still injured and exhausted from the Watch's harrying of Trevarde, and nearly a thousand years behind the science of magic, he'd be easily defeated.

The only thing Thelyan wasn't confident of was his ability to fully assimilate Ka'an. He'd failed, last time. He'd only been able to cut Ka'an from his power and kill his body. Though he could easily do that this time, it would mean another long period of watching for the evil one's possible incarnations. He would far rather break Ka'an's will and take him in whole. But the methods by which Thelyan had broken the others hadn't worked on Ka'an. The others had loved their worshippers, and thus were vulnerable to Thelyan's threats to their populations. Ka'an, on the other hand, was perfectly selfish. When Thelyan had warned that retaliations would fall on the Iavaians as a result of Ka'an's stubbornness, Ka'an had been unmoved. *If they can't defend themselves, let them die*, Ka'an had replied.

Well, perhaps something would come to mind. Until then, it was better to plan on keeping the body alive, using the null sphere. Having three of his enemies in one sphere wouldn't be secure; he would have to build more.

Then there would be no chance of anyone spoiling his plans. His people would continue to spread across the world, bringing order and righteousness. Gradually, rebellion and sin would be weeded out. There would come a time when all was clear, all voices raised in unison to him, ordered and regular, grateful for the bliss of perfect obedience. There would be no more of the pain caused by conflict. No more pride or lust or anger. Ka'an's diseased legacy would be erased at last.

Thelyan was surprised to discover that a fine tremor had begun in his hands. With an effort, he stilled himself. It wouldn't do to get excited. He still had to give orders to his people, predicated on the assumption that there would soon be a Burn here. All nonessential personnel would be evacuated. He would have the prisoners locked down; they could go hungry for a few days, if necessary. If they were killed, he could simply collect others later. Did he want to bring extra troops in?

Yes, why not. They would probably die, but they'd weaken Ka'an in the process, lessening the likelihood that Thelyan would be harmed. Loyal men would be grateful for such an opportunity. Even if they didn't know what Thelyan was, they knew they were dying for their God.

Chapter 27

Ash watched warily as a stranger's senses spread out beneath his own. It was not quite like Empathy. There was a pressure building, a point of tension; nervously, he waited for this new thing to push through him, as he'd sensed Ka'an doing to Kieran. It didn't push him, though. It found a kind of tense equilibrium, and there it stopped expanding.

At the same time, a memory was nagging at him. A scene: a beach. A green, wet place, dripping with mist, the sound of the sea. It invited him to daydream.

He frowned. Was this a trick, meant to lull him so he could be taken over?

The weird kid was watching him expectantly. Ash had to assume he'd been telling the truth about what this bubble thing was, at least in terms of it stopping aging. The kid's hair was longer than he could have grown it in his life, if he was the age he looked. And what he'd said made sense, in its crazy way -- about what Ka'an was, and the thing in Ash's own mind...

And if Ka'an was harming Kieran, then there weren't any other options, were there? He had to know.

He closed his eyes and let the scene open before him.

Hazy at first, like remembering, but solidifying quickly into something more like a dream. Then something even more real. He stood on a cobblestone beach beside a cold sea, the surf sound rushing in his ears. Above, a steep hill thickly covered with oak and brambles. A thin drizzle was falling, chilling his naked flesh.

He was so tired of being cold and wet and naked. It seemed he'd been some combination of those things for ages. Well, true vision or not, he believed he ought to be able to at least imagine he was clothed. Thinking back to the state of his closet before he'd been arrested, he took his favorite clothes and remembered what they'd felt like on his body. Trousers of heather-colored wool, a bit scratchy but nicely warm. Cream linen shirt, soft from many washings; the green and gray brocade vest; his elastic-sided boots, which were out of fashion but well broken-in. His winter coat, russet wool, with the collar that turned up, and -- why not -- the silly red scarf his aunt had made him, with the fringes all falling out.

Despite the strangeness and sadness of everything, he smiled. He'd missed these clothes. It was so nice to be comfortably dressed, for once. He felt much warmer now.

A footstep crunched behind him.

Steeling himself, he turned to face --

"Aunt Isobel?" He took a step back, incredulous.

"I'm afraid not." She smiled, and it was the wrong smile. Aunt Isobel's smile was a toothy, crinkly thing, wry and cynical. This woman's was sadly serene. She held herself differently, too. This woman stood straight, head high, hands at her sides. His aunt was always in the middle of some movement, her hands never still.

But there she was, dressed in her blue serge suit with the side-button skirt, collar wrinkled, hair coming down at the back, the way he'd last seen her. The lines of laughter in her face were just right, and the sparkle of her eyes, the same color as his own. Homesickness punched him in the gut.

"I'm sorry," she said, sounding as if she meant it. "This was the only clear memory of a woman I could find in your mind. If it distresses you too much, I could construct a face for myself, though it would be a bit hazy."

Ash shook his head. "I'll cope. You'd be this Medur person, then."

"Yes." She inclined her head gracefully, like a queen.

"What are you doing in my head?"

"That's actually two questions, isn't it? What *was* I doing? I was waiting. What do I intend to do now? That's largely up to you."

He narrowed his eyes suspiciously. "What does that mean?"

"I'm not impatient. If you don't want to merge yourself with me, I can wait for another life. We should discuss this thoroughly before you make a decision, though."

"There isn't time. That Ka'an thing is killing someone I love. I need to find out what's going on and get out of that bubble place."

She raised a hand to stop him. The more she moved, the less she looked like Isobel. "Don't worry. This isn't taking up as much time as it seems. Like a dream, in which you might live a lifetime in one night. We have all the time we need. Shall we exchange questions?"

"If I can go first."

"Please do."

"All right, then: what *are* you?"

"The short answer is that I'm a goddess. Somehow I sense, though, from the flavor of your mind, that you're not inclined to awe."

"That answer doesn't satisfy me, no."

She gave him an approving nod. "It has never satisfied me either. I was born in the ordinary way, perfectly mortal, and what I became, I became through my own efforts. That doesn't taste properly of divinity to me." She stepped closer, reaching out to him. "Walk with me."

He hesitated, but placed his hand in hers, and let her turn him along the shore. It felt strange. He hadn't held his aunt's hand since he was much shorter than she; now he towered over her. But this was not his aunt, of course. She didn't walk like Isobel, or smell like her, and now that he looked more closely, this version was younger.

"In my first life," she said, "I was a queen. In that time, magic was a sign of divine favor, even of divine parentage. For we had our gods, in the sea and in the wood. My people were poor, often hungry, often at war. I was determined to change that. Though the priests told me it was sacrilege to examine magic too closely, I made experiments, I studied my abilities. I discovered ways to help my people. I improved the soil; I improved the laws. I saw into their hearts and helped them to help each other. In this I was a great ruler.

"When my time to die drew near, I was not satisfied that my sons would continue my work. My people still needed me. I told them I would remain nearby after my death to guide them. They believed me. It was true. I must have been something like a ghost at first, half-aware, for I recall nothing of it. I learned later that I had been called to give advice on many occasions, through ceremonies that grew up around that purpose. I must have answered well, for my people prospered.

"In time, I grew more aware. The devotion my people sent to me gave me strength. More often, I was able to help them even when I wasn't called. I watched over my line as my little kingdom grew into a nation."

"Yelorre?" Ash guessed.

"Yes. Does it still exist?"

"No. You're not done answering me, though."

"True. Well, then, there came a time when all that remained of my descent was a blustering bully of a king whose children were born dead, three in a row. The next time his queen quickened, I watched over the child, healing it in the womb, keeping it alive. But when it came near term, I saw that its mind had not developed. The people needed a ruler, and would not have one, because this child was not a fit heir. So I inhabited it. I imprinted my own pattern on its vacant brain, and I became the child. However, when that happened, I lost much of my context. A child's brain is not capable of holding the memories and thoughts of an adult, let alone one who has been aware for many generations' time after her death. It was not until after I had married and given up rulership to my husband that I remembered who I was.

"I shouldn't bore you with the story of how I took my sovereignty back. I got children with several men other than my husband the king, in order to invigorate the line --"

"Ceriamme? You were Queen Ceriamme?"

"So you know your history."

Ash chuckled. "The racy parts, anyway. So you figured out how to take over babies in the womb. Then what?"

"I did so only once more, in fact. In that case, the child was not destined to be an idiot, and I had to make my peace with the soul already there. We came to an agreement, however, and she was absorbed into my substance. It was necessary; a god from the south had spurred his people to spread his worship by fire and sword. The people called him Tellin."

"Thelyan."

She nodded. "Yes. In time, I met him in battle. I was defeated. He could have swallowed me, he told me, as he had many others, but despised me so that he would not have me in him. Instead he stripped me of my power and cast me adrift. From then on, I was born many times, lived many lives, as a passenger in many minds. I lived both male and female, good and bad, powerful and weak. Those who gave me shelter in their souls were always of my line. I saw little of the world; I have no idea how much time has passed. From your manner and the way you've clothed yourself, I suspect my descendants still retain some standing in the world, although -- forgive me -- I think you are not a prince."

Ash laughed. "No, I'm not a prince. Well, ask your question, it's your turn."

"Very well. Tell me about yourself."

"That's pretty vague."

She waved a hand, unconcerned. "Just a long view of your circumstances. Your name, your age, what titles you hold, whether you're married..." She gave him a thoughtful look. "Somehow I doubt you're married. This aunt of yours is the only female face you remember clearly."

"You won't get any more of your line out of me. I'm only interested in boys. Only one boy, actually, and he's the one that Ka'an --"

"That, later. You, now."

"Well, at least you're not shocked."

"I've lived a long time, child. Come now. Your name, at least."

"I'd think you'd know. You really were asleep. My name's Ashleigh Trine. I'm eighteen -- no, I think I might have turned nineteen by now. I just realized I don't know what the date is. What was the rest of it? Titles?" He snorted. "There are no more titles. My aunt told me my great-grandfather had been something semi-important, a baronet or something, but none of that matters anymore. I'm an orphan; my parents were killed by Commonwealth soldiers when I was four, and I went to live with my mother's younger sister. She happened to be a member of the Resistance, and raised me to be a rebel too. We did propaganda. Wrote pamphlets, put up posters, spread rumors. I got arrested. They found out by reaming out my mind that Aunt Isobel was in on it too, but she got away. That was our agreement -- that if one of us got caught, the other would run." He took a deep breath, swallowed a salt taste. "That way, whoever got caught could know that at least the other one was free somewhere. I sort of made the same deal with Kieran, just a little bit ago, and I thought I could be glad he's free. But this goddamn Ka'an creature is -- look, it's my turn now, right? Tell me about Ka'an."

Medur took his hand in both of hers and squeezed it gently. "Calm yourself, son. We have time, remember? Yes, I'll tell you. It will frighten you, if your lover is involved with him, but you must be calm."

Ash set his jaw and nodded.

"Ka'an is the oldest of us. He was the first to gather power after death; the first of the immortals. I have encountered him several times. What I've learned of his origin is that he began so long ago that men had not even learned to make metal. All they had was bone and stone, wood and clay. Their houses were pits dug into the ground. In his mortal time, weaving was a new art, and sacred. That is how old Ka'an is.

"How he came to be considered divine, he tells proudly, though it's an evil gift: he taught men how to cultivate the poppy to increase the potency of its sap, and use the plant to enter a trance, to dream."

"He was the first junkie?" Ash gave a disbelieving laugh.

"I'm not sure what you mean. In any case, he was a product of a desert people. They worshipped him, and he became very strong. He interfered directly in mortal matters. He constructed for his people an empire of great grandeur and great cruelty; slavery, vice, and human sacrifice were its foundations. Other immortals who stood against him were absorbed or destroyed; this is how he took dominion over death and storms as well as his first power of dreaming. There were friendships among immortals, if you can give that name to a communication as tenuous as ours, and I recall the names and patterns of many who also feared him. None of us were anywhere near his level of strength."

"But -- then how come he was hiding in Kieran's brain, like you were in mine?"

"Thelyan." She shook her head sadly. "When he first proposed to ally and defeat Ka'an, many went to him. You must understand that Thelyan represented justice, fairness. Retribution as well -- he arose from within a tribe of slaves, freed them by his power. Ka'an represented only evil. Thelyan convinced several of the younger and weaker immortals to weld themselves to him, and he swallowed them. Then he began to take us by force, still in the name of defeating Ka'an. His armies attacked our people, and he threatened to slaughter them to the last child unless we surrendered. Only I was left, because he didn't want me, and the Observer, the Silent One, Chaiel, who --"

"Chaiel? That lunatic with the hair?"

Medur raised an eyebrow.

"He's in the bubble with me. He's been there a long time, his hair's about ten feet long. He's not what I'd call silent, either. So he really is a god?" Ash gave a wry grin. "I clocked him on the jaw."

"Oh, dear." Medur sighed. "The poor child. You mustn't bully him, Ashleigh. He was never very strong."

"Yes, ma'am," he said contritely. "Please, finish your story. You got knocked out, Chaiel's in the bubble -- I assume Thelyan put him there -- then what?"

She spread her hands. "I don't know. I sensed a great battle. Thelyan must have won, if Ka'an is coexisting with a mortal mind."

"You don't think he might have just decided to live there, the way you did once?"

"Not Ka'an. He would have done as he always did. He would have destroyed the child's mind in the womb, driven its soul out so as to have sole possession."

Ash shuddered. "That's what he's trying to do to Kieran."

"My question, then. Tell me about this Kieran. From his name, he sounds Yelorrean, or perhaps Eskaran."

"No." Scowling, Ash decided not to get off on a political tangent. "He's Iavaian. His real name is Kai. I love him more than life. I don't mean that as a sentimental expression. He's better than breathing and seeing and thinking. If I lose him -- I shouldn't tell you this. I'm relying on my judgment of you. If I lose him, you can have this body. Do anything you want with it, just make sure I don't have to live with missing him."

Medur's smile was indulgent. "This is a new love, I suspect."

"Yes, I see what you're getting at, it's fresh and raw, but it's real enough for all that. If you're going to belittle what I feel for him --"

"I didn't mean to insult you. Please go on. What sort of man is he? A man grown, or a youth like you?"

"About a year older than me. He's lived a lot more than I have, though. He's had a hard life. He's terribly strong, and terribly lost -- he's been fighting all his life just to survive, he's never had a moment's peace, and I want to be that peace for him."

"A warrior?"

"Definitely. Not a soldier, not in the sense you mean it. But he sure as hell can fight."

"Is he strong in mind, or only with a blade?"

"Blade?" Ash raised an eyebrow; then shook his head to Medur's questioning look. "Never mind, long explanation. Yes, he's strong in mind. He doesn't care what anyone thinks of him... or he didn't, before I got to him. Oh, hell. You don't think I weakened him so it'll be easier for Ka'an to beat him?"

"I don't know, child. I think, if you love each other, it might strengthen him." Her look softened, becoming very gentle, a strange thing to see on his aunt's face. "He must be truly kind, to win such devotion from you."

Slowly, Ash shook his head. "Kind... no. No, he can be downright mean sometimes. He's had to be, you see. He can be cold, and rude, and thoughtless, and he's got the filthiest vocabulary you ever heard. But he's *true*. That's what you have to understand. He's -- he's *pure*, not in the sense of innocent, but in the sense of -- distilled, wholly himself. Pure iron, pure diamond, pure rage. There's nothing like him in the world, and never will be again after him, I think. To be near that, part of that -- do you see?"

"I do. In a way I envy you. If I had not already meant to help you, I think I would have decided to, seeing how intensely you feel. Thelyan and his type believe emotion is a weak thing. But it gives strength, does it not, when it's honest?"

Ash nodded. "So you'll help. How?"

"We'll decide that shortly. I must know more first, but it's your turn to question me."

"No. I've learned enough. Let's talk about what we can do to save Kieran."

"This 'bubble,' then. You said you and Chaiel are in it; I assume Thelyan put you there."

"That's what Chaiel said. I was in kind of a trance, I don't remember."

"Tell me what it's like. A prison?"

"Yeah. A weird one." He described it to her, but from her expression she was as baffled as he was. "And I can tell you I'm not enjoying being stuck naked to a crazy kid, even if he is supposed to be a god or something. He's even more ticked off about it than I am. At least I can appreciate that he's cute -- too young, mind, and I would never cheat on Kieran, but you see what I mean. He doesn't even have that consolation. I think he's going to wig out on me any minute."

Medur seemed amused. "We shall have to see if we can prevent that. Now; how is it you know Ka'an is battling your Kieran-Kai? Have you seen this?"

"Yes." He shuddered. "I was connected with him, when Ka'an first came up. At least, I think it was the first time. We fought him down, but Kieran said he was going to come back. Then -- long story short, the White Watch caught me but not Kieran, they tranced me, I'm pretty sure they dug through my brain and got everything I know -- the Watch, those are Thelyan's army mages. He's Director of the Watch now. And Chaiel said something about Ka'an running Kai to death.

Starving, hypothermic, he said."

"It may already be too late," Medur said gently.

"I refuse to consider that. What am I going to do, give up?"

"I see your point. Very well. If we're to help your Kai fight free of Ka'an, we must pierce that bizarre prison." She sighed. "I will never understand how Thelyan thinks. What a cruel device to have invented. I should like to see it for myself, but to do that I would have to take possession of your body."

"Permanently?"

"That depends on whether you can retain selfhood while I do it. Perhaps it's better not to gamble on that. You could be killed or driven mad."

"Are there any other options?"

"Two. The first is that you could surrender yourself entirely to me. I would do my best to save your lover, but this would do you no good. You would be, effectively, dead."

"If that's what it comes down to, I'll take it."

Respect narrowed her eyes, and she nodded. "I see. Yes, I see. The other possibility is that I could surrender myself to you, and you would then be in possession of my abilities. Thelyan stripped me of my power, and I've built up only a little more since then, so you would most likely survive it. What I question is whether you would be able to get any use from it. My knowledge would not be passed on intact. You might keep some shreds of it, but not enough to tell you how to be what I've been. It would probably not make you an immortal."

"And you'd die."

"I would." Her shoulders sagged a fraction. "Please understand me, Ashleigh Trine. I've held on so long only for the sake of my people. Now it seems Thelyan has conquered them. Could I free them if I took possession of you? Perhaps; perhaps not. You say you're an orphan, and a homosexual. My line of descent is finished in you. Could I force your body to sire children and continue it? Perhaps. But I'm tired. I'm far behind the times, it seems. I don't understand half of what you tell me. I'm an old, old woman, Ashleigh. I would gladly end... *if* I had some hope you could accomplish what I wish done. The return of my lands and the posterity of my blood."

He stopped walking the endless beach, turning her by her hand to face him. "Let me get this straight. If I agree to do my best to free Yelorre from the Commonwealth, and -- what, have a child? Somehow? Then you'll give me all your power and vanish. Without a fight."

"I've done my fighting, child. It's your turn now, I think."

"It's... a lot to think about." He chewed his lip. "I don't think I could even -- with a girl -- I don't even know any girls."

Medur laughed. "That's the part that worries you? To free a conquered nation is such an easy task?"

"Hell, I'm a rebel already, ma'am. I was going to do that anyway."

"As for continuing my line, if you swear to make the attempt, I shall be satisfied. Or perhaps you have some living relatives, close kin -- siblings, cousins?"

"Nope. It would have to be me. Aunt Isobel never had kids, she's too old now, and we're all that's left of the family. Oh, hell. All right. I promise. I'll do what I can -- but Kieran comes first. Then Yelorre. Then the kid thing." He grimaced. "He's not going to like that."

She patted his arm reassuringly. "From what I've seen, your kind often wishes for children strongly enough to sire them, though at a later age than you are now. You'll manage. But I'd like to be more certain that you can take my power and keep it. What magic have you? Are you a wizard trained, or only a vessel?"

"No training. Not sure what you mean by the other."

"Does it only pass through you, or do you control it?"

"Um... I can turn my Empathy on and off, sort of. If I don't get too worked up."

"So you've never shaped a spell."

"I made a sort of charm thingy for Kieran once. It seemed to work. I just made it up as I went along. The Watch has a monopoly on pattern-magic, you see. They own thaumaturgy. Nobody gets trained unless it's with them. But I kind of get the idea that I could do a lot more if I had some time to study."

She thinned her lips, doubtful. "It could be worse. You seem an intelligent boy. Calm enough, and clear-minded. Do you think you can experience something strange and perhaps painful without pulling away from it?"

"If I've decided to."

"Have you ever seen the figures -- the shapes -- I seem to be at a loss for a word. There was a more accurate one, once. The shapes of life, like interwoven designs surrounding a thing or a person. Have you seen that?"

"I... think so. Through Kieran, when he was calling a storm. He was better at it, he just dived right in."

"Ka'an must have been close to surfacing." She paused for a long moment. Tilting her head, she took his chin in her hand and studied his face. "I find myself stubbornly reluctant. Are you a fit successor? I know so little about you. It seems irresponsible to make this decision without knowing more. Have you even a hope of succeeding?"

He let her look for a little while. Then he gently pushed her hand away. "Ma'am, if there's a way, I'll find it. Giving up is not an option. And if I get half a chance, I'll not only save Kieran, spark up the rebels in Yelorre, and pass on the blood somehow, but I'll kick Thelyan's ass for you as well. Honestly, if I don't have a chance, I doubt you do either."

"You're very confident."

"Call it determined. I'm also seriously scared, but I've kind of gotten used to that lately."

For another minute or two, she stared at him. Then she looked at the sky and took a deep breath. "Yes," she said.

"Thank you," he said sincerely.

"When you have the power settled, follow the designs, the symbols. They'll show you what you can do. If you reach your Kai while he still struggles against Ka'an, remind him who he is. Ka'an will be undermining his personality, eroding his identity. Remind him of his name, tell him his memories. This while adding your strength to his. Do you understand?"

"Yes."

She gave him another one of those serene, sad smiles. "You're a good lad. I wish I could have known you better. Please mention to Chaiel that all people are his. Are you ready?"

Ash nodded. Medur took his hands.

The scene of the shore went thin, began to smear.

Confusion crashed through him, like the dazedness after a blow to the head. Whirling thoughts and shapes and sensations. He felt too small to contain it, and at the same time stretched thin, scattered. He couldn't grasp it, it was spinning by too fast, he was losing himself --

Kieran. For him. Take it, Ash. Ride it.

A wire, a light; a solid center; himself. He reached, catching at the flying sparks of wordless ideas. Little by little, they began to fall into place. Spirals, spheres, braids, key-toothed fronds, clinging vines, settling along the limbs of his mind, grafting there. He healed the joins. He welded. He swallowed. He made room, and things flowered in the space he made. As the task progressed, it changed from pain to pleasure; the quiet pleasure of an intricate task. It was just like a cipher. Once he worked out the key, the rest was already deciphered in principle, and changing it to meaning was only a detail.

He opened his eyes and drew breath. Yes. There it all was. The cipher of himself, and the cipher of Chaiel, and the cipher of the sphere. The latter was a very deep code. Not the same language as a living pattern at all. More like math worked in a strange base. Base thirteen and a half or something. But he could get it. He was sure that he could figure it out, in time.

"Medur?" Chaiel leaned close, peering into his eyes. "Is that you?"

"No." Ash paused, then corrected. "Partly. She gave me her power."

Chaiel froze, horrified. "You *ate* her?"

"We discussed it, and decided that was the best course. She told me to tell you that all people are yours."

Inhaling sharply, Chaiel pressed his hands to his mouth. A quiet sound came out of him, its meaning unclear. His pattern had drawn in, small.

"This means something to you, I take it."

Chaiel nodded without taking his hands down.

"Much as I'd like to give you time to ponder it, I have a really long to-do list now. So what do you say we pop this bubble and get out of here?"

Chapter 28

Kieran felt it when the edge of the Burn touched him. He was barely there, a helpless passenger in his own body, but the first brush of the Burn's raw energy stung him nonetheless.

What are you doing, asshole? You're going to get me killed!

Ka'an didn't reply. For the first part of the night Kieran had been able to get a rise out of him, but after a while the arrogant spirit had stopped responding. Ka'an was taking them straight into the Burn. That was where he'd been going the whole time. Kieran had never stopped fighting him, and was now so tired that he felt like a tissue-thin shred of himself. He was starving, he was stumbling, his head was stuffed up. Ka'an didn't care. All Ka'an cared about was getting something out of the Burn and then, for some reason, killing the Director of the Watch.

Kieran could be all right with that last bit, Thelyan was a prick and might as well die, but he was going to rescue Ash first. That was the plan. This was just a little setback.

All around him, Ka'an swelled with pleasure at the sensation of the Burn surrounding him. He was doing something with it as he walked. Somehow taking in strength from it. Walking straighter, seeing more clearly. Kieran couldn't sense the patterns now the way he had yesterday -- no, day before yesterday -- but he thought he had an idea what was going on. The Burn had looked inviting, when he'd sensed it in the distance before. Probably that had been Ka'an in him, wanting to do whatever he was doing now.

So maybe two could play that game. It was hard to think how to do it, there was no analogy. It wasn't inhaling, because he couldn't reach his lungs; it wasn't grasping, because he couldn't reach his hands. It was like swallowing without a mouth. Sporadically at first, then more strongly as he grew more confident, he copied Ka'an and took power from the Burn.

"Clever, Ghost," Ka'an muttered. "But I've been doing this far longer than you have." His Iavaian was archaic, with double vowels instead of cut vowels. Kieran thought he'd probably pronounce his name something like Kaaaan, like the sound of a kettle falling down stairs.

The thought gave Kieran courage; irrational, to build himself up by mocking his enemy, but if it worked it worked. He accelerated his grasping of power, growing more real by the second, more aware. Ka'an reeled it in harder as well. At the same time, walking sped to running, and the running got faster and faster.

Now Kieran was beginning to be able to see. Rather, to think about what he saw, for he'd been watching scenery crawl by the whole time, but without making sense of it. He'd never been inside the Burn before. He'd heard rumors about what it was like: dead, deader than a salt pan, without even the hardiest plants or insects. And that was what he was looking at, all right. Bare rock and rippled sand, across which Ka'an forced his body to run at an ever-increasing pace. Soon the ground was flashing by at a speed he wouldn't have thought possible. It was as if he didn't weigh anything at all. He was taking six, ten, fifteen feet at a stride. His coat was cracking like a whip. The soles of his boots were getting hot.

And the sun was going to come up any second now. He'd overheat, his heart would burst. *Slow down, shithead, you're going to pop if you keep this up!* Of course Ka'an didn't listen.

They were going gradually downhill. On the left, a low squarish shape cruised past and was left behind; in the twilight, it looked suspiciously like a ruined building. A little later, they passed another one, and Kieran realized it really was a ruin. Then they topped a rise and started ripping down the other side faster than an express train on a straightaway, and the growing light showed a city grid spread out below. The ruins rayed out from the shore of an immense lake, the biggest body of water Kieran had ever seen. He could just barely make out that there was land on the other side, just a faint line of purpled hills to prove this wasn't an ocean. Ka'an was driving them straight for it, while the pressure of power from the Burn's whirling pattern increased with every step.

Kieran could feel his skin now, and it was far too hot. Dry, no longer sweating, dehydrated. He ran helplessly along a straight street between dune-buried walls, some broken off at the lowest course of stones, some intact enough to still have a bit of roof on them. He passed a square well that was filled to its brim with sand. A mile jagged by in two breaths.

He took the water's edge in a flat leap that carried him thirty feet from shore, and when he hit he skidded two yards on his steaming heels before he sank in.

The lake closed around him, cutting off the main force of impinging power. It cooled him, and when he bobbed up for a ragged breath he gratefully swallowed the water in his mouth. He could see the pattern arrayed above him now. So huge.

A moment of pure terror seized him. The Burn filled the sky from horizon to horizon, and all the space between. Its largest form was a many-armed spiral, ponderously rotating. Within that shape, smaller shapes spun, and smaller ones within those, faster as they got smaller. And it saw him, wanted him, beat at him, tried to change him. He could sense the patterns of his body being buffeted by this great power, knew that any moment the walls of his veins would give way, the delicate web of his brain would fray, and he would die in one bloody instant.

But it didn't happen. He stood neck-deep in insulating water, and somehow he didn't die. Ka'an was preventing it. They were both simultaneously in occupation now. Kieran could see what Ka'an was doing, how he was doing it.

Carefully, but with increasing dexterity, Ka'an was pulling in the power as it came. Some of what he took, he used to shore up the body's systems so the Burn wouldn't kill it. The rest, he fed into his own thought-form, so that he expanded within the Burn's shape and took its place. The process was accelerating, going faster as Ka'an got bigger.

That doesn't look hard. If a spoiled brat like you can do it... Kieran copied him, but he left maintaining the body to Ka'an. The spirit wouldn't want to kill his only vehicle, so he'd have to pay attention to keeping it alive. That would free Kieran to work faster.

Doubt nagged, a little; he'd never done anything like this before, never imagined it, never had any idea that stuff like this existed. But what did that matter? He'd discovered long ago that he couldn't expect any warning or practice before the shit hit the fan. Learn fast or die, that was the rule. He was a fast learner.

He reached. He caught. He organized. He went past the point of pressure, to where the power was no longer forcing itself at him, but just beyond him, and he grew to meet it. With half a thought, he put in an order to his body and walked it out of the lake to get a better handle on the pattern. His mind's eye focused wider and deeper at once, grasping the intricacies of the greater whorl and its component movements. He disassembled the clockwork. He understood the Burn, and he swallowed it whole.

Then he was standing on the shore of a sterile lake, beside a ruined city, in the slanting gold of dawn. And so was Ka'an. It was hard to tell which of them had taken more power. Neither was in full control of the body they shared. Stalemate.

It would have to be dealt with. No compromise was possible. Their mutual hatred was like a balanced stone, poised to crush whichever weakened first.

We have business, Kieran sent.

Ka'an agreed with a mental snarl.

The body crumpled to the sand as they leapt into the battlefield of dreams.

Thelyan paused in mid-word when he sensed the surge of dark power to the west. His subordinates looked at him curiously, concerned. They had never seen such an expression cross the Director's face. Some of them had felt a pale shade of what Thelyan had sensed, but none of them knew what it meant. They were already confused by his preparations.

He pulled himself together, wrapping himself in the chill calm that was his strength.

"Gentlemen, it seems the Situation is, in fact, occurring. Warren, begin evacuating the research section. Vaughart, I want the northern wing cleared and locked down. Rine, contact Strindner at Splitwood; have him leave a four-man team on standby and pull the rest back here. Liss, prepare your men for deployment."

Sergeant Liss hesitated as the others scattered. "Sir, do you have a time estimate?"

Glancing at the map, Thelyan performed some calculations. If Ka'an were in a hurry, he might use wind and Kinetics to 'fly' here; in such a case, his speed would be governed by the kind of wind he could summon. That method was wasteful of power, though. More likely, the evil one would simply run, and there were limits to what a body could do, even with a god's power in it.

"Six hours," Theylan replied. "Expect Strindner to reinforce you."

"Thank you, sir." Snapping off a salute, Liss removed himself.

Satisfied that there would be troops enough to weaken

Ka'an, and that what could be preserved would be, Thelyan left the meeting room by a different door. He would wait outside, atop the mountain. He didn't want anything interfering with his senses now.

Just because he expected to win didn't mean he'd make anything less than a full effort. He had nothing to prove by holding back. No one but he and his enemy even understood the conflict.

☙ ✵ ☜

Ash grunted as Chaiel let him fall. They'd been standing on the soles of each other's feet so Ash could probe the bubble's surface, when Chaiel had suddenly curled up like a pillbug. Ash collided with him, getting tangled in the ludicrous ropes and nets of Chaiel's hair and grazed by his overgrown toenails.

"Damn it, would you pay attention?" But just as he said it, he sensed what had set Chaiel off. A thing like tugging and pressure both at once, a rolling wave of needles. It washed over and through him, left him gasping. "Kieran," he breathed. He'd tasted Kieran's personality in that. And the greasy menace of Ka'an as well.

How had it reached him here in the bubble? A thought snapped into focus, and he followed it without taking time to analyze. Shot his attention down the wave's backtrail, searching. Somewhere out there was a bullet with his name on it, his scratched initials resting against the skin of Kieran's throat. That connection, somehow, was on a different level from the null sphere's blocking, just like Chaiel's visions. That meant that he and Kieran weren't completely cut off from each other. He would have wept in gratitude if he could have spared the attention.

Dimly, he sensed Chaiel babbling. That wasn't important. He was going to find Kieran and help him, even if he used himself up doing it.

☙ ✵ ☜

Kieran stood barefoot on a white limestone floor, beneath a roof painted scarlet, between pillars carved in the shape of bundled reeds. Before him, above him, Ka'an sat on a gilded throne. The dark god wore a body like a pampered version of his own; smooth of skin, attenuated and graceful, impossibly beautiful. Scarlet cloth brocaded with gold draped the god's slender body, leaving his chest bare to reveal a collar of gold and gems that spread across his shoulders. Bands of gold circled his upper arms, wrists, ankles, and waist. Atop his intricately braided hair sat a tall, sun-rayed crown of soft gold, its points decorated with looping strands of lapis and ruby.

A tight sense of anticipation bubbled up in Kieran's throat and came out as laughter. There was going to be a fight. He felt it coming, like a hot wind, tensing his stomach, baring his teeth. The indignant expression on Ka'an's face just made him laugh harder.

The god rose slowly from his throne, jingling. "You will regret your laughter, Ghost," he rumbled.

"You have no idea," Kieran gasped, "how stupid you look."

"See how the vision has dressed *you*." Ka'an pointed theatrically, arm straight out. "Deep down, you know yourself to be a slave."

Kieran glanced down, and saw that all he had between himself and the world was a loincloth. All his scars and tattoos were on display. He looked up grinning. "I'll whup your ass buck naked if I have to, boy."

"I think not." Ka'an passed his arm through the air, and a golden shimmer coalesced into a curved sword in his hand. He stepped down from the throne platform. Green lightning crackled in his eyes, and his robes fluttered around him in an intangible wind.

That was a nice effect. Kieran watched the god stalk toward him for a moment, to see how it was done. Then he pushed with his mind, clothing himself in half a second, not bothering with theatrics. The same stuff he'd been wearing before; he doubted Ka'an would be intimidated by flashy clothes.

He reached into his pockets and held up what he found: three spare magazines in his left hand, the Hart all cleaned up and loaded and chambered in the right. He spun the gun on his finger, showing teeth.

Then he aimed it at Ka'an and put five slugs in him, center of mass.

Pillars rippled and light tore as Ka'an's overdecorated body jerked. When it fell, though, it fell not as a dead body but as a multitude of snakes. A susurration of rattling arose as they multiplied across the floor.

Kieran's grin turned to a grimace. He couldn't shoot them all. What did he want, a net, taller boots, some kerosene and a match?

Wait, why was he letting Ka'an set the stage? It was the same as clothing himself, really: he moved the dream with a thought, and instantly he was standing on a lone rock in the middle of an endless stretch of water. Snakes thrashed and drowned.

His rock lurched, crumbled. As he fell, he grabbed the idea of frost. He fell on ice.

Ice turned to stone. Bare desert, now. As he scrambled to his feet, Ka'an's shape coalesced before him. They glared at each other for a long moment.

"Well played, for a beginner," Ka'an said. "But you have not yet felt my true strength."

"Bring it," Kieran growled.

Everything happened at once, then. Too fast to analyze. He countered instinctively, shifting himself and the world in flickers as Ka'an did the same. Storms raged. Armies charged. Fire, earthquakes, floods. Serpents, insects, sandstorms. One moment he was drowning in blood, the next he was miles above the earth and falling. Freezing, burning, deafening, blinding.

He was on the defensive from the moment it began. All he could do was keep coming back to images of safety. Empty desert -- but that was where the storms found him. City streets -- which cracked to chasms. Familiar buildings went up in flames. Green fields erupted with boiling masses of scorpions. Kieran was pushed farther and farther back into himself.

He was losing. Ka'an was going to win.

Of course I am. Did you think you could fight a god?

His dream-body was shredding, going to mist. A thousand different kinds of pain beat at him. He could endure it, but he couldn't find a place to attack from. This was no good. He had to think of something -- but Ka'an was giving him no time to think.

Surrender, Ghost. Why cling to this painful life? Death is your home.

He was a ghost? He remembered being dead, remembered dying. But then there was living after that. Ka'an was lying...

So why did the word ghost sound like it named him?

No, he had a body... somewhere... this dream-body was

modeled after it, this torn and tattered thing... he had arms and legs, he had skin, he had scars...

Taking a step backward into himself, he clutched at his memory of flesh. Hands, feet, clothes, something hanging around his neck -- he grasped it --

Bright as a scalpel, a thought cut through the fog:

Fight him, Kieran! Beat him and come back to me!

In a rush, he remembered. Eyes, hands, mouth, words, thoughts, Ash. Ka'an threw more horrors at him, but he realized that they were repeating. Ka'an had run out of ideas. They weren't doing anything, anyway. He'd gone past that part of the battle. Ka'an had won that part.

It doesn't matter. You're still you. Remember. Kieran Trevarde. Your name is Kai, which means courage. Do you remember?

I remember, he returned, and let the pains and horrors wash by him. Why had he let them matter in the first place? He didn't even need a body, in a dream. Or, if he wanted, he could have a body that just plain wasn't affected by all this weird shit Ka'an was doing.

At the moment he realized this, it all stopped. He was alone in a dark place. He swallowed down the urge to tense in expectation. Whatever happened, it wasn't going to affect him, because this was a dream.

Oh, really? That was Ka'an, sounding smug. He had something up his sleeve.

Kieran sent the sense of a snarl. *You waiting for an invitation? Do your thing. Let's see if you can touch me.*

Light swelled. Dim, flickering. It outlined a rounded, uneven space: a cave. Messy little lamps burned here and there, and the air was filled with a complex stench of rotted meat, burned meat, fresh meat, and unwashed bodies. In the middle of the cave a frail figure sat crosslegged on a wad of greasy fur.

It was even weirder seeing this version of Ka'an than the clanking emperor in gold. Seeing his own face smeared with yellow ochre, dotted with black. Yellow grease matted his hair into dreadlocks. His wrists were like twigs, his ribs standing out, his feet looking ungainly at the end of legs that were sticks of bone. He was dressed in nothing but blue beads. Ropes and ropes of little turquoise beads. His eyes were closed, the eyelids decorated with the smeared remains of dots meant to make it look like his eyes were open while he slept. Before him on the fur, between his feet, there was a stone bowl encrusted with something brownish. Food?

Opium. Kieran had almost lost himself in wonder, but the realization of what was in the bowl jerked him back to himself. He knew, abruptly, what Ka'an was showing him: a past so distant there were no records of it. This was what Ka'an had been once. Mortal, and on the nod.

Vertigo hit him as he began to sense the enormous weight of time involved. Thousands upon thousands of years. How many thousands?

"Too many to count," the emaciated figure said without opening its eyes. Its voice was hollow, otherworldly. "Time is a figure like any other. Past and future are the same. Behold, I have dreamed: the People will grow greater than the number of seeds in a field of grain. All good things will come to them. For many years, it will be thus. Too many to count. Then will come a dark time, when the People fail and become less. In that time, I too will fail and become less. But it will only be as a sleep. I will return to bring the People back to the light."

Ka'an opened his eyes and fixed them on Kieran. Hollow, sunken, brilliant green. "I was given these eyes that I might see into the spirit world. I am holy. None may touch me. You may not touch me."

Loneliness snaked out from his words, threading a chill through Kieran's veins. He wavered as it struck him. A loneliness so immense no human soul could carry it. Holy and outcast. A whole life, and then life after life, without human contact. Any who touched him would be put to death. They had to do this, or the contamination of Ka'an's dreams would draw ghosts and sickness, and the people would suffer. All things pertaining to the otherworld had to be sequestered here with the Dreamer, and only the shamans dared even speak to him. It had always been this way.

Caught in the tide of Ka'an's memory, Kieran was whirled along. Life after life sped before him. Hidden in the dark, sacred and untouchable. Change came slowly; a tent rather than a cave, then a temple built of stones. Then there were battles, and the People triumphed. New arts rose. Cities spread and fell and rose again.

The People conquered to the east and north, many lesser people, enslaving them. Gold and jewels came; strange animals came; there was music and dancing, there was blood and crying, there were beautiful whores in his temples and cruel visionaries in his palaces. There was magic and wonder. Those who rose against him were destroyed. Those who venerated him were rewarded.

He was worshipped. He was adored. He was feared. He was always alone.

Time; the weight of all that time; it was unbearable, it was crushing him. He didn't want it. Better to give it up, let someone else take it. To be mortal, singular, to die, it was a blessing, and he yearned for it...

Kai! I can't hear you anymore! Kieran! Where are you?

Names. He'd had so many names. What did names matter?

Fight him, Kieran. Are you there?

He didn't want to fight anymore. He was so tired. Let someone else fight.

I love you, Kieran! Fight! I want you to come back to me!

So someone was talking about love. That didn't have anything to do with him. It couldn't. He was holy. No one could touch him.

The voice came again, and this time it was angry. *Are you giving up? You don't ever give up! Loser unity, Kai! Don't you read? The underdog always wins!* Confused, he groped after the source of this voice. It reminded him of something, maybe a time when he'd been happy...

Time? How could he find one moment among the years and years and years?

Kai, it's me, it's Ash, don't you remember? Remind him who he is. Damn it. Are you there? How am I supposed to do this? Kieran! Kieran Trevarde! Kai, Green Sky, Suneater, each one of these dots is a dead man, do you remember? You died and came back, you called the storm, do you remember? You're too mean to die, too beautiful to die, you don't care what anyone thinks except maybe me and I love you so much, I won't let you give up, damn it --

Wistfully, he listened to the voice rant. Was that meant to describe him? It sounded like such a strong person. He wished he was strong like that.

Hey Ka'an, are you listening? Let him go, or I'll personally reach down your neck and rip your balls off. Let him go, he's mine! Kieran, don't you let Ka'an win, you deserve everything good and he's just a spoiled child!

He was a spoiled child? Or was he the one that was too mean to die? Was he Ka'an, or the one who was supposed to be fighting Ka'an? He was drowning in this loneliness, the loneliness was Ka'an's, Ka'an who was a spoiled child, he didn't *want* to be Ka'an --

Shock. Perspective. A jolt like being shot. The smothering of years broke, leaving him light and empty and blind.

Rage boiled up to fill that space. The son of a bitch had almost won that time. Sneaky fuck.

I got it now, Ashes, he thought fiercely. *You just sit tight.*

For convenience, he built a scene. The barroom of a roadhouse outside Canyon, where the miners went to waste their pay. He didn't people it, left it deserted except for himself and a sort of clockwork bartender to work the taps. He leaned back against the bar and waited. He could feel Ka'an blundering around, trying to change the dream, but Kieran held it. A place this familiar was easy to make solid. Ka'an's many lives were working against him, here -- the god had trouble distinguishing between all the places he'd seen in all the lives he'd lived.

A minute later, Ka'an stormed in, furious at being made to use the door. He was wearing his emperor getup again. "You look like a twit," Kieran told him before he could speak.

"How dare you," the god fumed. His voice was low and menacing. "How *dare* you. You've seen what I am. You've felt how small you are. Yet you persist in this, this *satire*. I will make you suffer for this."

"Uh-huh." Kieran raised an eyebrow. "You done?"

"I am not."

"That's too bad, 'cause I'm just not impressed. Hey." He knocked on the bar. "Get us a bottle of the hard stuff."

As the clockwork bartender produced a chilled bottle of bootleg gin, Ka'an calmed himself. "You're very stupid, mortal, to speak to me that way. I felt your fear. Are you trying to make me angry?"

Kieran shrugged. "Have a drink with me. We haven't actually talked. You know, you really do look like a moron in that getup. Let me fix that for you." He had to push through some resistance to change how Ka'an looked, but it was only a matter of letting his familiar dream smooth over an anomaly, and in an eyeblink the god was clothed in a white linen suit like the tar runners wore. He could feel Ka'an's fury building.

Though this little success tempted him to get cocky, he reminded himself that he couldn't afford to. He knew where the battlefield was now. The real fight was still ahead of him, and he suspected it wouldn't be a messy slugfest like what Ka'an had hit him with. It would be like a gunfight. Twitch the right way and live. Freeze and die.

He pushed a filled shotglass along the bar at Ka'an. "So tell me. If being immortal is such a pain in the ass, how come you're so keen on coming back?"

"Why should I explain myself to a mortal?" Ka'an sneered.

"Okay, you need to get over that. Because obviously you can't just squish me, like you thought you could. I'm as tough as you are. My guess is that I'm a lot tougher. See, you had all that ammunition, you had all that skill and time, you did this a bunch of times before, and I came into it totally raw. But here I am. And there you are."

"If you count stalemate as such a victory --"

"Nah, we can fire it up again anytime. I'm just curious. Aren't you curious?"

"No." Ka'an spat the word contemptuously.

"Point for me: reason to live. Oh, now you're mad at me."

"I *am* rage, Ghost. You will learn that soon."

"Point for me. Kept my cool. What are we playing to? Three? You wanna drink that, gin's nasty when it's warm."

Ka'an's eyes narrowed. "Very well. You've chosen the game. My move: I submit that you're too weak to survive the power you seek. Your mortal mind can't possibly encompass the immensity of pain and pleasure that is my lot. It would break you."

"Doubt it."

"You tasted just the merest hint of what I --"

"You're bluffing. I got into that pretty deep. I think I saw the whole thing. What do you want, you want me to feel sorry for you?"

The air rippled around Ka'an as the god's anger swelled. "Pity is also a weakness," he said, tight and low.

And Kieran suddenly understood. "Shit, you *do* want that."

"I'll waste no more time here!" Ka'an pushed, but could not change the dream.

"You *do* want someone to feel sorry for you. Poor pitiful critter, he's had such a hard ten thousand years. Oh poor me, nobody loves me. Look at you getting pissed at me, you're just proving I'm right!"

"I am *holy*," Ka'an hissed, swelling larger, glowing. "I am *sacred*. No one may touch me!"

"You know what? You don't deserve my sympathy! In

all those bazillions of lives you showed me, you never had the balls to break loose. You believed your own press. You made slaves of people, and then you feel all put-upon because no one could comfort you. And you're still doing it. Look, here I am right in front of you, the only person who could possibly know you for who you are, and you're trying to kill me for it. And then if you managed that, you'd just go on with your pity party. 'Oh I'm so lonely, oh I'm so high above everyone.' It's your own damn fault, Ka'an. Fucking get over it."

The god was all teeth and eyes now, snarling. "You have no concept of what true pain is."

"Yeah?" Kieran felt his own face going feral too. "Try this on."

His hand shot out and grabbed Ka'an's head, driving a path through between them, and down that connection he poured his life.

Ka'an cried out in disgust, then in anger, then in dawning fear. Kieran sent him image after image of squalor, degradation, and pain. But he didn't send it to show how sad his life had been. There was no self-pity in it. After each beating, each rape, each hungry day and freezing night, each trick, each loss, he got up and kept going. Out of pure stubbornness, pure lust for life, he pushed himself onward. And bit by bit, he forced his way from defense to offense. He made himself strong. He made himself hard and cruel. He took what he needed, got rid of whatever blocked him. He was very close to being evil, when he first met a pair of pale blue eyes behind smeared glasses.

Ka'an's struggling weakened, uncertain. This was not pain. The hurts that came after this were small compared to much of what he'd suffered before. He didn't understand why he was being shown this.

Then he began to think again that it was all about pain after all, when Kieran dragged him through being shot, the sickness and festering wound, helpless under the shadow of death. And then came the memory of dying. When the two of them together looked down on Ash's grief, Ka'an ready to leave the body behind, Kieran unwilling to abandon the one person who had ever come anywhere near knowing him.

And Kieran had won. They wouldn't be here now if he hadn't.

Kieran released his enemy, watched the spirit's image reel and clutch the imaginary bar. "Get it now?"

Pulling himself upright, Ka'an glared, speechless. Lost.

"Do you know why I won that time?"

In a growl, Ka'an said, " I suppose you'll tell me it was because someone loved you, and no one loved me."

"You've got it backwards. I won because I love someone, and you never loved anyone. Not even yourself. That's why I'll always win. Because I give a damn, and you don't. You'd surrender the first chance you got if you could get past your pride."

"You don't know what I want." Ka'an's voice faltered.

"Actually, I do. You've been waiting all this time for someone to say: You're done now, kid. You don't have to be holy anymore. You did your job, it's time to quit."

"And you'd take my place? You'd do my work? No one will thank you. They don't understand that they need me."

"They *don't* need you, Ka'an. They don't need me either. Doesn't mean I can't help without being asked. No, I won't be the Prince of Pain. The Dreamer can rest now." He offered his hand.

The former god's voice was thinner now, his shape fading. "What will you be?"

"Human."

"My enemy..." Just a whisper.

"I'll get him. Trust me."

Ka'an's form was just a blur now, the hand he reached to Kieran's little more than a wisp. The murmur of his voice was almost inaudible. "I was beautiful..."

"Yes. You were."

With a sound like a sigh, the last resistance gave way. The fragment of smoke that was all that was left of Ka'an flowed over Kieran. For a breath's time it clung there. Then it was gone.

He took a deep breath, waking. Aches washed over him; heat, thirst, hunger. The sun stood overhead, burning down hard. There was no wind. The sterile lake was smooth as glass.

But he could feel the power inside him. So much power. All marshaled and ready to do whatever he wanted. It was exhilarating. He could almost see how having this power had made up for Ka'an's misery, made him hang onto it through life after life. For a moment he regretted it a little -- having killed something that old, that strong.

That full of pride and malice.

No, he didn't wish he hadn't done it.

He closed his hand around the bullet that hung at his throat. Gave it a little power and felt it pull. Pretty much due east. *I'm coming, Ashes. Don't you worry about a thing.*

Chapter 29

"Quit worrying and hold still."

"They're very busy out there, Ash." Chaiel kept twisting his head around as if he could see. Maybe he could. It wasn't helping, though.

"And I would be very busy in here, if you would *hold still*. And control your hair, would you? Tie it in a knot or something."

With a wordless grumble, Chaiel tried to obey. In the process, he threw them both off balance. Ash curled up as he fell, to avoid a repeat of the incident that had given him a bloody nose a few hours back. As a result, it was Chaiel who got an elbow in the eye. Chaiel reacted by howling and thrashing for a while. Ash was getting really tired of this. He believed he'd punch the kid out if he didn't need him for a stepstool. He considered that maybe it was time to voice this thought.

"I'm not really a violent person," he said quietly into a lull in Chaiel's tantrum. The lull didn't last, but he kept talking. "Normally, I'd try to calm you down in a much nicer way. But Kieran is on his way here. From what you said, Thelyan is more than ready for him. Which means he's going to need my help. Is this making sense to you? There are things going on that are a lot more important than your stupid eye. So if you don't pull it together here, I'm going to give you a matching shiner, and then I'm going to hurt you some more after that. Are you getting this at all?"

Chaiel's complaining turned into laughing. "You know we don't have a chance. Nothing can get out of this thing, don't you understand? Nothing can get in or out. Thelyan had a long time to design this -- this torture device -- and you think you're going to break it in a matter of hours."

"Yes, actually, I do."

Chaiel laughed harder.

"Look, it's just math. You've heard of math, right? It's that stuff you do with numbers?"

"It's not *math*, it's *magic*!"

"Same thing. You don't have to understand it, okay? Just

trust me."

"Trust. Trust? Trust you!" The kid's laughter was increasingly hysterical. "Why should I trust you?"

Ash felt his face harden. Though it took some doing, he collected Chaiel's wrists in one hand and a fistful of hair in the other, and brought the thrashing creature to a halt.

"Because," he said carefully, "it costs you nothing to do so. If hope hurts that much, be bored. Stand there smiling your superior little smile and telling yourself how funny it's going to be when I give up. Now do something with your goddamn hair and give me a lift again."

Calmer now, Chaiel sniffled and met his eyes. "You don't get it. I do think you can do it. I just don't think you can do it in time. And when Ka'an dies --"

"Kieran won. I felt it."

"Then when *Kieran* loses to Thelyan, you're going to give up. Then I'll be stuck here knowing you could get us out but you won't try."

"That's the kind of person you think I am? Let me explain how you're wrong. Thing one, Kieran's going to win. Thing two, I *am* going to get it in time, if you cooperate. Thing three, if Kieran loses and I don't get it in time, I'm going to bust out anyway so I can take it out of Thelyan's hide. And finally, you could do this yourself if you'd just pay attention to what I'm telling you. This magic is math. It all is, if you look at it right. I just have to figure out what kind."

"And then you'll, what, *subtract* it?"

Ash sighed. "If you like. Here, let me do that for you, you're just getting yourself tangled." He spun Chaiel around and collected the ridiculous length of his hair. It was too matted to braid, and too long; he couldn't separate the strands with his arms at their full stretch, there was that much of it. So he settled for twisting it into a rope so he could tie knots in it. As he worked at that, he sensed Chaiel calming; apparently more visions were coming, and these weren't incoherent enough to set him off. "What are you seeing?" Ash asked, more to keep him present than because the answer mattered.

"Oh, he's figured out how to go invisible. That's sort of clever."

"Who has?"

"Who do you think? The Dreamer, whatever you want to call him now."

"Invisible? I didn't think that was possible."

389

"Not *invisible*. You can still see him. But they can't sense him. They don't know he's coming."

"*Who* can't sense him?"

"Watchmen. It looks as if Thelyan sent them out to the end of the line to get near the Burn, but I guess he's recalled them now because they're getting back on the train."

"There's a rail line that goes there?"

"Didn't I just say there was? Within a dozen miles anyway. Oh bugger." Chaiel bit the base of his thumb as a stutter of confusion ran through him. The visions had switched.

Much as Ash would have liked to keep hearing what Kieran was up to, it sounded as if things were well in hand on that end, and there was the little matter of the null sphere to deal with. He tied one more knot and let go of the now more localized mess of hair. "Okay, let's get to work."

Chaiel sighed unhappily, but he cooperated. They put the soles of their feet together and slowly, carefully stood up. It was a very strange feeling, the way the sphere pulled them together. It made them topheavy, and every movement swung and spun them around their common axis. Reaching their hands above their heads, they stretched out until they could press their palms against the sphere's surface. That stabilized them a little.

It was slippery as a repelling magnet, though. Ash couldn't give it his whole attention, because he had to keep adjusting his posture to keep in contact with it. This would be a long piece of work even if he'd been able to concentrate fully. Seeing it as a cipher had been a simplification. The math used to break code was fairly elementary, once one knew the methods. This was a deeper kind of equation. It balanced inside and outside so perfectly that from within it seemed there was no outside. Almost as if it declared that the whole of the universe was inside the bubble. Presumably, from outside, the inside was the part that didn't exist. But from its own point of view, the skin of the bubble didn't exist, which was why it couldn't be affected, at least not directly.

What gave him a hope of breaking it was the fact that it had intermediate states. Thelyan had left it in one of these so that light could pass. Currently, the defining equation was ignoring light. From what Chaiel had said, it had variables for sound as well, and for objects to pass through. It also had a repelling effect, which accounted for the way they were pushed toward the center.

Ash had read a theory once, in a book about fluid dynamics, that sound propagated through air by means of vibration. Following that thought, he supposed that in order to pass sound, the sphere wouldn't have to allow air through, provided it acted as a resonating membrane.

Which meant that the sphere itself was an object. It didn't have mass or thickness, but because it could be made to transmit vibrations, it could be treated as a solid object in some cases. Because it didn't have a thickness, it was a two-dimensional object, despite being spherical. Ash wished desperately for something to write on. He was starting to think that resonant effects were going to be the key, though. That and the fact that in order to do its job, the sphere had to balance its input and output exactly.

"Well?" Chaiel sounded impatient.

"Can you analyze a deterministic system?"

"A what?"

"Then I suggest you shut up and let me work."

Chaiel gave a haughty sniff, but didn't reply. Narrowing his eyes, and his field of mental vision as well, Ash dived back into his task.

❧ ✦ ☙

Crouched behind a pile of broken ore carts, Kieran examined his options.

There were Watchmen swarming all over the place. He'd crunched his pattern down small to keep them from sensing him, but they'd certainly see him if he came out. Which was a problem, because he'd have to come out if he wanted to get on the train.

A number of methods of transport had occurred to him. He could do the really fast running thing again, but he didn't like it. The sun was high now and the air shimmering hot. He wasn't sure he could keep from overheating. It had crossed his mind to summon another storm, let the rain cool him, but he wasn't sure he could get one together in under a day. Whatever he'd done before seemed to have undone itself.

Stealing a horse would be worse than useless; it would mean confronting these Watchmen, for one thing. Powerful as he felt, he hadn't lost sight of the fact that every fight was a gamble. Then he could ride the horse to death within a dozen miles if he was unlucky, which would leave him right back at square one.

So he'd hit on the idea of hopping a train. A train would be ideal. Faster than the other options, with the added benefit that rail interference would hide his approach. The Splitwood mine's spur was the nearest track to the Burn -- or the place where the Burn had been -- and he guessed that there must be a regular run from there to either Burn River or Trestre. The right direction, anyway. Once aboard, it wouldn't be hard to stick a gun in the engineer's face and make him take the Churchrock loop instead.

But there were these Watchmen. They'd corralled the mine workers and shunted all the mining company's engines off on a siding. They had an engine of their own, a handsome sleek thing with nothing behind it but three passenger cars, but even if Kieran could manage to steal the thing he'd have to pick up its crew as well. He had no idea how to drive a train.

He ruefully examined his gun. Removing the jammed round was easy enough, but poor thing was just a mess, what with mud and water and dust, and he didn't have anything to clean it with. Not to mention how he didn't trust his ammunition. And while he'd managed not to lose his spare magazines, his pockets had been full of mud.

Crouching down, he peered through a space between two of the rusty carts. After a moment he cautiously poked his head up for a moment to confirm what he'd seen. Most of the Watchmen, a couple dozen of them, were getting back on the train. A few still stood outside, conferring. Under the direction of one of the officers, a mining company engineer was throwing switches. Apparently they were going to turn the train around and go home.

It would take them a while, though. Meantime, he wanted to do something about his poor neglected Hart. Could magic substitute for gun oil? More to the point, could he do anything without alerting the Watch? He chewed his lip for a moment, thinking, and concluded that it was worth the risk. He really didn't want to try to do this unarmed.

Stripping the Hart gingerly, wincing every time he heard a gritty sound, he ran his fingers over the pieces. He could distinguish the textures in his mind, the difference between dirt and oil and -- he grimaced -- rust. If he let the power trickle out of his hands, if he didn't project it at all...

There was a crackling noise, and a puff of vapor blew out from between his fingers.

He looked through his peephole, but no one seemed to have noticed. The ones who'd been getting on the train were now aboard; four of them stood aside, making no move to board. None of them were looking in his direction.

Going a bit more gently this time, he divested his gun of everything that didn't belong in it, and reassembled it. He did the same to the magazines. Then he turned his attention to the bullets. He guessed that duds ought to look different to his magical senses than viable rounds, and he could indeed distinguish two different types of bullet, but he couldn't tell which was which. There were a lot more of one kind than the other. Hoping that the more numerous type were the ones that would fire, he loaded up with those, and rearranged the clips so that he had a full magazine of the rarer kind and two full of the other, with two spaces free and two bullets left out since he didn't want to mix them.

A grinding, groaning noise had been swelling up while he finished this task. He ignored it until he was done. Then he looked out, to find that the White Watch engine was being turned around. Through the windows of the passenger cars he could see the Watchmen who were leaving. That meant, of course, that they'd see him if he tried to get aboard. And there were still those four fellows standing clear.

Half an idea occurred to him. He chewed over it while he watched the engine grumbling around the switching loop. Risky. But all his options were risky. He really hoped he'd loaded with good rounds.

The short train emitted a series of clatters as it switched onto the main track facing east. A ball of black smoke jumped from the smokestack, and the engine roared as it began to pick up speed. Kieran forced his eyes away from it, watching the four men left behind instead of the departing train. Two were watching the train go. The other two were talking to each other. As the engine's noise diminished, they all turned toward where they'd left their horses.

Time. Kieran stood up, aiming with a two-handed grip at the nearest of the Watchmen. He pulled the trigger as their heads began to turn. There was a small clack sound.

"Shit," he muttered, ducking back. There wasn't time to care where they were or what they were doing; he cleared the jammed round, dropped the clip of duds, and shoved in his solitary clip of what he hoped were good bullets. As he worked the slide, he suddenly flashed on a parallel. Shooting from behind cover, low on ammunition... he just knew that if he stood up now he'd die the same way Shan had.

Well, fine. He wasn't hiding anymore. And he had all this power, just *itching* to rearrange the world.

The Watchmen yelled in surprise when the pile of broken ore carts suddenly erupted, half-ton square buckets on wheels whirling across the ground like dry leaves in a wind. The noise this made almost covered the sound of their wildly fired shots, their desperately blurted shielding spells. Two men missed their spells and were smashed; Kieran felt their deaths the way Ash must have felt the deaths of the ones he'd shot on the Canyon road. He had to admit it was unpleasant. Like a splash of cold kerosene in the face. One of the men had got his shield up in time but been shoved across the yard. The last had held his ground, and was readying his rifle and gathering power at the same time. Kieran aimed at him, then hesitated.

He could taste the type of spell the man was beginning. A fire pattern. The man wasn't a natural Pyrokinetic, he was using thaumaturgy. It was easy to see, now, easy to counter.

Kieran reached out and tripped the fire spell just before the man would have released it. The soft bang of expanding hot air -- a moment's glimpse of the heat-shimmer that was all the visible evidence of the colorless flame -- was followed by a sharper explosion as the pattern exciting materials to heat was sucked into the rifle. A rippling clatter as the whole magazine went off at once, and chunks of wood and metal flew spinning through the air.

For a moment, the Watchman stared at the ruined remains of his hands. Then he gave a short grunt and folded up.

All that had happened so fast that the man who'd been shoved over the tracks was just now getting up. He'd made it as far as his knees. He didn't bother standing all the way up before sending a blast of dust flying in Kieran's face. No spell; Kinetic. Coughing and squinting, Kieran dodged sideways as he threw down a bit of a pattern to settle the dust. He heard a shot, and another. Then the dust dropped as if every particle were a fist-sized stone, clearing the air, and he saw his quarry.

He fired twice. The man crumpled and lay still.

Kieran took the time to load his two spares. Now he had precisely ten bullets. There had been upwards of thirty men on that train. He suspected that if he came aboard, they wouldn't give up their seats for him. But he thought he had a way to do it that would keep them from even knowing he was there.

Calling a wind was easy enough. Because of the recent rain, there wasn't as much dust as he'd wanted, but he didn't need a sandstorm, just a smokescreen. Yellow-gray wisps rose around him, became billows, rolling off east down the tracks. He tied his kerchief over his nose and mouth, then set off after the dust cloud.

When he moved up onto the railbed, he felt the rails snatch his power away. That was all right; once started, the wind should keep up for a while. And it was only power outside himself that was disrupted. The power that remained within him, speeding him as he began to run, worked just as smoothly as it had when Ka'an had done it in the Burn. The heat was going to be a problem, though. Could he do something with it? He felt like he was juggling eggs, but just as his heart began to labor he grasped the pattern. Twisted it around and fed it back into himself in a different form. Chill washed over him. He accelerated.

There was dust everywhere now; the wind he'd begun had spread, lifting opaque veils across his path. His eyes watered. Some dust got into his lungs despite the kerchief. It didn't slow him down. Magic was substituting for breath and nourishment now. He wasn't even panting.

How long could he keep this up? It had been three days since he'd last eaten. Several hours since he'd had any water. One hour of sleep in the last thirty-six. Maybe he was using himself up. Killing himself. There'd be more exertions, too, maybe much harder ones, before he was done. Maybe it would be better to sleep and eat before he tried Churchrock? It would be terrible if he reached it and then lacked the strength to free Ash.

But the thought of leaving Ash in the Watch's hands for another day choked him. No. He'd do it now. If it broke him, then it broke him. No holding back. *There's only one person in the world brave enough and forgiving enough to care for me. If I saved myself at his expense, what the hell would I be saving myself for?*

He smelled coal smoke, then heard the sound of the engine ahead. The dust was still thick. The back of the hindmost car loomed ahead before he was ready for it; he nearly collided with it. There was a white uniform standing watch on the little balcony-thing there, eyes widening as Kieran vaulted the rail. The Watchman opened his mouth to give warning, but Kieran's hand smothered his shout. A twist, a crunch; the man sagged, neck broken. Kieran tossed the body overboard.

With magic running along his muscles, it was easy to climb up on top of the car. Easy to stand firm against the wind, though the train must have been going forty miles an hour. Stepping carefully, so as not to alert the men below with the sound of his feet on their roof, he walked forward. Checked carefully at each linkage to make sure there was no one who could see him go over, then leapt across the gap between cars.

Kieran crouched atop the engine just ahead of the smokestack. He watched the desert rush past, and wondered how much of himself he'd used up to get here. It was hard to judge; unfamiliar as it was, this new magic looked infinite, but he knew it wasn't. He saw ways to increase it, though, even when the patterns around him were distorted by engine and rails. He couldn't send any energy out without it being snatched away, but he could take energy in. There were plenty of sources. The sun's heat, the wind's motion, the vibration shaking through the soles of his boots. Even the noise.

Coat and hair thrashing behind him, eyes streaming, he collected power and waited to arrive.

༄ ❈ ༅

Chaiel was trying very hard to be still. Ash had said he needed quiet to think; it was implied that if he didn't get this quiet, he would become violent again. They were back to back, something between sitting and sprawled. Ash had said he was on to something. And also that if he ended up with Chaiel's hair in his face one more time he'd pull it out by the roots. So Chaiel held his bundled hair in his arms and worked on silence.

The visions made it so hard, though. Something had broken loose in the world. Everything was disordered. Sights and sounds and thoughts were coming in stutters, too fast to make sense. Vertigo made his stomach roll. He wondered, if he vomited, what would come out? *No, don't think of that, or you will. Think about something else* -- But not about what it might be like to get out of the bubble, because if Ash's idea didn't work -- if he'd been hoping and those hopes were dashed -- he wasn't sure what would happen, but he was sure it would be the worst thing possible.

But what else was there to occupy him? He had tired of his own body long, long ago. Picking at his hair, chewing his nails, even hurting himself no longer afforded any distraction. The only interesting thing was Ash, and Ash was too busy to be entertaining. The warmth against his back was pleasant, though. Unfamiliar skin, dry from too much time outdoors, a bit gritty. And the new smell. Not what would normally be considered a nice smell, kind of muddy and sweaty with just a hint of gunpowder and blood. But it was good to smell something, after being locked up with himself so long that he'd thought his nose was numb.

He wondered, if this plan failed and they were stuck here forever, whether he'd learn to want to have sex with a boy, just for something to do. He wouldn't get any satisfaction from it, because of the way the null sphere paused his body's functions, but it might pass the time. Sordid thought, that.

Chaiel surprised himself by giggling. *When did I last care for the propriety of my thoughts, or my actions for that matter?* Then he froze, fearing retaliation for having made noise.

Ash didn't react. A sense of involved concentration was trickling out of him. He'd got his mental fingers into some complex knot, and was picking it apart. Chaiel envied him.

"Right," Ash muttered. "Size and distance. They'd be proportional. Then it wouldn't matter, if it's parabolic. Okay. Hey, Shy."

"Chaiel," Chaiel corrected.

"Yeah. Which one of those doodads out there is the one that he turned off to let me in?"

Chaiel twisted around to point over Ash's shoulder. "There, with the glyph *tacheth*."

"The one that looks like a three-legged elephant in a big hat?"

"Uh... yes." Chaiel snickered. "It does, rather, doesn't it?"

"Someday you'll have to tell me what the hell it really is. Right now, though, I'd like to know whether you can muster enough power to break the switch."

"It's outside the sphere, stupid."

"That's not what I asked you," Ash said patiently.

Chaiel's heart began to beat faster. He swallowed, mouth dryer than usual, and his answer came out hoarse. "Just barely. If you could get the spell through the sphere." He swallowed again, no longer quite able to keep from hoping. "Can you?"

"Yes. Whether I can do it on the first try, though..."

"Oh." The sound jumped out of Chaiel's throat without his intention. He found he was curled small on Ash's back, fingers digging into the redhead's freckled shoulders. "Oh. Are you sure. Are you. How could. How did."

"*Breathe*, Shy," Ash said in an exasperated tone. "You're not going to be much use if you're hyperventilating. I know this is a big deal for you, but can you put off thinking about it for a minute? Take a deep breath. Count to ten or something."

Obeying, Chaiel gradually calmed himself. Another burst of visions helped, oddly enough, by putting something between the moment he was in and the moment in which he'd realized he'd be free soon. When he trusted himself to speak in complete sentences, he said, "I assume I wouldn't understand if you explained how you're going to manage it."

"Maybe you would. It's not a hard concept. See, the sphere is set to pass sound and light right now. But sound and light aren't going straight through. They're gathered and then emitted by the sphere. The skin of the bubble actually absorbs and then generates them." Ash's tone was admiring. "It's really a very robust design. But I think I've figured out the way it transmits energy, and it's something we can use. I'm going to make a pattern like a sort of lens, and then have you throw your spell through it. The energy will focus wherever I aim the lens -- that is, in the middle of that chunk of stone that acts as a switch. Did that make any sense?"

"I have one question."

"Shoot."

"What if he's designed it so that, if a seal is broken, it's simply stuck *on* forever? You'd be trapping us inside."

"No, the switches -- seals -- they hold the pattern in place. They're foci. Break one, and its particular variable is removed from the equation."

"How do you know?"

Ash chuckled. "Well, *now* I have to say you wouldn't understand the explanation. I'll show it to you sometime when I have *lots* of paper."

"Ah." Chaiel took a deep breath. "Is there anything else I need to know?"

"Wait until I have the lens made. I'll tell you when I'm ready. Then you work up a gob of raw power and fling it into the lens. Your aim isn't important; if it hits the lens at all, it'll go where I want it to go. Pure energy, mind you -- anything else will be stripped off as it goes through the bubble, and it might wreck our focus. Can you do that?"

"Yes."

"Okay, hold still for a minute, the placement has to be just right."

Chaiel watched tensely as his new ally began to construct a small, tight pattern in the air between himself and the seal. *It's as tidy as one of Medur's,* Chaiel thought at first, but as the pattern continued to form he realized Medur wouldn't have thought of this. She would certainly have thought of something, she'd always been the creative one, but what Ash was doing... Chaiel had never seen magic used quite like that before. Spell patterns were complex, sprawling things, in his experience. Unless the mind that built them was supremely disciplined, they tended to skew and fade, fur themselves with sub-patterns, so that no spell was ever exactly the same twice. The thing Ash was building, though, was simply a stepped series of concentric rings of force. As smooth and solid to Chaiel's magical senses as if it were built of glass. It seemed to have no urge to change itself. It held itself in perfect tension, perfectly in place.

Ash studied it for a time after he'd made it, apparently not needing any effort to keep it there. Stretching out a hand, he gathered a pebble of energy and flicked it into the lens. Chaiel couldn't see what happened to it, but Ash turned the pattern a fraction of a degree and sent out another tiny spark. He repeated this procedure five times before he was satisfied.

"All right," he murmured. "I'm spent. I hope you have enough steam to get the job done."

"Now?"

"Now."

Chaiel's hands were trembling. He rolled them into fists, bit blood from his lip, telling himself firmly: *There is no future. There is no next minute. If you think of the next minute, you're sunk. Just do this one thing, and then you can think again.*

Slowly, he uncurled his hands. Steadying himself against Ash's body, he put a kernel of pattern between his stretched fingers and wound power around it. He didn't know quite how much it would take to break the seal, so he supposed he'd better give it everything he had -- which wasn't much. His mind hadn't been clear enough to gather and store as much as he could have from the visions. But he had what had been on Ash in the form of Thelyan's binding, and a little from his own body.

Goosebumps crawled across his skin as he stole from himself. His toes and fingertips began to go numb. Still he kept spooling it out. Only when lethargy began to creep over him and threaten his concentration did he stop.

Please, please let me not have any visions in the next two seconds...

He detached the ball of energy from himself and shot it into the lens.

A sharp crack rang through the room. Flying chips of stone stung him.

The seal was gone. There was only a charred spot on the beam where it had been fastened, and bits of it pattering and bouncing across the floor. Chaiel let out a wild screech of triumph.

Ash's simultaneous victory cry turned into an indignant yelp, and he twisted away. "Right in my *ear*, Shy. *Ouch*." He held Chaiel at arm's length. "Okay, boost me up."

Eagerly, Chaiel obeyed. Rather than standing with their feet together as before, Chaiel grasped Ash's ankles. With his arms at full stretch, Ash could just barely get his hands around one of the struts. The sphere's repelling effect was still in place; cords of muscle stood out under Ash's skin as he strained to pull them free of it. Bit by bit, he climbed out onto the floor, curled around a strut to keep from being hauled back in. Bit by bit, Chaiel was pulled out after him. At last Chaiel popped free and tumbled onto dusty stone.

Ash gave a breathless laugh. "Well, it worked."

Chaiel drew breath to reply, but was stilled by how difficult it was. He lay sprawled where he had fallen. His limbs felt like lead. He wasn't sure he could move at all. And the aches -- all the aches, hunger and thirst and torn nails and torn skin -- he whimpered in alarm. Had he been freed only to die?

"What's wrong?" Ash bent over him, concerned.

"I can. Hardly. Breathe."

"Oh. I guess you've been floating for a long time, haven't you? It's just muscle memory, Shy. Your muscles can't have really atrophied, if your body was shut down."

"Stop. Calling me. Shy."

"I just realized something. We weren't really breathing in there, were we? I mean, we were breathing, but we weren't using up the air. And now we are." Ash glanced around the small ovoid room. "And there can't be all that much in here. We need to go."

"Wait. Just. A little while."

"Can't. If the air thing isn't enough to get you moving, I bet you anything Thelyan's going to know we're out. Aw, hell, I weigh a *ton*." Groaning, Ash labored upright. He went to the corner where he'd left his clothes when Thelyan had made him disrobe. Chaiel numbly watched him put his glasses and trousers on.

Any second now I'm going to realize I'm out of the sphere. Any second. It's going to hit me, I'll understand it, and then -- feel something, I suppose. Happy? I might be happy.

"You can tie my shirt around your waist, like a kilt. You want the coat? I think you need to be warm more than I do. I bet your feet are pretty tender. I can go barefoot." A pile of filthy clothing hit the floor in front of Chaiel's face.

With great effort, Chaiel rolled onto his side, then curled up to sitting. He picked up one of the socks, but immediately dropped it with a cry of disgust. It practically bounced. "*How* did you get your stockings so *dirty*?"

"A mudslide was involved. Also a broken ankle and a jammed rifle and Kieran leaving, so mud in my boots wasn't exactly foremost in my mind." Ash was over by the door now, running his hands around the edge.

Gingerly brushing the worst of the dirt off, Chaiel clothed himself. He still felt too heavy, but at least he could move now, albeit slowly. The boots were much too big, and the shirt-as-kilt idea didn't work as well in practice as in theory. Nevertheless it was wonderful to be covered. On hands and knees, he put a little distance between himself and the sphere. He was afraid it would somehow grab him, pull him back in.

"Can we smash it?"

"What?"

"The sphere. Let's smash it, so he can't use it again."

Ash spoke without turning. "Sure, hand me the sledgehammer. Or you could use that keg of gunpowder, if you brought your earplugs."

"There's no need to be sarcastic," Chaiel sulked.

"Sure there is." Palms flat against the door's metal, Ash bowed his head and sighed. "Well, we're not getting out this way. He's got the door rigged somehow, might just be a weird lock but for all I can tell it'll blow up in our faces. Help me feel the walls for thin spots."

"What, you're going to tunnel through stone?"

"Yep."

"With that keg of gunpowder you mentioned?"

"Oh, so you can dish it but you can't take it?" Ash shot him a grin. "There's all sorts of power floating around loose here, can't you feel it? I mean, not enough for anything flashy, but if we're smart we don't *have* to be flashy."

Chaiel crawled to the wall and hauled himself upright

against it. Now that he was looking, he could sense the power Ash mentioned. With skills rusty from disuse, he started gathering it in. First he strengthened himself. Then he sent his senses exploring into the rock under his hands, trying to feel its dimensions.

Then he took a step and tripped over his hair.

Ash's hoot of laughter angered him at first. He'd landed hard on his hands and knees, skinning them, and it hurt. But as he opened his mouth to say something sharp, it suddenly struck him: he was on solid ground, he had the *option* of skinning his knees, he was *free*.

Little giggles welled up in him, then turned to real laughter. Sobs of relief and gratitude mixed into it. Tears rolling down his face, he laughed until his stomach ached.

When he finally wound down, he looked up to find Ash watching him with a small, sweet smile. "You're welcome," Ash said. He offered a hand to pull Chaiel to his feet, and they went back to work.

Inching along the curved wall, they gathered power as they searched. Nearly opposite where they'd started, Chaiel found what they were looking for. "I'd say it's about ten feet thick here. There's a tunnel on the other side. I don't understand how you mean to get to it, though."

"Think small." Ash came to run his hands over the place Chaiel indicated. "Really, *really* small. We're lucky this isn't marble or granite or something, we'd be screwed." Without further explanation, he spread his hands across the rock and closed his eyes.

With a faint crackling noise, a few chips of stone broke off and pattered on the floor. Then a hand-sized chunk, followed by a pouring of sand. Just as Chaiel was about to comment that they'd run out of air before they got through at this rate, the whole room boomed like a drum. Chaiel's ears popped. Sand and pebbles poured out of a fresh crack in the wall, wide enough to wedge a hand into. The sound of crumbling stone was a constant sizzling now, the hole deepening until Ash was in it to the elbows, then to the shoulders.

Belatedly, Chaiel realized that all this rubble would have to go somewhere. Falling to his knees, too excited to feel the sting of the skinned places, he began scooping aside sand with both hands.

Pretty much the first thing I said to him was that he wasn't very bright. When he remembers that, I'll be sure to let him laugh for a good long time.

Chapter 30

From atop the mesa, Thelyan combed the world for a sign of his enemy. He had sensed Ka'an for a time, but then the trace had vanished. It was possible that the evil one had discovered some way to cloak himself, but Thelyan doubted it. Such spells had not yet been discovered the last time Ka'an had been active. So that implied that the enemy was moving along the blind zone created by the train tracks.

Since the interference of the rails would prevent Ka'an from repelling from the ground to ride the wind, he must be running. It would probably be full night before he arrived. That would suit him; he reveled in darkness, after all.

A puff of black smoke in the west caught Thelyan's attention. That would be the troop train, with Strindner's reinforcements. They would arrive in plenty of time. Going to the edge, he looked down to see that Liss had his men formed up near the platform, ready to merge in Strindner's unit and brief them. The neat ranks of white uniforms pleased Thelyan. The White Watch were the most disciplined men in the world, thanks to the harsh training he had designed for them. Even when Ka'an began killing them, they would hold their formations and return fire. Thelyan doubted that Ka'an would be harmed in any serious way by the hail of lead and spells the Watch would throw at him, but he would have to use much of his power to prevent his body's destruction.

Then it would only remain for Thelyan to break and devour him.

The Director's thoughts were interrupted by a sparking alarm in the back of his mind. He sought its source, and frowned. The null sphere had been damaged. Perhaps breached. He hadn't thought that was possible.

Perhaps putting Medur in with Chaiel had been a mistake. The Green Lady was weak, but might have sacrificed herself to give Chaiel the power to break free.

Well, he had time to deal with the problem before the joining of battle. Thelyan turned toward the entrance to his hidden stairway, away from the ant-small ranks of his troops below; but something in that direction nagged at him. He paused, trying to puzzle out what it was. He could sense the lives of his mages, he could sense that the prison ward was intact, he could hear the troop train approaching --

Whirling, he gasped -- the first involuntary sound he'd made in centuries -- as he realized what was wrong. The sound of the train. It should have been slowing. It was accelerating.

Despite the distance, his eyes picked out the dark shape crouched atop the engine just before the train derailed. Throttle jammed open, the train hit the switch just before the platform at its maximum speed of sixty miles per hour, jumped the track, and crashed tumbling and screeching into the massed men there. Some tried to run; some threw useless spells at the grounded mass of iron; all to no avail. Thelyan watched helplessly as his men died for nothing.

His mouth opened without his command a second time, and a cry of rage leapt out. How? How could the evil one, that vestige of a barbaric prehistory, have managed to use Thelyan's own machinery against him? How?

"Where are you?" Thelyan growled. "Where are you, you snake, you sneaking spider?" There -- he found the dark shape again, leaping and dodging among the few survivors beyond the still-skidding train. As the burning engine tore through the outer fence and dug itself to a halt half-buried in sand, Ka'an in Trevarde's skin neatly turned the spells thrown at him by the last few Watchmen. Then the dark one produced a pistol and fired off three shots, leaving no one to oppose him.

Again, he should not have been able to do that. What did that ancient serpent know of modern weapons? He shouldn't even have known what a gun could do, let alone how to use one so neatly.

Scowling, Thelyan stretched out a hand. Sent a thread of force down into the carnage below to snare a discarded rifle.

Ka'an glanced up, following the motion of power. Thelyan could see the glint of his eyes, and of his teeth -- the mad creature was grinning eagerly. It was not an expression he had expected to see on Ka'an's face. Fury, arrogance, megalomaniacal posing at grandeur, yes; but not this wild-dog smile. Something had changed. Ka'an was no longer what Thelyan remembered. It began to seem possible that the outcome of the fight was not predetermined.

Men held in reserve were pouring out of the compound. Ka'an looked between them and Thelyan. He threw out his own thread of power, catching at the rifle before Thelyan could receive it. Thelyan retaliated by following that thread back, snagging at Ka'an's body. Ka'an copied the action.

With a simultaneous, counterbalanced pull -- ironically cooperative -- they jerked Ka'an's body from the ground and flung it high into the air, toward Thelyan.

Ka'an landed lightly on the mesa's top, long hair and coat settling around him like dusty black wings. His power was spun tightly closed, defensive; another thing out of character. He studied Thelyan with eyes that held more curiosity and wariness than malice. The pistol in his hand -- a new model, of the kind that Thelyan didn't yet trust enough to issue to his troops -- covered Thelyan before the Director could bring his own rifle to bear.

"You seem like a smart guy," the dark one said. "Has it crossed your mind that we don't have to do this?"

Thelyan's eyes narrowed. What did he mean, spouting such nonsense? "If you're trying to negotiate a truce, Ka'an, you're a fool. I will not let you return the world to chaos."

"Whoa." The enemy's eyebrows climbed. "Wait a second. This is starting to make sense. You're one of these immortals too. *That's* why Ka'an wanted to kill you. How many of you fuckers *are* there?"

"This is a ruse," Thelyan frowned, but as he said it a scenario presented itself that might explain this. Could a mortal vessel possibly have bested Ka'an and taken his tainted power? No, that was impossible. "This is a trick."

The dark one shook his head. "We're not understanding each other. Look, here's the deal. I owe you a kicking for messing with my head a while back, and I guess I wouldn't mind seeing you dead on account of your job title. But I just took out about fifty of your guys, and I figure we can call that even. Let Ashleigh Trine go, and I'll leave."

"Unbelievable," Thelyan snarled. "No. I don't believe it. You end here, Ka'an."

The enemy's lips quirked. "Oh, I see. So I guess we fight, huh?"

Thelyan answered with a slash of power in lieu of words. The enemy twisted aside and replied with a blast of his own, and the battle was joined.

☙ ❈ ❧

The last thin shell of sandstone crumbled away under

Ash's hands. He sagged to his knees, smiling despite his fatigue. A fresh-smelling draft stirred his hair. He was rather proud of himself. Breaking through the wall by main force would have been impossible with the tiny trickle of energy he'd been able to pull, but he'd used the principles of steam power to do the job. Finding tiny pockets of moisture in flaws among the rock, he'd jolted them to heat, cracking the stone. Far more efficient. Even so, he was tired.

Chaiel climbed past him, hair dragging in the dust. The little light Thelyan had left in the room bobbed along obediently behind him. The kid looked ridiculous, bare-legged in Ash's overlarge boots, drowned in Ash's mud-crusted coat, with the matted rope of his hair snaggling behind him. But for all his weirdness, he'd turned out to be a solid ally. He looked up and down the hallway they'd broken into, then glanced back at Ash, gray eyes round as a kitten's.

"I smell outside. Which way? I can't tell which way."

"Pick one, I guess." Ash took a steadying breath, made himself get up. He chose a direction at random, and set out toward the left. That one seemed to be slanting down a little, so it was more likely to let them out, since he sensed they were high up in the mountain.

He could feel that Kieran was near, and the sense of him made Ash's head spin with an anxiety of need. Every moment, he had to fight the urge to act with frantic haste. He wouldn't help Kieran by panicking. Calm persistence was what he needed.

Are you fighting now, Kai? Are you in danger? I'm so tired of being afraid for you. Be smart, defend yourself, hold on, and I'll find a way to join you.

He thought he sensed a flicker of emotion in response. Just a confirmation, thrown out of a state of concentration. It conveyed something along the lines of: *Busy. Doing fine. Patience.*

It was reassuring. But then, it took a lot to scare Kieran. He might not even begin to fear until he was already too deep in trouble to dig himself out. Ash's help -- and possibly Chaiel's -- might be necessary. And the sooner the better. Ash forced his weary body to pick up the pace, and heard a groan behind him as Chaiel followed suit.

The hallway made a gradual curve left and down, then ended in a metal door. This one, unlike the one that had sealed the sphere room, had a handle and lock, and was painted white.

Ash put his hand to it, then his ear.

"What --" Chaiel began.

"Ssh." It was almost silent beyond the door, but there was one puzzling little noise. A dull thumping in irregular rhythm.

No voices, though, or sounds of feet. Ash put his hand to the lock plate, but discovered that his senses slipped and skewed within the metal. He moved to the wall, contemplating the feasibility of tunneling around.

Chaiel went past him, grasped the door handle, and turned it. The door swung open.

Ash slapped himself on the forehead. "I'm an idiot."

"You're a genius," Chaiel countered. "I expect you frequently miss the obvious."

"Let me go first." Ash peered cautiously into the dimness beyond the door, then stepped forward, allowing Chaiel to follow with the light.

This was a large, ominously laboratory-like room, with a series of doors along the far wall. It smelled rank, like a hospital and a kennel combined. The doors opposite were like jail doors, each with a small barred window at head height. The thumping sound came from behind one of these. Ash crept toward it, into a growing miasma of pain and despair as thick as the smell.

"What *is* this place?" Chaiel breathed.

"Light." Ash beckoned. He followed the thumping to look through one of the barred windows, from which came a strong stench both physical and emotional.

The faint gleam of the light revealed a cell occupied by a single, deformed figure. The figure was crouched in a far corner, banging its overlarge head against the wall. Its upper limbs were useless paddles, its legs short and fat as an infant's. It was a little larger than an ordinary man, squat enough to weigh three or four times as much, and its skewed face was blank. It did not react to the light.

Ash reeled back, choking. As he struggled not to throw up, he sensed Chaiel's echoing shock as he, too, looked into the cell.

The thumping didn't pause.

"What are they *doing*?" Ash gasped, when he could speak at all. "Oh god, what do they think they're doing here? And --" He straightened. "Are there *more* of those things?"

Chaiel shook his head in dismay. "What should we do about it?"

"Do?"

"Should we put it out of its misery?"

Ash spread his hands. "How? We're unarmed."

Then they both jumped as a sharp clang sounded from one of the other cells. Spinning to face it, Ash saw a pair of eyes glittering behind another barred window. The clanging noise came again, and he realized the cell's occupant was tapping something against the metal door.

The face retreated as Ash came forward. It backed off just enough that he could see that it appeared human, small, a child. White face, dark eyes, dark stubble on its scabbed scalp.

He swallowed sour spit before speaking. "Um. Hello. Can you talk?"

The figure shook its head. It made a small whimpering sound.

"Hold on, I'm going to try to get you out."

Whimpering again, the figure nodded frantically.

As Ash fumbled with the mechanism that barred the door, Chaiel grabbed his arm. "Is that a good idea, Ash? What if the creature's dangerous?"

"What if it is?" Ash returned. "It's aware of its situation, not like that giant fetus in there. I can't just walk away." Setting his teeth, he finally got the wheel to turn, and the bar cranked back. He hauled the door open.

The prisoner wobbled out, smiling gratitude, and Ash's heart squeezed small with pity. It was a young girl, no more than twelve or thirteen years old, naked, emaciated and bruised. Attached to her shoulderblades, surrounded by swollen and suppurating flesh, was a pair of enormous, greasy black wings.

"Oh." The meaningless syllable was all Ash could get out. He reached to steady her, wincing at the way she flinched.

Chaiel's face twisted. He spit on the floor. "This place is sick. I want to leave."

"Wait. Are there... are there others?"

The girl shook her head. She pointed at the cell that held the head-banging creature, then made loops by her head with her finger: crazy. She gestured at the other cells and drew her finger across her throat: dead.

Ash nodded. He took the child's arm to help her walk, avoiding the hideous taxidermy on her back.

Moving more slowly now, they followed the hall the other direction. This time what they found was more encouraging: a stair leading down. No discussion was necessary.

☙ ✵ ☙

Kieran wasn't afraid, but he sensed it wouldn't be long until he began to be. Fighting Ka'an had been a bar brawl compared with this. He was in over his head.

Thelyan was powerful, and he was *fast*. Far too fast. And he knew what he was doing. He had a repertoire of spells that he could just rip off in an instant. He'd bark out a phrase, trace a shape with flickering fingers, and suddenly something nasty would be flying at Kieran's face -- a hissing gout of invisible heat, or tendrils of pain groping for his nerves, or a clap of eardrum-rupturing concussion. No matter how tight his defenses, some of it always got through. Kieran had learned the hard way that by the time he saw what the spell was, it was too late to avoid it. The air reeked of singed hair and burnt leather, and the palms of his hands were blistered.

But he'd learned. He had a sort of strategy. He'd decided that since it was impossible to tailor his defense to the attack, the best he could do was to throw something out at the same time, it didn't matter exactly what. He didn't try to make these blasts into spells; just did his best to get them into the right place to disrupt whatever Thelyan was making. It mostly worked. So far.

But it just went on and on. They stood facing each other, hands slashing the air. Thelyan spitting spell words; Kieran muttering fragments of obscenities. To an unmagical eye, they must have looked like a couple of railyard bums having a lunatic argument. Kieran was getting tired. He couldn't tell if Thelyan was wearing out; it was possible that the Director could go on all day.

When he'd felt Ash calling for him from within the mountain, he'd hoped that it meant this fight was only a distraction. Keep the Director busy long enough for Ash to get out, then run for it. But when he'd been able to spare the attention to check his surroundings, he found that there was a lot more of the Watch left alive than he'd thought. Even though Ash was moving within the mountain, which meant he wasn't stuck in a cell, he still wouldn't be able to walk out the front door. Kieran would not only have to beat Thelyan, he'd have to do it with enough juice to spare so he could take down whoever was guarding the compound.

As things stood, that just wasn't going to happen.

He'd wasted a couple bullets finding out that Thelyan's shield against projectiles was a lot better than Ka'an's had been. Thelyan had again moved to snatch up a rifle from below, and this time had succeeded, but Kieran had seen how the shield thing was built and so the gun hadn't done Thelyan any good. It was down to this flicker-fast chess-game staring contest, which Kieran knew he wouldn't win. He had to find a way to move the fight onto better ground. Make it physical, somehow.

This realization came without words, gradually building in the moments between attacks and deflections. He had to be realistic; plain determination wasn't going to beat skill. *And I'm thinking too much. I've been thinking way, way too much today.*

I'm a thug, damn it. What the fuck am I doing playing brain games with this bastard?

Managing the shape of his power was taking up too much of his attention. Thelyan seemed not to have to consider it at all. He had it trained to his hands and voice. He spoke and gestured, and it leapt from him already formed into some lethal shape. Kieran tossed out random bursts, tangling Thelyan's spells as they emerged, scattering them. Sometimes he was too slow. As his resolve to shift the ground firmed, he missed one, and knives of air tore across his chest, ripping clothes, welting his skin.

A button, sliced from his coat, fell to the ground and bounced. It seemed to take a long time.

"Don't cut the tattoos, asshole," Kieran said. His cheerful tone surprised him a little, and pleased him. He knew what that meant: this was starting to feel like a fight. Whatever Thelyan was doing, he didn't know what to call that, but a *fight* he understood. If there was going to be blood flying around, then the thing made sense. *And if someone's going to spit teeth, it won't be me.*

Hauling his power in tight around him, letting it develop a bit of a spin, Kieran stepped forward. Another set of invisible blades met him halfway; only partially deflected by the whirl of his pattern, it struck him in the side. Now his left sleeve was hanging in shreds. But he'd decided to take the pain. It could have been a lot worse. The coat was a loss, but his skin was barely scratched. Relishing the wary way Thelyan stepped back at his approach, Kieran closed the distance between them until their patterns overlapped. Tangled, clashing, like kite strings fouled together.

The Director's eyes widened in outrage in the instant before Kieran's fist caught him across the cheekbone.

Kieran followed this with a hard hail of fast blows to any target he could see, trying to keep the man off balance so he couldn't form a spell. There was a bitter joy in him now. *Where's your fancy magic? Where are your pain spells and your headgames?* He battered aside Thelyan's arms, followed the Watchman's attempts to back away. The pale-haired man was far shorter than Kieran, and weaker. Thelyan cringed, he cried out; things broke, things bled, fingers, an ear, and now he was the one off guard, unable to summon a defense.

When Thelyan was staggering, slack-faced, punch-drunk, Kieran hopped back half a step to finish him off with a nice solid kick to the temple.

Mistake. In that split second, Thelyan threw out a wall of solid force -- half-formed, no attempt at subtlety this time, just pure Kinesis. It caught Kieran right in the face and lifted him off his feet. The world flashed white as he flew headfirst backwards in a long arc, then flashed again as the back of his skull hit the ground with all his weight behind it.

He lay stunned, looking at the sparkles. There wasn't even pain. And then there was; all at once, fat and dull from behind, small and sharp in front. Something tickled inside his throat and he tasted metal.

Bloody nose. Concussion? Don't have time to puke. As soon as thought re-formed, he was moving. His head throbbed in big slow waves as he stood up. Hot blood rolled out of his nose in a sheet, down his lips and chin, threaded itching down his neck. His eyes wouldn't focus, but his mind's sight was working just fine. When he saw what Thelyan was doing, he laughed.

The dumbshit was taking time to heal himself. "Can't you take a few bruises, buddy?" Kieran's voice sounded thick, but he was only amusing himself anyway. "Tell me, you ever been smacked in the kidney with the back end of a rifle?" As he talked, he was gathering up his pattern, shaping it more carefully this time. Blood spattered from his lips with his words. "If you're not pissing pink, you can't really say you got beat up. You should have those guards of yours give you a demonstration. You know -- for science."

Thelyan wasn't listening. He was watching Kieran warily, but his attention was turned inward. The injuries Kieran had caused him were righting themselves, and all the power he wasn't using for that was shaped into a shield that looked as solid as a brick wall. He clearly thought they'd reached a stalemate, declared a momentary cease-fire to lick their wounds.

Kieran finished his preparations as he finished talking. He wasn't going to try to get through that brick wall. Instead, he took the hungry, gnawing pattern he'd fashioned and shoved it into the ground at Thelyan's feet.

The Director stumbled as the stone beneath him began to crack and crumble. He scrambled aside, but the crumbling followed him. Leaving off his healing, he sent a spell of his own to block Kieran's, then spread a wide net of force above Kieran's head, which started to radiate a blistering heat.

Spells again, Kieran thought disgustedly as he countered. But they weren't quite back where they'd started. It was a little different now. And he thought maybe he was starting to get the hang of it.

☙ ✵ ☜

"What's that?" Chaiel balked, pointing. "I'm not touching that."

Ash studied the strange pattern before them. It cut through the hallway at an angle, a slanted plane of regular, interlocked shapes. While he examined it, he stated the obvious: "There isn't any other way to go." At the foot of the stairway, they'd found this hall, and there had been no doors or branches from it in all the long way they'd followed it.

The child with wings grafted to her back sank to her knees. Ash reached out to her, concerned, but she shook her head. Just resting. Her pale face was sheened with sweat; he didn't think he'd ever seen a little kid sweat that much. She was really sick.

He pushed pity from his mind. Once they were out, then he could try to get her some medical help. Right now, he had to figure out whether the thing that crossed the corridor was dangerous, or maybe something they could use. Its pattern was geometric, and its workings were less complex than the null sphere had been. But he'd spent hours on the sphere, and he wasn't sure if he had even minutes now. Brushing off a protest from Chaiel, he went to put his hand to it.

There was no sense of resistance. His hand went right through. The pattern didn't react to him at all. "I think it's safe," he said, and stepped forward.

Blindness snapped down around him, patterns vanished, the walls of his mind closed in. With a short cry of dismay, he scrambled back. To his great relief, nothing prevented him, and his magical sense returned as soon as he was back on the right side of the pattern. Understanding dawned.

"It's the ward."

Chaiel frowned. "What ward, what do you mean?"

"The ward that -- we must be near the prison section. Go through for a second. Go on, it's harmless, you can walk right out again."

"You'd better be right." Chaiel did as Ash asked, and came back out even more quickly than Ash had, looking even more shaken. "That was awful," he said with an accusing glare. "Why did you make me do that?"

"So when I tell you that's where they keep the Talents, you'll know what I'm talking about."

"Why do I care?"

"Well, I'm just thinking, if that ward came down, a few locks and bars wouldn't do much to hold those guys. I'm thinking it might do Kieran some good if the Watch were distracted by escaping prisoners."

"It might do us good as well," Chaiel said thoughtfully. "Can you do it?"

Ash shrugged. "Let me think a minute."

Sighing resignation, Chaiel turned to the child and explained to her. "That means we have to be very quiet for a long time, until we're thoroughly bored, and then he'll suddenly come up with some genius idea he can't explain."

The girl nodded solemnly and folded her hands in her lap.

Ash hid a smile and turned to study the ward. After a moment he forgot his amusement. There was something familiar about the way this thing was put together. It had some design elements in common with the null sphere, but that wasn't what nagged at him. Something about it made him think of Dawyer's experiments with electricity; he could see the page in his mind, last spring's issue of the North Bank Technical Quarterly. There'd been diagrams, he'd been frustrated because they weren't labeled right, the experiment couldn't be reproduced without further information...

Batteries. The ward was a battery. That was how it kept anyone inside it from doing magic -- it snatched away any free power within its boundaries and used it to strengthen itself.

And that meant... yes, it was a simple hexagonal matrix... must be spherical, or at least domelike... so if any of the nexus points were removed... "But how do you get at it? If it just eats anything that comes near it -- from outside, but -- no, that trick's not going to work here. Just make it stronger."

Behind him, Chaiel sighed again. Only then did Ash realize he'd been talking out loud. He turned, catching the gray-eyed boy in a theatrical yawn.

"Hey Shy, if you want to do something to something but the something just grabs whatever touches it --"

"Something something?" Chaiel's tone was mocking, but Ash had already answered his own question, smacking himself on the forehead.

"Another battery. Duh."

"You're making no sense at all. And I *wish* you'd stop calling me Shy."

"Hm? Sorry." Ash's reply was an absent mumble. He was already building his own battery. It didn't need to have a structure like the ward's; a simple layered pattern would suffice, transparent one way and opaque the other. He constructed it in the palm of his hand. Just as a precaution, he took the time to arrange his own pattern as receptively as possible, in case his one-way membrane drew out more than one nexus point.

When he was finished, he stretched out his hand... and hesitated.

"You might want to step back," he said. "There's a remote chance that my head will explode."

"You're joking."

"Mostly." Nevertheless he waited until he heard Chaiel and the child moving away before he plunged his hand into the ward.

He heard the beginning of his own scream before he went deaf. Energy leapt into him with terrible force and speed -- agonizing -- distantly, he was aware he must pull his hand out of the flow, but couldn't find it. Couldn't find his body. Couldn't find himself at all.

༄ ❀ ༅

Kieran heard Ash cry out in his mind. In the moment of distraction this afforded, Thelyan got a direct attack through, knocking Kieran tumbling across the rough stone of the mesa's top. Kieran didn't care. Something had happened to Ash, something bad, and now Ash was in pain.

What is it? -- the thought was incoherent, just a burst of fear sent nowhere. Huddled crouching with his head behind his arms, pattern meshed tight around him, Kieran didn't care what Thelyan might do to him in the next second. If Ash was being killed right now, then it didn't matter who won this fight. The sense of pain and fear from Ash was mounting. Kieran took a hitching breath, tasting stale blood and dust, and sent out to him again. *Will my power help? Take it!*

When he touched the bullet charm at his throat to send his power out, though, he sensed immediately that the problem was something opposite. Energy flooded along their link, coming from Ash's direction. It was jetting through, like steam from a pinhole punched in a boiler. Ash had encountered a surge of some kind.

It didn't matter why. All Kieran needed to know was that Ash was being burned out by it, drowned in it.

Give it to me, he thought desperately. Knowing that words wouldn't make it through, not sure whether the sense of his intention would carry. *Send it here!*

"Exhausted already?" Thelyan's smug voice was an irritating distraction. "Get up, Ka'an. We've barely started."

"Shut up," Kieran said through his teeth, not looking up. He couldn't spare the attention for his adversary just now. He needed to reach out, couldn't find a direction in which to reach -- was suddenly sick to death of all this magic, all this vagueness and sideways thinking. Groping with his mind at the leaking energy, he bullied his way into the part of his pattern that was joined to Ash's, wrenched it wide, flung more strands into it. He robbed his shield to do it, and was buffeted by fragments of an attack from Thelyan, but he didn't care. He could sense the pressure on the other side of that divide, the agony and fear, Ash screaming, he couldn't stand it --

With a soundless sound and a prickling across his scalp, the dam burst. Power shoved into him. It hurt, even more than taking in the Burn had hurt; it was not his own power, not fitted to his pattern. It was something icy and sawtoothed and regular, and he couldn't find a place to put it. No wonder it had pained Ash so much. He heard himself panting, blood from his broken nose gurgling in his throat as he gasped for breath. It seemed, for a time, that he might have sacrificed himself.

That wouldn't be so bad. But it would be better if he

lived, better still if he could find a way to keep this power and use it... and with this thought, an instinct rose in him, some vestige of the dead god.

The process was violent. Stone cracked beneath his knees. Dust blew away from him in a widening circle. Thelyan intensified his attack, but Kieran ignored the cuts and blows. He tore apart the power as it came, smashed it out of alignment, forced it to follow the rules of his own mind. Sweat beaded and ran, stinging broken skin. His eyes were useless, his limbs frozen, his whole attention focused on this one task.

There was too much -- a river turned to an ocean, a bullet between the eyes, a firehose jammed down his throat -- he couldn't keep up, his brain was going to melt, it was all over --

And then it stopped. There was no more.

He opened his eyes, realized he was lying facedown on the ground. Shoving himself up to kneeling, he scraped his hands across his face, examined the mud of sweat and blood that came off. Looked around for his enemy, to see why Thelyan hadn't finished him off.

The Director was staring at him with an expression of angry awe. "How?" The one syllable was nearly a whine.

Kieran coughed his throat clear, spit, grinned. "Pure sex appeal."

Thelan made a jerky gesture dismissing this flippant answer. "It's not possible. It simply can't be done."

Laughing a bit, Kieran climbed to his feet. His pattern still wove its wall around him, but it was now thick and thorny with the new energy he'd pulled in. He could feel that Ash was alive and no longer hurting. Weak, maybe unconscious, but alive.

"Okay," Kieran said gamely. "It can't be done. So I didn't just do it. *Damn* you're dim."

"*How?*" Thelyan stepped forward with clenched fists, angrier by the moment. "I've studied power for centuries, and you -- but you're a primitive, a savage! Our last battle -- you couldn't adapt, you weren't smart enough, you were *nothing* like this, *nobody* should be able to do what you just did!" He pointed at Kieran, and the pointing finger shook. "You are the soul of darkness, Ka'an. You have no place in the light. How... how *dare* you change!"

Kieran shook his head. He pinched the bridge of his nose with his fingers, pressing hard, dragged down, felt the broken place snap right with a sharp pain behind his eyes. It was easy to trickle in just enough power to heal it. Now his voice came out right when he answered. "I'm *not* Ka'an, all right? I swallowed him. We fought and I won. I got some of the story from him, but not the part about you. I don't know what you guys were fighting about -- though I bet it had something to do with the fact that Ka'an was a self-involved jackass who pissed off everyone who had to deal with him. Anyway, he's dead now. Can you get that through your head? Or do we have to go around again? Because I'm game, if you wanna. But it's getting stale."

For a long moment, Thelyan just stared at him. The Director looked young, just then, with his white skin pink-blotched and his pale hair darkened with sweat and dust, straggling out of its queue and into his face. It occurred to Kieran that the body Thelyan was using couldn't be much older than Kieran was. And Thelyan must have pushed out the soul that was born in it, killed whatever towheaded boy that face would have belonged to. At this point, one more death probably mattered less than pocket change to him.

He deserved to die. He deserved to be beaten in the most humiliating way and then squashed like a bug. Kieran didn't feel like doing that, though, which didn't make a whole lot of sense.

Thelyan was apparently having the same thought. With narrowed eyes, he said, "Even if that were true, why would you want peace with me?" After a moment's pause, Thelyan's face relaxed, conflict gone. "If you're Trevarde and not Ka'an, then the beast's power is in the hands of a sexual-deviant multiple-murderer from a race of brawling, squabbling savages."

"Well." Kieran snorted, wiped clotted blood on his knuckles. His pattern spiked out all over in a forest of thorns. He heard his voice from a distance, slow and drawling. "That was kinda the wrong thing to say."

The Director moved his hands, had time for the first syllable of an attack, and then Kieran sent spikes of power shooting deep into Thelyan's shield. He aimed not for the forming spell but for the pattern itself, tearing its fabric, grasping and breaking.

Thelyan cried out and lost his spell. He wrenched at the attacking thorns, formed slicing shapes in reply. Locked together, wrestling power against power, they bent all their attention to destroying each other.

Chapter 31

When Ash screamed and fell, Chaiel's only thought was that he should have expected something like this. Things had been going too well.

He was able to get his hands under Ash's head before it hit the stone, but snatched them back immediately as a cold burn of power snapped at him. The little girl was whimpering, hiding her eyes. Ash lay slack-mouthed, twitching, while the structure of the ward dissolved and reeled into him in pale, roping strands. This went on for a handful of long seconds, and then the ward was gone and Ash lay quiet. Chaiel made one more attempt to reach out to him, to see if he lived; what he sensed when he came near, though, made it impossible for him to offer any help. All of Ash's natural aura was replaced with a high, tight vibration of foreign energy.

Chaiel bowed his head. The blue-eyed boy was not yet dead, but it seemed his mind had been burned away. Such a shame. It had been a beautiful mind.

"There's nothing more we can do for him," he said softly. He reached for the child's hand. "He sacrificed himself so we could escape. Let's not waste it."

She obediently put her clammy little hand in his and let herself be pulled to her feet. Walking slowly, as much from his own fatigue as from consideration for the child's weakness, Chaiel led her past the place where the ward had been. His thoughts turned ahead: there was chaos all around, above and outside, and it would be difficult to get through it unarmed and with a sick child in tow. It would have been better if Ash hadn't let his ambition outrun his abilities. Still...

I won't forget what you did for me, Chaiel thought reverently. *Or what Medur said through you. All people are mine; mine to care for, mine to watch and learn from. I'll begin with this child.*

༄ ❈ ༅

It began as a headache. Everything was just a little too loud. Moving a little too fast. Duyam Sona thought it might be just the onset of one of his periods of despair, at first. They had been more frequent since he'd been recaptured. He sat listening to the distant sounds of running and barked orders, not really trying to imagine what might be going on out there, ignoring the muttering of his cellmate. Gibner was acting a bit odd. The bald, bearded man who was his only remaining friend generally responded to every stimulus with the same surly silence. Muttering wasn't his style. But then, they'd all been a bit more insane than usual since that bastard Trevarde had got some of them out and then left them to their own devices.

The problem with his head was getting worse. His brain itched. He felt the walls pressing in, felt Gibner in the cell with him, agitated. Like a jittering flame, like the spitting spark on the end of a fuse. Sona could almost smell the smoke.

"God's balls!" Gibner leapt to his feet, looking more like a monkey than ever. "Motherfucker! Fuck!"

Sona turned, scowling, and then his jaw dropped. Gibner's bed was on fire.

"Holy shit," Sona breathed, awestruck. His head-problem jumped into focus, and he suddenly understood that it was not a problem at all.

Gibner raised his head slowly to meet Sona's eyes. The understanding was mutual. "You're a Kinetic," the bald man said. "Ain't you."

As an answer, Sona spread his fingers across the lock plate in the cell door. There was a faint creaking, as of metal under stress, and then a heavy clank. The door swung open.

The next few minutes were a smear of noise and movement. Others had realized it at about the same time -- the ward was down. Their magic would work again. Kinetics, Pyros, Entropists, all the destructive Talents came swarming out of the cells, to find only a quartet of fearful guards between themselves and freedom. There were some shots fired, but Sona didn't see who fell; the guards lasted only a breath's time beyond that. Torn apart, burned up, and melted down, all at the same moment.

Those who had been present for Trevarde's stunt after the storm, which was most of them, would rather have died than be recaptured again. No one said it out loud, but all had the same idea: make certain that this prison could never enclose them again. Deafening noise rose up as debris showered down. Some Kinetics, Sona among them, had the presence of mind to steer the falling rubble toward areas where no one was standing, but they couldn't catch every boulder or glass shard. There were screams, and sobbing whimpers afterward.

Desperate men ignored wounded ones. The roof came down. The walls crumbled. A slope of crushed stone formed at one end, the one with the door that led to the mess hall and exercise yard, the direction most of them associated with 'out.' Men began swarming up it before others were finished making it, and more injuries resulted. Sona was one of these, though he didn't remember deciding to climb up. One moment he was realizing that escape was possible -- then there was a mess, and catching falling things, and then he found himself twisted beneath a slab of stone and howling.

He bent everything he had to lifting the stone off him, but it wouldn't budge. It had crushed one of his legs. He could see, in the flickers of lucidity between swarms of pain, that his left leg was utterly gone, not just broken but smashed to paste. He wanted to separate himself from it, certain that the pain would go with it. Tugging at it made him scream, but he couldn't stop doing it.

Somewhere above, guns were barking. Shouting and flickers of power. He rolled his head, but it was aiming in the wrong direction. Back toward where his cell had been. *Please all the gods, don't let that be my last sight. Urotu help me -- haven't I always been true? Haven't I always resisted the Dalanists and their heresy? Is this my reward?*

Something moved, something pale, in a hollow of broken rock. Up above the shells of the cell tiers, up where the gun post had been. *A soldier? Watchman? Left alive to shoot me dead?* The figure went to the edge where the floor had broken off, stepped out onto thin air, and drifted gently down. *I used to be able to do that...* Sona wanted to play dead, but couldn't keep his sobs behind his teeth. The pain was unbelievable.

Bounding lightly over the strewn floor, the figure came nearer, and Sona began to doubt his senses. Not a soldier. The paleness was not a white uniform, but white flesh, crowned with something that in Sona's blurred eyes glowed like a streak of fire. Flickered, as the figure moved through bands of falling sunlight.

"Can you speak?" The voice was gentle. A young man's voice, and oddly familiar. "Can you hear me? Do you remember me, Sona?"

Sona clenched his teeth, blinked fast to clear his eyes. The bright figure's face jumped into focus. It was Trevarde's redheaded bumboy. It was Ash Trine.

"I'll have to make a tourniquet, or you'll bleed to death when I take that rock off you. It's going to hurt, but you have to try to hold still. Do you understand?"

"You came back." Sona's voice came out in a thin whine. "You came back for us. Is he here too? Trevarde?"

"Yes. I'm going to use some of your shirt; I don't have a lot of clothes left." Trine barely touched Sona's arm, but the sleeve of his sweat-soaked prison shirt flew away in neat strips. A brush of power trailed it along his skin, and that tiny touch was enough to clear his mind and ease the pain.

With full consciousness came a different kind of confusion. Trine's face was unmistakable, nobody else had a beaky freckled mug like that, and for all the dirt in it his hair was still a dead giveaway. But somehow, Sona was certain that if he thought of this as the same person he'd brawled with before, he'd be wrong. Power breathed from Trine like the cool of evening. His pale blue eyes, no longer frightened, held a kind of wry serenity that Sona had seen in the eyes of very old men. The pain in Sona's leg as Trine knotted twisted fabric around it wasn't nearly as bad as it should have been.

He would have been afraid, remembering how nasty he'd been to the kid, except that he had a feeling that this version of Trine would never harm him. Was too powerful to have to do harm.

"This is going to hurt a lot," Trine cautioned. "Are you ready?"

"Thank you," Sona said. Just in case something kept him from saying it later. There was no use in wondering how Trine could be so different, or even whether it was enough to help. "You don't owe me this and I know it. I'm ready."

With no sign of effort except a slight frown, Trine pressed his palms to the slab of stone that pinned Sona, and it shattered to gravel.

Pain fizzed up Sona's spine and burst in his head in a galaxy of spinning sparks.

When he woke, he was alone. He was dizzy, nauseated from loss of blood, but nothing hurt. By inches, he raised himself on his elbows to look at what was left of his leg. Ready for anything, not sure what he expected. He gagged at the sight of the mess of bloody meat and splintered bone that stretched out before him -- but it wasn't attached to him. Beyond where his trouser leg had been neatly sheared, the brown skin of his thigh gave way to pink, shiny scar. The stump looked as if it had been healed for years.

Beside him, placed neatly to his hand, was a length of steel bar from one of the skylights, one end melted and fused into a shape like the handle of a cane.

☙ ✺ ❧

Colonel Warren had gone past the point of having his hands full about fifteen minutes ago. Five minutes ago, he'd stopped trying to contain the breakout. Now all he could hope to do was save as many of his men as possible.

Rifles were a little use against the escaping prisoners, but not much. For the most part the weapon of choice in this fighting retreat was magic. Warren had only a handful of men left -- he'd counted twenty-one, but a few had gone down since then. They were backing toward the only intact building he could see, firing and casting as they went; he could feel that they were exhausted.

"That's it, boys," he kept saying. "Just a few more yards." He hoped they couldn't hear his fear in his voice.

The prisoners flinging themselves against his line were a snarling mass, all filthy skin and stringy hair and blue-gray rags. Rabid. Not like last time, when they'd all bolted as far from the compound as possible. This time they were determined to tear the place apart. Warren didn't have time to wonder how the wards had come down. He didn't have time to wonder what he'd do when the few men he'd managed to chivvy out of the shaking mountain reached the guardhouse that was their goal. They'd be boxed in, but at least they'd have cover... cover which would come down on their heads if they didn't spend energy keeping it up...

A breath of wind ran across his sunburned skin, and with it came clarity and the smell of cold brine. At its passing, a change fell over the sound of the battle; not a hush, not at first, but a faltering of fury. Then, one by one, the prisoners straightened their backs, took deep breaths. Their magics went from attack to defense, then ceased completely. His own men began by crouching to reload and check their ammunition, but lost interest in the process partway through, and they too were still.

Warren felt his own spine straighten, his own lungs and eyes clear. Peace grew through him. It was a spell, of sorts, but not a heavy hand of passivity like the spells he knew. He still had the option of fighting, if he wanted to. It was just obvious to him, suddenly, that fighting was the least logical of his options, provided this cease-fire lasted into the next few seconds.

Waves of murmuring went through the prisoners. They parted; someone came through. Someone tall, bird-boned, pale as new ivory, with eyes like sea ice.

"My God," Warren breathed. "How, of all the -- what --"

"Empathy, Colonel. Just Empathy." Ashleigh Trine's tone was conversational, but his voice penetrated the mind without seeming to pass the ears. His expression wasn't that of a man possessing this kind of power; he looked a little worried, a little angry.

So why were some of the prisoners sinking to their knees? Warren felt his own exhaustion keenly, and the urge to bow his head in respect was part of that.

"I think," Trine said kindly, with a graceful gesture of his hands, "that you should go that way, and these men should go *that* way. And none of you should look back."

"What did -- what --"

"And I think *now* would be a good time for that to happen."

Some of the men were already taking this apparition's advice. Prisoners in one direction, Watchmen in another. Warren remembered his duty clearly enough, but it didn't seem as important as his life at the moment. He spoke to convince himself as much as to answer Trine. "I'm a soldier of God. I don't desert my post."

Trine tilted his head like a bird. "What's God need an army for? No, don't answer, I'm sure you've got an argument but I don't have time." He sighed. "It's strange, but I'm glad you don't know what it's like to have your mind gang-raped. If you did, you'd want to undo it, and you can't. Go away now, Colonel Warren."

Against his intention, Warren took a step back. The terrible thing was that he knew Trine wasn't influencing his mind with anything but words. Everything was too clear. "I --" He meant to say something else, but what came out was: "I do know. It's part of our training."

"Go away," Trine repeated gently. The curve of his mouth was kind, but his eyes were like diamond drills.

Warren turned on his heel and ran.

Cut, twist, block, break, dodge, cut. There was no more thought. There was no time to have an opinion. No time to wonder whether he could win, or what would happen if he lost.

He barely knew that he was kneeling, hands fisted in the sand. Blood and sweat running into his eyes had no effect on the senses that mattered. He couldn't be bothered to wipe away all the things that ran out of his nose and eyes and mouth, tears and snot and blood and spit. The sounds he was making had nothing to do with anything. His enemy's body was just the nucleus of the shape he was trying to wreck, and the fact that this nucleus still stood upright and did not fall was of no importance.

He could barely remember his name anymore, but knew his pattern better with every moment.

What had once been a shifting shape in his mind's eye now stood out more clearly than earth or sky. Its colors gave light. Dark light, most of it; his enemy's was all pale and glittering, but his own was full of a thousand shades of black, the darkest greens, streaks of crimson and deep blue. No doubt it looked like the soul of an evil man. He was aware that his tactics were also those of an evil man; he caused as much pain as he could, using the distraction it afforded to press home the most damaging attacks he could devise. As he began to understand the structure of his enemy's soul-shape, he chose his targets with more care: self-image, sight, thought, hope. He knew that he was confirming Thelyan's certainty that he had to be defeated for the good of the world, but he couldn't care about that.

Only one thing mattered: Ash was moving again, out among the chaos, and any moment some stupid accident could take him away.

The act of sharing that power surge had connected them even more strongly. There was now a constant circuit of energy and emotion running between them. Kieran knew Ash's intentions despite the distance between them, and knew that he was sending his own struggle in return. He was afraid that if he was killed in this fight, his death would wash back along that connection and harm Ash -- and he couldn't pretend that a power backlash was the only hurt his death would do. He was the reason for everything Ash was doing, just as Ash was his own reason for fighting.

Still fighting, though beaten to his knees. Though his skin was a mess of cuts, though his muscles ached, though he'd been thrown tumbling across the stone a dozen times. He thought some bones might be broken, knew for certain that things inside him were bleeding. Unless he could keep enough energy for healing, he'd die even if he won.

There is no if, he snarled at himself. *I will win. A world in which I don't doesn't matter.* And the world got smaller every second.

Smash, slice. Bite and scratch. Shoulders hunched and creaking with repeated blows. *We're killing each other by inches.* Whenever he managed to steal some power away from Thelyan, he had to use it to repair himself. No time to heal properly, just barely enough to stop the worst bleeding so that he could keep going.

Ash was nearer. Nearer than he should have been -- nearer than Kieran wanted him. Coming up, somehow coming up the side of the mountain, faster than climbing, had now figured out the Kinetic's ability to lift himself.

Don't! It's dangerous up here, everything is knives --

Kieran's incoherent message met the sweet calm of Ash and brought back a reply strong enough to contain words:

It's time to trust me. Do as I say, now, and we'll win. Love, will you trust me?

Yes. No other answer was possible.

Pull in. Shield yourself.

Kieran obeyed without wondering why. He yanked back all his thorns and blades, walled himself in tight. Suddenly his body mattered again, and it hurt all over. He wiped his eyes clear, took a creaking breath.

Thelyan was standing, but in a staggering posture, white uniform red-speckled. Some of Kieran's needles had gotten through. The Director was frowning, turning, as Ash rose over the mesa's edge and alighted weightlessly.

The scene was too familiar.

Something seemed to burst open in Kieran's heart. He had seen this before. He'd seen Ash shining like that, glowing like precious metals, his eyes brighter than the sky, walking as if touching the ground was optional.

No. Not this. Not this dream.

But he knew what came next. As Ash went to stand between Kieran and Thelyan, the message he sent was no surprise.

Pick up your gun now. Don't hesitate. Don't argue. This will work.

A thin, high sound rose up in Kieran's throat, but his hand closed around his gun. It seemed to take forever, but Thelyan had just begun to open his mouth to speak, and the dust raised by Ash's footsteps was still floating.

Ash spread his arms, meeting Kieran's stare. His pattern blossomed around him, for a split-second unfurled as a golden chrysanthemum with ten thousand petals, so bright Kieran could almost see it with eyes alone. Then it contracted, spinning itself glittering around the thread that linked them.

And the path it made went through Ash's chest, and speared toward Thelyan's throat.

Ashes, no! You're the one thing I can't spare!

Ash smiled, and it looked like a goodbye. He had never been so beautiful as in that moment. His voice had never been so sweet as in the one word he spoke:

"Now."

No. No. But it would only work in this moment. One second and the chance would be gone, Ash had his unprotected back turned to Thelyan, Thelyan was readying something big and full of whirling knives of air --

Kieran brought the gun into the path Ash had made, and fired.

Thunder echoed forever and ever. It took years for Ash's loving smile to turn to slack, stunned nothing. The hole in his white skin stood empty for ages before blood began to roll from it, so brightly terrible, so slowly that Kieran could see it bead before it ran.

Ash's knees bent, balance lost, somehow still graceful as he fell, reaching one hand to catch himself, the other coming to cover the wound, its movement like a bird's flight.

Beyond him, Thelyan was still standing, staring, and everything below his chin was wet red chaos.

Then time snapped right and Kieran was on his feet, flinging himself to Ash's side. In the corner of his eye he saw his enemy wavering, about to fall, but didn't care. Dropping his gun, he grabbed Ash's shoulders, trying to lift him from his kneeling slump. Babbling, words discarded half-formed, eyes blurring -- so irritating, he needed to see Ash's face -- and when Ash lifted his head it was such a relief to see him still alive that the blur turned to pouring tears.

"Got him?" Ash's mouth was too red. Crimson drooled out with his words.

"Yes. Yes. Oh god Ashes, why --"

"'Splain later." Frowning in an effort to focus, Ash groped across the ground until he found Kieran's gun. Fitted his fingers around it; used the wrist of that hand on Kieran's shoulder to push himself up. Kieran, belatedly understanding, helped him stand, though they were both reeling. Ash nearly fell over when he turned to Thelyan.

The Director was still standing, though the whole front of his white uniform was now sheeted wetly red. His pattern was beginning to fragment. Some of it still moved with purpose, though. Moved toward his torn throat, healing. His eyes, impossibly, were still full of terrible intelligence, though the white of his spine was showing.

Ash brought the pistol up. Kieran took his wrist, steadied his hand.

Five shots thumped out. Thelyan jerked with the first shot, fell with the third, but Ash went on pulling the trigger after the bullets were gone. Kept clicking on the empty chamber after Thelyan lay sprawled on the ground. Crumpled like discarded clothing, eyes rolling, then empty. Flecks of dust stuck to their clouding surface.

The shards of his pattern swirled for a moment, settled, turned to flimsy veils. Fluttered in an intangible wind. Then began to grow, to reel out like silk from a spool, creeping across the ground.

Eyes narrow with intense concentration, Ash took his hand from the bullet hole in his chest and spread the bloody palm toward the pattern billowing from Thelyan's corpse. Kieran's arms were wrapped around him from behind, holding him upright. He took a gurgling breath, and as he let it out a shape spread from his hand. A sphere, a glittering honeycomb of force scribbled with intricate equations interlocked. It closed around the corpse, and where the growing power touched it, it glowed brighter.

"There," Ash said. A sigh of deep satisfaction. Then his eyes rolled up, and he slumped.

With a wordless cry, Kieran caught him, scooped him up. Ash still lived -- blood bubbled around the wound, streamed from his nose and mouth. But when Kieran tried to spin the wound closed, his power wouldn't adhere. He wasted precious seconds pouring out his energy to no effect, before an idea occurred to him: the Watch. There were healers among them. They'd help, he'd *make* them help.

Gathering up what little power he had left, he took a running leap from the mountain's edge, pushing himself away from the ground just enough to break his fall. His ankles jarred as he came down; he went to his knees to avoid jolting Ash. Then he was up and running.

He could sense where they were, the people with magic clinging to them. The desert was a blur. He leapt wreckage and bodies. Blasted a fence out of his way, saw figures in the distance. Closed at the best speed he could manage, ready to turn away whatever spells or bullets they sent at him.

Ash coughed a little, shuddering in his arms. One pale hand still clutched Kieran's empty gun, holding to it as if terrified to let go. Beneath the streaked blood, his lips were going purple.

Kieran plowed right into the midst of the knot of startled men, shield thorn-spiked and attacks prepared, before he realized that these were not Watchmen. These men wore prison-gray, and some of their faces were familiar. Those familiar faces looked amazed, some a bit alarmed, some muttering his name in confused tones.

He knelt to lay Ash on the sun-hot ground, propped up against his knees, to have a free hand to press over the bubbling wound. He looked up at the circle of faces, pleading.

"Tell me one of you is a Healer. Please."

They talked, but he didn't hear the answer he was looking for, and none of the rest of it made sense. Questions, recriminations, distrust, demands.

"Please." He could feel Ash's life draining away under his hand. He set his power's hooks in Ash's soul to keep it from fleeing, but the blood kept pouring out, filling lungs, and he knew he couldn't hold Ash to life forever. "Please." He couldn't stop saying it, and they were all just making noise. "Please!"

One of them loomed closer; a slap rang Kieran's head.

"*Listen*, boy." It was Duyam Sona; Kieran recognized him when the slap cut through his panic. The man was leaning on a crutch now, one leg missing. With his free hand he was pointing emphatically at Ash. "*He's* a healer. He'll heal *himself*, that's what I'm trying to tell you. But he's worn out." Sona gestured to the stump of his leg. "From doing stuff like this. If you can share your power with him --"

Kieran saw the truth of it before Sona was finished

speaking. He didn't waste time acknowledging. Through his hands slicked with Ash's blood, through the cord spun between their souls, he let the power run. A trickle at first, until he was sure Ash was taking it. Then he opened the stops. But there was too little of it left. There was no time to comb it out of the air.

Dimly, he sensed a hand come to rest on his shoulder. Then another. From these hands, more power came. The energy spread, linked from source to source. A chain of hands and minds; exhausted men, newly returned to their Talents, poured their life into him, and through him, into Ash.

At first it seemed to disappear, as if the wound was an endless void that couldn't be filled. But little by little, Ash's failing pattern began to brighten. Things torn and broken began to right themselves. Warmth grew and spread from him. A sense of well-being, as strong as a lungful of opium but bringing clarity instead of dreams, threaded into Kieran and spread from him to the men around him.

Pain faded. The pain of his body and the hurt in his heart. He could feel his own injuries healing, and saw the bruised and battered faces of the prisoners returning to health. All the world glowed gold, and just a little green.

At last the glow settled to the normal light of afternoon, and Ash smiled up into Kieran's eyes. "Kai," he murmured. "You trusted me."

Swallowing a sob of gratitude, Kieran crushed Ash close and kissed him. His mouth was still stained with blood, and in it Kieran tasted the truth more clearly than words could have conveyed: *We will never be lost again. This is permanent.* Ash's arms came up to encircle him, strength returning. He buried his face in Kieran's shoulder.

"It's over." Kieran stroked his dirty hair, his bare back streaked with blood and dust. "It's over now. Let's not ever do that again, all right?"

"Okay." Ash's laugh sounded a bit choked. Then he pulled back, and an unpleasant realization showed in his eyes. "Wait. Where are we? Which side of the tracks?"

"What?"

Struggling out of Kieran's embrace, Ash stared back at Churchrock. Kieran followed his stare, as did those of the prisoners who weren't already looking that way. On top of the mountain was a flaring light, as if some huge mirror was catching the sun. But he knew there was nothing reflective up there. Whatever it was, it was glowing on its own.

"The ward I made," Ash said. "All Thelyan's power is inside it. It's overloading. It's not going to hold."

Sudden understanding made Kieran jump to his feet, hauling Ash up after him. "Across the tracks," he ordered. "Everyone. Now!"

The prisoners didn't ask questions this time; they obeyed. Kieran turned to run, but Ash's hand hauled him back. Pointed him at Sona, who was grimly struggling along with his cane. Kieran met Sona's eyes. Sona grimaced and nodded. Kieran set his shoulder to Sona's gut, hefted him, and in this undignified posture jogged away with him. Ash staggered along beside, carrying the cane.

"It's about to go!" Ash yelled. "I can feel it!"

Kieran had thought he had no power left, but he found just enough to speed himself for the last hundred yards to the rails. Men were struggling up the embankment, some helping each other and some leaving the rest behind. Ash seemed to have found power of his own, because he was grabbing the worst stragglers and *throwing* them up the slope. Kieran was only halfway up with his burden when he felt the soundless explosion behind him.

"Go!" He was shouting himself hoarse, not paying much attention to what he was saying. "Go, go!" He dragged a final burst of speed out of his worn-out nerves, and tumbled down on the other side of the tracks. Dropped Sona sprawling, scrambled to see whether Ash had made it, charging back until he saw the redhead with a straggler's arm clutched in each hand skidding heels-first down the gravel slope.

Then the sky flashed white, and a cold prickle scraped across his skin.

"Keep moving!" Ash was yelling, shoving men along. Groaning, Kieran picked Sona up again.

"I don't like this any more than you do," Sona grunted as he bounced over Kieran's shoulder.

"Let's not talk about it," Kieran returned.

With Ash herding them, the men dragged themselves about a quarter mile from the tracks before they refused to move any more. Kieran managed to set his burden down a bit more gently this time. He straightened, wincing, to look back at the mountain. He half expected to see a chunk bitten out of it as if mining charges had exploded it.

There was no such physical damage. What he saw with his eyes was nothing but a bit of smoke streaming from the train he'd wrecked.

With his mind's sense, though, he saw what they'd been running from. A new Burn, boiling out from where Thelyan had died, the sphere of it centered on the mountaintop, angry jags of thought-lightning roiling in chaos. Where they neared the railroad tracks, the streaks of energy smeared and bent. A secondary Burn, linear, rushed in either direction along the bands of steel.

Ash came up next to him, and with an arm around his waist watched with him until it was certain that the new Burn wouldn't overflow the rails. Once they were sure the danger was past, they leaned into each other and stood embracing. There was nothing that had to be said out loud. They just held each other for a long time.

It was Sona's bald friend with the beard who finally got their attention. He stood around clearing his throat until they turned to him.

"Hate to bust up your romantic moment," he said, "but we're all kinda wondering -- what now?"

Kieran raised an eyebrow. "You're asking *me*?"

"Well, yeah. I mean, it's true not everybody likes you much. And to be honest, looking at you boys grabbing on each other is making me sorta sick. But you came back for us. We ain't gonna forget that. So if you got us out to do something for you, like fight or something, looks like we're up for it."

Kieran opened his mouth to protest that he hadn't freed them, but Ash touched his lips to silence him and answered for him. "If you want to fight, that's up to you. We all have reason to be rebels. But be smart about it. Don't waste yourselves. As for us, we're used up."

"Fair enough." The bearded man glanced around at the other men who were watching this conversation. "We got no food or water, though."

"Food's a problem," said Kieran. "You white boys better ask the Iavaians to help you with that. As for water..." He rolled his eyes up to the sky, sent a brush of thought out to see whether anything was coming. He smiled. "You got about five hours to find something to catch it in."

"Wait!" That was Sona, calling out as Kieran turned away. "What are *you* going to do?"

He glanced at Ash, who grinned back at him.

"I don't think you really want to know."

Epilogue

"Funny how things work out." Ash gave a weary laugh to hear that cliché come out of his mouth. "What I mean is, I can't get my head around it."

"Don't have to, I guess." Kieran glanced up at the clouds that had been creeping out of the west for the past hour or so. The sun had gone behind them, and the shade eased the heat a little. Ash was still not sure he could keep walking. He hadn't asked where they were going. Kieran seemed to know, and that was good enough.

Since leaving Churchrock and the former prisoners behind, they hadn't talked much. There would be time to talk later. For now they needed their breath for walking. Ash had very little power left. Kieran seemed to be worn out as well. What little they could gather as they went was just enough to keep them upright and moving in the face of their thirst and hunger.

There was a time, Ash thought bemusedly, *when being this hungry, this filthy, this tired, would have been the peak of misery for me. But I have my Kai, I have his hand in my hand, and so the rest of it isn't important.*

Though he hadn't sent his thoughts out, Kieran turned to smile at him. "I'm sorry it's such a long walk. It'll be like when we busted out before, I'm afraid. Eating snakes and sleeping in caves. At least until we get there."

"Is there food where we're going?"

"Um." Kieran's smile turned wry. "I thought we could steal something from the miners. But it just occurred to me that the rail spur that went there -- well, it would be part of the new Burn, now."

"Maybe it spread out enough..."

"Hope so. There were people there. They had nothing to do with this." Kieran bit his lip, bowing his head. After a few minutes, he went on, "I'm sick of death, Ash. I must've killed more than fifty men today. More in one day than I did in my whole life before. I'm so tired of being the bad guy."

Ash raised their joined hands to his lips, kissed the tattooed dots on Kieran's skin. "I don't want you to start beating yourself up over this. They were Watchmen. Soldiers. And I -- I killed someone too, you saw -- even if the first shot was yours, I set it up, and then I finished him."

"It had to be done."

"Did it?"

Kieran nodded. "I have a lot to tell you before it'll make sense. You were sending me strength when I fought with Ka'an, but I don't know how much you understand of what he was, what Thelyan was..."

"And what you are now? And what I am now?"

Questioning, Kieran turned to him, step faltering. "You? Is that how you did those things?"

"It's confusing as hell. The thing you saw curled up in me, that was a sort of goddess, a thing like Ka'an but not cruel like he was -- an old woman, not so powerful, and there was Chaiel in the bubble -- he woke her, and she told me things -- gave me her power, what there was of it, and I think I have a new way of doing magic, I'll have to show you later -- so we got out, and there was this little girl with wings, and then we ran into the ward -- that's when you helped -- and I guess Shy thought I was dead, but I woke up with so much energy and it all seemed so *obvious* --" He broke off, finally realizing he was babbling. He gave Kieran a lopsided smile. "What I mean is, I don't think I've become a god or anything. But I'm not just an Empath anymore."

"Yeah." Kieran chuckled. "I gathered that."

"It's a little scary. I don't know what I can do. I have a new theory, though. About how magic works, I mean. It's how I got out of the bubble."

"You realize none of this is making a damn bit of sense to me."

"Sorry."

"Start at the beginning. When I left you -- god, I hated doing that."

"I know. I didn't think you'd be able to come back for me. I just wanted you to get away. I figured I could handle whatever happened, as long as I knew you were free somewhere."

"Ashes..."

"Anyway, when they found me, I started shooting. I got one of them in the hip and clipped one across the scalp. Then my rifle jammed. I'm surprised it worked at all, it was so full of mud. I got shot in the arm, right here." He showed a scar just above his elbow. "It didn't hurt, though. I was too worked up. They dropped some kind of spell on me. Next thing I know, I'm floating in the middle of a little stone room, with a naked kid sitting on my chest. That Chaiel person I mentioned."

"What? Why was he naked?"

"We both were. I guess Thelyan took our clothes so we couldn't use them to make a rope or something."

Kieran's face darkened. "How old was this 'kid'? Was he attractive?"

"Are you jealous?" Ash laughed, but the laugh faded as he realized how he'd have to answer Kieran's questions. "Um, he looked about fifteen. And yeah, I guess he was cute. And -- just to get all the unfortunate implications out of the way, the bubble that imprisoned us shoved everything in it toward the center, so we were sort of stuck together. You don't seriously think that was anything but an inconvenience to me, do you?"

Kieran gave a laughing sigh. "I get a little irrational about you, you know that. Go on. You were stuck together."

Ash told the story carefully, relating conversations as close to verbatim as he could manage. Kieran listened quietly until near the end, when Ash explained how he'd tried to break the ward and swallowed it instead.

"I got some use out of what you sent me," Kieran interrupted. "Just about killed me, though, before I got it broken down into something I could work with. How did *you* do it?"

"Math," Ash answered simply. "It's all mathematical. I'd explain, but I think I'd have to teach you calculus first."

Kieran shook his head. "Never mind. You're a genius. Let's just leave it at that."

"For now. I bet you could learn, though. You're smarter than you think you are, love. It's just that nobody bothered to teach you."

"You think so?"

"I'm sure of it."

"And you'd teach me?"

"If that's what you want."

Kieran gave a crooked smile. He seemed surprised by his own joy. "We have time, don't we? There's... there's a future. I have a future, and you're in it. Sorry, I'm getting sappy."

"You think I mind?"

"Go on with your story."

"There's not much more. I walked around, found myself

in the cell block. The place was wrecked. There were some... I found some dead men. Falling rock killed them. I found Sona alive, with a rock on his leg. I helped him. I just meant to stop the bleeding, but I found I had so much power, it was easy to fix it all the way. If there'd been anything left of his leg I could've saved it, but the flesh was dead. I went out looking for other people to help -- I wanted to come to you right away, but you seemed to be winning, and there were injured people everywhere. Then I found where they were fighting, and I stopped them."

"Just like that."

"Well, yes." He shrugged. "It was just projective Empathy. I thought it was pointless for them to be fighting, when all any of them wanted was to get away. So I showed them what they really felt, and they stopped. I sent them in opposite directions."

"And at the end there -- I'm afraid to ask. Did you know what you were doing? Did you know what it would do to you?"

"I saw the shape of his shield. It blocked solid matter. If I'd had a bucket of water or an apple or something, you could have shot through that. I considered using my hand or some other part farther from vital organs, but I was afraid you'd cripple me. I tried to put the path through the same place where you were shot, because you survived that -- or would have, if we hadn't been on the run -- but I guess my aim was a little off." He hung his head. "Sorry about that. I didn't plan to sacrifice myself, I swear."

"You're saying your blood breached his shield?"

"Just long enough to let the bullet through."

"You are really something, Ashes."

"We used it all up, though. All that power. If we have to deal with anything else, we're in deep trouble."

"Only if it happens tonight. We'll build up our strength again. You *are* taking in power, right?"

"Just enough to keep walking."

"Maybe I'm better at it, because I'm getting more than that. Want to try taking some?"

When Ash nodded, Kieran closed his eyes for a moment. A trickle of strength flowed through their joined hands. Ash's fatigue abated. They shared a smile, and went on at a better pace.

"So where exactly are we going?" Ash was only curious.

He was getting to enjoy the walking a bit, now that being tired wasn't a problem.

"You remember how you told me once, if we got out of prison, we should find a lake and swim around until we get all pruney?"

"Yeah. We swam in the river, but only for a few minutes. If we're going back to that temple, it'll be all mud still..."

"Nope. This place is better. It's got this lake in it that's just -- you'll see."

Nodding, Ash didn't have to reply. This was all right. Walking. Talking or not talking. Night beginning to come down as the clouds rose up.

They trudged on into darkness.

Sometime after full night had fallen, rain came. Spatters at first, then a downpour. They tilted their heads back to drink it, caught it in their hands. It washed them clean, washed out their tracks. Chilled them, then tapered away to a gentle spattering that didn't keep them from drawing enough power to warm themselves. Kieran wrapped his shredded coat around Ash's bare shoulders, and they went on.

They reached a stream as clouds cleared and released the moon. "This is Burn River," Kieran told him in an amused tone, before hopping across.

"Is it safe to drink?"

"It should be now."

So Ash waded into the water, warmer than the air, tendrils of mist curling around his legs. He scooped up handfuls to finish off his thirst. It only came up to his knees at its deepest point. When they had both drunk enough, they moved on, upstream.

It took Ash several minutes to figure out what he was seeing: a lake, an endless sheet of still water running out to the horizon. He breathed his amazement, and Kieran's smile was proprietary, proud to show off his discovery. And there were further wonders; circling the lake's barren shore, they encountered tumbled walls, ruined buildings that hinted at a forgotten grandeur. Toppled pillars, slumped jetties and seawalls, stairs that led down toward the water and ended ten feet above its surface.

"This wasn't always a desert," Ash guessed.

Kieran just nodded.

They threaded their way through the traces of narrow streets, heading for an area where the buildings looked a little more intact. They were moving west, toward the mountains that were just now tipped with gold, toward some flat-topped ruins from which a thread of smoke climbed...

Kieran stopped, hauling back on Ash's hand. He gave a faint groan. "Oh hell. I don't want to fight anyone right now."

"There's not supposed to be anyone here, is there?"

"No."

"I'll go look."

"No!" Kieran's hands clutched his arms, unwilling to let him move any closer to the mysterious smoke. "We are *not* going through that again!"

Warmed to his soul by those words, despite their impractical implications in this situation, Ash took a moment to lean against Kieran's shoulder before answering. "With my mind, I mean. I should be able to tell what kind of person it is. At least, whether they have magic."

"I'll do it."

"We need you alert if it comes to a fight."

Kieran nodded, but he didn't look happy. "Be careful. Be *so* goddamn careful, Ash."

"I will." Ash closed his eyes, and sent his senses creeping out. Gently, tentatively, ready to sink away at the first sign of recognition.

A moment later, he opened his eyes laughing.

"What?" Kieran demanded.

"It's Chaiel. And he has that little kid with him."

"The one who was in the bubble, right? What the hell is he doing here? Can we trust him?"

"He's a friend."

"A *friend*?" Kieran frowned at him for a moment longer, then relaxed, sighing resignation. "I should've figured. You could make friends in Hell. You could make friends on the moon." He let Ash tow him toward the rising smoke.

When the smell of cooking food reached them, the last of Kieran's resistance crumbled. Soon he was the one leading.

They got a bit turned around when they got close enough that the mostly intact walls around them blocked the sight of the smoke. Ash was about to cast out again with his mind, weary though he was, when a tiny figure bobbed around a corner and waved to him. A tiny figure with wings.

"Whoa." Kieran faltered. "*That's* not normal."

"Hello again," Ash said as brightly as he could manage. "You're here to take us to Chaiel?"

The child nodded. Solemn-faced, she grabbed their clasped hands and tugged. When she turned away, he saw that the infected swelling around the grafted wings was gone. The scars of stitches were clearly visible, but other than that it looked as if the wings had grown there. She took them through a maze of dust-choked alleys, brought them into a courtyard strewn with piles and bundles.

Beside a small cookfire in the center of the courtyard, Chaiel was just in the act of standing up. Ash smiled to see how different he looked. He'd cut his hair neatly at his shoulders, and was wrapped in layers of mismatched, ill-fitting clothing. He nodded welcome, gesturing to the objects piled around him, and the pot full of what smelled like stewed chicken.

"You'll want to eat first, no doubt, but I've clothes for you when you've finished. Medur, please set out blankets for these gentlemen."

The child nodded. She went to scramble among the baggage.

"You named her Medur?" Ash sank gratefully down beside the fire, reaching for the bowl Chaiel offered.

"It's the best name I know."

Ash passed a bowl to Kieran, whose questioning frown was threatening a tirade. "Kieran, this is Chaiel. He's an immortal, Thelyan was keeping him prisoner. Try to remember not to shorten his name. For some reason that's hard for me. Chaiel, this is Kieran, who is absolutely not Ka'an."

Chaiel nodded. "That's obvious. It's in the eyes."

The corner of Kieran's mouth quirked up. "Thelyan didn't think it was obvious."

"He needed you to be Ka'an, I suppose. It justified him. You do realize, don't you, that you haven't destroyed him? You've only bought a few years of peace."

Kieran chuckled, spoke around a mouthful of food. "Years. Hell, I can't think past sleep, just now. I just might be able to wrap my brain around the concept of tomorrow."

"Besides," Ash put in, "he won't know who he is, will he? If he's reborn at all; I gathered that they aren't, always."

"You can count on that, if you like," said Chaiel. "I won't."

Ash gave half a shrug. "Anything can happen in a few years. Hell, anything can happen in a few *months*."

"Yep." Kieran grinned. "But I never saw a kid grow wings before, what's up with her? And not to be ungrateful for the food and all, but how the hell did you -- what was your name again?"

Chaiel rolled his eyes. "Oh, for pity's sake. Why can't you people manage to remember my name?"

Kieran dismissed this with a wave of his spoon. "How'd you get ahead of us, and with all this junk? Ash can't have told you to meet us here, he didn't know about this place." He turned to Ash, frowning. "Did you?"

"No."

"Well, I call that suspicious."

Ash leaned to scoop more stew out of the pot, and to hide his smile. "Kieran's tired, and it's making him a little snarky. But I'm pretty curious about that myself."

"I know spells you don't. Spells I don't intend to teach," Chaiel added quickly as Ash opened his mouth to ask.

"I'd teach you how to use math for magic," Ash said in a hurt tone.

"That's up to you. I won't strike a bargain. All this --" again he gestured to the piled baggage -- "is my way of repaying you for freeing me. No doubt we'll meet again someday, and perhaps that debt can't be repaid, and perhaps you'll have a favor to ask of me then. But I can't make extravagant gestures of gratitude today. I have Medur to think of. I have..." Chaiel's eyes went distant, a little bit frightened. "I have the future to think of. That will take some getting used to."

Kieran grumbled, "You're saying you don't trust us with this stuff you know."

"Not at the moment, no."

After a long moment, Kieran shook his head and went back to eating, not interested in arguing. Ash finished his second bowl of stewed whatever, and offered the bowl and spoon to Chaiel. That one gestured refusal and stood up, reaching for the child's hand. Little Medur came to him instantly. Ash could sense the trust in her malformed mind; she'd imprinted like a baby bird.

"Good luck to you both," Chaiel said.

"Wait." Ash stood as well. "Before you go... I'm not sure how to explain this so it won't sound condescending or stupid. But I just want you to know, I don't think we should owe each other anything. If there's anything you need, or even if you just feel like talking to someone who has half a clue what your world is like... you see?"

A smile spread slowly across Chaiel's face. "Medur was more eloquent, but I see her in you nonetheless. As you wish; we part as friends, with no debt between us." He offered his hand, and Ash clasped it.

Then, draping a frail arm around the child's frailer neck, he turned away and began walking, and the two of them grew distant much more quickly than the ground they covered allowed. Within moments, they were wavering in haze, and then gone. He hadn't spoken a spell, or made any gestures, and Ash had felt no spill of power. Kieran made an appreciative sound.

"Not bad. Your buddy there is quite a mage."

"He's been around a while." Ash reached for Kieran's hand. "Oh Kai. I'm so tired. Are we done now?"

"Yeah. We're done."

They helped each other to the blankets that little Medur had spread for them in the shade of an intact corner of roof. Too weary even to undress, they flung themselves down, curled together, and closed their eyes.

Several minutes later, Ash admitted with a sigh what they were both thinking: "I'm too tired to sleep."

"So just lie here. We can lie around all day."

"For how many days? How long until something else comes along to mess with us? I can't believe we're safe now. I can't believe the world will just let me spend my life with you. Things that good don't happen. Do they?"

Kieran whispered a laugh. "So that's where my cynicism went."

"I'm not being cynical. I don't think I am. I'm just trying to reassure myself. Where are you going to live, Kai? Because that's where I'm going to live too, if you'll let me. Burn River? What about those gangsters? And there are still warrants out for us, even if Churchrock's wrecked, and --"

Kieran silenced him with a kiss. Drew back to catch his eyes, brushed away a curl of his hair, smiling. "You worry too much about stuff that doesn't matter. Between us, we have just about all the magic there is. There's nobody in the world who can beat us now, except maybe that Chaiel kid, and he seems decent enough. And don't start with that 'if you'll let me' crap. You want me to promise? You want a ring? I'm not giving you up. Not for anything. I'll swear on anything you want."

"I thought you didn't like to make promises."

"I changed my mind."

Sighing happily, Ash settled into his favorite place on Kieran's shoulder. "Even with this new magic, though, we can be hurt if we're not paying attention. Wherever we go, things will get dangerous. We can't be on our guard every moment."

Kieran was quiet for a while, toying with Ash's hair, turning something over in his mind. Something that filled him with hope, but which he thought Ash might not like. Ash didn't mean to eavesdrop on his feelings, but when they lay together like this the bond was too strong for anything to stay hidden.

"Whatever you're going to ask for," Ash said, "the answer is yes."

"Well, I was just thinking -- how would you like to stay here?"

"Here?"

"Yeah."

"If you want to. Yes. But... there's nothing here."

There was a smile in Kieran's voice when he answered. "There will be."

Printed in Great Britain
by Amazon